A PLACE of SAFETY
(Volume Two)
New World For Old

Kyle Michel Sullivan

KMSCB
Buffalo, NY

Disclaimer

This book is a work of fiction. Though it is written as if an autobiography and is set during a difficult period of history in Londonderry, Northern Ireland, and Houston, Texas, the main characters and their names, places, incidents, and situations are products of the author's imagination. References to actual historical events, real people, and real places are used only in a way to illuminate or further the story. Any resemblance by the fictional characters to actual events or places or persons, living or dead, is entirely coincidental. All rights are reserved to the author, including the right to reproduction in whole or part in any form, manner, or concept.

Cover design by Emily Jackson
ISBN: 979-8-9923177-1-8

LIBRARY OF CONGRESS CATALOGUING IN PUBLICATION DATA
Sullivan, Kyle Michel (1952-   )
A Place of Safety - New World For Old / by Kyle Michel Sullivan
Buffalo, NY : KMSCB, 2024 | Summary: Set between 1966 and 1981, Brendan Kinsella just wants to live his life, but he was born and raised in Londonderry, Northern Ireland, and history keeps intruding.
Library of Congress Control Number: 2024911743
(print) ISBN: 979-8-9887577-2-6 (Hardcover; alk. paper)
Historical-Fiction | Narrative Fiction

Acknowledgements

Thanks to Carrie Armstrong for assisting in the editing and proofing of this book.

Thanks to Eamon and Martin Melaugh for allowing me to pick their brains and use their knowledge of the times to keep it as true as possible.

Thanks to CAIN, PRONI and *Derry of the Past* on Facebook for their excellent attention to the period and collection of images and information.

A Place of Safety
(Volume Two)
New World For Old

Table of Contents

About the Author

Other Books by This Author

Rebirthing

Drifting...
I was drifting...
In an ocean of blinding white.
Gleaming and swirling around me.
Real but not real.
Alive but not alive.
Nothing anywhere.
Nothing.
Until...
A thick line. Black and breathing. Drawing close. Building from the hideous white. Evil white. Ghostly white and...and...

Slowly...

Slowly sharpening into focus to cut through the middle of the white, white horror smothering me. Surrounding me. Hot and vile. Wrapping me in a prison of nothingness.

The dark line expanded. Details filtered in. My focus sharpened. It revealed itself as...

As...

The painted sill to a pair of narrow windows. Both open. With mesh screens held in place by a small hook connected to an eye-hole screw, allowing the barest of breezes through.

The black was strips of paint that remained on the windows' sills. Weather-beaten. Dried. Bleached by the sun. Curled into little shreds to reveal creviced lines in the wood, gray and deep and dark. Some bits picked away by wind and rain, making the color inconsistent in tone. Others maybe helped along by someone's careless pulling at the splinters?

Was I that someone?

I shifted my gaze to my fingernails. They were long. Ragged. Chipped. Unclean. Not like mine had always been.

So it *was* me who did that. I could tell, and was I pleased with myself. The wood was lovely in its weaving grooves and interlocked patterns. Care taken to place each line just right, next to its brother. I felt as if I were gazing upon the work of an artist. A work I helped finish.

The flow of it was emphasized by a steady line of little black ants scurrying back and forth from one corner of the frame to the center post. Then they swirled over what was left of...

Of...

Was that a half-eaten sandwich?

Could be.

Whatever. It now churned with the little beasts, like something alive and breathing. I caught glimpses of what vaguely looked like some sort of meat salad on light bread. Oh, and there was part of a crust next to it, well-bitten into.

Had it been mine? There was a taste on my tongue that was rather fishy. Salmon? Tuna? Anchovy? I chuckled. I hated anchovies. All I could say for certain is, it definitely was not haddock.

A near sense of awe whispered around me as I watched those swarming little creatures continue their quick dismantling of what I'm sure they considered a fine offering. It was on a dish. With crisps. The greedy little buggers wanted those, as well. Danced over and under and around them, making them move a bit, almost as if another living creature was trying to escape their casual destruction. Were my hearing sharper, I'm sure I could have made out their screams as bits were torn away.

A chuckle whispered.

I jolted and tensed...but heard no more.

Was it me did that?

Yes.

Yes, it was. It was.

I let my focus shift back to the plate, on my side of the center post. Plain and simple with a yellow band around its edge. And in my left hand was a short bottle of *Coke*. Sweaty and half gone. Barely chilled. In my right? Half a crust from a portion of that sandwich and—

The tea and cakes I shared with Joanna were so gentle and tart and real, and she loved them as much as me as the whiteness surrounded us and—

Lightning tore into my heart.

I coughed and coughed.

Eyes closed.
Eyes closed!
Breathe, Brendan.
Deep.
Long.
Slow.
Long...
Slow...
Until the coughing ends.
Let it end.
Let it end.
And slowly...slowly, my heart also ended its screaming.
And I could open my eyes, again.
Could see the windowsill, again.
See the black and gray still there.

Ants still swirled and raced back and forth. The sandwich and crisps still a living breathing mass of the little beasts.

My breathing was harsh, like I've run ten miles.

I coughed.

Drew in a deep breath. Held it, for a moment. Released it.

I felt the need to keep still. Let myself think of now. Only right now. Think of nothing things.

Think only about...

About...

About being seated on a chair. With arms. I let the fingers of my right hand explore its wood. Smooth. Polished. Old and creaking. Not happy when I moved.

A bit of oil would take care of that.

Dowels in the back ran from the seat to a curved banner and that was my anchor. I needed it. Needed something to brace myself against. To hang onto so I wouldn't float back into that destructive whiteness.

Next, the windows, narrow and tall. Their frames also black, as were those of the screens. The lower panes raised halfway. Sounds of the outside so normal and real. I was up off the ground, almost as if I was floating until I saw—

No, noticed—

No, realized—

I was on the first floor of a house, in a gable window, looking down at a fair-sized yard that was nothing like what you would find in Derry.

And which could have used some tending.

Half was covered in red bricks set into the earth, with grass forcing its way between them in ragged strands. A large rectangular swimming pool held the other half, more bricks and mortar encompassing it. Leaves and twigs were scattered about. At the far end was a large hutch built of similar bricks, with French doors under a narrow porch and a slanted roof made of tin.

I'd never seen a hutch like that in Derry, before. Brick, yes. Roof, yes. But not with doors that were so large and fragile. Was this some new construction up Creggan? Pennyburn, maybe? Out the Strand Road?

No.

No, there was nothing new about it. Thick strands of ivy twisted up its corners and across the top of that porch to finally enmesh themselves in a wire fence that ran along one side and behind it. Then its leaves mingled with deep green vines that drooped with fragrant yellow and white flowers. Those vines also wandered up two fat, crooked trees that flanked the little house. Trees that offered lovely deep cool shade under their grasping branches. A bunched-up strip of colorful cloth was strung between one of them and a post of the porch. An old Schwinn bicycle, rusted, was propped up against the other and—

Tommy rode up on a Schwinn, Shane on his Huffy, and they threw stones at the Paras off William Street and the bastards were shooting and there were waves of blood and—

Cough.

Deep breaths.

Repeat.

Repeat.

Let my heart stop its racing. Let the quiet, dark stillness of that corner whisper through me. Let it settle me. Bring peace and easiness. Keep me from thinking.

From feeling.

Feeling? I almost laughed. Feeling what? I had a terrifying numbness behind my heart. Nothingness. It made me weak, so I had to lean against the frame of the window to keep from toppling out of the chair.

That little building...so quiet, dark and still...it was like a haven. A respite from the hell in my mind. A hideaway. Like the hutch Danny and I made over for Tur and Mairead, where you could live apart from the madness and never have to think ever again and—

No, Brendan, stop it!

No memories.

None.

Don't think, don't think, just look. Memories only shatter you with grief from the second they land till they withdraw to their corners and lie in wait for the next chance they have to spring forth and wreak havoc and damage and leave you torn to bits and lost in weariness.

Fight them.

Look to the shed to your right, the other side of a tree, standing unto itself. Large and well-kept, also under a tin roof. Could it be a second hutch?

No.

There were two large wide doors facing a well-tended gravel drive. A garage, with an old Volvo parked in front and—

"Ye know cars, do ye," the bloody para snarled while fingering his gun and his mate grabbed me arse, sneering so happy as he whispered, "Where'd youse come from and tell us why's your mate hurt there and did you really work on a car an' weren't you at Magilligan tossin' stones an'—"

Sharp gasp.

Deep breath.

Long and slow.

Long.

Slow...

I coughed. Tried to clear my throat. So dry. Then I managed to chuckle, almost indignant.

Tossing stones? Jesus, who didn't on my side of the Foyle? Arrest anyone who'd picked up half a brick and the whole of Derry would be at Long Kesh. Stupid bastard.

Why were people always pushing in on you? Demanding answers from you then not happy with your answers, no matter how true? Taking from you, and taking and taking, without asking what you wanted and not caring about your worries and hopes and dreams? Like those bloody fucking ants, grabbing the last of my meal without so much as a by-your-leave. Just taking it, the bastard things.

The motherfucking beasts!

I used that Coke bottle to crush half of them in the line. Spilled some of it on them. They scattered and scurried about.

I chuckled. Deep. Cruel. Greedy little fucks. No care for anything but your own belly. I unhooked the screen and brushed most of them off the sill into the air. Sent the plate flying with them. Watched it float out of sight then heard it break as it hit the bricks, far below. Then I sneered, thinking, *Take from that, you bastards,* as—

Ma slapped me, screaming, "What's this? What's this?" waving my note before me as Da grabbed my hand and near crushed it so I'd hand over the pound I got for my birthday and it was mine and—

I bolted up from the chair—

To smack my head against the ceiling! Hard. I felt dizzy, for a moment. Saw stars. Beautiful stars, gleaming and sparking, and wondered if I was flying. Then I dropped back in the chair and the stars slowly drifted away.

As did the dizziness.

And the memories. The thoughts. Even the raving beast snarling inside me, that laughed at my pain and confusion. All of it backed away, and my thoughts wandered into thinking *Brendan, Brendan—if you'd but paid a bit of attention, you'd have known you were in an alcove.* Cut into a roof that slants forty-five degrees. Starting two feet up from the floor, atop a short wall. It kept that angle halfway up then cut across to the other side of the room in a normal ceiling, nice and flat and...

And...

What the bloody hell? Was I in a bloody attic? A bloody attic room? Stored away like unused furniture?!

This time I chuckled in full...and coughed.

I turned away from the window to look about the room. Just as I'd probably done a thousand times. But this was the first time I really saw it. It was near the same area as Ma's, with a fair-size bed and frame against the wall, opposite the window and twice the size of the one I'd shared with Eamonn.

Eamonn—

Tumbling across the pavement as Mai threw him from her home and not having seen him, since, as lads I knew were shot and blood flew and...

I wrapped my arms around myself and jammed my eyes closed.

Tight.

Gasping.

Gasping.

Breathe in.

Soft out.

Slow.

Steady.

Over and over and over until finally...

Finally...

Finally, I could open my eyes, again, and see everything was still in its same little spot. If this reaction was to be a habit, I did not want it.

I slowly let more of the room become visible. Shadows filled it, the only light coming through the windows. A table in the corner beside the bed held a lamp and a digital clock that read 1:42. A shelf above them was lined with books that looked too neat to have been read. To its other side was a door, and against the wall to my right were a massive wardrobe and another door.

The walls were covered in paper, soft lines of gold and brown and orange and green. The half-ceiling was done with plain tan paper. Slapped on quick and cheap, I'd say, since corners were coming loose, here and there. The slanted part was smooth wooden beams holding up long, wide planks, all stained a deep brown. Pictures in black frames hung on the walls, black and white photos of hillsides and lovely skies and—

Clouds passed below me and I could not believe the beauty of it all as I sang "The Banks of Claudy" and walked in the cold, clear night, Joanna beside me...but I'd not met her yet, and...and how could I have known and—

"He should be in a grave."

"You do that, I'll see to it you follow him."

I froze. Those were voices. Real voices. Voices cold and angry. I fucking heard them. I could not move. Could not breathe till my lungs were bursting for air, then I gasped air in.

It made no sense. None of it made sense. This room was like one from a manor house, but why would I be here and what had happened? It tore at my mind in little ways I didn't understand, and I ran my hands through my hair and rubbed the back of my neck and—

Hang on.

I had no hair. Only stubble. Short and prickly. While I'd always cut it close it was never like this and...

"Cut off much as you can, first." Was that Colm's voice? *"It's me Da's razor and I gotta clean it 'fore I give it back."*

"Keep goin'. Shave it all off." In a voice I didn't know.

Shite shite shite!

I couldn't breathe. I gasped in and whimpered out and told myself over and over just look about the room. Don't think. Just look. Just look. Pull together information.

Like-like-like-like the books on the shelf, I could just make out the titles in the gloom. *Catch 22. East of Eden. For Whom the Bell Tolls. When Worlds Collide.* That's all. Just titles. All in paper-cover. Books to read, sometime.

That's all.

Or had I read any of these? I didn't recognize them. But why would they be here if I hadn't? Well, since I didn't remember them, I would have to read them, again, I suppose.

Finally, I was able to release myself and let my eyes drift around and down to the bed. Its covers were mussed. Slippers and a robe lay on the floor, atop a large rug, and—

I was in pajamas! Bottoms only as—

The Paras dragged me outside and I was only in my pajamas and they were down to my hips as he threw me in the van and—

I grabbed them and held them tight to my waist. Searched for the top...then noticed the air was warm and thick, not at all like fall but like—

Milk fresh from a cow poured into our tea, in Malcom's tender farmhouse, and Joanna sipped it so much like a lady as children laughed and a boy and girl chased each other from a shop, dancing about in full happiness until the boy fell against the car and—

I gasped and bolted up to pace the length of that room, my breath harsh and sudden, my arms wrapped around me as panic filled my entire body and I put my hands to my ears.

The laughter haunted me.

Echoed after me.

Mocked me as I walked, back and forth and back and forth and back and forth, shaking and coughing and stumbling until the sound faded and my pacing could slow and my arms were willing to curl down so my hands could cup my face. And just hold it and...

And...

An odd smell was on my skin. A scented soap so clean and fresh.

I turned to look at the door beside the wardrobe. Somehow, I knew it was for the toilet.

Which is when the urge to piss grew rather strong.

I saw no chamber pot in the room, so I moved towards that door. Slowly.

Carefully.

The door was far enough away from the slanted ceiling to keep from hitting when it opened. And creaked.

Could use a touch of oil, whispered through my brain. Then I looked inside.

It was a short rectangle of a room, far too clean and happy to be real, with a wash basin to my right, jammed under a single gable window in the slanted roof. A small round mirror was attached to the side wall, just above it. Next to it, a low cabinet and shelf with toiletries. Across from it was a small cubical shower stall with a detachable nozzle and hose half hidden by a curtain. And between that and the door was a toilet. There was a door at the far end that I knew, somehow, was not to be opened. Everything was as if it had been freshly bought, it was in such fine condition.

I entered and did my business, then turned back to my room. I noticed a rack of clean towels attached to the shower stall. Glorious towels, thick and rich. I took one and smelled it. Found the same lingering aroma of that soap.

Well, Brendan, could it be more obvious you are not in Derry?

But where was I? And when was it? I had no sense of time. It couldn't be the day after, could it? A week or two seemed more probable. So was I in a manor house in the Republic? Down to the south? Did it grow so much warmer, down there?

No.

No, this was to the point of hot and the stillness of it oppressed almost to where you couldn't breathe. This could not be winter in Ireland. Nor even summer. Was I in the tropics?

I made myself turn to the sink. I turned on the faucet and whisked cold water over my face, then cupped my hand to drink from it, over and over and over. Finally, I looked in the small round mirror—

And froze.

Staring back was a hollow-eyed stranger on the cusp of starvation, from the way his cheekbones showed. The hollow circles of his eyes. Scruff as a beard, in the places it would grow. Hair all but shaved. Skin pale. Scars on his chest and neck and left shoulder as well as his scalp. All healed. He was like photos I'd seen of concentration camps in Germany, with gaunt, newly liberated men standing around and...

And...

And was it me in that mirror?

No, that wasn't right. It couldn't be right. I couldn't look like this in only a few days. It must be I'm still caught in that nightmare. I knew it, I knew it, I knew it, and the faucet was still running and steam was whispering up from it and I began to shake and my knees gave out and I dropped to the floor and—

I flew through clouds of the finest mist molded into perfect playthings, with the sky above them as blue as could be, seen through a small window with rounded corners that distorted everything but I didn't care because the clouds were my prayers and wishes filled them to bursting and hopes danced in the shadows of their billowing tufts as they soared past like dreams and a hand touched me and I looked around and—

Someone entered the room.

Without knocking? How rude.

At least, I hadn't heard them knock.

"Bren?" asked the kindest voice one could imagine. "Ya all right, son?"

I couldn't answer. Couldn't think of the words to say.

A woman wandered into view, looking about. Short and round and hair black as coal, with eyes as kind as any you'd ever witness.

Aunt Mari. Ma's sister. I'd not seen her since Da's wake.

But what's this? She was in Houston.

In Texas!

America!

What the bloody hell was this!?

She saw me in the toilet and came over, wiping her hands on a dishrag. "What ya doin' on the floor, there?"

I made myself shrug. I tried to pull myself back to my feet but did not succeed, so she came over to help me.

"Come along, me boy, to bed. Ya need time to rebuild yer strength."

She took me under the arm and guided me back into my room.

Somehow, I found enough voice to croak out, "Aunt Mari? What-what's this?"

"Don't ya remember, Bren? Do ya recall anything?"

I shook my head as—

Ma slapped me, screaming, "What have you done? What have you done?" and Danny was to one side whispering with some men I didn't know and I'd never seen him so white and afraid and near weeping and bleeding, he was bleeding, and a man was patching him up and those men were angry and furious, but why was he in my home when he was in Armagh, only these weren't my rooms and why was I here when I was in the Waterside waiting for Joanna to have tea and cakes and—

I coughed. Over and over.

Aunt Mari sat me on the bed. Gently guided me to lie down. Pulled a sheet up to cover me. She dug into a box on the table and pulled out a small tablet and held open my mouth to set it under my tongue, like I was a dog being given a pill. Then she turned to set a small circular fan to going.

Shite, I hadn't even noticed the bloody thing.

"Amazin'," she murmured, shaking her head at the fan. "Ya did such a fine job with it."

What? "Me?"

"Aye. It rattled, but last week ya stopped it."

A strip of torn metal in my hand to undo the screws, reset the front cage and screw them back in. All while the bloody thing was running.

I looked at my hands. No recent cuts. So when had I done this?

She chuckled. "Who knew the front grill needed to fit a certain way?"

"I worked it right?" I managed to croak, leaving the pill to dissolve where she'd put it. Automatically. Like I'd been trained.

"Just after I brought it up. That's when we knew ya'd be fine, again."

And I barely remembered it. "Where-where am I?"

"Good. Two coherent questions in a row. There's more proof yer comin' out of it."

"...Aunt Mari...?"

She gave me a look that could mean a thousand things, then she said, soft and easy, "Yer here, Bren. My home. In Houston. Brought here to be treated by a heart specialist after—"

White filled the air with smoke and debris and a single child's leg flipped towards me, twisting over and around like some form of ballet and Joanna fought to free herself as the flames danced, danced, danced closer and closer and filled the world and the sound of someone screaming in my voice crushed my ears and—

I gasped. Gulped in air. Coughed. Sharp hideous whimpers burst from me. I rose to sit and almost tumbled from the bed.

Aunt Mari sat beside me. Calmly wrapped me in her arms. Held me close. Ran a smooth hand over my head.

"Shh-shh-shh-shh-shh, me boy. Yer all right now. Yer safe here."

Safe here.

Here?

How could I be here? Was I having some ridiculous dream that was meant to make sense but didn't?

It took me some moments to stop breathing fast and sharp, but her holding me did much to slow my pain.

Slow it.

Until I could manage to whisper, "I-I-I'm not in Derry? I'm gone from Derry? I'm here? In Houston?"

Her eyes grew kinder and even more gentle. "Yes, yer here. T' let yer heart heal."

And *"That should have been tended to, years ago,"* cut into me. A voice said it and I jolted, for it was a voice I didn't know.

But my coughing. And shortness of breath. Brought on by trouble. Or fear. Mainly thanks to Ma. Had it been my heart the cause of all that?

"A bad heart? Like what happens with an old man?" I almost laughed.

She smiled. "All these questions. They do show a great improvement. They're coherent. Specific. When ya first arrived, ya were a zombie. There were concerns ya'd not come out of it."

When I first arrived—

A wall of heat slammed into me, and I knew I was in hell.

"I was-was-was brought to you. All this way? How long. How long. Have. I been. Here?"

"No need to worry 'bout that, Bren. Just rest, some more. Let yer mind catch up to ya in its own time. I'll bring ya up a little TV and ya can—"

My voice grew hard and demanding. "How long?"

She sighed and murmured, "Near six month."

Her words sliced into me.

Six months.

Six bloody months gone to nothing?

Six months since...

Since—

White filled the world and silence with it and—

No!

No, no, it wasn't right, it couldn't be right, it couldn't be.

Except...

Except it explained that thing looking back at me in the mirror. Its eyes. Its skin and bones. Like death had become my reflection.

Death.

Oh, dear God.

That meant Joanna was no more.

That this was no fantasy. No nightmare. None of it. She was long buried. Food for those bloody fucking ants and other creatures that feasted on those gone from us, with no thought of how they'd dreamed with us and hoped with us and prayed with us and loved us and...and—

Joanna kissed me by the door, light and easy as spearmint whispered about her and smoke enveloped us and flames laughed around us and—

Somewhere, someone was keening a howl of hideous pain and suffering and fury until that hideously wonderful blinding white finally returned to fill my world with silence.

Breaking the Surface

That ceiling of plain tan paper slowly blended into the cruel white-white nothingness. Soft shadows drew across it, almost like they weren't there. The sun was low and the room had gained a gentle aura of dusky gold. The circulating fan worked at cooling the air as a bright soft beam of light cut past the branches of a tree to whisper in through one window. Specks of dust danced within. Sparkling. Twisting. Swirling in the air as if rejoicing that I was finally back with the living.

I sneered at the foolish thought.

I stretched out across the bed. A space large enough for all four of us boys, but it was mine, alone, and I luxuriated in that understanding. Sheets still crisp and clean even after having been slept in. Mattress firm yet comfortable. Two soft pillows! I never wanted to rise from it. This was far, far better than even my stay in hospital, so long ago. I could live the rest of my life in this bed and never have to face the world, again. Never have to think about anything, ever again. Oh, what heaven that would be. What a glorious thing.

There's an erotic aspect to not feeling the need to join in with your life. A sensual beauty that seduces so easily. Just lie here and be calm. Never worry. Never even have to give in to thought. Just rest. And sleep. And let tomorrow become the years to follow. No concern. No need to care.

No need to do anything as—

My face was covered by something that stank of sweat and I couldn't see or breathe and Ma was shouting "Is this what you want?" and she was holding it down on me and I couldn't breathe but I wasn't fighting because I didn't care and—

I gasped.

Gulped in short, sharp breaths.

Easy in.

Easy out.

Let calmness surround you as...

As...

There was noise. Whispering...drifting from somewhere, breaking the chaos in my thoughts. Laughter. Soft. Happy. Distant. Pleasant and human. Joyous, even. I could also make out what almost sounded like a telly playing some program.

I held tight to it. Let me help slow my beathing and calm my heart. Help me walk away from the tears and fears and pains and horrors of that moment. Let me just be. Just lie there and listen.

Listen.

It was far too muffled to really understand. But with the laughter came the aroma of something rich and fine and—

In The Diplomat, in the back, waiting for Joanna as the combination of various aromas danced around me. Nothing harsh and greasy like a chippy. Just lingering beauty, toying with me, as my focus kept to the entrance, waiting to see if my world would be made complete or shrugged away by a girl I barely knew and could never know and...

And suddenly I was bloody perished from the hunger. My belly a snarling, raving, growling, demanding thing. I wondered if the kind person fixing such a heavenly feast would be willing to feed a poor traveler. I could ask, at the very least. I had money put aside. And manners enough to not drag stares from other patrons and...

Wait.

No.

No, I couldn't.

I wasn't in Derry, was I? In that cafe enjoying the rich full air wafting around me as I waited for Joanna. Nor in Marianne's and the beauty of her pastries.

That was forever ago.

No need for money. No need for my finest manners. No need for me to do anything.

Except lie here.

If my belly would let me. But the damn thing was bloody insistent. *You get some food into me now or I will make you regret it.*

And was that the hint of a cigarette, mingled in? Tickling a memory in my psyche? Whispering gently to draw forth a sweet urge?

That last did it. Now I had no choice but to cast aside my laziness and confusion and venture out to see if I might join in such simple pleasures as food and tobacco.

I rolled over to one side, propped on an arm, then rose, slow and aching. Some foul taste was on my tongue, and my throat was as dry as dirt. I maneuvered myself from the bed, found slippers right at my feet and a light robe draped from a corner post. I picked it up. Looked at it. Simple and plain and blue with white trim. The sleeves long. The material lighter than cotton.

I finally figured out that if I put one arm in one sleeve and the other in the other, I could actually wear it. Which I did. And felt as if I'd accomplished some great thing. It was cool and crisp on me, and I breathed deep from the pleasure of it. I then shuffled into the toilet like a man five times my age. Neither steady nor unsteady; just slow and careful.

I drank from the faucet with my hand. A toothbrush and toothpaste were in a holder on the wall, both looking very new. So I broke them in.

I never would have thought the simple act of brushing your teeth could be so damned exhausting. And bloody. And painful. And exhilarating. And unusual and glorious. I felt as if I were the Dagda washing his sins away in the waters off the coast of Clare.

If I got that right.

It was a story from one of Rhuari's books and—no. No, it had been one of Da's stories. Hadn't it? But Rhuari'd said it wasn't right...or something was wrong.

Rhuari and his books. His way of dealing with the world. Vanish into them instead of oblivion. Keeps you safe and to yourself. No one to hurt. No need to face anything.

The opposite of Maeve. She would butt heads with the devil, and happy to do it. Like a little billy goat—or were nanny goats the same? I didn't really know.

I could ask Eamonn.

Eamonn?

No, he was caught in the causes he followed and the groups he chose and certain of his righteousness in them. How long had it been since I saw—

Him pulling Ma away. She was still holding the pillow and spitting vicious words at him and he eyed her in horror and—

No.

No, Eamonn wasn't there.

Was he?

No, it was—it was—

A man I didn't know pulled her off me as Colm yanked the pillow away and she was screaming at the both of them, "Isn't this what you want?" and the man was snarling something and—

NO!

No, no, no, no, no, not now, not now, NOT NOW!

Deep breaths.

Slow and easy.

Think of Kieran. Still forming. More stubborn than any in the family and more difficult to talk with, even by the age of six. His face a perpetual snarl, and the neighbor ladies thinking that telling him he's too fine a lad to have such a look about him would mean he'd stop having it. But anyone could see he was born as angry as Da had been.

Da, whom he'd never known. Who I didn't really know. About whom I only had ideas and thoughts, with contradictions that offered no real truth.

Thanks to Ma.

Had she always been angry? Growling at life? Filled with hate, with me her sacrificial lamb to it?

Had she really tried to smother me?

No.

No, something else had been going on and—and I couldn't think of it and—and—

STOP IT, Brendan!

Shut your mind.

Shift your brain.

Reroute this trend of thought and task it with something more tangible. Wonder something like-like-like what would all of them think of *me* being *here*?

What *did* they all think?

Hell, what did *I* think? That was quite the question. When my brain had settled itself, I'd have to ask it. Write my brothers and sisters. Pick at their thoughts about everything. Everything I couldn't ask them in person. I suppose. If that was such a thing that could be done, but I couldn't think of how to do it because the toothpaste was digging at me, its taste so familiar and—

I kissed Joanna atop the wind-swept fort, long and deep, with the lovely scent of spearmint about her and—

I gulped and swallowed some of the foamy paste. Choked on it. Gagged. Coughed. Yanked the brush from my mouth and spat. Still coughing. Breathing hard. I drank more water from the tap to settle me. Left the water going. Rinsed the brush.

And worked my teeth over, again.

And again. Each time with fresh paste on the brush. Each time more gentle. Until the last, which became like a glorious parting kiss from her. And brought tears to me.

My breathing was hard as I put the brush back in its holder. I was aware enough to understand my gums were bleeding, so washed my mouth with water, twice more, and spat more blood out. And did not move.

Could not.

It was all too much to face. To remember. To accept.

After some minutes, I looked at the toiletries. Bandages. Toilet tissue. Bars of green soap called *Irish Spring*.

That brought a chuckle.

A stiff brush was mingled in so I wetted it and ran it through— no, *over* my hair, careful and easy. This actually felt good to my scalp, so did it again and again and—

Ma checked my hair for nits, every other day, because it was so thick and so many other kids had them and weren't being tended to right, she said, and they loved tangled hair like mine, the little bastards, and she was hurting me as she did it, but she did it to all of us and washed it with vinegar and Eamonn hated even the smell of it but it seemed to do well, only Paidrig wouldn't come into the house because he'd face the same from Ma and—

And I was out of breath, again.

I turned and leaned back against the sink. In the small mirror, I finally looked hard at the marks on my face and chest. Pockets of tiny scars, with one large that cut through my left eyebrow in such a way that the hairs didn't meet right. It looked like it was perpetually cocked and—

I flew back in the blast and slammed against a wall then tumbled across the pavement and—

I dropped the brush to the floor.

Deep breaths.

In and out.

Slow and easy.

Slow.

Easy.

Step by step.

Step by step I was finally able to focus back on the mirror. Focus on my face. Then on my chin. I wasn't fond of the scruff on it, but as

I could find no blade to shave with that would have to wait.

I left the toilet and opened the door by the bed. It led into a dark wide room that made up the rest of the attic, with the same types of windows cut into the other side. Boxes, toys and furniture abounded, like it was a warehouse, of sorts. Now I knew that I *had* been stored away like some unwanted table or chair, and almost let myself chuckle.

Along the wall immediately to my right was a door. I opened it to find stairs leading down to darkness. The voices were only a hint louder.

Well, Brendan, standing here is getting you nothing, and this is the way you must go. So I used the wall for both guidance and support and made my way to a landing. Then it was left ninety degrees—no, a hundred and eighty, to another set of stairs that led down till I came up against a door, which I could tell only by touch.

I found the knob and opened it...and saw a toggle switch on the wall so flicked it—and let there be light in the stairwell! Glorious light! Showing bare wood walls and naked stairs, and suggesting that me not breaking my neck coming down them was a miracle.

I now was in another hallway that had carpet and a bit more lighting, thanks to yet another stairway leading down from the end of it, to my left.

I hesitated, stunned at the size of the place. Obviously, it was three levels, and there were several doors to the right of me, leading to more rooms, to be sure. Now I was even more convinced it was a manor house.

Let's move it, mister, screamed my belly. As did my want—no, *need* of a cigarette, so I made my way to the stairwell, as soft as I could. I desperately wanted to see what this led to before I met with anyone, but as I crept down these steps the damn things weren't willing to be silent. Each creak was like a gunshot to me, making me pause to see if anything more might happen.

Before I was to the middle landing, a large golden hound greeted me, sniffing and wagging its tail as if in greeting and—

I was in bed, a golden mound of hair lying close by, as the door opened and someone said, "Angus, what you doin' in here? C'mon, out."

"Angus?"

And I think it was me who said it.

He stuck his nose in my crotch. Brought a yelp from me.

"Angus, downstairs!"

The dog huffed and scurried back to where he'd come from. Then a solid bulk of a man appeared at the bottom of the stairs. Taller than me, a smiling face with cold, laughing eyes, a flock of freckles still evident on his nose and cheeks, short sandy hair going white. My Uncle Sean, from photos Aunt Mari had sent.

"Look who's up," he said, his voice long and slow, like he was thinking of every word before saying it. He met me at the landing, and it wasn't till he took my hand that I realized I was shaking.

And coughing that bloody cough.

I let him guide me the rest of the way down and through a wide foyer back to a pleasant sitting room twice the size of ours on Clíodhna Place. It had two settees placed at ninety degrees to each other that met at a table. A lamp was atop it. There was also an overstuffed chair that turned out to be a recliner, a small table in the middle of them, all on thick carpet and facing a wall of shelving that held a hi-fi setup, television and shelf after shelf of books.

Seated on the floor watching the telly were two girls of about ten, both blond, slim and bright-eyed, like twins. Angus was situated between them. I vaguely recalled Aunt Mari had two daughters, and she'd been in my room but a few hours—or days or weeks before, so I remembered where I was and smiled at them.

Uncle Sean said, "Brandi, Bernadette, want to meet cousin, Bren?"

Bernadette? Like Ma?

"We have," said one, and the other chimed in, "Twice."

I frowned at the casual dismissal and—

I lay on the bed in the dead of night, a single lamp on, as Aunt Mari placed a cool cloth to my forehead and the door opened and two blond heads peeked in as one asked, "Is he gonna cry all night?"

I cringed. Looked at the floor, embarrassed. Ashamed. I managed to say, "I-I-I haven't been the-the best neighbor to you, have I?"

They shrugged and turned back to their program.

Uncle Sean sat me in the overstuffed chair, saying, "Scott's back in a moment, and we'll have dinner. You hungry?"

Hungry? Put cow feed before me and I'd go for it. I managed a nod. Uncle Sean placed a glass of Coke in my hand, ice clinking in it. I smiled my thanks and sipped some. It felt sharp and real on my throat and slaked a hint of my hunger. Before he could sit down, I managed to say, "Uncle Sean, could I—could I get a smoke off you?"

He shrugged and offered me his pack of Camels and a shiny new lighter. I took one, fired it up, inhaled—and coughed. It was a harsh cigarette and I'd forgotten I hadn't had a single one in months. Oh, but did the smoke in my lungs give me a fine new center of gravity.

"You smoke?"

It was one of the girls who said that.

The other chimed in with, "You didn't smoke while you were upstairs."

I ignored them. Just drew in, again, with more care and let it drift from me, and already I felt steadier. I could focus on that, for the moment, and on the telly. Some program about people making bids on cars and clothes and appliances. It was confusing and gave my brain no time to settle as lights flashed and bells rang and people yelled as—

Danny looked around, his eyes filled with horror and I knew and turned and I was being rousted by that bloody Para, with Colm, and he was grabbing my balls then grabbing Danny's arse and I had to walk and walk and walk to Claudy and tried to warn everyone but that car was in the ditch and no one would stop and listen and—

I put the glass to my head. Let the cold of it jolt me. Realized my cigarette was gone, already, without a thought. How did that happen? Finally, I asked, "Have I been like-like this the whole six month?"

"Seven," one of the girls shot at me.

The other huffed and said, "No, he's right—six."

"You don't know how to count."

"He didn't come till Halloween, so October doesn't matter."

"Yes, it does!"

"Don't be silly!"

I frowned at them. "But I-I-I thought..."

"You've been out of it, Bren," said Uncle Sean. "We're in April."

I shrank into myself. *Out of it?* A year older and not knowing it? Christ, I wanted another fag, but I couldn't think of how to ask and I began to shake and the ice was clinking. I had to sit the drink on the table before me before I dropped it. I wrapped my arms around me to lessen the shakes.

One of the girls noticed, gave a massive sigh, and got a small cork pad to move the drink onto.

"I'm sorry," I coughed, my voice barely able to keep even. "God knows what you had to put up with."

"Cut it out, son." Then he took in a drag off his own cigarette and added in a lesser tone of voice, "We're just happy we could help."

Funny, but I got the feeling he really meant the opposite.

The two girls looked at me with questions on their faces. One asked, "You sure you're from Ireland?"

That confused me, so I looked at her. "What d'you mean?"

"The way you say stuff," said the other girl.

"Mommy's from there but we can understand her," said the other.

"Same for all those other people."

"Yeah, your accent's kind of weird."

I near spat back, *And the way you speak is bloody damn well impossible to figure out,* but I caught myself and instead only said, "Yeah. I am. From the—"

"Brandi," Uncle Scott snapped. "You're bein' impolite."

"Just wondering, daddy."

"Your cousin is from Ireland, and that is all you need to know. Do you understand?"

They smiled and the first girl turned to me to say, "You weren't all that bad."

"Just when you first got here."

"You really bugged Scott."

"Only 'cause your room was above his."

"Then he moved in the pool house and they drugged you up, and everything was fine."

"Valium," I heard Aunt Mari's voice say. I turned to see her coming in from the kitchen, wiping her hands. "Which ya've had none of in near a month." She turned to Uncle Sean. "How long's Scott gone?"

"Half-hour," he said, not really paying attention.

"It's a five-minute drive to Weingarten's, five minutes for a head of lettuce, pay for it, and five minutes back. What's he doin' that takes so—?"

A car with a powerful motor thrummed up the driveway, its tires crunching over the gravel and—

The car squealed to a halt, behind me, and Charlie and his mates boiled out to pummel me and yell, "Fookin' Taig bastard!" and—

I crushed back against the settee, shivering, again.

No one seemed to notice. Aunt Mari just shook her head and returned to the kitchen, shooting back at us, "Food's on in a few minutes. Wash yer hands. Girls, set the table."

"In a minute," the girls chimed in unison.

Angus barked, happy and wiggling as he ran into the kitchen and two lads about my own age busted in from there, one pale blond and one dark-haired, both with it long. The blond looked at me and I could see strong hints of both Aunt Mari and Uncle Sean in him, though he was not as large as his father. He wore shorts and a pullover shirt with sandals on his feet and was taller than me by a few inches. The other lad was darker, stockier, wore athletic shorts and was only as tall as myself, but had much stronger lacings of hair all over his arms and legs.

The blond one saw me and spoke first. "Dad, he's up!"

"Cool," said the other lad.

"So, Cousin Bren, I'm Scott and this is my best bud, Jeremy."

Jeremy shot his hand forward and I made myself take it. He was looking hard at me as he said, "Jeremy Landau. An' it's about damn time I met you. I's thinkin' you guys had a *Jane Eyre* situation goin' on here."

One of the girls hopped up and said, "Yeah, it *is* kinda like that."

And the other chimed in with, "Don't be silly; that was a girl they kept hidden, not a boy."

To which the first one said, "It's similar, nitwit."

And got the reply of, "I know, I know, but it's still not right." And they argued off to the kitchen.

I'd no idea what any of them were going on about, so I just shrugged and said, "That's the Irish for you."

Jeremy laughed and Scott rolled his eyes, so I guess I said the right thing.

Uncle Sean got up and motioned for me to join him, but his eyes were on Jeremy. "Didn't expect you. Stayin' for supper?"

Jeremy shook his head. "Thanks, but mom's fixin' Kosher. Wants me ready when I'm on the kibbutz. Besides, I kind of need a shower."

"He was out runnin', dad—well, walkin', so I picked him up. Poor lilttle feller was just give out."

Jeremy jostled him and headed for the front door.

"Say hi to your folks, for us," Uncle Sean said as he guided me to the kitchen. Scott and Jeremy were halfway down the foyer before I remembered my manners and turned and turned to say, "Jeremy, it's a fine thing to meet you."

And I saw a smirk pass between the two lads

He looked at me and nodded. "Same here." Then he left and Scott bolted past me to the table, followed by the hound. I caught a hint of pot on him, barely layered over by cigarette smoke and—

Danny strode up to me, fag in one hand and joint in the other, his mates jostling around behind him, and—

That actually made me smile to myself and think, *If I can get some of that, this might not be so bad.* Even a decent cigarette. Oh, but shite, how would I pay for it? Did I still have my money?

Ma waved my note in my face, howling, "What's this? What's this?"

Probably not. And thinking...it'd be British pounds. How can I change those, here? So better not to have it and borrow from Scott till I could make my own scratch. But could I do that in a country I'd never been to before? And what could I charge for anything I might do and—and—and God, I've got to stop my brain from nattering.

It helped that the kitchen was painfully bright and airy even in the dimming light of outside, with a pair of sliding glass doors opening to the back yard. Appliances and the sink were spaced neatly apart and a tall counter sat in the middle of them all. Everything was done in yellow and white. Even the plates were sunny and cruel.

I was led to a large dining table with six chairs that matched the rest of the room and was sat at a corner. Then a blond girl appeared next to me. I couldn't help but ask, "Which one're you, again?"

"Brandi."

The other girl sat across from her and sighed, deeply. "No, she's Bernadette. I'm Brandi."

"I'm Brandi, Bren. She's messing with you and that's not right."

"You're the one doing the messing, nitwit."

"Cut it out. He's probably still kind of crazy and—"

"GIRLS!" That shot out of Aunt Mari as she set bowls of cheesy pasta and salad on the table. "Bren, yer seated next to Bernadette. And, little miss, if I catch ya makin' sport of yer cousin like this, again, ya'll not hear the end of it." And her brogue was stronger than I'd heard, before.

Scott softly chuckled and leaned over. "Oh, Berni, you got mom's Irish up."

"Sorry, Bren," she said so sweet. "I forgot about you being nuts."

"BERNADETTE!" That came from Uncle Sean, and the look on his face was murder.

I was starting to shake, again, and—

Ma slung my dinner onto the floor and Kieran wailed and Joanna ate a bite of the cake with such delicacy, it hurt me to watch her, and

Mrs. O'Cannain put a bowl of stew before me and I ate what had to be manna from heaven and—

I coughed. My chest was tight and my breath fast and I had to do something to make it all vanish or I'd sink back into that white nothingness and never come out, so I barked with laughter.

They all jolted and looked at me, which made me laugh harder. Then I leaned in close to Bernadette and loudly whispered, "You're right, little miss. I'm mad as a March hare, so have a care with me or I might snatch one of your dollies and split her."

Both girls shrieked, "That doesn't make sense!"

Aunt Mari laughed. "All he means is he'll bash her head in." But she was blushing. She knew what I was truly saying.

"He wouldn't dare!" said Bernadette.

I growled a low laugh and whispered, "Then test me."

Their eyes grew round and they said nothing more.

Uncle Sean helped himself to the cheesy pasta, not trying to hide a grin.

Scott silently chuckled and grabbed some bread as the girls took tongs full of the salad. His silent chuckle turned loud and he said, "That's the quietest those two've been at dinner in months."

Both glared at him, but still said nothing.

Finally, Aunt Mari put pan-fried chicken before us then sat at the end of the table, next to me, and said a short grace over the food. The moment she ended, everyone dove in. I hadn't touched a thing, yet, so she took my plate and set a chicken leg on it.

"Best to start light, Bren," she said. "We've had some trouble gettin' food down ya, so yer belly won't be used to a lot. Can I have the Mac and Cheese?"

The bowl of pasta was handed down to her and she put a spoonful on my plate. Then added a few bites of salad.

"Yer already set for a doctor's appointment, Thursday next, so I won't try to change it. The girls in the office'll be happy to see yer better."

A round woman wearing white with a halo of yellow hair kissed me and pulled back to look at me and smile and wipe her fingers over my lips.

I began to breathe heavy. This was too confusing. Too normal. Too simple. It was wrong to not be howling with pain and sorrow and-and-and—

"What day is it?" I gasped out.

Uncle Sean looked at me. "Thursday's the 19th."

"No, today. Today. Today. What's today?"

Aunt Mari cast me a gentle look. "Monday. April 9th."

"Nineteen and seventy-three?"

Brandi cast me a confused look and said, "Of course it is."

I glared at her and she shut it. Didn't look at me, again. Nor did her sister. They had poked the mad rabbit and found him to be dangerous, so best to let him be.

The date made it official. It was six months, almost to the day, since my world vanished into that blinding white nothingness. Six months since my life was shattered. If I'd stayed up in my room, I could have continued to brush aside what had happened as a nightmare to overcome. Nothing more. The date made it absolute. The normalcy of this table made it impossible to refuse. And my physical state only emphasized the reality of it.

Joanna had been lost to the world for six months. And I could do nothing to change it.

Nothing.

The understanding welled up in me like a flood and my breathing stopped and my hands shook, and—

The para knelt and aimed and fired and Hugh crashed to the ground and the para laughed as he chased more down the street and Eamonn lay in the hospital bed, bandaged and wrapped in white and blood was everywhere and people sat around so quiet and kind and tender before Da's closed casket only the color was soft and green and I could smell spearmint and—

Aunt Mari gripped my arm, tight, jolting me from my spiral into madness.

"Eat somethin'," she said, smiling but with an urgency in her voice. "Please. Show me ya can."

I hesitated then nodded, laid my face in my hands and silently offered a prayer for the souls of the dying and the dead. The words I used are lost to me, but they let me return to myself, take my knife and fork, cut into the chicken's leg as—

Miss Hill showed me how easy it was, and I did it at Joanna's when I was invited to supper and before Charlie revealed me for the liar I was and—

"That's not how you eat a drumstick!"

I jolted.

It was Bernadette said it—I think.

I must have had some expression on my face, for she gulped and looked away and left me to myself. Brandi cast quick glances between her sister and me as Scott just watched me lift the meat with my fork and set it in my mouth, wonder in his eyes.

It wasn't easy, but I managed to chew the food that I knew tasted wonderful yet was meant only to keep a ghost alive.

Moving on

More than a week after that dinner I still struggled to climb all those bloody stairs without being winded. Of course, I would go down for meals, only, and did nothing else to really strengthen myself. Scott gave me a pack of Chesterfields and I spent my days seated at the window, smoking the occasional cigarette, or lying in my bed. Fighting thoughts that would appear. Memories slashing in. Sorrow cutting deep. Sadness washing over me. Pain with all of it.

I fought to remember—

Maeve serving tea to me and Rhuari...and working out a striker's path then stopping a goal during footy...and seeing my work-around on Mr. Keenan's camera properly advance the film without tearing it...and the photos he made from it...and walking to the circle fort...Joanna with me...and kissing me on the Ha'penny Bridge...and her kindness to Malcolm in her quiet ways...and rushing into The Diplomat or Marianne's for our secret meet-ups.

Each was still a stab to my heart, knowing she was no more. Each another layer of anger built against Colm and Danny. And guilt. But I continued to drag them into my mind. Use them to build a wall against that last horrifying image of her.

To keep me from crashing into madness.

And hate.

And despair.

And fury. While I knew in my head Colm and Danny were not the ones who'd arranged the bombing, that mattered little to my heart and soul.

I also read the books on the shelf in the room. And poked about in the attic to find more in boxes with cut-in handles. Paperbacks, for most part. I asked Aunt Mari if I could pick from them and a bright smile came to her face, as if she'd not known me capable of reading, prior to this.

"Help yerself," she said. "They're put aside for a bookfair month after next, so best to read them now. But if there's any ya want to keep..."

There weren't. A fair portion of them were from various romance series and well-worn, but I did find some action ones that were good, like *Airport* and *Day of the Jackal* and *Odessa File* and *The Godfather*. There was also *The Exorcist*, but I found it kind of silly. I'd seen evil true enough, thanks to the Christian faith; didn't want to read some fabrication about it.

I cleaned myself daily now, for taking the nozzle and washing the hot water over me was like a spa, of sorts. A razor and scissors were provided to make my face clean and smooth, again, so I might present something of a civilized look. But I kept to wearing pajamas and a robe, and while in my mind I knew the food Aunt Mari served was nothing but tasty, in my heart it seemed inappropriate to enjoy.

And dear God, it was rich beyond belief. A chop, three bites of creamed potatoes and a half-dozen string beans stuffed me, while Scott would have twice that much on just his first helping.

When I finally asked him how he managed to keep so bloody tight and trim his response was, "Basketball. Tennis. Swimming. That kind of crap. Wanna join some games after school?"

I just shook my head and walked away. I had neither the strength nor endurance for anything, nor was my belly yet able to accept what little food it was getting.

Apparently, I'd lived on broth, meals of porridge, rice mixed with shredded meats, and cheeses and eggs and bread till but a month ago. So long as it was pale in color and easy to chew. I worked out that Aunt Mari had once tried to feed me a pasta with sauce that was red and I'd started crying that it was blood. Then I'd shown myself willing to eat a sandwich, she'd shifted to those. Egg salad. Tuna salad. Chicken salad. Cheese salad, even. Nothing that looked like real meat.

Christ, what a handful I must've been.

I found Scott to be pleasant enough but not very attentive when talking with you. He was nearing his final days at school before heading off to university, and his sole concern was to make ready for that. It was my pacing and God knows what else that made his parents agree to him living in that building in the back, called the pool house.

A number of lads from his class were to join him, at university. Many of them would come over some afternoons to laze around in the water, to smoke and talk out plans for what they would do in Austin or Dallas or College Station. My cousin made no offer to introduce me to them, nor did I express any interest. They all had cars and money and lives with little trouble and hearing their light happy voices echoing about the yard brought forth a dark anger in me at their casual attitudes about the future. They had no idea of the evil in the world. That, or they felt themselves to be apart from it. Or above it. I don't know which. I'd just look out the window at hearing their voices, see them and return to my bed to read.

The only one of Scott's mates I felt any ease with was Jeremy. He lived but a few houses down, and he was off to Israel for a year, the end of July. His time at university would not begin till he had returned and—

Joanna had thought she might do a gap year, and I'd thought it so wonderful a thing to consider and felt I could join her with little trouble for I was leaving—

Cut through me when he mentioned it during the first of the two times he joined us for dinner. We were having fish fingers and string potatoes baked in the oven. Not quite like chips. Red sauce only. Lemon. No vinegar, like Eamonn hated and I loved. It confused the girls when I asked for it, but all they had was clear and that was not good. The lemon was acceptable.

I'd never known a Jewish lad, before, and he hardly fit what I'd been told of them. He was willing to take in what you said, when you spoke with him, and always easy-going and polite. His nose was small, his grin wide, his eyes brown, and while his torso was sturdier than Scott's, there was little fat on him. Nor was there anything sneaky to him; just pleasant to be around. He and Scott made an odd pair, as friends.

"Mutt and Jeff," Uncle Owen had once called them. I didn't think to ask what he meant, for it didn't really matter.

The second meal with Jeremy was a brisket and spuds, cooked over the coals.

Like home.

Off Nailors.

Well...spuds in the hearth. Never a fine cut of meat like theirs. Sometimes the potato had been the full dinner. But I'd been happy with it.

Jesus, was I actually missing the deprivation? Never!

The girls weren't twins, I found. Despite their best attempts to fool me. At eleven, Brandi was ten months older, and Bernadette was well jealous of that. She'd do all she could to make people think they were the same age while Brandi would treat her like a little doll she carried about. And they were always yapping at each other over nothing.

The one good thing was both stayed somewhat apart from me after that first meal. I thought it's because I'd scared them, but I soon learned they were merely taking time to determine who I was and how best to make sport of me.

I caught a glimmer of it when Brandi (I think) was glancing between me and Jeremy during that first dinner a few days after I'd returned to this world, and she'd finally said to him, "You look like Bren's brother."

"Don't be silly," said the other. Bernadette? "He's Jewish, not Catholic. They can't be related."

"I'm not saying they are. But Bren looks more like him than us."

At which Bernadette huffed and said, "He looks like mom, idiot."

"Not in the face, nitwit, and he's not as big." Which brought a cool glance from Aunt Mari and a hidden smile from Uncle Sean.

"But his hair's curly and thick."

"How do you know. He doesn't have any."

"When he came here, idiot. It was like Jeremy's."

"I'm just saying—"

Jeremy chuckled and said, "Well, nobody in my family's even been to Ireland."

I was confused by the whole conversation so said, "I'm after me Ma."

Both girls frowned at me as one said, "What're you after her for?"

"What d'you mean?" was all I could think to say.

Aunt Mari cut in with, "He's just sayin' he looks like his mother, and enough of that. Why would ya even be mentionin' such a thing?"

Brandi shrugged and muttered, "I just thought Jeremy and him looked alike, that's all."

Bernadette rolled her eyes and shook her head, which usually irritated Brandi, but before she could say anything more, Jeremy grinned at her and said, "Both of you know *my* brothers. Does he look like any of them?"

"Kind of," she said, scowling at Bernadette, who rolled her eyes, again.

"Dunno how they'd feel about that," he laughed, then he looked at me. "So what are you, Bren? Member of the tribe?"

By this point I was completely lost and starting to shake. They were talking about me, I knew that, and seemed to think I wasn't really part of the family and it was digging at me, and suddenly Jeremy was watching me so carefully, as if he knew some secret I wasn't privy to and—

Aunt Mari set down her fork, with a clack, and cast both girls a strong look, saying, "I don't think it's funny, makin' out that yer cousin is not one of our family, after what he's been through. I am very disappointed in ya both for doin' it."

Both girls drew themselves up to argue but Aunt Mari's expression grew darker and they both turned back to their plates and focused on their meals.

"As for you, Jeremy," she continued, "yer the only Jew at this table, right now. The rest of us *are* Catholic." Then she added, with a sweet smile, "Though I do get the impression our Bren is more lapsed than not."

Aw, shite, what was that for? Just because she'd asked me if I'd like to join them at Mass, this Sunday, and all I'd done was say no? Why would I want to attend a church where I knew no one? Did she expect me to say the rosary every day and kneel at the virgin's corner before I went to bed? I knew lads whose families were like that. Hell, Danny's could be. So what did this mean? Why was I being picked at? My shaking was growing worse.

But then Jeremy laughed, his eyes kind.

"Y'know, Rachel," he said, touching my hand, "she's my sister; she says I'm not really much of a Jew. I like cheeseburgers at Champs too much."

That cut into my slide towards chaos and gave me a line to latch onto. "Jews can't—they-they can't have cheeseburgers?"

Jeremy shrugged. "Not if you keep Kosher."

I made myself smile. "I-I-I'll have to try one, sometime."

Jeremy near dropped his fork of creamed—no, *mashed* potato and gave me a look so comical, I almost laughed. "You never had a Champs' cheeseburger!?"

I just sort of indicated *no*, so he nudged Scott. "Let's take him, tomorrow."

That's when Uncle Sean finally butted in and said, "Um, Jeremy, I don't think that's a good idea, yet. Bren's still kind of iffy, so..."

"Oh, right, right, right—we'll bring you one. Okay?"

"I-I-I'd like that," I said. "Thanks."

Then Uncle Sean cast a cool look at the girls and said, "Now, did you see that? He didn't even need to be prompted to say *Thank you.* That's what manners is like."

I glanced between him and the girls, saw them cast me quick little glares of irritation, and quietly focused on my meal. I had the feeling I was now very much on their wrong side.

Which was proven that weekend, when they had a number of their friends to a sleep-over, as they called it. Half a dozen girls of eleven, all cut from the same cloth in looks and manners, chattering over pizza and sodas about school and boys and God knows what else on a Friday night. Their rooms were across the hall from the door up to mine, so I heard some of their knocking about and music playing jumpy, happy pop songs about tying a yellow ribbon around an oak tree and another about lights going out in Georgia. They must have had some special meaning to them, because I heard those two over and over and over.

I had begun reading *Catch 22* but found it truly difficult to follow Yossarian's growing panic, Colonel Cathcart's absurdity, Minderbender's casual avarice, and Major Major Major Major Major's nonsensical concerns striking me too much as non-fiction. Which I wanted none of. That and the soft whispering of the revolving fan and the incessant murmuring of the music may be why I managed to drift asleep and—

There were two priests in the confessional and I was dragged in by Ma, telling me I was going to hell if I didn't explain the gun no one knew about when Father Devil reached through the screen to put his hand on mine and I slapped it off and stepped away and saw him change his focus and it was Danny next to me, who couldn't move as the bastard caressed his face and chin and murmured something in a language I didn't know as fire enveloped the confessional and—

I woke to find eight little faces standing around my bed, watching me. My heart near stopped, as did my breathing, till one of the B-girls said, "Told you he talks in his sleep."

Before I could even think of what to say, they whispered out like so many tiny ghosts, muttering things like, *How weird,* and, *Creepy,* and *He looks so sweet,* to which the other B-girl replied, "When he's sleeping."

I actually could not move. My heart was now pounding, I was coughing, and it was a real fight to get my breathing back to normal. I had a tin of pills on the table by my bed that Aunt Mari had said I should take should I have a spell like this, so I slipped one under my tongue and leaned back in the pillow. After a few moments, I felt calm enough to look around my room. I could make out nothing had been touched. Nor had I heard them head down the stairs, which I should have despite the door being closed. So I said not a word to their parents because, in truth, I wasn't positive it hadn't been part of that horrific dream.

Until Brandi (I think) came up to me in the kitchen, just before leaving to Mass, and asked, "Who's Father Devil?"

Her sister was at the sliding doors, watching me, wary.

I only turned away and took a cinnamon roll from a covered pile on the table. Then I fixed my tea, with my movements being steady but mechanical. I was still in my pajama bottoms and robe, and I felt oddly vulnerable.

"Told you he wouldn't tell us," the other said. Bernadette? At least, I think that was their order. At that moment, I still couldn't tell them apart, which is why I began calling them the B-girls.

They left through the sliding doors, Brandi saying, "He will."

I coughed and shook my head, thinking, *Like the devil, you little beasts*.

Which told me they *had* been in my room, that night, and God only knew how many other times while I was still lost. I took my tea and pastry upstairs. I had no lock on the doors, so they could come in any time they wanted, and to say that built a paranoia in me would be simplistic. I sipped a bit of tea and nibbled at a part of the roll, trying to think of what I could do about this casual invasion.

Well, Bren, how do you keep a door closed without a lock?

I remembered a couple of wooden chairs in the attic that had struck me as solid. In I went and found they were easy to clean. So from that day on, each night I put them up against the knobs to keep both the hall and the door to the toilet shut. I can't swear to it, but I think I half-woke at someone trying to get in. Twice.

But never was a word said about it.

Now both girls claimed sole possession of Angus. He was as gentle as they come, and seemed to prefer to sit at my side or lay his head in my lap as I watched the telly. He was an oddity to me, as we'd never had a pet, but I found I liked him being close by. Running my fingers up and down his back, light and easy, with an occasional scratch behind the ears, was oddly soothing. However, this bothered the B-Girls so they would wind up calling him to come to them and he'd sulk and go, casting me a plaintive look now and then, the poor beast. But while they were at school, he was usually in my room and I grew used to him as a companion.

Aunt Mari managed the house, including the cleaning. Scott swore they could have brought in a maid, but she felt herself better equipped to do the place right. And it was well-done. Older yet neat furnishings arranged in comfortable manner in all rooms. Tiny clear works of spun glass graced shelves in a corner of the front sitting room—*living* room, another space twice the size of our entire house on Clíodhna. Not counting a large bay window facing the street and a fireplace taking up half a wall.

Flowers and plants were in abundance, and photos of the family were hung about, including a shot of us that Aunt Mari'd taken when she was in Derry for Da's wake. Grouped together in front of the old house. A bit of the Bogside showing below, on the right. Kieran still in Ma's belly. She had a copy of it hung on the stairwell. I didn't like it; I was realizing with Da gone we were better off, as I recall, and I was smiling wide so actually did look simple in it.

What with five bedrooms and three baths, not to mention the living room, family room, kitchen, breakfast *nook* and dining table, I wondered at how Aunt Mari had time for it all. For she also helped with a charity in the Fourth Ward, as they called it, not far from where we lived, and saw to it her family attended Mass, looking bright and polished. Not as Ma would, to show us off, but calm and quietly insistent that they have some *moral* instruction.

Moral instruction from the church? After dealing with Fathers Devil and Jack? I had to shake my head at that.

I think she knew Scott would slack off the moment he was at university, but still asked him to herd the girls out the door as they sniped at each other about which was more properly dressed for Sunday school.

Uncle Sean would dress in a fine suit, without enthusiasm. I had the feeling his time there was more for socializing. Maybe business. As I had done.

He was quiet in ways I'd never seen in a man. His waist wasn't as trim as it probably should be, as he loved to point out, and while his smile was easy, I got the sense he was not one to be crossed. He spoke with a slow drawing-out of his words that, at first, I found hard to understand but soon got used to. He owned two pubs and was talking of taking on a third, and from the looks of the house and his children having all they could want or need, he was doing well with them.

So all I did for ten days was eat, read and think as the days grew warmer and more still. To call me lazy would have been stating the obvious.

Then one morning, I woke to the chugging of a motor, outside. A car motor. Trying to catch once then again and again and—

Josiah O'Shea's jeep wouldn't start on damp mornings and he'd had near everyone he could think of check into it, at no small cost to himself, until I found the problem and—

I laughed. Startled myself, remembering Josiah. A man who personified the image of a leprechaun. The first time I'd had a happy memory without having to specifically seek it out. I nearly sighed with joy from it. Then I recalled his was the jeep that had taken Joanna and myself partway to the circle fort. And our lovely walk, that day. But this memory didn't hurt.

I looked at the clock and it was just past nine. I'd been rising about this time, anyway, so sat up, felt the fan's cool breeze whisper over me a couple times, then got out of the bed and went to the window. It didn't hurt that the constant irregular noise was beginning to drive me mad. If a car's not working, why keep trying to make it do what it won't do?

There was a light mist in the air, keeping the heat from becoming smothering. Through it, I saw Uncle Sean was at the Volvo, under the bonnet—the *hood*, as it were; might as well use the American terms for all things. It was a dark blue 544 and looked like it had the twin SU Carbs to it. A decent car it was, but in need of a wash and attention paid to the rust spots developing between the passenger door and front wing—*fender*. The interior wasn't in quite as good of shape but wasn't beyond saving.

From here, the motor looked fine. But when Uncle Sean got behind the wheel to turn the key, I could hear telltale creaking that meant some lubrication would be needed. Maybe a fresh set of dampers—*shocks*.

Angus lay on the grass, nearby, watching him patiently.

I saw him try to start the motor, again, and it chugged along, working really hard to catch but not managing. It was flooded. So he took a drag on his cigarette—which was not smart to do around an engine in that condition—then went back under the hood, unplugged the spark wires, re-plugged them and tried once more. Only to get nothing. So back under the hood to undo other connections and redo them and try again. It was comical, for he did not sit easy in that car.

Finally, I had enough of it and was in need of some smokes, so I went all the way downstairs and out the back door. Angus bounced up to greet me and I gave him a scratch behind the ears.

The bricks were wet and sticky, and the air had reached the edge of smothering. I wore only pajama bottoms, still, no slippers even, so the soaked grass tickled my feet and I loved the feel of it—

Caressing the back of my neck as I lay on the hillside, Joanna beside me, our complaints about life in Derry so simple and pure.

I stopped, halfway to him from the house, took in a deep breath and forced myself to say, "Having troubles?"

Uncle Sean jumped to look at me as if I were madman. "Bren, what you doin' out here? You ain't dressed."

I shrugged. "Would you care for me to look at it?" I said, motioning to the Volvo.

He grimaced, in response. "Dunno what you can do. Does this every time there's a fog in the mornin'. Then in the afternoon, it starts up fine. But I need to get to *Liam's* and this is the only car left."

"Liam's?"

"One of my bars. *Liam's Trough*. Not so far from here."

I looked around and saw two dry spots where the other cars had been. "When's Aunt Mari back?"

"Dunno. Guess I'll grab a cab. Lookin' at buyin' 'nother bar up in The Heights and the owner's droppin' by to talk. I'll get it towed to the shop, tomorrow."

"Can I score a ciggie off you?"

He let me have one of his Camels and I fired it up off his, then I just leaned over the motor—and quickly moved the Camel away, for it reeked of petrol—*gas*. He *had* well-flooded it, and I'd almost pulled the same foolish stunt as himself.

The engine was in fine enough shape. The cables were on the old side, possibly original. Same for the coil. I pulled at it without gripping the glove and it nearly come out. Of course. "Try startin' it, again. But no more petrol!"

He shrugged and sat behind the wheel and the car creaked. Definitely lubrication. I had no place to set the Camel but in my mouth so killed its fire. Then I pushed both ends of the coil's cable into their gloves, and the motor fired right up.

Uncle Sean bolted from the car, startled. "What'd you do?"

"You need a new coil," I said. "It's comin' apart inside the glove, so you can't see it. Dampness keeps it from makin' the connection. Is there an auto shop nearby?"

"On the way to *Liam's*. I can stop off."

I nodded. "You might want to think about havin' all the cables replaced. They're about due."

"Damn, Bren, where'd you learn that?"

"I've been at this since forever. Clocks, tellys and the like. Cars. Made money. Had a job."

"Your mother never said a—" Then he seemed to give himself a mental kick and added, "I mean—well..."

"It's all right," I said. "She thinks me simple." Then I headed back into the house, feeling vague and sleepy but also hungry for breakfast. Both Uncle Sean and Angus let me go.

There was no one about to ask after food, so I dug into the cooler. Found neither eggs nor sausage for a fry-up. Instead, I fixed a sandwich from the wealth of things available. Flaps of cheeses and a round, thin-sliced thing called bologna that didn't even begin to look like meat, and lettuce so crisp it could cut you and some sort of mixed sauce called *Sandwich Spread* all piled high on two slices of white bread that felt as light as a feather. There were also tomatoes, but they were so rich and red they made me uneasy. I found only a couple cans of *Dr Pepper* chilled in the fridge's door so took one, opened it and returned to my room.

I sat on the bed and ate, feeling very luxurious, and thoroughly enjoyed the *Dr Pepper*. It wasn't as sharp and biting as *Coke*. Then I finished that Camel and dozed a little before rising, again, and for the first time found myself weary of having nothing on me but sweat and pajamas. It was time to work out a way to pay for my own bloody cigarettes.

I took a long hot shower. Let the steam boil through me. Watched how it caught the light from the window and made tiny rainbows of beauty and gentleness in the clouds. Loved how it filled my lungs and wiped away the world long past. This was such luxury.

Then I toweled off—and had to towel off twice more, thanks to the humidity bringing out my sweat.

"No wonder Americans bathe every day and there's non-stop ads on the telly about deodorant," I muttered to myself. "If they didn't slather themselves with it, they'd reek."

So I did as they did. Some kind of spray called *Right Guard*. It filled the air and stank of chemicals, and I wound up coughing my way out of the toilet—*bathroom* from how it near choked me to death. I may have used a bit much. I'd best ask Scott to show me the right way for it.

I dug through a drawer at the bottom of the wardrobe to find y-fronts and socks and undershirts and athletic shorts and wondered when these had been bought for me. Then I figured they would be some of Scott's things. I pulled on the y-fronts and was surprised they fit, seeing as how he's taller than me and thinner, but reminded myself I'd lost a fair bit of weight and was only just beginning to regain it. When I was back the way I used to be, I'd need a size larger, for these, and shorter on everything else.

I dug into the wardrobe and saw—

My boots!

I slipped on the wet pavement and the car vanished into whiteness and I flew back and hit the wall as dust and filth and bits and pieces of metal and engine rained down on me and that leg...that fucking leg...floated towards me—

I stumbled back to half-sitting against the bed, shaking, soft, pained squeaks whispering from within me.

The bloody things were sitting on a shelf.

In the back.

Cleaned and with nicks in the leather and...and...and...

Come on, Brendan. Breathe in; breathe out.

One of your pills. Quick and easy.

There now. There now.

Breathe in.

Breathe out.

Slow and easy.

Steady.

Oh, dear God, did my mind take its time catching up to my racing heart. And despite the heat of the day, I was chilled. Shaken. But my breath managed to calm and my heart whispered back to normal.

I don't know how long it was before I could even look at the wardrobe. Knowing what was in there. Of course, any clothes I might want were in it, as well. Maybe I didn't want to get dressed, after all.

Except...

Except, I'd shuffled about in these bloody pajamas for ten bloody days, and it was not my way to avoid doing what must be done. Maybe...maybe that memory had hit me so hard only because I-I-I hadn't been expecting it.

Maybe.

The only way to be sure? Get up and return to the damned thing.

So I held my breath.

And I did.

But this time I opened the other door and found a pair of sandals on the bottom of it. So I took those. They were on the large side, but an extra pair of socks helped them fit well enough. Scott's flared jeans were rather undersize, but not buttoning them at the waist and using a belt to cinch them did well-enough. They also bunched at my feet so I had to roll the legs up, a bit. Which looked pretty stupid. On a hangar next to them was a pull-over shirt with a soft collar. On that went, and now I felt presentable to the outside world.

I was also weary, but in too stubborn a mood to give in. Especially since it was near noon. I made myself head downstairs then out in the yard to find the Volvo gone. I'd not heard Uncle Sean drive off.

I was alone.

Jesus, Christ, outside and alone.

No one close by to lean on.

No one to ask anything. Not even Angus was around. Had he gone with Uncle Sean? I heard hammering echo around me, and far overhead a jet passed by, its engines sending a soft growl down to break the last of the silence.

It felt odd, being out of doors, which was not at all like I'd been in Derry. I'd go walking any time, day or night, alone being as fine as with my mates.

Me Chinas.

Who'd set the bomb that-that-that—

NO!

No, that will not take me over, now. Not now. Not out here.

My breathing still grew ragged but I stopped it. Drew in a deep breath and held it. I no longer forced myself to be soft and easy with it; I'd found if I just relaxed and let myself do it without thinking, I was soon able to just—to just be.

I focused on the heat. How it worked with the damp air to carry the overpowering scent of those little white and yellow flowers. Strong as the most powerful perfume and—

Me and Eamonn in Austin's...a lovely store...cannisters of money racing about overhead and escalators up and down and just...just a place for living...him buying rose water for Mrs. McKittrick.

I went to the vines covering the fences with thick velvety leaves.

Close up, they smelled more like a jar of jam and surrounded me with their fragrance and filled my heart and brought to mind laziness and gentle meanderings. Honeybees danced around the flowers, focused on their day's work, all but radiating the thought of, *Mind your business and I'll mind mine*. The elegant simplicity of it made a smile fill my face.

If only the world could take a cue from them.

Shafts of light dashed between the branches of the trees to happily flicker over the foliage, as if to remind me there was a sun, above, and I loved the joyous moment.

Despite sweating under it, again.

I took in the back of the house. It's odd, but while inside it felt large, outside it seemed smaller. It was two levels but also had five matching gable windows cut into the roof for the second story—no, *third*; they counted these differently in America. The walls were a gray brick of many tones softened by thick clumps of ivy climbing up its corners. The bay window for the family room was to the left side and the sliding glass doors for the kitchen to the right. The chimneystack jutted to the sky from the other end and more trees shaded the sides and front of the place. Another wing and it could have been a manor.

I wandered over to the pool house's porch to find its shades were drawn, which had a *Don't bother asking* attitude about them. So I shrugged and turned to the pool. Its water was clear of leaves and had neither wave nor ripple, nor hint of a breeze to cause any sort of motion. Just the gleam of the sun off the edges.

Quiet edges.

Unmoving.

Not real.

The stillness of it bothered me.

A lot.

It grew to be oppressive, so I had to crouch down and slap the surface into motion. Tiny waves danced away and sent shadows crisscrossing along its basin. The chaos of them felt right.

I turned to the bicycle and looked it over. Its gears were rusted near to solid. Some oil might be enough to loosen them up, but I wouldn't know until I'd started in on it.

Then I noticed dustbins resting under a canopy of vines behind the garage. Atop one's lid sat a steam iron with its cord half off. I slipped over and picked it up to look at it. There was only a section near the base where it had been burned through, looked like. It would be easy to mend, so I kept it.

"Creature of habit, aren't we?"

I jumped.

Looked around for who had said it.

But then I-I-I grew to think it was me actually said that. Aloud, and it was only the sound of my own voice startled me.

That or I AM mad as a March hare.

I headed down the drive in front of the garage. Gravel crunched under my sandals, filling the thick oppressive silence. Steam iron still in hand. The fence stopped halfway down the side of the house, and a long gate crossed the drive. It was in two halves that opened from the middle, by motor, to let vehicles pass through. A narrow gate was positioned between it and the house, to allow foot traffic, and there was a lock on it.

A combination lock.

That stopped me.

Froze me to the spot.

I could not think of what to do about it. I had no idea of what the combination might be, but that was of no importance. I simply was unable to imagine what that lock meant except I could not go through. It might as well have been an army patrol holding me in place.

It's just...I wanted to go in front of the house.

I wanted to see it.

I needed to.

And for some odd reason, I did not even consider returning into the house and simply going out the front entrance. I caught a glimmer of thought that if I did go back inside, I'd never come out, again.

Well, I could not be cowering here. Not be afraid. I was determined to regain my life, and allowing such nonsensical fear into it was not acceptable.

But my breath was quick and sharp, and my heart was pounding as if I were in a panic, and my pills were in my room.

No, no, no, no, no, no, no, that would not do!

That could not do.

Joanna would not have been afraid of a simple lock on a simple wire gate. She'd have gone straight up to it and climbed over without a thought. No question in my mind.

I was so sure of it—well, that's what I did.

Reclamation

To climb a wire fence like that in sandals? Not smart. I pinched a big toe in one corner, but thanks to the second sock it wasn't so bad. I also tore a hole on the inside thigh of my jeans, thanks to the twisted wire along the top. Well, Scott's jeans. Left leg. Cut into my skin. Again, not so bad even though it bled, some. I'd had more blood than that come out of me in my life.

I did have to rest, once done. Find my breath, again. It was only then I realized I still had that bloody iron in hand.

Christ, Brendan, could you have made it any more difficult?

I sort of half-chuckled at myself as I looked around...and around and around while wandering down the drive. In full shock.

The front yard was as wide and spacious as the back, if not more-so, with a straight brick walk leading from the entryway to a street wider than Strand Road. Thick green grass framed it. Bushes crouched against the trunks of three additional trees, all laced with more flowers than I'd ever seen outside a florist. Angled bricks lined their beds as well as the walk while the gravel of the drive ran right up to the grass.

Five large windows on the second floor and five gabled windows above mimicked the back. On the ground floor, a massive bay window was to the side of an ornate entry. A roof of black tiles matched the windows' trim. It was all so neat and proper it was more like a picture from a magazine than real life.

I continued to stumble in a circle, overwhelmed, as I took it all in. All so perfect in order. How did Aunt Mari and Uncle Sean have the time to tend it all?

The street curved around, with a number of homes lining it, all of them massed with shrubbery and trees of crooked branches bursting with leaves and bright green grass. Paved walkways lined the road, crisp and clean as if laid yesterday, with everything on as large a scale as Aunt Mari's. I'd have thought myself in a dream were it not for the gravel crunching under my feet and stones hopping into the sandals to irritate me and keep me caught in reality.

Then there was the next to total silence. Oh, birds were singing and insects dashed about, mixed with the occasional dog's bark or cat's call, but those sounds were really lost within the withering peace...to the point of being oppressive. Was there anywhere in the world as calm and quiet as this? Could such a fairy tale of a land truly be possible? It was as if I were the only person left living on the face of the earth. The massive extent of it made me feel more than a little dizzy, and I finally had to stand still to keep from falling over.

I mean, it's not like I didn't know *where* I was. I'd seen Aunt Mari get in her massive estate car and drive off. A Chevy Kingswood Station Wagon, she called it. I'd seen Scott roar up and leave in his six years old GTO. I'd known the expanse of the house I was now living in and had watched programs like *The Partridge Family* and *The Brady Bunch* on the telly as the B-girls argued over whether David Cassidy or Barry Williams was the cutest. They also lived in fine homes and drove cars as big as barges on the Foyle and-and-and all of them had this sense of richness to them, subtly filling me with the absolute certainty that America was the wealthiest of nations that had ever been.

However, it wasn't until actually standing out there and seeing it with my own two eyes that I felt as if I'd been taken from hell and been handed to heaven, and I feared if I so much as twitched it would vanish and I'd be back to the simmering heat of the devil's domain.

Or worse—Derry.

I don't know how long I was caught like that before Aunt Mari drove up and honked at me. I realized I was standing dead in the middle of the drive, so stumbled aside to let her pass and followed the estate car—no, *station wagon* back to the garage. Made it through the large gate before it closed and trotted up to her like a pet dog.

"Look who's out an' about," she said as she opened the door.

"Aunt Mari," I croaked, "this-this neighborhood. The space of it all..."

"Oh, this is nothin', Bren. What ya doin' with that?" She motioned to the iron.

"Thought I'd mend it. Spare you the need of a new one."

"I already bought one, but if ya'd like to fix it, that'd be nice. I could take the new one back."

The rear of the car used some sort of amazing design to vanish into its tail and she pulled out bags of groceries, saying, "Carry these in, will ya?"

I nodded and ferried two full bags to the kitchen's sliding door. She followed with another. Since I still had the iron, she had to open it. We set everything on the center counter.

"Now you sit, lad. I'll put these away."

"I could help..."

"No, I know where everything goes. And we've plenty of time before we leave."

"Leave?"

"The doctor's. Isn't that why yer dressed?"

I'd had no particular reason to put on clothes; I'd just wanted to. But thinking about it, I remembered her mentioning at some time or other there was to be a visit. So I shrugged. "Is this all right, what I'm wearin'?"

"Sure it is. He's very informal, this man."

"You say I've seen him before," I said and—

The round blond lady dressed in white caressed my cheek with the backs of her fingers and said to Aunt Mari, "Lord, his eyes, so big and hurt, they cut right to your heart."

I tensed. Made myself turn to inspect the iron, carefully. For some reason I felt a bit sick from that memory.

Aunt Mari was putting vegetables into the fridge so didn't notice. "He's your heart specialist."

I had to make myself say, "You-you said-you said I was having problems with it."

"Yes. Somethin' ya were born with but hadn't been tended to. I'm not sure of the full name. The pills ya got are for it."

I nodded, still a bit uncentered. "There was mention of it, I think, when I was in hospital. But the doctor spoke with Ma, not me."

She started putting tins of vegetables in a pantry. "Well, yer doctor's name, here, is Gilbert, and he come to the house, a couple times. Then I took ya to him, three times. He told us yer break from the world was good because it helped keep ya quiet and gave yer heart space to mend."

"Was I so bad off, then?"

"There's problems, but Dr. Gilbert can better fill ya in on them."

"I doubt I mended from the quiet," I huffed. "The B-girls say I was anything but."

She cast me a smile. "The *B-girls*?"

I grimaced. "Your daughters. Well, I-I can't tell them apart, so..."

She chuckled. "That actually fits those two. Ya'll learn how to handle them. And keep in mind, they both love to exaggerate."

I shrugged and focused on the iron, fingering the iron's back panel.

She continued with, "What I can say is, ya got a severe shock and yer brain couldn't handle it so shut down, that's all. He said it was somethin' like an—oh, what was it? Akino—no, no. Akinetic catatonia! That's it." She dug more tinned goods from the bag then looked straight at me. "Do ya remember anything since ya got here? Any of it?"

I just shook my head. The iron's back panel wasn't easy to remove, but I managed to get it off to reveal the connections. "Have you a knife I can use?"

She handed me a strip of metal holding a razor's blade. "This do?"

"Aye." I unscrewed the fasteners and got to work on cutting the wires and stripping off the casing so I'd have bald wire to use for reconnecting. I slipped the newly bare parts into their holder then tightened everything down with the thick side of the blade before replacing the panel. Finally, I looked around for an outlet to test it only to find Aunt Mari staring at me.

"What?" I asked.

"Ya've not heard a word I've said," she replied, a bit peeved.

"When?"

"For the last five minutes. I've been talkin' along an' ya offered up an occasional grunt to suggest yer listenin', but ya've been so focused on that iron, ya haven't heard a thing, have ya?"

Shite.

I shrugged. "I-I-I can get like that. On occasion, Ma had to flick me with her finger to snap me from it. But it's only because she'd go on and on at me, and I'd just stop listening."

"And ya think I go on and on like yer mother?"

"No!" Now I was irritated, her making me feel awkward, like that. "I just—I have the habit when I'm working. I don't mean anything by it."

"Don't worry," she said and rubbed my hair. "Lord, ya had such lovely curls, once. Ya like yer hair like this?"

I nodded. "I think I'd prefer it in this heat. I already feel the need of another bath."

"Oh, this is nothin'. Wait till August."

"August?"

"That's usually the worst month for heat and humidity, with September almost as bad. And the hurricanes..."

All of a sudden it was as if my feet were no longer touching the floor. I dropped the iron to the counter and just managed to ask, "Aunt Mari, now I'm better, when am I to go home?"

She did not look at me. Just busied herself with folding the paper bags. "Oh, I...um, it's not time to talk with ya 'bout that, yet."

I did not like the sound of that. The meaning of it.

"Am I not doing well? Is there some other illness in me?"

"No, no, Bren. But I'd prefer we go into the whole of it, later. After the doctor's visit. Have a nice dinner and-and let's see how it goes."

I could barely breathe. "Am I banished?"

She only sighed and put the bags into a cabinet drawer.

"Why? What did I do?"

She took in a deep breath and turned to me. "Nothin'. It was just an accident and—"

"Accident? It was a bloody bomb that took down half a—!"

Her eyes grew sharp and she snapped, "No! *You* were nowhere near that bomb, and ya need to remember that! It was just-just a farmin' accident. Ya saw yer father decapitated and—"

"What the bloody hell are you on about?!"

She bolted over to me. "Whist that talk and listen to me. We-we-we needed to protect ya, so ya-ya were not brought here as Brendan Kinsella. So far as everyone knows, he...he left Derry before that bomb. He'd got himself a passport and his mother got his note, showin' he left. He even bought a train ticket. It was after that—after that when the bomb went off."

Not one word of which was true.

"How can I not be who I am?"

"I-I-I'm sorry, Bren. Sean and I thought it best to wait till we had the okay from Dr. Gilbert that yer heart was strong enough and could face what had happened and...I should have waited. Explained it better. From the beginnin'. Lead ya into it."

Lead me? Like a dog being trained? Like a criminal trying to escape his past? Like I was hidden away? A lad lost in madness kept apart from the world? I couldn't think of what to say. I felt like I was sinking into a bath of ice, yet I managed to whisper, "But I (cough) I-I-I am Brendan Kinsella..."

She put a finger to my lips, her eyes filled with meaning and pain. "Not. While you. Are here. So far as all are concerned, we don't know where my nephew is, or where he went. We've no way to contact him, and he's said nothin' to us, at all. He left no information, and the British Army and police services are satisfied that yer not him."

The peelers and Brits were looking for me? Because of that bomb? I was hidden away and not under my name and—

Uncle Sean and two men in suits looked down at me, in the bed. Himself saying, "As you can see, all his papers're in order."

"They appear to be," said one in a fine British tone.

The other just frowned and they vanished into white nothingness and...

I gripped the kitchen counter to steady myself. No words came to mind. Nothing made sense.

Aunt Mari continued with, "Try to understand, that is how it had to be, and how it needs to stay, for now. Not only for yer own sake but our family's. If it comes out we helped hide ya? well, that's why—yer name is now Brennan McGabbhinn. My third cousin. From a farm in Donegal. I learned of him through my brothers. Seamus and Michael. Seamus is in Toronto and has met my niece, Mairead. Michael is in Sheffield and knew the McGabbhinns and heard of the accident..."

Accident?

Accident?!

ACCIDENT!?

My brain spun into chaos. What she was telling me made absolutely no sense. Seventeen years on this earth and I was not who I claimed to be? And I had not seen what I saw and—and—

Danny looked around at me, startled, his eyes wide, and I turned and started to run for the shop but I slipped on the wet pavement and the world vanished in a cloud of white smoke and fire and silence and I was lying on the ground and that leg was in front of me and its blood covered me and I was screaming from the pain and horror and Danny was grabbing me and forcing me to my feet and holding me as Colm punched me and—

The ceiling filled my eyes. Cold and white, with yellow trim. My heart pounding like the devil. I was lying back on something hard. Unyielding. It took me a moment to realize I was stretched out on the kitchen floor. Aunt Mari was kneeling over me, a portable phone held to her ear by her shoulder as she tried to shove a pill in my mouth.

"...When he just keeled over," she was saying as I half-choked on her fingers. She noticed and shifted to, "Wait-wait-he's comin' 'round. Bren? Listen, son, can ya hear me?"

Hear her? It's as if she were screaming, me head hurt so. But I nodded.

"Here, take this. Take this. Under yer tongue."

I accepted the pill, as I'd been trained to do.

"Can ya get up?"

I'd rather have done anything else, but something told me I had little choice. So I forced myself to rise, slowly, to where I could sit. A rag fell off my face, and it was bloody.

"Aw, shite, I hit me head?" whispered from me.

"On the counter." She turned to the phone. "We can make his appointment, if ya think we should." She nodded. "We'll head straight over so Carla can check him. See ya soon, doctor."

She hung up and turned back to me. "Can ya stand?"

Again, I'd rather not, but now it was a case of damn me if I'd give into it. So I took hold of a chair and pulled myself up, Aunt Mari hovering over me in case I fell, again.

"I'm a right mess, aren't I?" I croaked, leaning against the counter and almost laughing.

She wet another towel and pressed it to my head. "I should've held off tellin' ya all that. Put it in a way that wasn't so confusin'."

"No, I-I-I understand, now. I'm not me."

"Don't be sayin' that," she said, her voice quick, soft and tender. "Yer-yer here as Brennan McGabbhinn, yes, but this isn't forever. It's only to protect ya. For a while. A little while."

Protect me? By making me a lie and—

I sat in a chair, my shirt so clean and starched it cut into my skin, and hands held me in place till just before a photo was taken, when they released me and I wavered and the click-click-click of the camera laughed through the silence before I tumbled over and...

And Aunt Mari was still talking. "It was the only way we could get ya away from all that—all that horror, by it not bein' you. Some people were very unhappy."

Unhappy?

"He belongs in a grave."

"He didn't know anything about it."

"He was there to warn 'em! Little traitor!"

"Then runnin' off."

"He's already half-dead. Finish it."

Ma screaming, "You do that to him, I'll make your lives hell, ion this earth,, by my word!"

Ma?

Fighting to keep me alive?

No.

No, she'd be happy I'm gone, never to vex her, again. My head was just confused.

"I flew over to accompany ya here," she said, far too bright and happy. "Just a lad in my family needin' medical care for his heart and mental health and glad I could help. Could sponsor ya. Fortunate enough to live in a city with the best heart specialists in the world. And physical and mental..."

My head was reeling. I tried to look around and—

I slipped on the wet pavement and the car vanished into whiteness and I flew back and was in a dark room on a bed, weeping, as the pillow came over my head and I could hear Ma's voice snarling, "This is what you want, isn't it?"

No-no-NO! No. Not that. Not now.

I felt ill. My stomach slammed hard against my insides. I was glad it had been hours since having that sandwich. Or had it been?

Aunt Mari was telling me, "Then with Brendan havin' already left, there was nothin' to connect the family to that—to what happened."

Already left?

Right.

Right. My note. The rail ticket. The timing was off, but it seems no one cared, and the remains of me had been taken away. Like refuse. Changed a new world for old.

I had to grip the counter to keep from falling, again, as I murmured, "So I'm not to go back."

"Now, that's not what I said, Bren."

I managed to chuckle. "Bren. Always called Bren. Now I see why."

"It was just to keep things as simple as possible," she said as she removed ice from a tray. Then she wrapped it with a small rag and held it against my forehead.

"So...so...so Scott. The B-girls. That's how they know me."

She hesitated then took in a deep breath and nodded. "But all will work out. Once memories are forgotten and life is settled and cleared."

Memories forgotten? In Ireland?

I must have laughed, for she smiled and said, "Much better. So till that happens, it's best if we focus on makin' ya well and strong, again. Now give us yer shirt and put on another. I'll set this one to soakin', see if I can get the blood out."

Mrs. Kieffer took Danny's bloody jumper as he pulled on my coat and came back to life and—

It probably would. Soaking out the blood. Many a mother in Derry had experience doing that for their sons and daughters. Especially of late.

I made myself focus and slip out of the shirt. Held the ice to my head and started for the stairs. I needed to be to myself. Needed to think. Needed to understand.

But Aunt Mari followed me, so I had to tell her, "I'm fine, now. Thanks. I'll be down in a moment."

"Are ya sure?"

I gave her half a smile. "If I'm not returned in ten minutes, then you can panic."

She swatted me arse and headed back to the kitchen.

I went up the stairs.

Slow, like an elderly man.

My world spinning as I mounted each step. A stark despair whispering around my heart. My head pounding as much from the fall as from the realization that my life had become a danger to me and my family. And that those I'd considered my best mates had nearly got me killed.

And *had* killed Joanna.

No.

My love for her had killed her.

Never mind her Da was UVF, and they were responsible for Catholics being killed. Never mind the growling, howling, screaming anger between both sides, now.

Then.

Always.

She was dead because I'd loved her.

And my family was no more to me because I'd loved her.

It was all on me.

The whole of this catastrophe was all on me.

And many were angry with me over it.

They thought I'd passed information to her Da, through her, so they'd targeted her Da's shop.

And her.
Thanks to me.
I could no longer hide from the brutality of that understanding.
But how in God's name could I live with it?

52

Reconciliating

I was standing before the door to the stairs leading up to my attic room and couldn't remember why I was there. It took a few moments for my mind to focus on the fact that I was without a shirt. Well, Brendan, let's get yourself dressed, why don't we? Now you begin by turning on the stairwell's light, so you can see. Then comes mounting the stairs. After that, enter the attic and turn left to grab the handle on your door. That will open it. No latch, so no key needed. The B-girls at school so no need for the chairs under the knobs. Just wander into the center of the dusty light.

All of which I did, in a haze, then stood still for a moment. Used a wooden chair to steady myself. Give my heart a chance to catch up to me. My head a chance to stop throbbing, at least a little. My brain to settle back into place.

Everything about the room was the same as but an hour or so, ago, except now it was alien. Not Brendan's temporary abode, but a hideaway for an unknown lad named Bren. The bed unmade and staying so. A book half-read on the table, beside it. An ashtray half full. An empty cigarette packet next to it, with a folding book of matches. Those had been Brendan's, I thought. But no, they couldn't have been. They were Bren's, only.

I managed to half-stumble into the toilet and hold myself before the mirror to check my wound. It was a nasty cut, still seeping a bit of blood. Some had trailed down my face and over my cheek. But then, I'd gotten worse from Da.

Who was no longer my Da.

A knot had already begun to form. There was nothing I could do to hide it. If I'd still had my old hair, I could have, but why did I care? I'd never made excuses for Da or Ma, over my injuries.

Except—

I was lying on the divan and told the ambulance attendant my bruising was because I'd fallen down the stairs, and with no question he didn't believe a word from me and—

I covered my eyes.

Everything began to flood back in on me. All Aunt Mari had told me—who was not my aunt, now, but a-a-a cousin? Did I understand that right? And the family? It almost seemed like no explanation had even been offered. I was just *Bren*, here for a doctor's care. Or was I merely a mad lad once treated bad who's too-too sad?

Oh, Christ, I couldn't keep my thoughts straight. It was all I could do to think about washing my face and sticking some toilet tissue to the blood, to help it clot better. Faster. Something. Before pulling on a fresh button up shirt from the wardrobe.

It's funny. This time when I looked at my old boots—boots that had cut deep into me but a few hours before—but they were no longer my boots. Is that why I felt nothing at seeing them?

The room was back to shifting under and around me, so I collapsed against the bed. Put the ice-cloth back to the cut. I noticed the hole in the jeans stained with blood, but there was so little I hated even the idea of changing them. Instead, I just lay back and let my thoughts spin around me.

Brennan. McGabbhinn. Who'd seen his Da die and gone off his head, for it, and—

One of the men in suits said, in veddy-veddy British, "Yes, medical reports seem in order."

"Immigration, too. His visa..." In Uncle Sean's voice?

"This photo sure looks like him," in a not-British voice.

"And half the kids of my wife's family. Check 'em all."

Still naught but flashes, yet I seem to have been accepted by those who needed to and—

"He belongs in a grave!"

"You do that and I'll make your life hell!"

"But he was there to warn his Proddy tart!"

"And how many times has he done it? "

No!

No. Anyone who knew me knew I never carried tales. If I'd known what was going to happen, I'd only have got Joanna away from there to keep her safe, nothing more.

But I didn't. Didn't know.

So how could the British have linked me to the bombing? How could they even know I was caught in it? In all that chaos? Could someone have heard me call to Danny, then added two and two? Were only the rumors about Joanna and myself all evidence enough to suspect me? Had they found my letters to her and come sniffing around for more Catholics to blame? Is that why my absence had been shifted to the simplest explanation? That I'd already left to the South to find work? Or Scotland? Or London, where it would be easy to disappear?

See, Brendan Kinsella couldn't be part of what happened. He wasn't here, so no need to waste your time, on him.

Then where is he?

No idea. He's just gone. No one ever knew what he was planning in that quiet head of his.

A response that anyone who knew anything about me would have easily confirmed to the peelers or the Brits was absolute truth. My note to Ma was in my handwriting, easy to prove by notes I'd made at McCloskey's and from school. And surely one of them had used my passport to leave the country. It would have to be checked through at some point, wouldn't it? Unless I'd got off in Belfast. Ferry to Stranraer. Train to London or Liverpool. Glasgow.

So was that why I'd been rebirthed? *Seek him out, yourself, for the good it'll do you.* And who cares if never he's found because—

"He belongs in a shallow grave."

"For what? Just bein' there?"

"Then why was he there? Right then?"

"Probably warnin' 'em."

"How could he, when he didn't know about it?"

Oh, Christ, that's what they'd been considering. Arguing about. Vanishing me one way or the other. I was bad hurt but couldn't be taken to hospital. The smartest move would be a shallow grave but—

Ma pressed a pillow over my head and I let her and it would all be fine but Colm pulled her back as she snarled, "Isn't this what you want?! Kill a lad who did nothin' to yous?"

Nothing.

Except exist.

The swirling madness in my head was slowing down and I could see that, now. *He's a danger to us and needs to be neutralized. It's gone or a grave. Just the way it has to be.* And the story would remain the same—*He left and we don't know where.*

"But you're nowhere, Brendan, so it's of no matter."

Said aloud. Possibly by me. I shrank a little.

It now amazed me that I was still living.

There had been rumors of that happening to—what was his name? Shane? One of Danny's Shantalow mates. He went off to a meeting and just vanished. No one had seen him for weeks. All he'd left behind was gossip and—

Wasn't he PIRA? Working with Colm? How'd he get that flash bike? Did he know anything to grass on? Does it matter to them bastards and—?

Ma was screaming, "It's you bastards responsible for him bein' here, like this! Give me time to handle it, meself!"

Handle it?

Ma handled it?

Had my mother actually kept me alive? Done it by hiding me in Aunt Mari's attic? No, I'd been erased. Had no one but her and Uncle Sean and the doctor known about me, here?

No, two of my uncles did. And it sounded like Mairead, as well. But Scott and the B-girls did not, and for good cause; I could not see them keeping the secret. It was also now obvious my meeting Jeremy had been by accident, so they could hide me from him no further.

Mother of God, suddenly everything was making sense. Why everyone called me Bren. Introduced me as Bren. Short my actual name as well as Brennan so it would cause no confusion in me. And on the few occasions where the issue had almost been raised, Uncle Sean or Aunt Mari had deflected it. That was probably why Aunt Mari wasn't taking me to hospital for to check my injury.

Christ, I'd have killed for a fag right then—*cigarette*, Brendan. Use the American way of saying things.

BRENNAN!

Bren.

Remember your name—your new life...

And that is when the full understanding of what it meant slammed into me so hard I actually gasped and could not breathe, for a moment.

It wasn't just my name that was new; it was me!

I was free.

I was here and I was free.

Free from the horrors of Derry, and the hate and the pain and the anger and the suffering and the never-ending brutality, both small and large. A sudden wave of happiness washed over me, cold and sharp, casting aside all other thoughts and worries and concerns! I'd been trying to escape Derry—and here I had!

I was able to build anew. Reinvent myself. I had skills that translated anywhere. I had family I could lean on for a bit longer, if need be. The heat was something I'd not be fond of, but I could adjust. It was like I'd been released from a cage to race through an open field, unencumbered.

I was fucking free!

From Ma. From the past. From all of it and—

And the horror of my sudden exuberance slammed into me.

I should not be so joyful about this! It should hit me as wrong. I should be embarrassed at the happiness I'm feeling. Ashamed of it. For it had come at the expense of Joanna's life, and that should not be acceptable.

Hadn't I loved her?

Of course, I had.

Wasn't I part to blame for what happened?

No.

No, she was not the target. It was her Da they wanted dead. Also, the bomb wasn't meant to explode till later. All the anger about her and me had come after it happened.

After.

Hadn't it?

Christ, I didn't know. My head was still too confused. All I knew for sure was, while I could never release myself from her or her memory...or toss aside the evil that had taken her away...I had been cut off from every part of what happened. It was as if I'd been reborn.

Dear God, I could grieve for her, now. I was fucking free to do so, openly and without complaint from anyone.

But it was wrong, it was wrong, how could I be happy about that?

To say it was confusing, having these two opposing emotions careening through me was fair simplistic. They tore at me. But what it came down to was, absolutely nothing bound me to Derry now and I cannot begin to convey the overwhelming joy that idea sent throughout my body. No more fear of being taken out to be damaged or killed. No more bombs going off wherever or gunfire getting closer or Paras out to destroy all in their path. I had a new life.

I'd have to verify much of this with my aunt and uncle, but surely there was a way for a wounded traveler to be welcomed to a land as open and rich and free as America, even under questionable paperwork. I'd heard on the telly that you could move anywhere you wanted, here. To another state, even, if you like and—

Shite.

No, no, I was wrong.

There was Mai and hers, in Toronto. Could I abandon them? And Rhuari, lost in his books. Maeve protecting Kieran from Ma's worst aspects. Could I accept being cut off from them? They were of my blood. So somewhere down the road I needed to figure out how to eventually regain contact with my brothers and sisters. A safe form of contact that would not lay waste to my new world.

A world to live in. No, not merely live. Make myself become more than I ever thought I could. Honor Joanna's belief in me...in what she thought me capable of. Expand. Grow. Live. Make the fullest use of this opportunity. I had a bright new future ahead of me, and I was close to weeping from the joy it brought me and—

A knock at the door was followed by, "Bren?"

I jolted, rose and was halfway to it when Aunt Mari opened it to peek in. I made my grin sheepish as I said, "Sorry, forgot the time."

"Ya ready, then?"

"Yeah. Let's go." Then I drew myself up, stood a bit taller and deliberately added, "And if you don't mind, Aunt Mari, could I have one of your cigarettes, and-and-and could you explain how I got here, on the way?"

Her look grew tender then she said, "I'll tell you what I can."

Tell me what you can?

Well, that walked me a few paces back to wariness. Maybe this new world replacing my old wasn't yet as open as I thought.

Little Bomber Boy

The city she drove us through was a tangled mass of homes, commercial buildings, empty lots, wide car parks and massive streets. And that barge of a car floated past it like we were on water. Seats as fine as I'd ever sat in. Air conditioning so icy it gave you a chill. Aunt Mari offered me a *Kool* as she drove. Bloody *Kools*? I quit before half done. The menthol only added to my head's pounding.

We passed a University called Rice that was across the road from a large, open park cut through by another boulevard. Behind us was the overpowering city center with its sudden office towers and cranes aiming to build even taller ones. Ahead of us was another mass of tall buildings she referred to as the medical center that made Altnagelvin seem a county clinic in comparison. But what struck me the most was how flat it all was, everywhere you looked.

This is to be my new home? That, I was suddenly not so sure of.

As for how I'd got here? Aunt Mari provided me with an idea as to what had happened.

I'd hit the wall hard enough to break my left arm, three ribs and get a concussion, along with a fair number of cuts and bruises. My rucksack being stuffed with clothing had cushioned me so I was not more severely injured. But the shock actually pushed me halfway into a heart attack. Colm striking me unconscious may have saved my life. Then they'd taken me to a safe house near the border, and Colm had fetched Ma.

"How?" I asked. "The Bogside'd be locked down after the bomb."

"I didn't ask," she snapped, "nor did either he or your mother say. She made it to your side to fight against a couple of men who wanted to finish ya."

"Why was Ma arguing against it?" popped out of me.

"What d'ya mean?"

I almost said, *Because she hated me*, but held back and muttered, "She's women's auxiliary, and so hard after Eamonn doing well, I'd think she'd go along with them with whatever they wanted."

Aunt Mari cast me a glance of shock and said, "Bren, you're her son. Her child." As if that should be explanation enough.

I merely shrugged, in response.

So instead of being assigned to a grave, I was attended to by a doctor they knew. Even put on nitroglycerin tablets! Jesus, talk about the *Little Bomber Boy*. And once they knew I wouldn't die on my own, I was snuck into the Republic and Ma was allowed to contact Aunt Mari.

"When Bernadette called with the news," she said, "it scared the breath from me. I had yer uncle talk to some people and he—"

"How did he know who to call?"

She huffed. "Does it matter? Ya were given time to heal, weren't ya?"

True. I was kept in an isolated farmhouse for well over a fortnight. Always medicated to keep me calm and let my heart work through its problems. Cardiac surgery was not an option, and I half believed they thought I might still kick off, thanks to it.

Mairead was included as a possible alternative to Houston, but it was decided that since she was immediate family that might arouse too much suspicion from the British. She learned from our Uncle Michael of a cousin who'd been killed in a farming accident, more than a year earlier, and that his wife had wasted away. They'd had a son who passed in a cot death, same year as my birth, so he was used for my papers and Irish passport. A bit of makeup to cover my scars for the photo. Then they used the excuse that I'd gone off my head at seeing the accident, and now my heart needed repair.

Without a doubt, a fair amount of money changed hands, for all of this. And half the reason I had time to heal from my injuries was to give them time to work up the new papers. Make everything look good.

"I flew over, through Shannon," she said, "once yer doctor said ya could travel, and brought ya here."

"You had no issue with the customs?"

"Immigration. Ya were provided a medical visa. Yer Uncle arranged that, with his lawyers."

"But why so much trouble for me?"

"Would ya rather be in a grave?"

To be honest with myself, no. But the tone of her voice all but snarled, *Don't ask any more questions*. Only I had to know, "So Uncle

Sean has my new passport?"

She hesitated then sighed. "Somewhere, I'm sure. But best to take care, now. While we did get an extension on yer visa, it's expiring soon. We're lookin' into askin' for another, but not sure if it's allowed. He'll need to find out how best to handle that."

She drove in silence for a few blocks, which I appreciated. My head needed a chance to settle. Then finally she continued with, "Bernadette showed me that note."

Of course she would. Just further proof of my unwillingness to help the family.

"Bren, what did ya think ya were doin'?"

No sense in hiding plans that would never happen now. "I was off to work on a ship. I had an offer."

"Without a word before leavin'?"

I shrugged. "I'd have sent money home."

"How? The way the British are bein' with the mail? I don't dare send cash, now."

To be honest, I hadn't really thought about it beyond that, so all I could do was shrug.

"Well, it's better that yer here. I think I've talked yer mother into openin' an account at the post office, so I can transfer money into it. It's expensive and is reported to Inland Revenue, but if it's needed..."

I nodded, which was a mistake. That and the Kool Aunt Mari was smoking made me feel a bit weak in the stomach.

I swallowed and said, "Ask Mr. O'Faelan or his missus about that. They have one with the savings—um—the Catholic—no—no, credit union. I-I-I can't think of the name." My head was back to pounding.

"Is that the one run by John Hume?"

"Yeah-yeah-yeah. Him."

"Father Jack mentioned them. It does sound the better idea. He sent me their information and said he'd keep workin' at Bernadette for it."

That caught me off guard. "Aunt Mari, it's been six month."

She sighed and nodded.

Good ol' Ma. Won't be pushed into a thing she doesn't want to do, no matter how smart it might be, or helpful. But I suppose it made sense. If it is reported to Inland Revenue the grubby bastards who administer the dole might cut her payment back. An alternative might be to send it through the church, but they were sure to take their percentage. Something Ma had seemed to finally understand before I left.

My head slowed to merely hurting, so I asked, "When you brought me, I-I-I feel like I was—well, was I drugged the whole time?"

She took a moment to reply. "On sedatives. For yer heart and the pain." That last sentence was said a bit too quick and sharp for me not to understand it was done to keep me from revealing who I really was or what had really damaged me and—

A cold bright room surrounded me. Stark. A man in a uniform before us, at a table, saying, "Can't he speak for himself?"

"He's not all there." A man's voice, not Aunt Mari's.

"Oh. Retarded."

"Well, when your brain's deprived of oxygen..."

Oh, Christ. Had I gone from being simple to being an idiot? I almost laughed. Probably the one true thing about me.

What was good about this is, without question the Brits did not think I'd been caught in the blast. Which released a massive wave of relief over me. For that meant at least my family was safe. Well, as safe as any can be in that bloody state.

Then Aunt Mari took in a deep breath and said, "I don't know that I should tell ya this now..." And grew silent.

I said only, "Tell me what?"

We stopped at a light and she flexed her fingers then said, "Eamonn's been arrested."

A chill cut deep into me. "Do you know why?"

"Somethin' about smugglin' arms in. Mairead wasn't sure. It's only recent it happened; came in yesterday's letter."

Oh.

"May I read it?"

"If ya like."

"Was he snatched on his own?"

"No, it was with a couple other lads."

Oh, Jesus. "Did she mention any names?"

She looked at me, wary. "Are ya askin' after anyone in particular?"

Oops, careful, Bren. "Not really. I just—just wondered."

"Ya sound like Scott when he's tryin' to work around answerin' a question."

"I don't mean to. It's just, the other two lads—I'm wondering—

might they...?"

I almost asked if they might be friends of mine, but I stopped. Despite my anger at Colm and Danny, I still had not the slightest interest in drawing attention to any of me Chinas. So I made myself cough to cover my hesitation and said, "Might they be lads who were friends of Eamonn's? I know most of them."

Her eyes became sharp. "Did ya know what Eamonn was up to?"

I laughed without meaning to. "Aunt Mari, you've forgotten how Derry is. Everything you do is everybody else's business."

"Which doesn't answer my question."

"I have no answer for you." My voice was sharp when I said it.

The light had turned and the car behind us honked, so she snapped, "Read the letter for yerself. All of them, if ya choose. There's a lot. She's been sendin' one every other week. Read 'em all." Said in a voice meant to end the matter.

But still I asked, "Can I read Ma's letters to you?"

She gasped and grew incredulous. "No! Those are between me sister and meself, only."

A moment later, we turned into a car park between an office complex and construction site. A new hospital was going up and I wondered at the need for it, until Aunt Mari mentioned Houston alone holds half the full population of Ireland and was growing larger by the day.

"Built on oil, cattle and shipping," she told me, her voice relieved she could talk of something unimportant. "Financed through Dallas banks and investment firms."

"It's massive," I whispered, still taking it in. "Is NASA close to here?"

"That's in Clear Lake, twenty-five miles on."

"All of it city?" I asked, as I got out of the car.

"I don't know. Never been."

"But you sent me a—"

"I know that cap!" Joanna snatched it from my head, laughing, and put it on and her girlfriends roared with laughter and then she gave it back, with a wink, and my love for her near exploded into nothing but white and red and—

I fell against the car door. Dizzy. Couldn't breathe. I had to force myself to gulp in some air. Christ, that one had come so sudden and sharp.

Aunt Mari took notice, put an arm over my shoulders and guided me into the building, saying, "Ya can buy those in any shop, just about. I think I got yers at The Galleria. Can ya ice skate?"

Ice skate!? Bloody hell? "Never have. It-it-it gets that cold here?"

"No, The Galleria has an indoor skating rink, surrounded by shops. If ya want to learn."

"Don't you ever want to go on to university?"

Joanna's voice drifting up to me. No image with this one, just the sound, and me answering, *"I've no head for university."*

"You never struck me that way."

Then I saw her gazing at me, so sure and gentle and this memory didn't hurt. It was almost like a caress.

Without thinking I said, "I do."

I didn't.

Not really.

It seemed silly to be dancing atop frozen water on slits of metal. But to have said *no* to learning something different now my new life was begun? It would have been a desecration of her memory.

We rode up a quiet lift—*elevator*, went a short way down a corridor, and stepped into an office that was simple and felt comfortable. Standing by the receptionist's desk was a round blond woman and—

"His eyes're so big and hurt."

Sliced into me.

I gasped and stopped, cold, at seeing a pair of cold black orbs surrounded by colored lines focused on me from behind fancy eyeglasses. Lips as red as blood. The skin of her face smooth and tan for the yellow-blond hair she sported. I had to close my eyes to let the pain whisper past. My head froze in its hurt, my heart raced and-and-and I bloody fucking coughed.

"Hallo, Carla," said Aunt Mari. "Look who made it under his own steam."

"Hey, Mizz Nolan, Bren," Carla purred, her voice long and slow with its words, like Uncle Sean's. Her lips smiled but her eyes did not. I mean, they almost seemed to, maybe just enough to be all right, but I wanted little to do with her. Then she added, "Looks like you got quite a bump."

I just shrugged.

"It's better now there's been ice on it," said Aunt Mari.

"Well, come on back," Carla said. "I'll get your vitals an' see if you need stitches."

Oh, I did not want to follow that woman anywhere. But Aunt Mari made no motion to go with me. I had to remind myself I'm a free man, now, and seventeen years, to boot, so it's time to have a pair on me. I made myself follow Carla into the back.

Coughing.

Bloody fucking coughing.

She did a simple checkup—temperature, blood pressure, weight and the like—and seemed satisfied. "Your pulse is a bit up but you put on a few pounds. That's good. You were gettin' too skinny." Then she looked at my head. "Knot should go away in a few days. Don't see no need for stitches." Then she cleaned and dressed the wound...and gave me what she called a tetanus shot.

In me arse.

Which bloody hurt.

All the while she chatted about what a nice kid I was and how glad she was to see my heart statistics were more normal and nonsense of that nature. Then she left the examination room and called for the doctor.

And that was all.

I wondered at how I'd feared more, from her. But now she was gone so was my cough, and that was a truer monitor of who to be wary of than anything else.

Moments later, a man near eighty came in, the little hair on his head white to the point of being clear, his thin frame covered with a black suit and tie over a white shirt and a white smock atop it all. His eyes crinkled with kindness, and I felt immediately happy to see him.

"Well, Bren," he said, his words inflected in a way I found both odd and sweet. "You're looking right good. Better color to your skin. Filling out a bit." I shrugged. "Remove your shirt, please." I did. "You remember my name?" I shook my head. "Dr. Gilbert. I understand you took quite a spill." I half-grinned and shrugged. "Are you unable to speak?"

Shite. Find some words, Bren. Find some words.

"Yes. I-I-I been talking." My voice was soft, but it was there.

He started checking me over. "Excellent. Do you remember anything that's happened over the last six months?" I shrugged. "Is that a yes or a no?"

Him, I felt a trust for, so I said, "I dunno. I get flashes of things. Dunno what they mean...how they're connected to me." Which wasn't entirely true, but true enough.

"I see. Well, your memory should return with time. I spoke with a few people familiar with cases like yours. Seems the Valium was the best way, for you." He felt my neck and raised my left arm over my head and pressed his fingers down my left side around to my spine. "You have a name tattooed on your shoulder. No one knows who it is. Do you?"

Oh, Jesus—

Joanna held my hand and I gazed into her eyes and the pain drifted away as I opened my heart and soul to her and we were given tea and biscuits and she watched me, in awe. Such lovely awe and—

It overwhelmed me and sank my heart to my stomach and my eyes closed and the words came out in a pained sort of whisper. "Girl I knew."

I opened my eyes to find him looking at me. He was even more kind as he said, "You must've known her real well."

I shrugged a sort of nod, then, "Loved her," whispered from me.

His eyes grew tender. "You should always remember those whom you loved." Then he put a stethoscope to my back. "Cough, please." I did. "Again." I did, and twice more. "Excellent. You were having some fluid build up in your lungs, but it sounds like it's pretty much gone. And while your blood pressure's still a bit high, your heart sounds nice and normal. Do you smoke?"

That caught me off guard, but I said, "Yeah, I do. I mean, I didn't for a—while I was—how did you know?"

"I can smell it on you, but I know Mrs. Nolan smokes, so just wanted to make certain. You might want to think about cutting back. Won't help your heart, any."

"So it's right that—that I have heart trouble?"

He gave a slight shrug. "You have a slight arrhythmia. I'd say you were born with it. Things just went a bit off-key, but not so bad that surgery was warranted. Carla says you coughed a bit, while she was examining you."

I nodded.

"Well, that can be an effect. But you're much better now."

"So I-I'm healthy enough for work?"

"Well, why not wait a short while to start looking for a job? Give that knot a chance to go down."

Then I had to ask, "How bad was I? When I first come?"

He looked at me, his kind eyes growing kinder, if that was possible, and he said, "You'd been seriously injured but healed well-enough. Though you responded to none of the stimuli I used. Do you recall what caused—"

The car dissolved into white smoke and flying debris and I flew back and could near nothing but a sharp singing and a child's leg flying through the air and...

I tensed.

And coughed.

He noticed but said nothing.

I wanted to remain silent, but his gentle manner pierced through me and I swallowed and heard myself say, "Bomb."

"A bomb? You witnessed it?" I nodded. "Where was this?"

No, don't say it, Brendan, don't say it. "Derry. Northern Ireland."

"I've seen the news. Some horrible things going on over there."

I coughed and nodded but could not find any words to say.

"I know someone who works with veterans who returned from Vietnam. She says they're suffering from serious battle fatigue, one that's worse than anything she's ever seen. You might want to talk with her." I shrugged. "I'll have Carla give you her name. Consider it. I would like to do a follow-up exam in about six months. Okay?"

"I-I come here every time?" I asked.

"No, the first few times I went to you, after office hours. Your cousins were very worried about you."

"How bad is it to be—well—Aunt Mari—I mean, well, she said something like I was-like cata...catter...?"

"You were in Akinetic Catatonia. It just means your mind had separated itself from this world, for a little while. But as you can see, it's rejoining us."

"Thanks, Dr. Gilbert. Sorry to be so much trouble."

"Don't worry about it, son. We're all happy you're doing so well."

And he left.

Carla came in as I was putting on my shirt and eyed me in a way I found even more uncomfortable than before.

And that bloody cough came back.

"Mizz Nolan's taken care of everything," she said, "an' I gave her that name an' number. So you can head on."

She had to stand there and watch me as she told me that? I nodded and started for the door, but she stopped me and slipped a fingernail into the hole in my jeans. "Looks kind of bloody, down there," she whispered, her nail pulling at the material. "Maybe I should've checked that, too," and—

Her fingers trailed down my shirt to my pants and—

I jolted, snarled and grabbed her hand and held it tight. "You think it right to mess with me, knowing how I was?"

She winced and whimpered, "I didn't mean nothin'."

"Oh, aye, aye, nothing meant."

I released her hand and pulled at her lower lip, smearing her lipstick. She yelped as I rubbed it on the left of my mouth and backed away, leaving her at the door. There was a box of tissue at reception, so I took one and deliberately wiped my full mouth with it in a way that Aunt Mari could not miss.

I have no idea why I did that except it just seemed—I dunno, necessary. Then as we rode down the elevator, I asked, "That Carla, was she with Dr. Gilbert when he examined me?"

Aunt Mari cast me a wary look. "No, he does those alone. Why?"

"Does she always do the—I dunno, the first exams?"

"*Preliminary* exams. She's his main assistant. Why ya askin' me this?"

I shrugged. "She just-she felt familiar—like there was more—I dunno..."

Aunt Mari looked away, now confused. "She took care of ya every time we brought ya here."

"Every time? Just her and me, alone?"

"Of course. She got all your vitals—what we could get from ya."

"We?"

"The first time, I was with ya, tryin' to answer on yer behalf, but somehow she got ya to respond to her questions. Only one or two words at a time, but they gave her what she needed. I let her take the lead from then, and she stayed with ya till the doctor came in."

"Her and me, alone."

Her hard red nails traveled from my lips to my shirt, and she unbuttoned it then undid my trousers, her voice soft and words meaningless and hypnotic as she—

The elevator doors opened and I damn near jumped through the ceiling.

"Bren, what's wrong with ya? Why're ya askin' me this?"

Why was I askin' her what? Her question made no sense. Nothing made any sense and-and-and—yes, it did it did it did. But it took me a moment to understand why she was asking it and in reference to what. Every thought in my head was bouncing about like mad and could only think to say was, "I-I-I dunno. My memories. They're all jumbled up and I dunno what they mean."

Aunt Mari led me from the elevator so others could enter, saying, "Well, at least they're comin' back. That's good."

"Yeah, it is," I said, not really meaning it.

I knew already there were many things I'd sooner not remember, but I had no choice in that, it seemed. Those images would fly at me without warning, cut into my heart, and dance away as if they meant nothing. Gone till I was back to not being ready for them, again.

What made no sense to me was, I actually dreaded the day they'd stop. Because it might also end the ones I liked.

This Carla, she must have known the damage I'd been done and could still be done to, and yet I was near certain she'd made sport of me in some way, when we were alone. Here I am a lad whose mind is gone and she's playing the maggot with it? Even now? When I'm barely able to lumber after Aunt Mari like Frankenstein's monster? Jesus God, that fucking bitch! I'd be happy never to see her, again.

Except from deep within came a voice asking, "Would you really?"

And my response to it? A quiet growl of, *Maybe. Maybe not.*

Which both scared and thrilled me.

Ground Rebuilt

The days following were taken up reading bundles of letters from Mai, written in her precise hand and each including Polaroids of her family. As well as queries on how *Brennan* was doing. As she wrote in her latest letter—

I'm so pleased to hear Brennan is doing so much better. You were such a saint for taking him in and getting him the proper treatment. I am sure it is far better than he could have got at home. As Eamonn has said, far more often than once, the best care within the NHS is reserved for Protestants, at Altnagelvin, despite London's assurances. I used to think that was an exaggeration of his. But no more.

A friend of our Brendan's, a rather chubby lad named Paidrig—you met him and his family at Da's wake—I learned one of his sisters-in-law was cleaning a house on the Waterside and got attacked by the owner's son. She became pregnant, and as her husband is still in Liverpool for half the year, she tried to handle it in private. Instead, she was brought into Casualty thanks to non-stop bleeding, was put to one side and died before they tended to her.

Saoroise! Now dead. Paidrig's brother had been off to work construction when I was leaving. Actually trying to make a living for his wife and wains. But why would they have just left her to die? I didn't understand. The care I got was fine, as was Eamonn's. Was that Scottish doctor not available? He seemed not to bother about what your religion or background was. He'd never have allowed that to happen. But then, it'd been so long since I was at Altnagelvin I didn't honestly know if he was still there. Of course, now it's no good to find out.

Mai continued with, *No one wanted to talk about it because of the circumstances, but it has made Ma so very angry. Two young wains without their mother, now being cared for by their aunt, who has three of her own, and uncle who's not known for one to take care even of himself. And despite Father Jack's attempt to intercede, she was buried in City Cemetery, not the family's plot by St. Agnes. I would say Ma was just as angry about this as she was when our Brendan was arrested, a couple years ago. It has been very upsetting for them all. Perhaps now she will stop giving so much money to the church.*

As well as this, I learned that Eamonn's been arrested. The Army's linked him in with arms smuggling and to that bombing on the Waterside six months back.

Arms smuggling. Like that bloody pistol. I was so glad I'd kept its hiding spots from him, for now he could not lead the Army to it, even by accident.

Apparently, there was Semtex with the shipment that was intercepted, and that is their reasoning. Which is nonsense. This shipment was stopped only recently, and it's been months since the Waterside bombing. What's more, at the time they said it had been dynamite in the boot. But thanks to the Special Powers Act, his attorney says to be ready for conviction and many years at Long Kesh. I must admit it seems truth and innocence mean nothing, these days, especially to the British.

The reference to it being dynamite going off in that Rover caused me to research the stuff. Aunt Mari had an Encyclopedia Britannica and what it described helped make some sense, but only if the sticks had been old and ill-kept. The nitroglycerin in them could seep out and explode for little reason.

I was taking nitroglycerin tablets, myself. Could that be the cause of my sudden surges of anger? Was I just as unstable? Explode with no warning? Wouldn't that be perfect?

Mai continued with—

I have convinced Ma to have a telephone put in. It took the possibility of Eamonn calling to get her to agree, and now I can be contacted quickly, should she need to. Ma's not completely happy with it after what happened during the strike, year before last, but I am paying for it. Father Jack helped arrange it through the Post Office.

Plus a fee of ten percent, I'm sure.

All of her earlier letters were written with the same care, and all carried far less detail than I would have liked. Bits about Rhuari taking courses in the Irish. Maeve doing well in her school. Kieran slinging stones at the Brits and being the best arm of them all. More sewing work coming Ma's way. Setting up a television subscription for Ma, which meant Mai'd also got her a telly.

She included stories of her own family, with Michael Paul being the brightest child ever at four years of age while Jordan Allen was growing fast and Aisling Marie had already begun to walk. There was also talk between Tur, Gerry and their Da about maybe opening a second store in Mississauga. And through every bit of it the new me was asked after, but in the least intrusive of ways —

How is Brennan doing?

Is Brennan's heart mending?

So happy to hear Brennan is better.

When do you think Brennan will be completely well?

Always the full name, as if I were a friend or acquaintance and not family.

The B-girls saw me returning some of the letters to Aunt Mari and decided it was time to fill me in that they knew all as regards matters of the mail.

"You never get letters, do you?" said Bernadette (I think).

"Haven't seen a one come through," said Brandi (maybe).

"Doesn't anybody write you?"

"Why should they?" I'd shot back. "Considering how I was for so long."

"Yeah, probably."

"Mommy gets letters here, but daddy don't."

"But we do."

"So does Scott."

"Just school stuff."

"Pamphlets from UT."

"That's what I said."

"I'm being specific."

"You're telling him the same thing I'm telling him."

"No, I'm just making sure he knows all about it."

And off they went on one of their little tangents. But in bits and snips I got more out of them.

"Mommy's got family all over Ireland," and I think it was Brandi telling me this.

"We had lots of visitors, before you," which would be Bernadette, if I was right. "From lots of different people."

"Lots of 'em." Said with a long, weary sigh that both of them had perfected.

"Guys and girls."

"But never together."

"Mommy don't like that."

"They didn't stay up in my room?" I asked.

Bernadette (maybe) looked at me as if I were completely mad and said, "That wasn't put in till you came."

"You're the only one mommy and daddy had up there," Brandi (maybe) snapped, as if it were the most obvious thing in the world.

"Daddy knows lots of contractors."

"They got it done real fast."

Bernadette took on a very concentrated air and said, "But y'know, it does sound like what Rochester did in Jane Eyre."

"A special room to hide her away."

"Until she burns down the house."

At which point one glared at me and demanded, "You're not going to burn down the house, are you?"

And the other added, "That could happen if you smoke in bed."

"Sister Mary Michael told us!"

"*Do* you smoke in bed?"

I just sort of gulped and gasped and muttered, "Never have." Which was true. Not for fear of the fire or health aspects but because I didn't want to burn holes in Aunt Mari's sheets.

"Those people who stayed in the pool house sure smoked a lot."

"They always had a cigarette, didn't they?"

"Oh, yeah. Even when Daddy took 'em to the bar to meet people."

"Like on St. Patrick's Day."

"Scott was really upset about them."

"He wasn't upset about them going to the bar."

"That's not what I'm saying. He was upset about them living in the pool house because he wanted to."

"That's what you said."

"No, it's not."

"Now you're just being silly."

And off they went.

Scott overheard some of this set-to and took me aside to say, "Don't listen to 'em. We just had some of your cousins come over from Cork, on business. Those two make it sound like a damn convention."

More cousins? First I'd heard—until I reminded myself they thought me a McGabbhinn, not a Kinsella. So the next morning, I got Uncle Sean off to himself and asked after them.

His response was to scowl. "Who told you that?"

Shite.

"I overheard it," I replied as evenly as I could. It was not rumors I wanted to be spreading or causing trouble for anyone. "Not sure whose voice it was."

He eyed me then simply murmured, "Yeah, well, I'd take anything those two say with a grain of salt. They're usually wrong an' love to exaggerate. It was just one of my wife's brothers, who lives in Sheffield. Michael, that's the one. Traveled through Cork on his way here."

That confused me. "Did he come by boat?"

"No," and he seemed a bit flustered. "My wife's diggin' into the family tree and there was some info there, an' he asked around for her. I mean, she's got seven brothers all over the world, all married..."

Fortunately, I'd already known that, so merely nodded.

"My...well, my side of the family's been in this country since the famine. Wanna know anything more about that side? Ask my wife."

Except when I did ask Aunt Mari about *the visitor from Sheffield*, her only response was, "Talk to my husband."

In short, *shut your gob*.

I huffed and puffed over it for a couple days, in my room. Finished off a second pack of Marlboros while scowling out the window till I finally got it into my head there was nothing I could do but let it go.

For now.

I thought about writing to the O'Faelans. Put my anger at Colm aside and see if he might fill me in on what had happened since the bombing. But that might bring the Brits to his door. The possibility they were reading mail as it came in made direct correspondence from myself to anyone anything but an option.

Dammit.

Thanks to the length of my mental collapse, news of that disaster had long been replaced with even more atrocities in Derry and Belfast and Armagh and Newry and on and on. I thought of checking to see if the libraries in Houston held old editions of newspapers, then realized I would have to read details of the bombing I'd been caught in. The mere thought of which made me ill.

Then came a new letter from Mai.

My mother and Rhuari were arrested, last week, for interrogation. Imagine! A slim, quiet boy of 15 interrogated by the

RUC and Brits! It was fully traumatic for him. Maeve let me know he is eating little and sleeping less since he came home, just buries himself in his books.

Ma was kept twenty-four hours, leaving Maeve to care for Kieran. That was a chore for her, I am sure. Still, I think she handled it well. What makes it funny is, some nuns came by the house to suggest Kieran be put in care, since Ma had no relatives local and she was now considered suspect and had led Rhuari into the devil's corner, as one put it. Our wee Maeve, who is but 13 years, all of five foot nothing and not even a hundred pounds, whisked them out the door with a broom while screaming curses at them.

Well, that was not acceptable, so they returned with Father Jack, both of them righteous and angry. Ma was home, by then, and cursed them even more for trying to steal her children away. When one of them said she had been arrested and could be, again, Ma fiercely pointed out the Brits would arrest anyone they felt like, and for those two biddies to accuse her of being complicit in death and destruction without even so much as a trial, and use that excuse to orphan her youngest? Well, that was against the rules of the Magna Carta! Magna Carta! I never laughed so hard when I read Maeve's letter.

Apparently, Father Jack agreed with her and led the nuns away. Maeve thought it hugely funny.

Now enough about the Troubles. Rhuari had already done well in his CSE and seems bound for university. I think. I hope this arrest does not throw him off course. Maeve is speaking of becoming a nurse, as well she should. She would be a good one. And I just received a call from the doctor; I have a fourth child on the way to join the three I have, already. Oh, joyous. But that means postponing my journey to see Eamonn.

Tur, his Da, and brother are doing better and better with the furniture business. It seems when Quebec began threatening to break away from Canada, a lot of businesses and financial interests began opening operations in Toronto, just in case. Uncle Shamus has joined with the new store, both investing and building cabinets and such. We are a part of the future, here, and it is glorious to consider the possibilities.

So there it was. Ma and Rhuari were now definitely under the eye of the British. That meant no contact, and I was left to know little or none. I could read the papers after Uncle Sean was done with them, but there was not so very much more in those. Which I suppose made sense. American news was the more important. So to keep from running mad, I dug through the items in the attic for things to fix, repaired sockets that didn't work, climbed onto the roof after a rain to seal cracks I found in the tiles, all without asking a penny. I was being fed, housed and provided ciggies, so it was the least I could do.

Aunt Mari also brought up a small TV so I could watch the nightly news. Which I did like a religion, even though there was little said about the North except when some atrocity happened. And every horror was first assigned to the IRA. Also not very comforting.

Or intelligent.

There were a couple of occasions where I saw a news snippet that showed Father Jack in some demonstration or march, also with little detail.

I began making a bit of money the same way I did in Derry when I saw a neighbor's char woman—*cleaning lady*—tossing an iron in the bin. I was in the garage and noticed she was trying to hide it. She spoke little English, but I figured out she'd dropped it and it had come apart. I managed to let her know I could fix it for a couple bob—um, two dollars. So did. Which made her more than happy, since I also did it quick. Word spread, and while nothing massive came from it, I could now pay for my own Marlboros.

I caught on that Americans preferred to toss out appliances rather than have them repaired. So if I went wandering on the morning of trash days, I could find toasters, lamps, fans, clocks, electric razors, hair driers, radios—Jesus, a full assortment of things that needed little work to be fine. I'd bring them up to the attic to tinker with and sell. Even pulled in a small table from the stored furniture, as my work bench. A gardener told me of a second-hand shop down Shephard that might buy some of what I fixed, so down I went. They offered no great money, but enough to buy a full set of screwdrivers and grips.

The end of May, Uncle Sean finalized his purchase of that bar in the Heights, and I happened to hear him talking with Aunt Mari about needing new help there. He wondered if Scott might do. He'd just graduated from his school so had the time. But she wasn't keen on the hours needed: Thursday to Saturday, six in the evening to two in the morning.

Uncle Sean laughed. "He's already out that late, most nights. This way he'd be of some use. Put money aside for college."

"In two months?" she'd said, "Ya'll not be payin' him so much."

"It's more about responsibility and learnin' the value of a dollar."

"If he don't know those things by now, he never will, and you givin' him a job will be the easy way for him, again. If yer so keen on him workin', let him find a summer job. They put up the notice for lifeguards at the pool, last week; and he can swim well."

"He needs to know first aid."

"Nelda says they teach 'em the basics 'fore they start."

Uncle Sean huffed and opened a bottle of beer to go with his Camel but said nothing more. That's when I tapped at the door. They both jumped and looked at me as if I were a ghost.

"I was passing—heard you," I said, "If it's all right, I'd like the work."

They glanced at each other, wary.

"Are ya up for it?" asked Aunt Mari. "Yer still..."

"I've worked before," I near snapped. "I can do what needs be done. And it's not like I've much else to do. Is it okay for you to use me?"

Uncle Sean hesitated then nodded and said, "Under the table."

Which brought a sharp glance from Aunt Mari as she said, "He's not old enough."

"He won't be bothered," was all Uncle Sean said.

I had no idea what he meant, but it sounded like I had the position. So I nodded and continued up my room to shower and change for dinner, after which Uncle Sean drove me up to the place and introduced me as the new bar-back. *Bren*, only. I was to replace a lad named Javier, and the sense I got was those working at the place were not full happy about it.

"Can't have no illegals working here," was Uncle Sean's excuse. Which suggested to me I wasn't one.

It was called *The Colonel's* and reminded me of *The Diamond Pub*, off Fountain in Derry—small and dark and thick with the smell of smoke, stale spirits and human sweat. A short bar ran along one wall, with tables and stools set about and a pair of tables for snooker— no, *pool* in the back.

Located up Shepherd past the Ten Motorway—*Highway*, I was to be paid fifteen in cash straight from the register, each night. The barkeep sighed and said he'd slip me a couple more, now and again, if I did an especially good job. Like it was so hard; just keep the beer and wine stocked up and the place clean, make sure there's a running count on the cases in the back shed, swap out the fountain drink cannisters, sometimes hand a bottle over to a lad at a table when the waitress was busy smoking or in the toilet, or both.

Its steady patronage was men working the warehouses and shipyards and refineries down in places like Pasadena and Deer Park and Texas City. Meaning miles they had to drive for work, sometimes in the wee hours of the morning, yet still they'd drop in for a beer or two and talk of their wishes and hopes and dreams as they smoked and sighed with a weariness approaching death.

The one-and-only barkeep was named Todd. Tall and lean with straight brown hair to his shoulders, tattoos up both arms and a Fu-Manchu moustache, as he called it. He didn't seem thirty yet, and he had this too-casual air about him that all but snarled, *Don't ask me anything, or else*. He knew most of the regulars by name and drove a pickup with a flag in its back window he called *The Stars and Bars*. He'd also give me a lift home, as he lived off Alabama.

I was happy to accept the arrangement, because before we left the parking lot he'd have a beer open for me. Apparently, it was legal for him to buy me one despite me not being of age because he had what he called *guardianship of me in his truck*. Which made no sense, but I was not about to argue. He'd also have some weed lit up...and a bowl with a cone of incense burning to cover the smell. Apparently, you were not to be caught with even a joint in Texas. Not if you wanted to escape the hell of the state's justice. Which I understood. Even in Derry, it wasn't something you boasted about. But what was best was, he never tried to get me to talk, and I gave him the same courtesy.

I did learn he'd been to Vietnam, thanks to a fat fella named Bidwell, one of the regulars who always had oil or grease staining his fingers and clothing. And soul, from my impression of him. He trapped me in a corner to whisper it like it's some major secret, casting wary glances at Todd as if in hope that he was being noticed. Like I was simple enough to swallow his shite. The man had something about him—it just put me off. I never said word one to Todd and saw to it one of the waitresses took him his *Lone Star Longneck* after that.

Two women came with the bar to handle the tables, the main one being Raquel, who was dark, thin, sharp and all business. She worked every night the place was open and was pleasant enough but had little to say to anyone and I was glad for it. How she said words made them hard to understand. Todd called it the *Lady Bird School of Diction*, which made even less sense.

Until I asked Aunt Mari about it. She laughed and told me it's just what some people called one of the Texas accents.

"Like the difference between Belfast and Derry," she said.

That made me roll my eyes, for I never had a bit of trouble understanding a Belfast man. So Scott filled me further.

"*It's lahk, this is mah par-rt of th' countreh,*" he snorted through his nose. "*An' I fe-yel down-home he-yer.* Then the twang's like this—*well, little feller, y'all got a lonnnng ways t' go, sti-yill.*" He used a deeper, throatier sound.

I scratched my head. "I'm supposed to understand this?" I'd asked.

That's when Brandi appeared and said, "Scott's got it all wrong."

Bernadette followed her, saying, "We can teach you better than him."

"Careful, Bren," Scott said. "These two are like terriers; once they get their teeth in you, they never let go."

"I'm not a dog," Brandi snapped. "I'm a girl."

"I'm a girl, too," Bernadette cried.

"That goes without saying," Brandi shot back.

"No, it doesn't, with you."

And off they wandered to have their own little craic. Thank God.

The other waitress was Lorraine, a nicely rounded lass with sleek brown hair who loved to flirt with anything male, didn't matter what age they were. Her way of talking was more like Todd's drawl, as he called it, and was a bit easier to follow. Her rear was handled as often as not and she never seemed to mind, but not once did I see anyone touch Raquel—Rocky, as she preferred. Lorraine was in Thursday, Friday and Saturday nights, like me, with the bar being closed on Monday and Tuesday and me making another tenner helping clean it and stocking for opening.

Both were stand-offish with me, at first, because they'd liked Javier. But since I kept to myself and made no demands, they warmed up.

There was a small kitchen in the rear, with a dirty stove and foul sink next to the cooler, which wasn't so clean, itself. This bothered me, so I spent three nights scrubbing them and making them useful, again. When Todd, Rocky and Lorraine saw how nice it all turned out, they brought in snacks, and would share some. I'd also purchase cans of soup to heat in a battered old pot atop the stove, so it was almost like a little home.

What made it even better was how Todd kept the makings for sandwiches in the cooler. Sometimes he'd work one up for a lad who was getting too deep in his cups, with crisps—*chips* on the side. Javier had refused, but I didn't care so I became what Todd referred to as *chief cook and bottle washer*. Uncle Sean even made up a price guide for it and bumped my wages to twenty a night. I felt like I was making a fortune.

The area the bar was in was hardly the best in town. Houses run down and streets gutted with holes. Long boring buildings of shops behind car parks overgrown with weeds and strewn with debris. But word was the city planned to *turn the area around*, as Uncle Sean put it, and since his other bars were doing well, I figured he knew what he was doing.

I actually worked six to two-thirty, my three nights, catching a bus up so no one need take me. Many's the time Aunt Mari or Scott or Uncle Sean would offer a lift, but I liked the solitude, and they allowed it. I began to pay fifty a month for room and board, and could only get Aunt Mari to take that by suggesting it be added to what she sent to Ma. I wanted to be owing nothing more to anyone. Uncle Sean said I was independent to a fault. Again, this made no sense as I'd always tried to be as independent as I could. I saw no fault with that.

As mentioned, I was also in demand with the neighbors. Never by the homeowners, mind you, but their maids and gardeners to fix a vacuum cleaner or lawn mower. Then they'd slip me a couple dollars and I'd add that to the pile I was saving. It was almost the same as home had been, except no need to hide it from Ma.

Dunno why I was saving money, other than a vague notion that if I wanted to open my own shop or move somewhere else, I'd need cash for it. I wasn't like Uncle Sean and could borrow from banks or build up investors, as he was planning to do with a row of vacant shops next to *The Colonel's*.

There were four of them, each with a large window and entrance in front and a rutted car park. I could get in through the back doors and found each one's interior was a fine size, just filthy and stinking of urine and mold. It would take a lot to clean them, but I could actually picture where to put a work bench and hang my tools and set up a counter and add storage. Yeah, I'm but a lad of seventeen, but I was halfway to eighteen, soon, so why couldn't one of those shops be mine?

That was something worth dreaming about.

Adjustments

By late June I was feeling quite settled in and more like I once was. I'd even been expanded to Wednesdays, at *The Colonel's*. I hadn't put back my full weight, yet, for in this bloody heat no matter how much you eat you'd sweat it off within the hour. That's why I began to take a second shower in the late afternoon. At dinner, I didn't want to smell as though I'd never seen soap.

Then came this one truly hot miserable Tuesday. I'd spent the afternoon in my room cleaning then rewiring an electric heater I'd found. Angus was lazing in a cool enough spot between a window and my workbench. The fan was doing little good for either of us and the sweat on me was irritating. But I got it done, saw the time was close to five so stripped down and hopped in the shower. I'd cleaned *The Colonel's* the day before so looked forward to an evening of the telly, for I enjoyed *Hawaii 5-0*, and then some reading.

Oh my God was it lovely, under the water's spray. While I did miss soaking in a tub, water dashing down on you was like a gentle massage, and I felt as if I were being reborn. I could have stood there forever.

Aunt Mari had mentioned she was preparing barbecue as she was laying everything out, which meant ears of corn and her hand-cut chips—*french fries*, Bren! I wanted to miss none of it. Not even Mairead's cooking at her best was this good. And simple. And abundant. God, the abundance.

My hair was long enough to begin showing its curls, now, as the water coursed through it. I'd filled in enough to where I'd had to buy jeans and y-fronts and shirts to fit me, from Sears and Montgomery Wards as they were cheap. I could now climb the full sets of stairs without being too much out of breath.

I finished and toweled off my hair, then walked back into my room, full naked, and—

The B-Girls were seated on my bed and—

Soldiers burst into my room like howling dogs, tearing me awake and grabbing at me, screaming, "Eamonn Kinsella!" as I was yanked down the stairs in my pajama bottoms and Father Demian was there, waiting and laughing as he sneered, "You thought you could get away, you wee bastard?" and they slammed me against a wall, kicking at my feet and—

"What the bloody hell!?" shot out of me. My voice was neither kind nor gentle. My body shook like mad, and I barely managed to whip the towel completely around me.

"Oh, Bren, I thought you were back to normal," said one of them, for I still could not tell them apart.

"Who's the girl on your arm?" asked the other, immediately after her, and my heart near stopped as—

Joanna looked out over the whole of Ireland from atop the fort, the wind catching her hair and making it flow in ways too beautiful to exist as the needle pinked into me and I focused on not gripping her hand too hard and words poured from me and—

"I know that cap," and her at the door of the auto shop and telling me she'd tried twice to see me—

Sliced into me like spinning blades and my mind was blank. I stared at the girls as they chattered on.

"Isn't it time you told us?"

"We saw it when daddy was bathing you."

"The first time."

"Mommy had us take up some towels."

They what? They what?! They fucking WHAT!? And—

Uncle Sean unbuttoned my shirt, but it wasn't my shirt. It was something gray and striped and I'd never have worn such a stupidity, and then he undid my jeans as fingers with red gleaming nails tugged at my zipper and a lovely hot cloth went around my neck and down my back and Scott bolted around to snap, "What're you two doin'?"

One looked at the other. "Wasn't that the first-time daddy was bathing him? Like a sponge bath?"

Who nodded, in response. "He used wash rag, not sponges."

"That's what he said it was."

They'd sneaked in on me more than once? This wasn't the first? As I'm naked and I coughed, my breath ragged and—

I sat in the tub, filthy, weary and drifting but we had won, we had the British on our side and the RUC were gone and I'd fallen asleep and then I was on the bed, awake and clean and Eamonn was beside me but he was in prison clothes and—

"It must've been the first time, 'cause those really ugly clothes were on the floor."

My heart pounded. I couldn't think. I couldn't move. I couldn't understand. This wasn't real. It couldn't be real.

"Right, daddy hadn't put in the stool, yet."

"And mommy threw everything straight in the garbage."

"But not his boots."

"Yeah, still in the wardrobe."

"Even though they're pretty worn out."

Danny looked at me, his eyes wide with horror and I turned and saw the car and I knew and spun to run back but I slipped and everything went white—white—white except for this doll's leg twisting and turning in the air as it drew closer and closer and red sauce was flying from it and—and—

"Get out," I coughed then gripped my head and slammed back against the wardrobe, still gasping, "Get out. Get out!"

Their voices grew cold and hollow.

"This is *our* house, not yours."

"We can go wherever we want in it."

"You're just a guest."

My head pounded and my heart screamed, and I was so bloody close to throwing both the little cunts right out the fucking window and watching them fall till they crashed to the ground and broke into pieces that I had to make myself tumble into the toilet so I could slam the door between us to keep from laying hands on them. I pushed my back against it and slid down to a crouch, arms wrapped around me, keening as—

The rain was light and easy and Joanna gave me the lightest of kisses and said she'd meet me at Marianne's and white filled the world around me and—and silence filthy with blood, red, red, red blood and—

Knocking at the door.

"Bren, c'mon," said one.

"We just want to know who she is," said the other.

"She must've been somebody really important."

"Yeah. Tattoos hurt."

Oh, Jesus God, could they not shut up? Could they not shut their fucking little mouths?

"Get out. Get out." I was thinking it but was I saying it?

"Scott was thinking about getting one but mommy said no way, José, and she was serious."

"Oh, yeah, 'cause you can't get 'em off."

"Are you mad? You can't take those off."

"I'll never want to, Joanna. You've branded me..." and she's looking at me in awe and—

"She must've been really important to you."

"Why won't you tell us about her?"

I finally managed to whisper, "Get out. Get out." And it was more like I was begging, now.

"You must've loved her."

"Yeah, putting her name on your arm, like that."

And I held Joanna's hand and looked into her eyes and told her everything there was about me and knew we'd have forever together but the devil had other plans and—and—

I heard Aunt Mari. "Why're you in Bren's room, an' him not here?"

"He's in the bathroom."

"Acting all weird."

"What d'ya mean?"

"We just wanted to know about the name on his arm."

"And he keeps yelling at us to get out."

"Of our house."

"Bren, ya all right, son?"

I managed enough thought to whimper, "Get out. Get out."

Aunt Mari's voice grew sharp and cold. "You two, down to th' kitchen. I'll be there in a moment."

"But mom—"

"NOW!"

I heard the girls scurry out. A moment later, Aunt Mari knocked at the door. "Bren? Bren? Can I come in, son?"

"Get out." I said it soft.

Those were the only two words I could think of.

"The girls are gone."

I said nothing. Made no move. I had no heart. I had no mind. I had nothing in me except a searing, screaming, slicing pain in my chest that burst from me with soft little grunts as I rocked back and forth and bumped my head against the door, over and over and over.

From a thousand miles away I heard, "I'll check on ya, soon."

And silence grew around me.

Blesséd silence.

Slowly.

Slowly.

Slowly allowing my mind to ease enough to join it. To let darkness blanket me and comfort me. Dear God, how I loved the dark. Hides the evils of the world, it does. Hides the ugly and vile. But there should be stars. Shouldn't there?

Why were there no stars?

Where were the stars?

They're my company. My guides. They watch over me and I never want to be without them and where were they? Where? The shadows were too cold and cruel without them and—and—and—

I finally opened my eyes. Focused on the floor. It was dark. I'd been sitting there for hours. I'd be awful late for *The Colonel's*—no, no, this was Tuesday. Tuesday. No need for me to go anywhere. Not today.

But dinner would be done. This late? Yes. I'd stayed here all through dinner. But wasn't I famished from the hunger? I may have been. Think I had been, but now? I-I-I couldn't tell.

I noticed my heart was finally soft in its hammering. My skin was clammy and cold.

Cold?

How can anyone be cold in this heat?

Was I even breathing? I had to be breathing. Yes, I could feel it. My head ached but didn't pound, not like it could when I'd forget to breathe.

I finally looked up. The room was naught but shadows. Only a bit of light filtered through the window. I shifted my eyes slightly to my right. Saw a corner of the window. Gray, not black. Not full dark.

It took a moment, but I reminded myself the stars would be there, waiting to be witnessed. It was not their fault that first they must wait until day was gone, in full, to shine. And even then only barely through the brightness of the city's lights. I could almost hear them calling, *We're here. Don't be concerned. We see you though you cannot see us. We will be here, always.*

Always.

Always.

Then they would offer all the solace I needed.

Finally, I was able to think about rising to my feet...so did. Bit by bit. Oh, dear God, how I ached all over. I'd stayed in that bloody crouch the whole time. I had to move slow so the kinks didn't become anything more than yelps of pain. God, how cold I was. Shivering cold. Colder than I'd ever been in Derry.

In this fucking heat? How? How?!

I leaned against the sink and looked in the mirror, and while I was nowhere near as bad as I had been little more than two months earlier, everything about me looked and felt blue. And my heart was still thumping deep. I started the shower and let it grow hot then stepped under it—and realized I still had that bloody towel on me, so got it soaked. And I had no other.

But the water steamed and wrapped around me as...

Clouds billowed soft, below me, gentle and kind and...

Gentle. So gentle.

So tender and caring.

Helping settle my aches and calm my head, if not my heart.

What amazed me was, not once since I'd come back to myself had I coughed. Or wept. It was as if I were petrified. A deeper fear was now gnawing at my heart.

I'd felt so calm and in control, that I was moving forward, but this one jolt had brought it all crashing in on me. And now I was fearful that it would happen, again. Something would trigger it and I'd careen back to madness. Relive that whole hideous moment, over and over and over. For the rest of my life.

I could not live with that.

I couldn't.

I needed to feel safe...and wondered if I ever would, again.

But under the water. Dancing against my head and flowing down me. Hiding me from the world. Letting me know that here. *Here. Here no one can touch you. No pain can cut you.* I could grow calm, again. I could take control of myself, again.

I could be warm, again.

I finally stopped the flow of water. Let the steam slowly dissipate. Let the world bring me back to where I could think, again. Be Brendan, again.

No, Brennan.

NO!

I'll be fucking Brendan till I fucking die. This shite is not forever. No bloody fucking way would I let it be.

I chuckled. What a childish thing to believe.

Still trailing water, I carefully went into my room to find the outer door open and Angus on the bed, his tail flipping light and welcoming. I scratched his ears and wondered if he saw me as a buffer against the B-Girls, being way up here. I would not have blamed him.

I closed the door then used a pillowcase to dry off, and I was back to being cold. Which was good. I sprayed on some Right Guard, dressed in my new clothes, slipped into my sandals, all without conscious thought. Brushed my hair. Brushed my teeth. Then made my way downstairs. Walking like a robot of some nature, Angus at my side, in solidarity.

I found everyone in the family room, as they called it, looking at me. Of course. Here comes the main attraction.

I stopped in the entryway, my eyes locked on the B-Girls in their usual place. Uncle Sean was seated on the couch, his usual cigarette in hand. Scott was in the lounger. They both looked at the girls, then Uncle Sean said to them, "Well?"

They sighed and Brandi, I think, said, "We're sorry, Bren."

"For going in your room without asking," said Bernadette, I presume.

"We thought you were normal, again, so—"

"Bernadette!" was shot from the kitchen by Aunt Mari. I'd got the two mixed up, again.

Scott just shook his head, trying not to laugh.

"Mom," Brandi whined, now that I knew it was her, "how were we to know he's still nuts?"

I just looked at them. Not glaring. Not angry. Not feeling or thinking a thing, really.

Aunt Mari huffed. "Bren, ya must be perished from the hunger."

"She went up five times to check on you," said Brandi.

"Six," Bernadette sniped.

"The first time doesn't count and—"

"Quiet yerselves, both of ya!" Aunt Mari snarled. Then she smiled at me. "Would ya like a bite?"

Without thinking, I said, "I can't live here. Not if this is going to happen."

The B-Girls sat up, in shock, and Uncle Sean said, "Bren—"

"I've no lock on my door. No way to keep anyone out."

"But you're safe, here."

"Safe? I come out of the shower to find them on my bed!"

Bernadette stood up, wary, "But we weren't gonna hurt you."

"We just wanted to know about—" Brandi started.

I cut her off with, "Whist. How many times have you snuck into my room? Whether I'm there or not?"

The girls glanced at each other, wary.

Scott gave a deliberate stretch and said, "They used to do it to me, too, till I bawled 'em out."

"Has this happened before, Bren?" Aunt Mari asked as she put a plate on the table. It was the barbequed beef on a bun and corn steaming and fries and looked like heaven, but I would not move till I got an answer to my question.

Aunt Mari sensed it and asked, "Girls, what's the answer? How many times have you done this to him?"

That she even had to ask only added to my uncertainty.

"Just a couple," said Bernadette.

"Like when daddy was bathing him," Brandi added.

That caught Uncle Sean's full focus and he growled, "What?"

Scott chuckled and said, "Don't worry, Bren, I stopped 'em before they got to the bathroom door."

"That doesn't count. Mommy asked us to take up some—"

"No," shot out of me. "No, I can't live here. I can't stay here. Not if I have to worry about this."

Angus nudged my hand, whimpering. I gave him an idle scratch.

Aunt Mari came over to me, saying, "Bren, ya look—ya look cold. Have ya taken your pill?"

I shrugged. She put a hand to my forehead and nodded then guided me to the kitchen table, saying, "Have yer dinner, before it's as chilled as you are. And tell me, would ya be happy in the pool house?"

That brought Scott straight to his feet. "Mom!"

"It has locks on its doors," she continued, casting him a look of warning. "An' blinds. We could even add curtains, an' there's a gate to use for yer own private entrance."

"But what about the people that come there?" asked Brandi.

"If any do come, again, they can have the bedroom in the attic. But we're not plannin' on more visitors, are we, Sean?"

He leaned back on the couch, his eyes locked on her, and shrugged. "Not at the moment."

"But, mom," Scott howled, "I'm in the pool house!"

"You'll be off to university, soon. I'd feel better if Bren had it and was close by."

She drew me to the table and the food all but called to me, but I had to say, "Why?"

She gave me a confused look. "What?"

"Why do you want to keep me here?"

"Bren, it's better for ya to be near us. Ya still have issues with your health. Your heart. I'd be so much happier if ya were close by. In fact, I don't like yer look, right now, so I'm callin' Dr. Gilbert and seein' if he can come over."

"Oh, don't, don't, don't..."

"It's for *my* peace of mind, not yours, and that is that."

Uncle Sean stood, stretched, and added, "Y'know, that don't sound like a bad idea, you bein' in the pool house. You could even move that junk of yours into it. Plenty of room. Work on 'em whenever you want. An' it's got A/C."

"Will ya think on it, Bren? For me?"

Honestly, I did not want to...but an idea grew in the back of my head that it made far too much sense. How could I afford a doctor's bill? And I'm sure were I to leave I'd lose my job at *The Colonel's*, so where else could I work? But still...

"We can help you decorate," said Bernadette, bright and chipper.

"You...will do nothing...of the kind," I snarled.

"We'll ask if we can come in," said Brandi.

"But will you wait for me to give an answer?"

That made them frown at each other.

"Don't you trust us?" Actually said in unison.

"Not in the slightest." And I was growling as I said it.

Scott glanced between them and me then huffed and stormed outside. Aunt Mari shook her head. Uncle Sean sighed and went up after him as I nibbled at one of the chips—FRENCH FRIES! Christ, Bren.

The B-Girls came over to watch me, and Brandi asked, "Can we still ask you questions?"

"No."

"Just simple ones," Bernadette almost whined.

"So you're giving me no choice?" was my response.

"We just wanna know why you eat with your left hand."

That surprised me. "What?"

"That's how mommy eats."

"Sometimes," said Bernadette.

"Not as much, anymore."

I looked at my hands and answered, "It's how I eat."

"But it looks kind of dumb." And I don't care which one said it, because I was about to snap at them, again, when—

"Girls!" shot out of Aunt Mari. "Leave your cousin in peace with his meal!"

They turned to the telly, one saying, "Maybe we should try it."

"I dunno. It's weird."

"But it's faster. You don't have to set down the knife after you cut something up, then switch the fork to your right hand."

"But why do I want to eat faster?"

"It just saves some work."

"But you have to learn a whole new way of eating."

And off they went.

Jesus, I would never have peace from those two. But reality was now making herself known to me. I could live in the pool house or be on the street. Which would be even less safe. I could see no other choice. The decision may have been simple, but still I had to force myself to accept it.

At least I'd taken a stand and won a small victory.

Silly, I know, but you take what you can get, in this world.

Celebration

I moved three days later, after Scott relocated back to his room. He huffed and sulked and growled the whole time and refused to accept my help. Nor would he assist me. And if either he or I had expected the B-girls to express the least bit of sorrow over what their selfish dealings had caused, we were sore disappointed.

It's not like I had so much or was going so far, but I did wait till Aunt Mari took the girls off to The Galleria—she'd given me the key to the place, the night before—and I made sure I was done in less than an hour. Which also made sure I was bloody wearied from climbing those bastard stairs a roundtrip of nine times. On top of it, I was working that evening.

It was one big room and simple, with two bean bag chairs, some floor pillows and a pair of Lava Lamps in corners. A small wet bar/kitchen was to the right as you entered, where I could store some of my findings till I chose one to fix. The shower and toilet were at the back. To the left, a long blank wall backed to the neighbor's driveway, and there the bed was situated. A bit smaller than the one I'd had— Aunt Mari called it full-size—but it was comfortable. Sure, the dark brown carpet was thin and an aging air conditioner in the window over the bar's sink put out barely enough cool air to make the heat livable, but I could lie in the middle of the floor and spread out and touch nothing. I vowed never to add a stick of furniture and to leave the wood-paneled walls bare. All very spartan, according to the B-girls, but just what I wanted.

Needed.

And I would work on the AC, once I understood how it worked.

A set of stairs were next to the toilet and led to a hatch in the vaulted ceiling, where you could climb out onto the roof. Since the house was on a rise, that gave view to the city's taller buildings beyond the trees. It was quite wonderful, at night.

My *own entrance* was Aunt Mari giving me the combination to the lock on the side gate, and I was still to come in for meals. But now I had a kitchen of my own, with a hotplate, and I'd discovered something called TV Dinners to heat in a toaster oven, so I kept that to a minimum.

After two attempts to sneak their way into the place without success, the B-Girls shifted their tactics to huffy silence. If they did happen to catch me as I was coming or going, they did all they could to show me how they were ignoring me. I simply paid no attention, which drove them into deep frustration.

Scott also refused to speak with me and was also perturbed I didn't care. I'd kept to myself, much of my life, so this was a welcome return to it.

I began to feel better about my new direction. The occasional flashes back to Derry still came, sudden and sharp, but they'd diminished before and I was finally at a point where I could believe they would, again. So I got back to thinking about what sort of future I wanted for myself.

A couple of times, I went up to *The Colonel's* an hour early to look through the row of shops beside the bar. Just walk around. Get a feel for each. Work out in my head what would be needed. And walks around the neighborhood helped me to understand this was an area that would prefer to buy second-hand, so I settled on the space farthest from the bar, at the corner of the next cross street.

It was a bit larger than the pool house and had a wash basin by the back door, next to an open toilet. The floor was cracked linoleum that would need replacing, but I could envision a counter half the way in with a wall with shelves to separate front from back and show off my works in a nice way. I actually began looking forward to presenting my idea to my uncle.

Until the first Wednesday of July.

I stayed in the pool house all day because suddenly the world was filled with little pops and cracks that were too much like gunshots. Aunt Mari called it the Fourth and said it would be going till well after midnight. I was happy to know it was just fireworks for a celebration and not a gunfight, but still I flinched at each, for each was like—

Snappers popping as people were laughed till someone screamed, "Those are real bullets," and young men collapsed to the ground and blood was everywhere and it was pandemonium and—

I would have to stop, take a breath and remind myself I was in a city safe from such evil. But the same images kept crashing into me, over and over. The same thoughts. Still, I was handling it. I was repairing a bloody Hoover—vacuum cleaner and I was bloody handling it.

Until dark.

I was at *The Colonel's*, stocking the bar, and Todd's country-rock had covered much of the noise. But suddenly the city went mad with explosions and gunfire, echoing from everywhere and—

Bombs. Another one. In the Diamond? In Brandywell? Wait for the smoke to rise, to see, and the Para aimed and shot and Hugh Gilmore crumbled to the ground, across from me, and blood flew from him and "Those are real bullets" and "He bloody shot a priest!" and a bomb went off on Shipquay and another on William and the pop-pop-pop of a gun battle on the Lecky Road and the car went white and the air filled with smoke and dust and the silence was tearing into me and that leg twirling closer and closer and—

I was cowering under the bar, shaking and gasping and had such a tight grip on a pair of longnecks, my knuckles were white. I had absolutely no understanding of how to release them. Todd was squatted next to me, saying words that were soft and easy but made no sense as he tried to get me to stop crying and more explosions and—

I turned and a Para aimed and shot at me but clipped the wall, fragments hitting my face so I fell and more gunshots through the growing dark as people chucked stones at the Paras snatching lads from their beds and they fired warnings in the air and—

Rocky put a freezing hand to my face, soft and gentle. It jolted me to where I could focus on the cold of it and hear her telling me, "It's just fireworks, Bren. Fourth of July stuff. Nothing to be scared of. Just fireworks, is all."

I wanted to believe her, but I knew what it really meant. Death. Destruction. Slaughter. I'd seen it and grown used to it till that day—that day—that day, and I couldn't believe no one was willing to accept the reality of it, for—

The blood ran like water and the madness in the Paras' eyes was too real, like crazed beasts set for a kill and buildings burned and people screamed and—

"What the hell's wrong with him?" cut into my thoughts. I think it was Bidwell's voice.

"How should I know?" Todd shot back. "I ain't his daddy."

That kicked me hard enough to where I could at least set down the longnecks. Shaking. Breathing fast and hard. Coughing. Rocky drew me out from my hiding place and guided me back into the kitchen.

The pop-pop-popping was nonstop, as was my cough. I saw the sink, staggered to it, ran the cold tap over my head. Water trailed down my face and into my nose and the shock of it made me sneeze, over and over. But that helped me come back to here and now enough to accept the explosions were only distant pops and cracks and the gunfire was miles away and variable. I still flinched at each noise, but I could now—at least now—I could handle them.

Rocky sensed it and patted my back. "You gonna be okay?"

I think I nodded. If so, it was jerky and unsure.

"Okay, I'll be out front. Just keep in mind, that stuff's gonna go on till early mornin'."

I gave another jerk of my head and gasped, "Thanks."

Todd slipped in after she'd gone and offered me a pill.

"Valium," he said. "Ain't hard to get. Just don't take it with beer or wine. It'll make you crazy."

I chuckled. "Had it. Before."

"Careful. You can get too caught by it."

I nodded and swallowed the pill, using water from the still-running tap to wash it down, and half an hour later I was back to myself. The rest of the night went well, despite the constant noise.

Todd drove me home, after we closed up. There was still occasional gunfire and popping about, but I did some smoke on the way, mixed with a Marlboro. That combination was actually more helpful than the Valium.

I wanted to stay silent and let the city drift past in the night, but it was only a ten-minute drive, that time of night, and I felt the need to at least whisper, "Sorry for that."

"You wasn't so bad. Just some whinin' then you're under the bar."

"Christ—like a dog."

"You seen some bad shit in Ireland, right?" he asked.

Some bad shit? I almost chuckled. "Yeah. Yeah." Then as we crossed the Bayou, I added, "You have as well."

He snorted. "Bidwell tell you that?"

I shrugged. Once again, repeating gossip and stupidly so.

"I was on an air base," he continued. "No combat. Just fillin' requisitions an' handlin' paperwork. It could still get intense, but..." He held the joint up and wiggled it between his fingers. "I know some boys come back from 'Nam just as jittery as you. There's plenty of people just can't handle the world's hate."

I only nodded. Remembered what Dr. Gilbert had said about battle fatigue and speaking to someone. But I didn't share stories with me Chinas; how could I share 'em with a stranger? Besides, I could see no similarity between a war in a tropical country and my slip of land, but I had no idea what more to say so let it be. And moments later, I was home.

I did like how mellow the Valium and pot made me, so scored more off him. At a price, of course. I got only beers from him for free, and I doubt he actually paid for them.

I said not a word to anyone in the family about my near collapse, nor did Todd or Rocky, from what I could tell. Uncle Sean just kept working unto himself, and the B-Girls were off to girl scout camp. Aunt Mari stayed busy with her life, and Scott continued to prepare for university and ignore me. All of which suited me fine.

Sometimes Jeremy would drop over, since he had no job. As he was soon to leave for Israel to work on a kibbutz and would be there for a year, his parents gave no complaint. Of course, it did not hurt that he'd already taken advance placement courses and tests for university, giving him credits enough to be in second year—sophomore, he called it—when he returned. That would save them a bit of tuition, something Scott shrugged off.

"I'm doing a business major, slanted for the oil industry," he told me one lazy afternoon, not long after the Fourth. He was seated on the edge of the pool, no shirt and what he called *cut-offs*. No Coppertone for him; he seemed to go more and more brown instead of red, like me.

Scott was face-down on a float and laughed. "Like you gotta worry 'bout that. You could have a nothin'-point-nothin' GPA and still get an oil job in this town. Nothin' else goin' on, unless you're into real estate."

"It's still gonna have its ups an' downs. So I'm learnin' Chinese, too. Mandarin."

"Chinese?" I asked. I was up to my chin in the water, letting it keep me cool as I sipped a beer. Scott had got some called Shiner Bock, from *Liam's Trough*, and I didn't ask him how. Apparently it was a big deal, because they didn't always brew it. Which was sad; it's the only American beer I truly enjoyed.

"Now that Nixon's opened it up, over there," Jeremy continued, "things'll be changin'. Bigtime. I bet in twenty years they're the world's biggest market. So I'm makin' myself indispensable."

"Hong Kong gonna be the capitol instead of Peking?" Scott sneered.

"Don't be surprised. There's already rumors the Brits'll give it back to China at the end of their lease."

"Lease?" I asked. "You mean they rented it, like a bloody flat?"

Jeremy cast me one of those funny, quizzical looks. "Don't they teach you that in Irish schools?"

"We're taught how the British treated Ireland as a bastard child, and buggered up everywhere they went."

He laughed. "Well, China's gonna need oil and if I'm gonna help 'em find it or buy it, I have to know the lingo. I don't wanna be workin' a rig when I'm fifty. Miss out on everything."

"Don't worry, buddy," Scott had said. "Your uncle's got plenty of connections, so..."

Jeremy gave Scott an odd look and said, "I rather not need 'em."

"C'mon, Jere, it's the way the world works. Who you know's as important as what you know. Maybe more."

"Then that makes me nobody, since I know no one," shot out of me. Don't know why I said that; I was just put off by Scott's comment, for some reason, and felt the need to cut him back.

Jeremy laughed and said, "Best way to be. Whatever you make of yourself, it's all on you and nobody else."

I nodded, finished the beer, set the bottle on the side and dipped deep into the water so I could hear no more of Scott's silly nattering. I'd learned early on that anyone who acts as if he knows it all, knows nothing. And in truth, I didn't agree with his belief. In Derry, I'd done well enough and not been a lad with connections.

Well, I mean, I'd not been connected like Father Jack. He sought out people on the councils and in Belfast and the Housing Authority, and I had to admit they helped him work over problems that came up. Then hadn't Eamonn done the same? Made connections to help him with money and other assistance at Queen's? And a connection with Mairead had got Paidrig's sisters-in-law on at Hogg's & Mitchell's, while her seeing Tur got us furniture and things at a discount. So maybe Scott wasn't so far wrong.

But little of my making the rounds in Derry had led to work. It had come more from good word going around about my abilities and people coming to me, like it was, here. That's not the same thing. Is it? I didn't really know. I just knew Scott saying what he had, to Jeremy, it struck me as rude, and I felt no need to accept it. Especially since he was still tight and cold with me over the pool house.

When I came up and wiped off my face, I asked Jeremy, "When d'you leave?" Change the conversation.

"Flyin' up to New York Sunday," he said. "El Al from there, then Temple in Tel Aviv." I must have given him a curious look, for he added, "Seein' some of Mom's family, in Brooklyn. An' Uncle David's hoppin' the shuttle up, from DC."

"DC?"

"Washington, Bren." That came from Scott in a tone too reminiscent of the B-girls at their most condescending.

"Jesus, Jere, you got family all over."

He nodded, his mind drifting as he said, "Austin. LA. Chicago. Four-corners of the country. What about you?"

I shrugged. "Here and there."

He chuckled. "You don't talk much about yourself."

"Little to talk about."

"Only people with lots to say, say that."

"Don't bet on it," Scott sneered.

Jeremy cast him a sharp glance then said, "Y'know, my dad's doin' up a brisket, on Saturday. Y'all're comin' over, right?"

"Pass up a brisket?" Scott said as he dropped into the pool...and, thankfully, said nothing more.

"If you don't mind having me," I said. Seemed short notice, to my way of thought. That, or no one had told me of it.

Jeremy laughed and said, "It'll be great. My last one, till Hannukah." Again, my expression must have been confused because he added, "I'm set to come home for ten days. Break this trip up. Make it seem like...I dunno...less time away."

"Don't you want to go to Israel?"

He shrugged. "Never been big on my list of priorities. But my rabbi talked me into it. See some of the world, history of our people and stuff. Somethin' different." He cast me a look I couldn't read and asked, "Kind of like what you're doin'."

I gave a sigh. "Mine wasn't by choice."

"See? You do know what I mean." Then he dropped into the pool.

And for some reason I felt as if he'd shared a secret with me. Which actually made me feel good. Perhaps people were seeing me as trustworthy, again.

The B-Girls

The Landau home was two-levels in light pink bricks with white columns and white shutters on the windows. A curving drive in front wound under an upstairs extension around to the back. They also had a pool. I'd been to enough other homes in the area to think there must be a rule that every house have one.

That cookout was lovely, as was meeting Jeremy's parents and his two brothers, Joshua and Jonathan, both older. Their wives were with them, and both looked like they were of the same family—dark-haired, solid, tan skin. It was a bit confusing.

His father was a surgeon, his mother a CPA, and they fit well, together. Joshua worked in oil and Jonathan in finance, and their wives handled the several children they brought. All were polite with me but offered little talk and even less attention. Which mattered not. The B-girls kept them busy with non-stop questions.

About me, I found.

I overheard Brandi (I think) saying to Mr. Landau, "It's just that Bren looks like one of *your* kids, not any of us."

Bloody hell, were those two little beasts still seeking a consensus as to whether or not I was a true part of the family?

He laughed and looked at me and said, "Only superficially."

"But you see him right next to Jeremy and—"

"Brandi, none of my family's in Ireland."

At which point Bernadette sneered at her sister and said, "I told you he'd say that."

"No," the other sniped back, "you said he'd say he wasn't. But that's not what he said."

"It's a nice way of saying he's not."

"No, it isn't. It's a careful way of saying it's possible."

"Oh, now you're being stupid."

"Not as stupid as you."

And off they went.

Mr. Landau and I exchanged shrugs then he came over to me and asked, "How's your ribs doing?"

Which brought a flash of—

The man lifted my right arm and pressed his fingers down my side as I whimpered, and him said, "They set well, but still healing. His arm should be back in a cast. Keep it straight."

I coughed, unable to remember if it had been or not, then managed to say, "I'll live."

He'd just nodded and turned back to his wife, and I was left to think, *Jesus, I had a full compliment of medical attention*. I almost followed him to ask more about his visit, but Uncle Sean got to talking with him about investments and money. Things I'm sure they figured I knew nothing about. So I just sat in a chair and enjoyed my chips— *French fries*, dammit! With a brown vinegar that was not like the kind I'd had in Derry, but was tasty enough and—

"Christ, Bren, you and the vinegar."

—made me jump. I'd have sworn it was said aloud. I looked around, but no one else was paying me any attention, so finally had to accept it was but my mind making sport of me.

I left for *The Colonel's* before Jeremy's sister, Rachel, came. As did Scott, to meet friends at *Liam's Trough*. So the next day, by the pool, the B-girls insisted I be filled in on the rest of the evening.

"She showed up after dark," said Bernadette (I think).

"The ugliest skirt and blouse I've ever seen," said the other.

"Rough knitting over some kind of linen."

"More like burlap."

At which they nodded to each other.

"She seemed upset that Scott was gone," said Brandi. Maybe.

"Do you think she *likes* him?" asked the other, not happy with the thought. "She's older than he is."

"Not all that much."

"But girls mature faster than boys, so he ought to be older than her. That way, they can be even."

"You mean like mommy and daddy?"

"Yeah. Kind of."

I was doing my best to maintain my non-listening mode. The heat of the day was like a blanket and even floating in the pool it was difficult to ignore their chattering.

"Did you put on *Coppertone*?" asked Bernadette. Maybe. And her voice was sharp with wariness.

"The real strong stuff," said the other, just as clipped.

"You got skin like us."

"Too delicate for a boy."

That twinged me, so I snapped, "What's that supposed to mean?"

"Your neck's already burned. And ears."

"And arms."

"You need to wear it, all the time." She held up a plastic bottle of the stuff, and I could smell the cocoa-butter from halfway across the pool.

"All over."

"You didn't have burns like that when you came here."

"Isn't there any sun in Ireland?"

All I could do is roll my eyes and say, "No. It's all rain and cloud."

"Well, it's not, here, so come on."

"We'll put it on your back."

I gave a deep breath and kicked to shore then jumped up to give them access. At least them smearing that stuff on me kept them focused on doing it right and not asking me questions.

My legs and front, I did myself.

After two weeks of this, the B-girls decided my general appearance was *not* cool enough, and I had to be made acceptable to them and their circle of friends. So a makeover was started.

I went along with it, though I'd never cared about that nonsense in Derry. But despite myself I'd begun to appreciate their non-stop chattering, for it helped build a barrier of sorts in my mind against those flashes of memory. By making myself think more about not listening to the B-girls, it was like...I don't know, it's like some kind of protection against the worst of it. So I let the fanatical two lead the way with one condition: we keep the price low. My ready cash was not so great.

"We could just ask mommy for her charge card," said one.

"Like for Joske's. Maybe Penney's," said the other.

"Oh, no! And no more Sears. No Montgomery Wards."

"Neiman's?"

"We gotta establish his style before we go upscale."

"What's upscale?" I asked, truly perplexed.

"Designers."

"No upscale, at all," I'd snapped.

"Well, we're not talking Yves St. Laurent," said one.

"Or Christian Dior," said the other.

"He doesn't have men's clothes."

"I saw one of his suits at Holleran's."

"That was Burberry. From England."

"You don't know what you're talking about."

And off they went. Until they came back to discuss my trousers.

"They're just plain ugly," said one, after I'd about given up hope of ever telling them apart.

"What's wrong with them?" I'd growled.

"They're for old men, not boys."

"And nothing but white t-shirts?" said the other.

"With stains on them!"

"And holes."

"From cigarette burns?!"

"You have to be around people."

"But we don't want you to be embarrassing."

"So this is for your own good."

"No hip-huggers, either."

"I don't know; David Cassidy still wears them."

"Not like he used to. They're closer to his belly button."

"I still think he'd look good in them."

"But they are so last year."

"Gracie Venable wears hip-huggers."

"Yeah, and look at her."

"Oh. Yeah. No hip-huggers."

Levi 501 jeans is how it wound up; no Wrangler, thank you. Dingo boots. Sandals. Madras button-ups, and undershirts with pockets.

"No tie-dies."

"Very last year."

"Worse, very 1970."

"Now that's just mean. We were wearing tie-dyes last year."

"*You* were. Not *me*."

"Now you're just being rude!"

And off they went into one of their arguments.

Of course, I could not completely forget about Derry and Belfast, because it seemed every night's news carried a new atrocity. Soldiers grabbed and murdered. Protestant workers killed, with the same done to Catholics. Bombs dealing death and destruction to people out and about at the time. Politicians nattering on and on with nothing to show for all their talk. Bleating from Westminster about how best to settle the matter and the planning of a new government beholden to none, after the June elections. Stories with little depth or understanding of what was happening. The intrusion of the B-Girls and their demands grew more and more to be like a sanctuary against the arbitrariness of what was happening.

So every Saturday at noon would be a quick lunch, then dragging me here or there, on the bus. Fortunately, the little beasts had accepted that *everyone agreed* second-hand shops were cool enough to consider. And were more my kind of cost.

"Sarah Wakeman told us about this great one on Bissonnet," said Brandi, one Saturday, "so we need to go."

"I'm due at *The Colonel's* by six," I said.

"Plenty of time," said the other, pulling out a bus schedule.

It took a bloody hour to get there. Then they took their time digging through racks of shirts and trousers and coats to seek out what was acceptable. Until they found a real leather bomber jacket in a wonderfully shabby condition. And with a name sewn in it! Oh, did they sigh over that.

"I bet this is from the Second World War."

"We're learning about that in history."

"Bombers flying over the Channel to destroy Berlin."

"Kissing the girls they leave behind."

"Sister Joseph played *A Guy Named Joe* in our class."

"I saw that one. So romantic."

Even though it was twenty dollars, it was settled I *had* to have it. And wear it home. And sweat my arse off in that bloody, never-ending Houston heat to the point I needed another shower. But it was that or risk their displeasure, and I'd melt before I'd do that.

They also took much pleasure at filling me in on what the newest sayings were.

"*Cool* is okay." said one.

"But *groovy* is dead."

"*Radical* is a fun word."

"So is *awesome*."

"But do NOT ever, EVER say *What's up, pussycat*."

"That is so middle-aged."

Fortunately, they were never concerned with music for me.

"Boys have to find their own songs."

"Usually pretty bad choices."

"Seriously! *Ramblin' Man*?"
"*Saturday Night's All Right For Fightin'*?"
"*Truckin'*?"
"*Money?* Really stupid."
"All barks and growls."
"And howls."
So they studiously ignored my eight-tracks, nor did I play any of them when they were over.

By this point, my curls had returned, but they weren't going to let me cut them...until they saw how thick and wild they became in the heat. Then they dragged me to a salon on West Gray, within walking distance, and demanded this amazingly patient woman find a way to make it smooth and well-behaved, while they instructed me on how best to care for it.

"A hundred strokes in the morning," said one.
"And a hundred at night," the other added.
"I'll go bald, like that," I growled.
"That's what Mommy told us to do."
"Are you saying she's wrong?"
Both carrying a great deal of hostility.
But the woman said to them, "Oh, but *your* hair is silk—"
Like Joanna's. Blowing in the breeze.
"—while his is more like cotton and needs a different way to be treated. You don't wash a cashmere sweater like your sheets, do you?"

That, they had to agree on. So the woman gave me a spiky sort of brush and said, "This'll be easier on you."

"Looks like what you use on a dog," I said.

She'd just smiled and winked, and the B-girls had giggled.

I managed to catch the woman to one side before we left and whisper, "You giving lessons on how to talk to those two?"

She'd giggled, patted my cheek and said, "Don't worry, honey, you'll catch on to it."

So on and on it would go, to the point I felt God himself couldn't have stopped them. Even Angus knew it, for on more than one occasion he would poke his head in the door, see them working on me and quickly turn away. Smart doggie.

At least they allowed me to shave the scruff on my face, but I had to leave what fuzz there was for my moustache. Even though it was barely there.

"Yours is better than Selena Bettancourt's father," said Brandi.

"His looks like cookie crumbs," said the other, nodding.

"That's how daddy described it."

"I know. That's why I'm saying it."

"You didn't say so."

"What for?"

"You're stealing it from daddy."

"Are you calling me a thief?"

And off they went. I think they actually took pleasure in their little fights.

But I kept that bit of fuzz, and by this point there were days when I'd look in the mirror, I had to remind myself it was me looking back.

They badgered me into ice-skating at The Galleria, where my awkward hugging of the sides gave them no end of merriment. And they introduced me to MacDonald's. Which was all right, for what it was, though their chips—*FRENCH FRIES*—were amazing. They also assured me the football team—*soccer* team was as fine as anything in Ireland.

It would be kind to say they exaggerated greatly.

Then Bernadette shifted to comparing me to Christopher Knight, since he was now her favorite.

"I think he looks more like the boy on that new Lucy show," said Brandi, and I was startled to realize I actually knew it was her.

"Her son? Please. The way Bren's hair goes, he'd be closer to that guy in *Room 222*," Bernadette shot back, eyeing me like I was about to be purchased. "Bernie something."

"There was no Bernie in that show."

"There's a redheaded guy."

"The Afro guy!? No way! Bren's hair is more like the boy in *The Waltons*."

"Not John-boy!?"

"No, no, the one with the ears."

"No, his hair's too pretty."

"What about Jim Morrison?" I asked, not really serious.

Brandi glared at me. "He's dead."

"I know that."

"And his face is completely different," Bernadette snarled.

Then Brandi frowned. "But his hair looks right."

Dear God, was this what it meant to be an American child? How I was missing Maeve's directness. She'd have shut the both of them down in two seconds, flat.

Well, that or she'd have joined forces with them.
And I'd have jumped off the Craigavon Bridge.

I regained enough of the weight I'd lost to the point I felt good enough to walk home after work. Not that I had much choice, anymore; Todd had taken up with a girl in Jersey Village, which was the opposite direction. So on the nights he had a date, I went *shanks mare*, as he put it.

Didn't matter. I truly loved the solitude of the street, at night. It almost took me back to my walk to Claudy. And the first time to the Circle Fort. Wandering about Derry. Back when I could still feel somewhat young and innocent. Hopeful, even. And while the air could be hot to the point of suffocation and the breeze inconsistent, having the dark mask the reality of the city while stars glistened above like watchful friends helped me find a connection to a sort of calmness within me.

It's odd, but sometimes I missed Jeremy, now he was gone. He was easy to talk with. Wasn't that a kick? I guess me being known as the Jew of the family made me closer to him than those of my own blood. Could one be Irish and Jewish at the same time?

Questions like that were no longer unusual, for me, as my mind could drift to odd places of thought. Like when I saw bats swirling in the night sky and half-wondered if people in Ireland had seen something like it and thought them fairies. Or if I caught sight of a stray dog skulking about like a beast, I'd wonder if he saw me as possible dinner. The more wary ones, I figured they'd just been shown who was boss by some cat they'd tried to corner. And walking across the bridge over Buffalo Bayou, I could see the glow of the center city to my left and compare it to Oz in the Wizard's book. Sometimes I even wondered if the world was dreaming me, or I it, and if I'd soon wake from all of this.

I'd have liked that. It would have meant nothing I'd lived through really mattered. Wouldn't it? I could have dreamt I was living in Boston or Paris or Tokyo. Or been the son of Aunt Mari and Uncle

Sean instead of Scott. Then none of this would have happened. Would it? I could have been so much happier. So much easier with myself.

But to be truthful, the best aspect of those walks was how invariably I'd find something in a dustbin—no, *garbage can* along the way. Items barely broken that I could repair and feel quite the *entrepreneur*; Uncle Sean's word, not mine. I didn't really understand what it meant, even after reading up on it in this massive dictionary kept on a stand near the telly. But I did like the sound of it. Made me feel quite adult.

Of course, even walking against traffic there was always the occasional car that would pull up beside me, and an older gentleman inside would ask if I'd like a lift. I always refused. I had no trust of strangers and in the back of my mind was a fair idea that at so dark an hour, no one has good intent.

Not even myself, truly.

The one issue came from a couple lads who drove around the Heights. They reminded me of Colm and Danny. From a distance. One dark. One fair. Always in a car. The darker one would smile and wave at me, now and then when he saw me heading up to *The Colonel's*, while the blond ignored me, complete. Catching sight of them driving by would jolt me back to that day, for a moment, and scramble whatever thought I was having, at the time. I'd have to stop. And breathe. And make a mental note to continue forward.

But oddly enough, seeing lads similar to me Chinas also helped me begin to accept a different perspective to that bombing. For in truth, they'd been little more than mules drawing a cannon, and if it hadn't been them to put that car there, it would have been someone else. I could now accept that the bomb had gone off prematurely, and that Joanna would have been well away from it had it done as was intended. I was still cut by knowing my best mates had destroyed the one person I'd ever truly loved, and I couldn't come fully to terms with that. But a lot of my anger was diminished.

Then on a day at the beginning of August, I was early to The Colonel's and waiting at the back door when those two drove past. The dark one cast me his smile and wave, and I started to dive into that hideous moment, but Todd drove up, startling me out of it. As he got out of his truck, he snarled, "Whoa, Bren, you know him?"

I was still partway into the abyss, so just shook my head and met him at the door. I had an old rucksack holding the makings for hot dogs and wanted to unload them into the cooler.

He unlocked it and as I followed him in he said, "That's one dude you wanna steer clear from."

"You think?" I said, paying little attention. Since I hadn't spoken word-one to the lad, how could we stand farther apart?

"Yeah. I dunno what it is about him, but—y'know, there's guys who'll be all nice and palsy-walsy with you till you're usin' their junk an'—"

"Junk?"

"Drugs. They get you hooked, make you a customer and soon you're goin' out stealin' shit or turnin' tricks for 'em. I think he's one."

All I did was shrug.

He kept on with, "I bet that older guy I seen him with's his dealer. They're connected to a few too many kids who run off from 'round here and it's just—just stay away from 'em. You want some smoke; come to me."

And let you do what you say they will, right? I all but chuckled as I closed the cooler door. Still, better the devil you know and all that.

I saw the two of them around once more, where he waved at me and I back, and that was all. No memory to avoid, for once, which was nice.

Until a week later, when their photos covered the front pages of both the papers. The darker one—Wayne Henley—had shot dead the older man—Dean Corll. Claimed he was going to rape and kill him. Then it came out that both him and his mate—David Brooks, the blond—were taking lads to parties to be tortured and killed by the bastard.

For two-hundred dollars a boy.

Of course, Todd had to crow, "Told ya there's somethin' wrong 'bout 'em. I knew it." Over and over, every time there was a new announcement on the TV.

Bidwell began spitting about how homosexuals wanted to rape and kill all straight men. Truly obsessed over it, he was, in ways that made me want to stay even farther away from him.

But he found a sympathetic ear in Lorraine. I actually heard her say, "All them queers oughta be locked up."

And Bidwell's response? "Naw, they'd have too much fun in prison."

Rocky just rolled her eyes every time they said something about the growing number of dead, until there were more than two dozen bodies. Then all she whispered was, "Those poor families. They kept askin' for help, but the cops didn't care. Nobody did."

To which, I had to agree. The B-girls had already suggested as much.

I'd been in the attic digging through a box of books for something to read when they'd found me, thanks to Angus coming up to sit at my side. I'd finally found a paper cover copy of *The Osterman Weekend*, by Robert Ludlum, and was putting the bloody romance novels back on the box when they'd appeared and launched into a complaint about the heat and how I was overdressed in a tee-shirt and jeans. All of which I intended to strip off soon as I was back down by the pool. They were nattering on about how unfair it was boys could be shirtless while girls couldn't and how sad it was Hot Pants were passé because this was the perfect weather for them.

Then Bernadette said, "Oh, did you hear? Angela Mireille thinks she knew one of the boys who was killed."

"But that's silly," said Brandi, with a huge sigh. "None of them were from River Oaks."

"We don't know that, yet."

"Don't be ridiculous. The boys we know would've known better than to go to those parties."

"She didn't say he was a neighbor! Just a handyman's son."

"Oh, of course. That explains it and—"

"Don't," popped out of me, sharp and sudden.

Both turned a hard glare on me.

"Don't what?" said Bernadette.

"Don't talk about the dead lads like they're worth less than you."

"But they were poor!"

"I mean it! Don't!"

I slammed the last of the books into their box and rose, truly angry.

That is when Brandi took on a condescending sneer and said, "You don't get it—they lived in the Heights, Bren. If even a couple of boys had gone missing in River Oaks, the police would have been all over the place, looking for them."

"That's what Sister Mary-Margaret said," added the other.

"They might've been able to ignore one or two disappearing and calling them runaways."

"But not dozens."

"Parents would've called the police, lawyers. councilmen, anyone they could."

"They did!" I snapped.

"They didn't know the right people," said Bernadette in so matter-of-fact a voice, it was like one of life's truths and she was shocked I didn't know it.

"That's what Sister Mary-Margaret said."

"And that's when Brother James told her to hush."

"So she did."

I needed to get down to some clean air, now, now, now, before I crashed into another chaotic mode, so I headed for the stairs, growling, "I'm not surprised. The Church loves to keep quiet about things that might cause problems for them or those they support."

"What do you mean?" asked Brandi.

I started down, fast. "Nothing. There's enough said about that."

They followed, one sighing, "You're right. Nothing more to say."

Except the little monsters had offered up one of those brutal truths that cannot be tossed aside. Some people *are* more important than others, in this world, and will be paid greater notice if anything goes wrong with them. In Derry, constables would let Protestants accost Catholics, but the moment a Catholic pushed back they'd be battering them and lifting them to Strand Road. I was shocked to find that sort of attitude extended to here. But it was obvious—the majority of the dead lads being from a poor area of Houston, where people were just trying to live their lives as best they could, meant they mattered little.

Nor would anything change.

What was most odd about it all was how fixated Scott became on the mass murders. Uncle Sean had both the papers delivered and Scott scoured them. Listened to stories on the radio. Watched the news. Apparently, it cut into him, as well, but I never talked with him about it. Not till the day before he was set to leave for Austin.

We were in the pool, it being a Tuesday, atop rafts in the tepid water, slathered with tanning lotion as the sun burned down on us. Of course, the day was hot as hades. Aunt Mari hadn't been joking when she said August was rough; even Angus was in the house to make use of the air conditioning. We were sharing a six-pack of Coors—which I didn't like, it was so weak. But it was cold and wet enough for the moment, and Scott's irritation with me had drifted away, now he was to be gone.

He had his radio playing, and the hourly news said the police had announced they were ending their search for more of Dean Corll's victims, now they'd hit twenty-seven of them. The families of lads still classified as runaways were not happy.

"An' still no explanation," he said.

I rolled my eyes and lit a fag—*cigarette*—shaking my head. Scott had led such a quiet, safe existence, he could never understand. I then splashed water on myself and said, "I doubt even *they* know why they did it."

"A guy in Austin says it's happenin' 'cause society's in turmoil. He says it was like this in Germany before the Nazis took over. Another guy says queers aren't bein' put in jail, anymore, an' that's why."

"Both sound like fucking idiots. The world's always in turmoil. Irish history, alone, shows the truth of that."

"What gets me is, they knew most of the guys they got killed," he said, his voice soft. "Henley and Brooks. They'd take kids they'd grown up with to a party and then it's—*hope you don't mind if we torture and kill you, for fun*. Then you're never seen, again. I don't get it. How can you do that to somebody you know? Known most of your life?"

I only sighed as—

Billy handed out tea to men building piles of stones that sent Eamonn to hospital and the bat swung down to smack against the back of Paidrig's knee as Colm watched, impassive and—

And Shane riding off to meet a mate...and enough said about that.

I thought of Da going out to tell his stories and sing his songs and get paralytic, fully intending to come home to a row with Ma. Instead, he'd joined with some men who offered him more of the devil's brew, but who really saw him as nothing but a toy to be torn apart. Then they'd dumped his body and run off to hide, hoping they wouldn't be found out. Like children. And when they were caught, they'd wept and cried and moaned, over and over, that *things just got carried away*. As pure a lie as ever was told, yet still accepted by those in power.

The same for Bloody Sunday. So many had doubts the Paras had truly aimed to kill anyone, but the monsters had arrived with real bullets in their guns and barreled in like a pack of mad dogs to murder thirteen men—fourteen, now—no matter what that lying Widgery Report claimed. The man who wrote that hadn't seen their faces as they gunned lads down. Hadn't witnessed the joyful gleam in their eyes as a bullet tore apart a fellow human being, in the back as he ran from them. They'd reveled in their slaughter. The reasons—the excuses—those bastards knew they would come later.

After all, doesn't everyone have excuses for what they do?

Oh, they'd be different for each person who flips from friend to foe. Protector to killer. Those who want to explain it all want to think people put thought into a course of action instead of simply rolling along with whatever came to them. Surrendering to instinct. Not knowing where it will end until it's ended.

Or caring.

What struck me was the arbitrariness of it. The men who killed my Da could have taken any of a dozen others, but he's the one they stumbled upon. And on Bloody Sunday, if that para aiming for me had fired a moment earlier, I'd have been number fifteen dead. It was all just luck of the draw.

Like with that bomb.

If I'd waited for Joanna at the back of her Da's shop, she might still have been caught by the blast, but I wouldn't have. And I might have been able to get in and save her.

Or if Father Jack had been our priest, Danny might have taken the mantle instead of growing cold and angry, over the years, then join with PIRA. Been willing to help set that bomb.

So all of it was just chance. Circumstance for it to happen to anyone at that particular moment. Just the rotten luck of the draw. Like those lads now dead. All for no real reason except they were there when someone decided to commit an atrocity.

What could I say but, "You ask for explanations when there are none. Things happen, and all you can do is hope they don't happen to you."

"No, that's not how it works," Scott snapped.

"Why not?"

"Because it don't make sense. One day you're best pals; next day some nut case gives you two-hundred bucks and you say, *Here, have fun with him.* That's even sicker, if you really think about it."

"Strikes me as a pair of uncaring bastards out to make a bit of scratch."

"Aw, Jeez. C'mon, people ain't that greedy."

I just rolled my eyes.

He continued with, "I think it had something to do with wantin' control over the life or death of somebody else. Provin' I can do what I want to you. It's how I show the world I'm important. I mean, it's not like either of those assholes had that much of a future in store for 'em."

Oh, God, that bloody crap, again. He was going to worry this like Angus and his rawhide toy. Keep at it till there was nothing left and he needed something to replace it. Scott wanted an explanation to make himself feel like-like the idea of knowing why it happened would help him make sure it never happened to him.

Me? I'd begun to think all men and women contained something in their souls that could destroy as easily as create, if given the right circumstances or opportunity. Probably easier. And that from it a cruel, uncaring blindness grew, and spread and brought exhilaration to those caught in it. And they wouldn't care about its effect on others. But that hinted at a religious aspect to his considerations, and I wanted none of that nonsense anywhere near me.

All I knew was, there was naught could be done about life's little cruelties. You just had to move along in your life knowing the best you could ever hope for was that such evil never touched you or any of yours. Nothing more to say.

"I wonder if they might be right?" he continued. "There's lots of pressure on queers here. I mean, it's illegal to be a homo in Texas, y'know. They can put you in jail for it."

Unless they're with the church and—

Father Devil put his hand on mine and I jerked away and he was gone with Father Jack in his place but Danny was frozen in place by the confessional and—

I kicked away from the side of the pool, snarling, "Must be why I've not seen any."

"You just haven't been in the right part of town."

I looked at him. "There's a neighborhood?"

A ghetto, like Bogside?

He grinned. "Can you keep a secret?" I shrugged and nodded. "Promise?"

"Jesus, Scottie." If he couldn't tell by now I'm not the sort who spills his guts, even when it suits him, he'd never know.

"Oh, cool it, Bren. You know what I mean." He dipped into the water, then jumped back onto his float to lie on his belly. "Now this is just between us. You and me." He kicked at the side of the pool, to drift closer to me.

I eyed him, growing wary. "Are you saying you're...?"

"No! Shit." He looked at me as if I were mad. "But Jeremy and me—we'd sneak in the queer bars, down in Montrose."

"Why?"

"If you're underage for drinkin', they're easier to get into than the regular ones. And they serve beer and wine coolers and you can dance as much as you want."

"They just let you pass in?"

"We'd have to latch onto a couple of guys and they'd work it, and sometimes there was a little give and take, know what I mean?" And he winked at me.

Actually, I had no idea but I wasn't about to admit it. "You AND Jeremy?"

"A couple other guys from school, sometimes. None of the queers ever tried to pull any shit with us." He took a drag off my Marlboro. "We'd dance with 'em and they'd buy us drinks, and if we were feelin' real horny, let 'em give us some relief."

"Relief?"

"Yeah." Then he moved his tongue against his cheek in a way that meant he'd been serviced, orally.

Paidrig's brother's claims brought a smile to my lips. But then I remembered Danny's response to what he said, which brought forward thoughts about him and Father Devil and Carla's use of me, and that killed the smile. So I said, "And-and you liked it?"

"It was no big deal. I'd just lean back, close my eyes, think of Charmaine Powell. She's this cheerleader at school with tits like you wouldn't believe—and bam, it's done. Everybody's feelin' groovy."

"*Groovy* is not cool anymore," I said, not really thinking. "As declared by the B-girls."

He shrugged and took a long sip of beer. "What those guys did— killin' those kids—there was somethin' wrong with 'em. And it wasn't that they're queer. That guy, Wayne, had a girl friend, and his buddy, David—he's married and about to have a kid. And besides, there've been lots of guys who killed girls, like that guy in Chicago—Richard Speck, killed all those nurses. Or the Boston Strangler. Guy named Starkweather, killed all kinds of people back in the fifties."

My voice was wary as I said, "Sounds like you've done a study."

"It's just interestin'. They were all crazy, man. Freaks who don't have feelin's left. Don't you have guys like that where you come from?"

The Para's face wrapped in a wild happy glaze as his bullet struck home and aimed to shoot me but I was on the ground, a cut to my head, and I stumbled around, bleeding, seeing another man lay nearby on the ground, in Glenfada, and you'd think him asleep were it not for the river of blood trailing from the back of his head and—

I kicked at the water to make myself float in a gentle circle under a shaded area. It had been weeks since those moments had cut into me, yet they were, back. Despite the heat, I was shivering and—

The car vanished into the white and I flew back and hit the wall and flopped down and looked and saw that bloody fucking leg whispering up and up and arcing down to aim for me and—

I took in a deep breath and rolled into the pool. Drifted down to sit cross-legged on the bottom, my eyes closed, in the middle area. Deep enough to swallow me but not so deep I'd drown. My shivering wasn't much seen, doing this, and I stayed under the water for a full minute before daring to rise.

Into air that was still smothering.

With Scott still drifting on his raft.

And the sky still a sharp blue.

And my bloody fucking Marlboro still in my lips! Now soaked and disintegrating. I threw it into the bushes and stood in water up to my chest, just looking at the sky.

The tenderness of the clouds was being whisked away by slow-growing shadows across their western edges, hints of gold and grey highlighted them to the east. The twisted branches of the oak trees grasped up at the sky like some evil thing. A gentle breeze worked itself through them. Birds danced about them, seeking a perch for the evening or one last insect to feed upon.

Control mine, again.

Control.

That was all one had was control of oneself, wasn't it?

I jumped back onto the raft and took in a deep breath. The honeysuckle smelled thick and more real than memories of the burned wood and cordite and waste of Derry. The warmth of the air felt right against the moisture on my skin. Soon we'd head in. Make sandwiches. Grab crisps—*chips* from a bag. Sit before the telly and let our minds focus on that stupid American baseball, which I found bloody tedious. Life untouched by hate or fear. Just longing and memory.

The sudden ache behind my heart was finally replaced with a wary sort of peace, once more. I was far, far away from all of that, now. And so would I stay.

Until I heard Scott climb out of the pool, water splashing happily about him. I looked around and he was already wiping himself down.

He cast me a bright smile and said, "Hey, Bren, you feel like goin' to a bar, tonight?"

"Why would I want to, while I'm workin' in one?"

"It's not your usual bar, dude." Said with a wink.

I knew what he meant and something about it spoke wrong to me. My inner voice was still saying, *Careful with this one.* And deeper within was a part of me saying, *I just want to keep the peace I feel, right now.*

But companion to that was another voice, nudging me with, *Why not? He's gone with Jeremy, and that lad is one you can trust. It's obviously done them no harm. What's there left to lose? Are you truly so afraid of what MIGHT happen after all that HAS happened?*

Then came the capper—*Joanna would go. You know she would.*

So I paddled back to the side and looked up at him, saying, "Be sure it's you sneakin' me in and no one else."

He laughed and helped me up from the water, then I went in to rinse off, feeling vaguely as if I were about to do something I really should go to confession for.

Which made me all the more determined to do it, peace of mind and spirit be damned.

Everett

Sandwiches before getting dressed, then me in Levis and a plain shirt; him in pants and athletic undershirt—and when he saw I was wearing my boots, he pulled on his. And down Shepherd we went to Westheimer, close to Houston's center city to find—

Cars backed up for miles, traveling slower than it would take to walk the length of the street. Seems we were on Westheimer and, as Scott put it, "People're just cruisin'."

"Cruising?"

He chuckled at me. "Yeah. Drivin' along to be seen."

I was incredulous. "We're barely moving."

"That's the point."

I huffed and popped my head out the window to look down a line of what must have been a thousand cars ahead of us, all big American beasts, a sea of red tail lamps in one direction, white headlights glaring in the other, all thrumping their motors as horns sounded and others stopped to one side or the other, or in car parks and stood about, calling to each other.

I just shook my head. "If we get to where you're going before next Saturday, I'll be surprised. Let's to home."

"C'mon, Bren," he whined. "I'm headed to Austin, tomorrow. God knows when I'll be back, so let's you an' me have some fun, here, now. Get to know each other."

"Bloody hell, we can do that in any pub you want."

"But you're a virgin."

That jolted me back into my seat. "Say again?"

"You're a gay bar virgin and can't get in without me, right now."

"Why would I want to?"

"Rite of passage, and I want to be there for your first time."

"Shite, Scottie, you sure it's that cheerleader you think of when you're getting polished?"

"No, baby, I think of you." And he puckered his lips at me and batted his eyes.

I only huffed and growled, back to full wariness. Didn't help that weariness was kicking in. I'd worked on cleaning up a vacuum cleaner most of the morning, in that fucking heat, and that sad excuse of an air conditioner was not doing the job, but I had yet to figure out its mechanisms to see if I could make it work better...though a neighbor's gardener had suggested adding something called freon. My plan was to look into that, tomorrow.

Fortunately, Jeremy had shown me that wetting a bandana in iced water and laying it over your head, then holding it in place with a cap kept things from growing too horrible. But I was still knackered. Even lazing in the pool had done little good, and I could also feel a burn coming on my back and legs despite the *Coppertone*. I'd so much rather have been asleep, with both a fan and the air conditioner pointed straight at me, than seated in his GTO with only the windows open to catch any hint of a passing breeze.

But after near an hour, we turned out of the line and found parking on a dark, narrow side street. It was crowded with cars and scared, ragged houses surrounded by overgrown lawns and midnight shadows. Better suited to Hallowe'en than a late-night ramble.

He led me along broken sidewalks and crooked fences that would have been an embarrassment in Derry, then up to an old two-level house surrounded by throngs of men, both young and old, half-hiding in the darkness afforded by a few ragged trees and shrubs of some odd lineage.

"Here?" shot out of me the moment I saw it.

Scott nodded. "It's one of the easiest."

The trick to get in was to wait till there was a line of lads headed past the doorkeeper and mingle in with 'em. Then you flashed a form of ID, got your hand stamped by the next lad and headed on past like you knew you belonged. Thing is, I had no ID, which shocked Scott.

"What about your passport?"

I shrugged. "Your Da has it."

"Well, let's see what happens. What can they do but say no? And there's a few other bars around."

He led me to the back door, which turned out to be the actual entrance, and soon as there was a rush of lads in bright clothes, we joined them. I got in; Scott was stopped. Seems there was a cover charge and one older, larger man had paid for a group; the doorman thought me part of it. Once inside, when I saw Scott wasn't right next to me, I stayed by the door, listening to this crap song called *Ring Ring* pounding through some speakers.

I looked around. The walls had been torn out to open up the whole of the main floor, emphasizing a twice-angled staircase in the center. Must lead up to private rooms. A bar to the right side was manned by two harried lads, beer or wine mixed with Seven-Up only. The place was packed with men of all ages, shapes and sizes, and a few birds, as well.

Including fucking Carla!

I all but dove into a shadowy area to keep her from seeing me, but a ball covered with bits of mirror hung above the staircase's lower landing and shot star-beams over me and every other dark corner. I kept a wary eye on her, but it didn't look like she had seen me.

There were some booths. Tables. Benches slammed against the walls. All were dingy, like a run-down pub on Lone Moor Road. I kept turned away from her and shook my head, not in the least impressed.

"There you are!" Scott appeared beside me, snapping, "Five dollars!" as he shoved his wallet away.

"Well," I managed to say, "the-the-the money's not for décor, that's for damn sure."

"Oh, honey," said a man's voice to my left. As I turned, a hand came up to caress my cheek and I found myself face to face with a woman weighing a good 30 stone and perfectly made up. "You should see it with the lights on," she continued—and that's when I realized *she* was really a *he*.

"Bloody hell," I whispered, "I'm living rock an' roll." In mind of The Kinks' *Lola*.

"No, tonight's pop, rhythm and blues," and he wandered off.

I turned to Scott and he laughed. "Oh, this is perfect! They're havin' a drag show!"

"A what?" was all I could squeak out before he grabbed a waiter, made an order and shoved me over to a set of benches. They were the opposite side of the room from Carla, and in shadow, but still I said, "Scott, I'm not so sure about us staying, for this."

"I paid five dollars to get in. I ain't goin' nowhere."

A few lads gave us the once over and made just enough room for one of us to sit. I made sure it was him and not me, for I was feeling more and more like that cat facing those growling dogs and wanted nothing to hold me back in case I felt the need to hiss and spin and get myself gone.

I scrunched against a post, my eyes darting about. The men were almost like members of an army—some divisions wearing fine trousers and shirts woven in fanciful designs; some in cut-off jeans rolled up and athletic t-shirts, with thick socks and sports shoes on. Fat moustaches were the norm, as was a mid-length cut of hair. My own jeans were now feeling a bit too snug on me, as was my shirt and—

A hand caressed up my leg as Carla kissed me, long and deep and felt me where no one but myself and a doctor ever had before and I wondered at it, because it felt nice and—

I jolted and looked down to find a man of maybe thirty years smiling up at me. My breath went sharp and low. I pressed against the post, but before I could do more, Scott leaned over to snarl, "He's mine, bitch."

The man shifted his smile to him. "I could handle you both," was the reply he got.

"Some other night," Scott smiled back, not missing a beat.

The man's hand drifted away.

I leaned my head against that post. Near shaking, I was. And—

Bloody fuckin' Carla was touching me and murmuring, "You're so cute, all over you, so sweet" as her hand was doing something to me and I was lying back on the bench and letting her and—

I bounced my head against that post, jolting the images from me. Why was I thinking of that now? Why was I so afraid? Was it because she was here and I worried over what she might say or do?

Oh, this was a mistake. It was a big, big mistake. I knew that for certain, now. I wouldn't be having that fucking memory if we hadn't come, and I nudged Scott, ready to say *I'm off, with or without you,* but that's when our drinks came—two plastic cups of bloody *Coors*; you can't get away from that fucking shite beer.

Now, he was full enjoying himself, our Scott, chatting up an older, dark-haired Latino lad next to him, letting the man's hand rest on his knee and arm drift over his shoulders. He seemed not to care a damn, and it didn't look like the man was trying to go where it'd be too familiar. It was as if this were some sort of dance and Scott knew the steps to keep it moving to a quick beat and not into something slow and personal. He seemed a bit too practiced at it, if you ask me.

A couple lads come up to me to ask my name or if I'd like a drink, but the man who'd first put his hand on my leg warned them off with a gentle, "Still too fresh." Then he'd wink at me and I'd jolt my eyes away.

Scott nudged me and handed me a second beer, saying, "This'll make you feel okay." I still had the first one, and to be honest I'd rather drink nothing than shite beer, so when he wasn't looking I handed both off to someone passing by. There was a lot of that, I'd noticed, so I did it every time he passed me another.

Never once did I see Carla look my direction. She was with a group of men and women, all dressed casual and chatting over wine coolers. I kept the post between me and her as much as I could.

Then the lights vanished and *The Happening* started up, and a woman—no, a man dressed as a woman in a long red gown covered with sparkles, hair done to perfection, face so much like Carla's it was disorienting, slowly descended the stairs and said, "Hi, boys," in a deep booming voice.

The crowd roared *Hello* back and the man began singing that bloody song, dancing about the landing and giving it his all—and damn, if he didn't sound just like Diana Ross. I mentioned that to Scott and he roared with laughter.

The man to my other side leaned over to ask, "What'd he say?"

"He thinks he's really singin'," Scott answered, his voice going thick.

So the lad wasn't? Sure looked it.

The man nodded, gave my thigh a soft pat and said, "Don't worry, honey, there's a first time for everything."

The show kept up for over an hour as one man after another, all in dresses I'm sure the B-girls would have died for, came down the steps and sang songs by Aretha Franklin and Dionne Warwick and Diana Ross and Ertha Kitt and Tina Turner and Peggy Lee and Karen bloody Carpenter and the like. It was all very impressive, I had to admit. And as the show wore on, I grew full relaxed and got to talking with the man at my side.

He was Everett Casterson and he worked in the advertising department of a grocers in the city, as a graphic designer.

"Meaning finding new and interesting ways to sell cabbage, croissants and *Coke*," he said. "The drink."

"And what else would I think it was?" I asked, not really joking, but he laughed.

"You're cute. How old are you?"

"What's this?" I asked. "I'm a used car, am I?"

He glanced me over, nodding. "No, I'd say you're fresh off the assembly line. A seventy-four model."

I rolled my eyes then leaned in close. "I had to sneak in."

"With your friend?" And he tossed a glance at Scott.

"Cousin. And he's of age. You gonna have me tossed?"

"I couldn't if I wanted to. You're too adorable. Both in looks and that brogue; that's what sells you."

"*Sells me*? Christ, you *are* in advertising."

He smiled at me and his eyes took on a hint of sadness. "Why'd you come here?"

"What d'you mean?"

"You're straight, aren't you?"

"Straight?"

"Likes girls."

I nodded. "I've never been around so many poofs, before."

"Oh, you have; you just didn't know it."

"How do you mean?"

"No one at my job knows I am. They'd fire me, if they did. And the things gay men like to do with each other, it's illegal. Not even married couples are allowed."

"That's what Scott's telling me," I said. "What business is it of anybody but you?"

"We live in a theocracy. Protestant Morality forced down the throats of all. Like in Ireland, where the Catholic Church determines the laws; here, it's the bastard Baptists."

I said nothing, since in Derry it was the C of E who ran things, and Paisley was a version of their religion referred to as Presbyterian. But they all come across the same to me, and since I'd heard that view from others about the church in the South, sick of the self-righteous priests and lying hearts of the nuns, and considering Fathers Devil and Jack, and what they'd done to Danny—well, I could see their point.

"So why *did* you come?" he asked, again.

I shrugged, because I had no real answer. The fact is, deep within, despite having to dodge Carla and understanding just how idiotic it was of me to do it, I was glad I had. Like I'd proven something to myself. Of course, had I been caught by a peeler—drinking underage and with no papers—Christ, there'd have been no end of trouble. I wondered if they had the equivalent of Strand Road in Houston.

"I shouldn't of," I finally said. I was all but telling the fates, *You've already fucked me over, once. Have at it, again, you bastards. See what happens. It's not like I have any choice in what's done to me.* And that's never a good idea to do.

Everett smiled. "That's reason enough."

By this point, the show was ending with all the *ladies* on the landing jostling for space while singing *Walk on the Wild Side* then strutting down the last steps to mingle with the audience during the chorus. The thirty-stone one came up to me and tugged at my ear. I laughed in response and Everett gave my thigh another pat.

Scott was deep in his Coors by that point—how I have no idea—but the crowd was joining in singing as away the *ladies* went. Then the lights came up. Not a lot, just enough to see by, and a number of the crowd headed for either the bar or the door.

And that is when bloody Carla finally saw me. Her face cracked into a vicious grin and she started over. Fortunately, the crowd was thick and hard to move through, so I said, "Time for home, Scott," then yanked him to his feet.

He flopped on me like he was made of rags. Not at all easy to maneuver. I staggered then aimed for the exit as that Latin guy grabbed at us, from behind, saying, "Wait, wait." I ignored him and mixed in with the crowd, trying to keep them between me and Carla.

Scott noticed we were moving and mumbled, "Where we goin'?"

"Jesus, Scottie, you're drunk off Coors? Bloody fuckin' Coors!?"

"Got some for free. Want one?" He turned back and called, "Hey, Juan, my buddy wants a—"

I spun him around and slapped a hand over his mouth. "I'm not in need of another, dammit. It's shite, anyway."

He moved my hand down. "Tasted good to me..."

And—

Da grabbed my hand and snarled, "Ya'll gimme the fookin' note, ya little bas'ard," and near crushed me fingers and—

Jesus, Christ, Scott smelled just like him. Sour and cruel. When did he bring out the whiskey? And why? It was making him bloody hard to handle for he didn't want to leave, and Carla had found me in the crowd, again, and was weaving closer and I was near to a panic.

That's when Everett appeared on his other side and said, "Show's done, honey." He took Scott's other arm and helped me all but carry him.

"Naw, guys," Scott muttered, "c'mon. Night's early..."

Out into the blasting heat we went and—

A wall of hot air hit me and I cried out and—

I stumbled. Kept myself erect only by holding onto Scott.

"He's like this off a couple beers?" Everett asked. I guess he thought it was Scott being so heavy, all of a sudden.

All I said was, "Uh, makes no sense to me."

Everett chuckled. "I wonder..."

"Won'er what?" Scott burbled.

"How many'd you have, honey?" he asked, patting Scott's cheek.

And got a chuckled reply of, "Not enough. Let's have more."

But he could not stop us from dragging him away. I chanced a look aback as we rounded a corner and saw Carla coming out, searching the crowd for me. I'd escaped her. Now it didn't matter what she said, I could deny it, thank all that was holy.

"Quite a little trip, isn't he?" Everett said, once we were by the GTO and had draped him over the boot—uh, *trunk*.

"We—uh, we've been out in the sun all day," I said back. "I'm sure it's just the heat and weariness."

"Uh huh. Did the sun also give him bourbon breath?" I just looked at Everett. He nodded. "He sneak a flask in, too?"

I made myself laugh. "In pants like that? Where'll he hide it?"

He cast a look over Scott and shrugged, then frowned. "Wait, he said *Juan*. Was somebody named Juan buyin' him those beers?"

All I did was shrug.

He nodded. "Tight-lipped. I suppose that's good. Usually. But this time? I know this guy named Juan Luna. I call him Luna-tick, because he's a little bit scary, especially when he's handing out boilermakers."

Now I cast him a very confused frown.

He smiled. "Bourbon and beer. Gets a lot of—oh, let's just say *conquests* that way."

I looked at Scott and pulled out a Marlboro. "Fucking shite. And after all that's happening with those dead lads?"

Everett nodded and motioned for a fag—no *ciggie*, dammit, now I'm in America. I handed him the pack and lit us both off one match.

Danny lit his fag and I said, You look like Steven McQueen, and—

I grimaced. Fucking Danny. Why was I crashing back into memories, again? Just as I'd thought I was past them. Was this what Scott had done to me?

Everett gave me a long look and asked, "Can you drive?" Smoke whispering from him like sprites dancing in the thick air.

I drew in a deep breath and eyed Scott. I was angry. He was in no shape to do anything, let alone drive that monster of a car. I thought about taking the wheel, but then I shook my head. "Right side only.

And I'm not sure exactly where we are and his car's got a real motor in it, so I'd not want to take the risk of windin' up the wrong side of the road and—"

Everett put up a hand to slow my words. "It's okay, honey, it's okay. I live 'round the corner. Let's take him to my place and I'll make some coffee, get some food in him. At least he'll be a wide-awake drunk."

I dug the keys from Scott's pants, making him giggle and mutter, "Naw, dude, not my thing." Then we managed to get him into the front seat. I sat next to him as Everett slipped behind the wheel, and the car thrummed to life.

We drove about four blocks to a row of semi-detached homes built in brick and surrounded by trees, hedges, and short parking spaces next to the entrances. It took both of us to maneuver Scott inside, where he collapsed on the divan.

"Whoof," he muttered as he put a hand to his head. "How much did I have?"

"More'n you think, baby," said Everett. "I'll make coffee."

"I don't drink coffee," I said, quick and easy. "Tea?"

"So long as it's Lipton's in your cup." Then he vanished to a back area.

I took a glance around a room that looked like something out of one of Aunt Mari's magazines—nice furnishings, curtains well set, framed artwork on walls covered in some kind of cloth, green plants all about, making it comfortable. A fine carpet lay across the tile floor and the only light was from lamps set in strategic places. I dropped onto an overstuffed chair and felt it was plush enough to sleep in, if need be.

Everett came back in, still trim and neat, even after a couple hours in a bar. His hair wasn't as long as mine and was thinning on top, but his eyes were kind and his expression gentle. I felt easy with him. Almost safe.

"So what's your name?" he asked. "You never told me."

"Oh, sorry. Brendan." Shite. "I-I-I go by Bren."

"How old are you? Sixteen? Seventeen?"

I rolled my eyes but felt it wrong not to say, "The second one."

"So your cousin's eighteen?" I shrugged, which he took as a *yes.* "One of those *Know-it-all* types?"

I just let myself laugh.

Everett nodded and sat on a fat stool, across from me. "You're older than him."

I blinked. "No, I really am—"

He cut me off with a shake of his head, saying, "He may be eighteen, but he's still a kid. You? Year younger, but with a head on your shoulders. I can see it in your eyes. How you act."

I had no idea what to say to that, so said nothing.

He looked at Scott, who was now asleep. Sighed, "Where do you live?"

"Up Shephard. River Oaks area."

"Slumming, were we?" he asked in a girlish voice.

I shrugged. The whistle for the kettle began to whine.

"C'mon. When I've had some coffee and you've had your tea, I'll drive you home."

"No, I'm sure when Scottie's had a cup—"

"He's too far gone; gonna have to sleep it off. But if you *want* to stay the night..." He batted his eyes at me.

I sighed and followed him into a nice enough kitchen. New appliances mingled in with cabinets and counters that had been painted over a dozen times, the latest in a sick sort of beige. We sat at a small extendable-top table and he gave me pastries and milk and sugar and we chatted for an hour over how he disliked his job and how I was a fix-it guy and the direction Houston was going and the rise of gay rights, my first awareness of that. Not once did he try to act like we were anything more than friends having a nice bit of craic, like Ma with the neighbor ladies and—

"What a chore it must be, raisin' so many wain's on your own, Bernadette."

"But with Eamonn it was easy, and he helped with the family finances, unlike some," and she cast a glance at me.

"He may be simple, but he's got a good hand with a turnscrew, and so quiet, as well, and—"

I found a surprising lump build in my throat. While I'd hated it at the time, I now missed hearing their gossipy voices and sanctimonious judgements, even when it led to Ma going wild on me.

Everett noticed I was suddenly silent so smiled and said, "It's almost two; we should go. What's the address?"

I gave it to him, and he was good to his word; he drove Scott and me back to Aunt Mari's and helped me maneuver him into the pool house then dropped him on a bean bag. He'd called to have a cab meet him there, before we left, for to take him home, and it drove up as we returned to the street. I offered to pay for it, but he refused. Just left me his number and said to call him if I needed anything. Then off he went.

The next morning—well, afternoon, for Scott didn't rise till near three, and then was so obviously in pain it gave me a wicked pleasure to make as much sharp noise as I could. I'd even been cruel enough to shove the second bean bag under his legs and let him sleep on that, with a sheet, though he was still dressed. I slept in my bed, and quite well, thank you.

When he finally asked me what had happened, I merely said, "What happened, you don't want to know. And the next time you want to show me a place to go drinking, don't."

He glared at me, stumbled into the house, and didn't say another word to me till he left for Austin.

Three days later.

Consistency

I liked working at *The Colonel's*. Especially it being night hours. The dark silence of Houston as I walked home, even though the air was warm and thick well into October. Sometimes the rain would pour, but I learned to have a light poncho with me so never worried about it, despite how harsh it could be from tropical storms. And I liked having my own entrance to the back, so as not to disturb anyone when I got in.

The pool house became my workstation. Neither Aunt Mari nor Uncle Sean minded, for I kept it clean, but the B-girls thought it *uncouth* and *uncool*. They had quickly mastered the art of sneaking in when I was deep into a project, then would help themselves to a *Dr Pepper* from the little fridge. It could be quite disconcerting to come back to earth and see them sitting on stools, watching me. Once they realized I was back amongst the living, they would proceed to correct everything I did or planned to do.

I could have closed and locked the French doors, but that would have meant suffocating in the October heat. And as a recharge of freon did not add to its coolness, I didn't want to take apart the air conditioner till it was cooler and I wouldn't need it, in case I made a muck of the damn thing. So, I chose to live with their intrusions.

"You're supposed to have a workshop," Brandi sniped at me, once, when I was rewiring a lamp for Aunt Mari. Though I think it was Bernadette; they were back to playing their little games, despite Aunt Mari's warning. The little beast kept on with, "Something like Mr. Holloman has, in his garage. He does all his hobbies in there."

"It's not a hobby," I'd replied, only half listening.

"He's right; it's a job," Bernadette sneered at her before shifting her focus to me. "And you need a store for that."

"It's a hobby if you don't do it all the time," Brandi shot back.

"But he makes money at it, idiot. That makes it a job."

"You can make money off a hobby, too, nitwit."

"Not the way people around here do it."

Then they fell into their back and forth.

Whenever that began, I could focus on whatever I was doing and let them have their fun. Until they realized I'd slipped back into my *not-listening* mode. Then they'd patiently wait till I came out of it and gang up on me, once more.

It was almost amusing.

Almost.

Maybe it was because Mai was so many years older than Maeve that they never had this sort of argument, for not once had I heard a truly cross word between them. Of course, that may have been because Mai was filled with naught but hope and support for us all, much like Aunt Mari, and had calmly presented herself as a buffer between those arguing.

Maeve, on the other hand—well, from the time I saw her go after a lad who was troubling her, I knew she'd have no trouble caring for herself.

Now it's true the family life at Aunt Mari's home helped to steady me, but what began to seal this new world in my head was how well I got along with Rocky, Lorraine, and Todd. The crowd could be thick and busy with men and women of all descriptions drinking beer, scream chatting and playing pool, but there were enough spaces where Lorraine could lean back at the bar and chat with Todd, the bangles on her wrists clicking as she waved her hands to emphasize whatever she was saying, which never was much. I got the idea she was interested in him, but he had his girl in Jersey Village so was having none of it.

He caught me glancing between him and her, one night, smiling to myself, so he drove me home and, between drags on the joint and sips of this new beer that we'd started carrying called *Anchor Steam*, he told me, "Y'know, I learned a long time ago—you don't shit where you eat."

In answer, I said nothing. While I think I know what he meant, I had since learned it's better to remain silent and be thought simple than to speak and prove you are. I'd heard Aunt Mari say something like that to the B-Girls when one of their arguments was becoming too loud.

Todd was absolute business behind the bar. He could pull pints without a thought—no, *glasses* of beer, for they were nowhere near the size of a pint. And he could fix a wine cooler that sparkled, or prepare a set-up, as he called it, while holding a three-way conversation, all without working up even the hint of a sweat. He was never dressed in more than a t-shirt and flared jeans, with dingo boots, and his ponytail floated around as perfectly as some model for Breck Shampoo.

Raquel was also total business. She always had a book with her and during slow times would read it under Todd's station light, at the end of the bar. She was deep into fantasy written by Ursula LeGuin, Andre Norton, Octavia Butler, Madeline L'Engle, and the like. She even lent me one of her books when she caught me looking at it.

"I read it, once," she said. "Just re-readin'. You'll enjoy it."

I thanked her. *A Wrinkle in Time* it was called, though it was a bit on the young side, for me. But the worlds it drew and the characters— Meg, Charles and Calvin, in their tug between good and evil—were interesting.

"I was in 6th grade when it come out," she told me. "She got me started in on readin' and I've got the whole series. Would you like me to bring the rest in?"

"No need for that," I said. "I've got a library card."

Scott's, actually. He'd left it in the pool house and I was making use of it. But that made Rocky and me mates, from then on.

I pulled back from following the disaster that was Derry. Mai's letters and poorly informed articles in the newspapers were more than enough to handle. But it's hard to ignore the atrocities of men when they happen in places I knew, in the North, as well as the Republic and the UK.

There were also the sky-jackings. Terrorism throughout Europe. Governments toppled by madmen. Murders over religion or politics, or the hideous combination of them, all around the world. It seemed everything was hurtling towards catastrophe, and fit tight into my feeling that making it from one day to the next was merely luck of the draw and not by plan or choice.

The worst of it was the Yom Kippur war and oil embargo, which made the last sane people go near mad with worry.

Like Jeremy's mother.

When he was yanked into the Israeli Defense Forces, she began hurtling in to speak with Aunt Mari of her fears, and with the pool doors open. I could hear her every word in the kitchen when she came by, regarding her terror for her youngest son.

"He's too happy a child to be on the front," she'd snarled at no one in particular. "How'll he scare any Egyptians?"

"I thought he was in the north of Israel," Aunt Mari said, just above a whisper.

"Not far from Haifa. But they sent him to The Sinai, and I just know he'll be killed."

"Oh, don't get yerself ready to bury him, yet. He's a smart boy who knows to keep his head low, and he's a fine shot, so he'll be all right."

A fine shot? I'd never have thought of Jeremy as one to hold a rifle, but that evening, as I was rewiring a tall revolving fan I planned to use, I learned from the B-girls he was a champion.

"Won awards," said Bernadette, claiming she was Brandi.

"He's been at it, years," said Brandi, claiming she was her sister.

And I felt no need to end their little game.

"He started when he was eleven," Bernadette continued.

"No, twelve, after his Bar Mitzvah. That's when Mr. Landau took him to the shooting range, the first time."

"He was eleven and his dad got him that rifle for their Christmas. That's why they went."

"They're Jewish; they don't have Christmas."

"They got something just like it, so why not call it that?"

"Because Christmas is for Christians."

"No, Christmas is for everybody!"

And they carried on, till I tested the fan. Its silence startled them silent.

For a moment.

"I've never seen one that doesn't sound like it's on," said Brandi.

"Me neither. Why don't we swap it for the one in my room?"

"You think mom'd let you?"

"The fan you got's on a cabinet, right?" I asked, wary.

"Yeah, and it's newer than this," said Bernadette.

"So it's worth more."

"Which is why it should *not* rattle."

"Why don't you bring it down and I'll look into it?"

Both squeaked "Cool," and bolted into the house. Two seconds later I had fans from both their rooms in my hands. I garnered even more amazement by making each stop rattling with but five minutes of tinkering. That shut up their nattering about my *hobby*.

The oil embargo, of course, messed with everyone but me. Aunt Mari's wagon was eight miles to the gallon and Scott's GTO not so very much better. He'd been coming home every weekend with laundry but that stopped, what with the price of gas. The old Volvo was doing twice the mileage of Aunt Mari's car, but it needed Premium, which was more expensive. Still, it was used more and more often, to the B-girls' dismay.

"It's old and rusty," said Brandi.

"And those seats are awful!" Bernadette chimed in with.

"Not at all cool!"

"Daddy was looking at getting a Pinto."

"But it's too small for him."

"Now he's looking at a Gremlin."

"It's better than a Vega. Those are dinky."

"Totally uncool."

"Totally."

Uncle Sean bought the Gremlin, which struck me as not so much a small car as a full one cut in half. But it was second hand and a good price, and was just for him to run about in. Aunt Mari continued to use her wagon. And the B-Girls kept up harassing me with their little games and gossipy chats.

As comfortable as it all appeared, I was still uncertain about continuing to live here. I did not know my status in the country, and I did not like being in limbo like this. I'd gained as much information from the B-girls as I think I could, and was certain half of it was unreliable, at best. But I had no idea how to go about testing it.

Mai's letters gave me nothing more than asides asking over *their cousin*. I'm not good at playing a charade and worried that I was wrong about being cut off from Derry. That eventually I'd have to return. I wanted to have firmer ground to stand upon, to make my decisions.

I was close to forcing the issue when Everett dropped by, one afternoon in November. It had finally started to chill down and I was walking up the street from selling an old cuckoo clock I'd snatched from the garbage and fixed up nice. When I saw him chatting with Aunt Mari at the front door, I called him by name.

He turned and smiled, as low-key as you can imagine, and said, "Hi, Bren. I wonder if you're up for fixin' somethin'."

"Won't know till I see it," I said, smiling and shaking his hand.

"Is that how you know him?" Aunt Mari asked.

"Yes, I'm friends with Henry Loudermilk," he said, without a hint of hesitation, "and was there when Bren brought in a Tiffany lamp he'd rewired."

I remembered the lamp; it had been sitting on my counter the night we brought Scott home, but it wasn't for some man named Loudermilk I'd fixed it. Still, I caught Everett's careful tone so just said, "I've done plenty enough for him. Pays decent."

"Well, he says you can work miracles, and I got this typewriter that's givin' me trouble."

"Bring it in," I said, heading for the gate by the drive.

Aunt Mari stayed at the door, watching as he slipped back to this new Chrysler that looked like it could be a barge on the Foyle and pulled an old manual beast from its trunk. She kept watching as he lugged it after me.

In the pool house, I had him set it on the counter as I pulled off my bomber jacket. Can't risk getting it dirty; the B-girls would destroy me. So I looked the typewriter over. It reminded me of Jeremiah's and I asked, "What's the problem?"

"Keys stick." I could feel his eyes on me as he continued, "It's my—it was grandmother's. I inherited it after she died 'cause no one else wanted it, but it's too old to make use of. Thought I might sell it, but Henry won't take it 'less it's workin'."

"Probably just needs cleaning," I said, ignoring his gaze. "Maybe a new ribbon. I can get her done, quick."

"What's it gonna cost?"

"Nothing. You helped me and Scott; I'll help you."

"Thanks, Pug."

I gave him a wary look.

He blinked. "Oh. Is it okay if I call you that?"

"Isn't that a dog?"

He gave a slight shrug. "My daddy used it for Irishmen. Something about the little noses they got."

That brought a snort of a laugh from me. "You never met me older brother."

"Scott doesn't have that much of a nose."

"He's a cousin and—"

"Why're you talking about Scott?" jolted us both.

It was Bernadette standing at the door, Brandi right behind her, both with their *Who the hell are you?* expression on and Angus between them, also watching us, wary.

Without a blink, Everett smiled at them and said, "They had some car trouble and I helped them out. Just wanted to make sure everything's all right."

"He's fine," I said then scowled at the B-girls. "And you both know to knock."

"Door was open," said Brandi.

"And from now on it'll be locked," I snapped.

Everett chuckled, let Angus sniff his hand then squatted before the girls once the beast gave him a lick and wag of his tail. "You know, I have never met such pretty twins, before."

"Thank you! I'm Bernadette—"

"No, She's Brandi," I shot out. "The other is Bernadette, and they're ten months apart, but you'd never know it from the way they act."

That got me a huffy glare from the both of them, but Everett just chuckled. "Really? My brother has twin boys, though they're a bit older than you."

"How old do you think we are?" asked Bernadette.

"Twelve?"

"I'm eleven," said Brandi, and pleased as punch, she was. "She won't be for another month."

"Then for two months we'll be the same age."

"So for two months you *are* twins," Everett said.

"That's right," said Bernadette, bright and happy, "we are."

"That's not how it works," Brandi shot back. "You have to be born at the same time."

"But we'll be the same age!"

"It doesn't matter."

And off they went back to the house, nattering on.

Angus stayed behind, casting me a weary gruff.

Everett rose, still chuckling. "God, those two'll be terrors by high school."

"As if they aren't now."

"How're you survivin' 'em?"

"Just let them go as they will. Life's too short."

He looked at me, long and quiet as I tested the keys of the typewriter. For some reason I couldn't ignore the sadness in his eyes so finally I asked, "All right, what is it?"

He blinked and asked, "What?"

"You looking at me. Why?"

"Sorry, Pug, it's just..." He took a step back and his voice trailed off then after a deep breath asked, "You mind if I take some-some pictures of you?"

"Pictures?"

"Yes. Head and shoulders, that's all."

"Why?"

"Because you're a boy, but there's an old man in your eyes. I noticed it that night. It's intrigued me. Can't seem to shake it. I'd like to see if I can capture it."

"In pictures?"

"A-a-a painting." Suddenly words tumbled from him. "My whole life I've been sayin' I'm an artist, but I keep lettin' things get in the way—like that stupid job, where I'm drawin' cabbage and carrots and cans of pork and beans and-and I keep findin' excuses not to really go for it and-and now I want to see if I've been lyin' to myself. Capturin' you would be a test, of a sort. See if I really am what I say I am, or if I'm foolin' 'round an' nothin' more, and for the first time I—you— you're the first person I ever felt strong enough about to try it with. You mind if I try?"

"I'm in an undershirt."

"Don't matter. It's your face I want."

It sounded odd, but he'd been fine with me and Scott. Nor did I sense misuse from him like I had Father Demian, so with a shrug I said, "What do I do?"

"Just focus on the typewriter. Do your thing. I'll probably take a hundred photos, so pretend I'm not here."

He ran back to his car to get an older Canon SLR. Then as I broke the typewriter down he took photo after photo. Probably changed film at least five times. I doubt the latter ones were of much use, because by that point I was filthy and lost in my work, but he left happy.

Of course, he couldn't get away before the B-girls burst from the house to catch him and pester him with questions as he led them and the dog down the drive to his barge.

"How well do you know Scott?"

"I don't. I know Bren. That's why I stopped to help them."

"How long you known him?"

"Just a few months."

"What kind of trouble could Scott's car have?"

"Gas. He was out of it. Happens to us all, now and then."

"Yeah, he's always complaining about how much it drinks."

"Do cars drink gas?"

"It's just a saying."

"I know, but it sounds silly. *Cars drink like we do.*"

And then they were out of earshot. I'd have run after and

apologized to Everett, but his voice was filled with the greatest of pleasure, talking and listening to them. I just made a note to let Scott know of these new events.

A moment later, Aunt Mari came to the door to ask about dinner—something she'd never done before. I got a funny feeling she was relieved at seeing me not only dirty but the typewriter actually being worked upon.

"Are you planning something odd?" I asked, wary.

"No, just wonderin' if you had a preference."

I hesitated then shrugged and said, "Whatever you're on for. It's just—well, sorry, but you'll have to give me half an hour to wash." I held my hands up to show her the ink slathered on my fingers. "If I *can* get it off."

"Ah, right, and some's on your nice shirt."

That made me tense. Ma had always criticized me when I got dirty, which is half what I'd expected from her. I'd first clean my clothes a little and let them dry before giving them to Aunt Mari for the wash, for fear she'd smack me around as Ma would. I couldn't have handled it, from her. "It-it-it's an undershirt," I said.

"I'll see what I can do, when I wash it," she said. "Sean has some Lava soap in the garage; try that. I think chilidogs. Toasted buns. Cheese. Onions. Homemade fries."

"Sounds fantastic. Thanks."

"It's a pleasure," she said, then added, "Oh, tomorrow's your appointment with Dr. Gilbert."

I tensed. Could just picture Carla and her vicious smile.

She must have noticed because she continued with, "Carla's no longer there, ya know, in case ya were lookin' for her."

A smile burst from me and I said, "Oh?"

She noticed the change in me and nodded. "I don't really know the..." And here she took extra care in her words. "Well, the *particulars* of why, but I've heard she...she may have had inappropriate contact with a patient and was asked to leave. Hope yer all right with that."

I was, and I nodded.

Her smile grew. "I'll get the dinner on."

I watched her head back in the house. I got the idea she had something to do with Carla's removal but couldn't say for certain. It was just the care she'd taken in how she told me I needn't worry about that bitch, anymore.

Whether she'd been behind sacking Carla or not, she knew more than she was willing to share, and she had supported me, in some way. It filled me with such a comfort, it was all I could do to not call after her with, *I wish you'd been me Ma.*

But I knew she'd not have liked it.

Still that little moment cast aside much of my uncertainty and reticence about staying here. Aunt Mari had offered me a sanctuary, with nothing but care and concern. And while Uncle Sean could be stand-offish, as the B-girls put it, he'd given me a job and provided for me in ways my own parents never did. So this wasn't such a bad place to be living in, that I needed rush away.

I finally began to feel as if I truly were in a place of safety.

Holidays

Jesus, was Christmas a massive affair at Aunt Mari's. Uncle Sean and myself fixed up the yard with lights, a creche, and a massive Santa atop the roof. That was not a joy to handle, for it was me up there putting it right, with Uncle Sean yelling orders that had little to do with reality. That I managed without a fall to break my neck was a miracle.

Through the week after a holiday called Thanksgiving, many of the neighbors also decorated their yards and seemed bent on outdoing each other. Big, colorful bulbs. Plastic Santas and snowmen in a place where it never snowed. Even the Landaus joined in with what they called a Menorah and blue and white lights, in front and over the house. I could only shrug at the silliness of it, but it did actually make me feel most festive.

The house was fully decorated, with a tree that reached the ceiling and filled with ornaments and tinsel to where I wondered at it being able to stand upright. I also helped string lights over the house and took great pleasure at how it all looked once they were done. We'd done nothing like this in Derry, not even a tree or creche, though Ma did add a candle to the prayer corner.

Shopping was at the Galleria, which was so decorated it was frightening. It was also far more costly than I liked when it came to just about anything I wanted, so when I was dragged there I'd ice skate and let the rest of the family off to carouse the stores. I got to be fair good at it. Even the B-girls were impressed and proudly touted how they'd taught me everything they knew as they danced in swirls around me.

What I never told them was, racing about on those skates in the cold of the arena...the *skritch, skritch, skritch* of the blades as I rushed along...around and around...clean and clear and crisp...my head grew much less troubled. For it was not part of my past. I almost felt I was leaving my history behind me and could scream to the future, *Come on, then; let's have at it.*

A stupid, childish thing to say, yes, but the joy of those few moments filled me with the purest pleasure.

Scott arrived from his first term, sporting a Madras shirt, polyester trousers and boots that zipped up the side. His hair was longer and he had a full beard on his face, which was disconcerting, because he was so blond it near vanished into his skin. Uncle Owen wasn't pleased at his new look and said so, but Scott just smiled, shrugged and noted his GPA was 4.0. Aunt Mari said nothing, but the looks she cast him more than hinted at her displeasure, while the B-girls swarmed over his new clothes like he was a new Ken doll.

I greatly appreciated the relative peace of it.

Jeremy returned for Hanukkah with a couple mates from the Israeli Army. The whole neighborhood was invited over for the lighting of the first candle, and I found I rather liked their jelly donuts and the fried potatoes. Never thought to make them in the way they did.

He looked worn down, our Jeremy did. Much like Jackie, Aidan and other lads I knew—young men caught in a war where there could be no winners, only those who lost less. I made no attempt to speak with them; I knew too well what they would have to say and needed nothing to bring back my own memories to match theirs. They seemed to tacitly agree and kept to themselves through much of the evening, chatting in what I think was Hebrew, visited only by Jeremy and his mother to make certain they were well fed and included as much as they wished to be.

What struck me was how deliberate everyone was in their manners. There were presents for us all, and vise-versa. Aunt Mari had let me know to expect this, so I'd checked with the B-girls on what best to bring—and spent an hour listening to their sniping and suggestions before we finally just went to Neiman-Marcus and found a nice set of glasses that looked engraved with trees and what could be winter-like places. Unimpressive, to me, and priced dear at twenty-five dollars for six of them! However, the giftwrapping was free and the B-girls satisfied.

"It's always better to give something safe to people you don't know," said Brandi, sagely.

"Our Aunt Judith is like that," Bernadette added.

"You'll meet her Christmas Day."

"She's daddy's sister and always has a few safe gifts in a back bedroom, at her house, when we go over."

"Handkerchiefs, usually."

"White cotton and plain," Brandi sighed, nodding.

"Bor-ring!"

"We figured it out when Cathy was with us, last Christmas. She gave her one."

"No, it was Christmas before last. You were nine."

"No, I was ten when I saw her sneaking back there to wrap them up. Real quick."

And off to the word-race they went. I just sighed, handed over my money, and led them to the giftwrap counter, their argument still going. I don't think it finished before we hopped the bus to home.

But the glasses were well-received and used straight off. Then I was given a small box to unwrap. And in it was a set of tiny turnscrews and—

Joanna gave me a set of small turnscrews and I was so happy—

I forgot to breathe and everything grew quiet. They were perfect for working on wristwatches. Small things. called *screwdrivers*, Brendan. American terms. I'd had the ones Joanna gave me in my rucksack and-and-and now wondered where they'd gone and...and...

And I managed to regain control enough of my mind to remember to say, "Thank you," then backed away from the rest of the gift-giving. No one seemed to notice, and I'm sure I spent the rest of the evening with a smile on my face. For it was that or weep, and I'm sure they'd not have understood my tears. Instead, I slipped into the back to have a smoke. Give myself some time alone, despite the chill.

Give myself time to—time to remember Joanna.

I'd had my eye on a pendant in Austin's that was near forty pounds, but so perfect for her. I'd planned to buy it as her Christmas present. When my passport arrived, I'd thought about getting it and giving it to her, early. But I was in a push to leave and-and-and stupidly felt it more important I keep as much of my money as possible available because I was sure we'd have a hundred more Christmases in our future.

I should have bought it.

Should have given it to her, right then.

That might have kept her at the back door for just long enough.

Or I should have dragged her to *Marianne's* with me.

For a moment, the white horror surrounded me, but this time in a whisper. Slow and easy. I fired up a Marlboro and made myself circle the pool, which helped me to handle it. Weeping was not allowed in someone else's home; merely sadness.

Sadness? What a silly word. Melancholy was better. I'd caught it in a book written by Arthur C. Clark and looked it up, and it gave title to some of my moods.

Moods that would drive me up onto the roof of the pool house so I could sit in peace and smoke anything I chose and let my mind stay silent and still. Whether it be raining or not. To keep gentle whatever thoughts came from the soft darkness. My poncho would protect my cigarette from the wet, and on clear nights I could see the stars fighting to make themselves known. I hadn't known a city could be so brilliantly lighted that it would hound the stars from the sky, but Houston was.

It wouldn't have mattered on this night. Clouds reflected the city's brilliance back at it. The air was chilled like a spring evening in Derry, my breath adding only a hint of fog to the cigarette's smoke.

Their pool was covered with a thick tarp, which made it seem smaller than the one behind Aunt Mari's home. I'd thought Uncle Sean should do this, as well, but he'd shrugged my suggestion off and drained it, instead. Seemed a waste. There were still the occasional warm days, even in winter, when it might be nice to float in the water and let that chase away my thoughts.

Like remembering it was now well over a year since that day.

That day.

When I'd thought I was off to find my own life, only to have everything ripped away from me. The fire might not dance around me, anymore. The whiteness down to thick billowing smoke. Almost as if that horrible day had happened to someone else and I was merely going over photos of it. Sickened by the death and destruction, but more in sympathy than actual pain or revulsion. Was it human to slide into so detached an emotion after only fourteen months?

Was I already losing all connection with Joanna?

No.

No, I wrapped my arms around me. Cupped my hand on my shoulder. Caressed her name. Brought up the image of her at the circle fort. Looking over the whole of Ireland. Wind whipping her golden silk. Cheeks smooth and red. Her expressions that of wonder and happiness. I could almost smell the soft Spearmint whispering from her. Feel the ache I had in my heart for loving her so much. Accept the joy of simply knowing her.

I could never lose that.

Never.

My soul was branded with her, as well as my shoulder, and that would do. Would have to do.

I'd lit my second smoke when Jeremy joined me, motioning for one.

"You-you're smoking now, is it?" I said, handing the box over, still a bit shaky.

He chuckled. "It helps."

I nodded. Scott had begun smoking just to look cool; it was obvious in how he used the cigarette once it was lighted. How he exhaled. All *look-at-me*, that lad. Everett was right, he was still a boy. But Jeremy? He sat on the edge of the diving board and inhaled the smoke in a way that spoke of need. And he held it close to him, resting his chin on a knee and letting the smoke drift from him like he was merely breathing. Almost like Danny had done.

Danny.

Christ, I did not want to be thinking of him, now.

I felt I should say something to Jeremy, but he was lost in other thoughts, and I didn't want to bring him any trouble. I would have expected the same courtesy from him, and somehow knew he'd have given it.

My cigarette was almost done, and I was just beginning to grow chilled, when he asked, "How you doin'? Here in Houston?"

I shrugged. "It's a place to live, isn't it?"

"Yeah. I guess. Funny. Y'know, I missed bein' here. But now I'm back, it's all different. Weird."

Before I could think to stop myself, I asked, "How're *you* doing, over there?"

He looked at me. "Don't you follow the news?"

"Why would I do that when I've lived through much of it?" popped out of me before I could stop it. I bit my lip and kicked myself for it.

He gave a near chuckle. "Answer a question with a question. Dad says the Irish are perfect examples of passive-aggressive."

I did laugh. "I've no idea what you just said, but it sounds right."

He smiled. "Shit, what I wouldn't give for a joint, right now. Yossi and Ofir were gonna bring some pot with 'em and it took me an hour to convince 'em it was a mistake. Especially in Texas. Now they're on edge."

Oh. Now this...this I could do something about. I opened the

Marlboro box, then carefully selected a ciggie from a corner of it and handed it over.

Jeremy waved it off, saying, "Naw, I don't want another—" Then he looked at it, his eyes growing wide. "Smoke?"

I winked at him. I'd repacked the paper like I'd seen was done by Danny.

He took it, almost reverent. "Do you have more?" he asked.

I shook my head. "It's no end of trouble to swap out the tobacco, so I only have it for emergencies. And isn't this one?"

He smiled. "I-I-I'm gonna show the guys the back of the yard. Maybe climb up-up to my old treehouse." Then he got up, but before he could slip into the house I handed him the rest of the box.

"For covering the aroma."

He laughed and scurried off. Moments later, I saw three very happy young soldiers scurry to the back of the yard as I headed inside. They were still there when we left for home.

Aunt Mari had us open presents on Christmas Eve and not the morning after, to my confusion.

"Because we're going to see Aunt Judith," Bernadette groaned at me when I asked about it.

"Tomorrow," said Brandi.

"After church and before dinner."

"Am I expected?" I asked.

Aunt Mari cast me a look and answered before the B-girls could. "If you want, Bren, but it's not required."

"But you'll get a box of white hankies," Brandi laughed.

"Oh, yeah, you *have* to have those," chuckled the other.

I chose to stay away.

I was given more clothes and—

Was handed a box and was expected to open it but I couldn't figure out how so Scott did it for me and it was a new pair of pajamas and I wept at how lovely and clean they were, so normal and human and Aunt Mari hugged me and—

The B-girls gave me coupons to the skating rink. Scott gave me ten dollars, which I appreciated but brought a disapproving look from Aunt Mari.

I gave her and my Uncle a small mechanical wind-up kissing couple I'd found at a toy shop, Scott a thick belt with a massive buckle, and mood rings for the girls, "So I'll know how to treat you when you come waltzing into my place," I said.

"We don't know how to waltz," said Brandi.

"We could take dancing lessons," Bernadette said.

"So long as it's not ballet."

"Yeah, that looks silly once you're our age."

"But we'll need partners."

"Larry Needham might do it. He likes to dance."

"Oh, right, he's cute. I'll ask him."

"No, he'd be *my* partner. You get your own."

"But he's a year older than me and two years older than you."

"So what? We're not gonna date; just dance."

And off they went.

Christmas Day was early mass, which I did attend and found the church pleasant enough. Then once they returned from Aunt Judith's, everyone lazed about the den, as they called it. Their aunt had fixed up a massive dinner and all had indulged, so the evening meal was light and easy.

No Boxing Day, it seems.

New Year's came and no one thought to warn me about the non-stop fireworks and gunshots on that day, as well. They were so massive and loud and—

The Para shot the man in the belly and the bullet hit the lad behind him and both crumbled and died on the spot and others were shrieking behind me and more Paras were running up but when did I see that happen or did I and only be told of it or was I hiding and saw the blood and-and-and—

Images played over and over and over in my head as I shook and, basically, hid in the pool house. Music turned up. Sitting on the floor with the bean bags protecting my back, one hand gripping a beer, a cigarette in the other. If the pool had been full, I'd have been sitting in it, deep under the surface as long as I could. And all that was despite me understanding it was just celebrations going on, like the Fourth of July, and not all-out war.

It took me two days to calm down, complete.

I became eighteen with some fanfare, both at the house and *The Colonel's*. Cakes and little gifts and cards from Mai, Aunt Mari, and the girls. I got one card signed by everyone at the bar, and Rocky gave me a copy of *Foundation*, by Isaac Asimov.

"It's part of a trilogy," she said. "If you like it, there's a bookstore in the Galleria that carries the rest."

"I'll pop in next time I'm skating," I said.

She nodded. "I used to love ice skating. I was pretty good. Thought I'd go for the Olympic team."

"Come along, sometime. You can give me pointers."

She gave me an odd look and said, "Let's see what happens."

But that was the end of the discussion.

I'd finished working on Everett's typewriter long ago, but he didn't come to fetch it till four days after, and he brought the portrait he'd done of me. It was framed and had a cloth over the front of it. Aunt Mari let him set it up in the parlor. Scott was in Austin, so once the rest of us had gathered around, he unveiled it.

And there was me. Head and shoulders. Face done right. Hair more wavy than curly but also more honest. And in my eyes was a certain wariness that did make me seem older than I was. I was bloody gobsmacked, it was so fine. Done in oils

"Jesus, Everett," I murmured, "this is what you can do?"

He blushed from the compliments. "It took a lot more work than I expected. Had a couple of false starts, and if you look close you'll see I made some mistakes, but..."

"It's lovely, Everett," said Aunt Mari. "Don't cut yerself down."

He beamed.

"Where you gonna put it, Bren?" Brandi asked.

"Not in the pool house!" asked her sister.

"But that's where he lives."

"It won't get seen there, and it'll get dirty."

I nodded and sneered. "Yeah, the way I work."

"We could hang it in here," said Aunt Mari. "By the fireplace."

She had me take down a nice enough painting of some flowers and hang it there, where it did look proper.

"Will you do one of us?" Bernadette asked Everett.

He took in a deep breath then said, "Do you have some photos you like? I could try to replicate those. See what happens when I'm commissioned to do a work."

Aunt Mari pulled out the family album then she and Everett spent the next hour going over it to find the right images to use, chatting like old neighbor-ladies—

By the front door, sharing a craic as they cleaned their stoops, hair tied up in a scarf, apron over their old shifts, feet in slippers, criticizing friends and approving of those they liked until they didn't like them and-and-and enough said about that.

By the time they were done I felt that she saw him as another son.

Which pleased me.

He was ordered to stay for dinner and marveled at me eating a drumstick with a knife and fork, which brought forth a slew of comments from the girls about how silly it was.

"But that's how kings and queens eat," was his response.

"C'mon," said Brandi, "the Queen of England doesn't know how to eat chicken?"

"Well," he responded, "can you picture her taking a breast with her hands and biting into it?" Then he chomped into one, like a dog, making the B-Girls giggle. "Or corn on the cob?" More chomping down and getting only half of it in his mouth. "Getting it aaaaaaalllll over?"

"But eating like Bren does is hard," said Bernadette.

"Not really." Then Everett proceeded to show he could eat it my way, as well.

That got the B-Girls to trying it, themselves, silent as they focused on their actions. Everett gave them little pointers and by the end they were cutting and trimming the meat off a drumstick as well as he or I. Aunt Mari exchanged a quiet glance with Uncle Sean, but nothing was said by either of them.

Then as he was leaving, Everett cast me a tender smile and said, "You're lucky, pug."

"I'd argue that," was my response.

"Don't. You got people here who love you."

"Yeah, but—"

"No, you don't get to put a *but* on that. Not when you have a family watchin' over you."

I had no idea what to say so just looked at him.

He took in one of his deep long breaths and continued, "When I was sixteen, my older brother caught me kissin' the captain of the basketball team. It's bad enough it was a boy; what made it worse was, he was *Chicano*. Mexican. I was told to get out. So I got."

"This the brother with twins?"

He smiled and nodded. "That was twelve years ago. My folks still won't talk to me. He and I—we're-we're better, now, and I think I've done okay, considerin'."

I nodded. "Well, if Aunt Mari says you're welcome any time, you are. And I know the girls would love you to be their latest pet project."

That made him chuckle, soft and low, and still with more than a hint of sadness. "Thanks." He cast me another tender look then headed down to his barge of a car.

Aunt Mari appeared behind me, as he drove away, and said, "He's who helped ya with Scott, that night."

What?! I cast a glance back at her.

"I saw ya comin' back, wee hours. My son paralytic as a fool. It's good his father was still at *Liam's Trough*."

Again, all I did was look at her.

She nodded and continued, "Ya *good* friends?" Her voice carried a meaning I did not like.

"He's been fine with me," I said. "And with Scott."

"That's good. Just be careful."

"I thought you liked him."

"I do. But men like that—they'll become yer friend, then lead ya places you never meant to go."

"Why do you think that of him?"

She gave a deep sigh. "It's just how those men are, Bren."

I finally realized I'd misunderstood why Aunt Mari had invited Everett to dinner. She'd wanted to work him out better, see if he was out to have me or Scott as his special mates, and he'd known and that's what his last comments to me had been about. I felt almost betrayed on his behalf. To me it seemed his was the soul of an artist, not a conniving bastard, and his meaning was gentle, not selfish or cruel or controlling. I'd had so sense that him helping Scott and myself was for selfish motives, or manipulative.

But then I remembered Billie Corrie helping his uncle prepare to attack Eamonn, sending him to hospital well-damaged, and not a word from him since. And there was Father Jack and his two faces, one Godly, the other political. And Colm setting Paidrig up for kneecapping over cigarettes. Bloody fucking cigarettes. I'd seen none of that-that—oh, I don't know—casual willingness to hurt others in any of them till they'd done it. Maybe Everett hid that cruelty as well as they.

Because I'd now caught a glimpse of that in my aunt, and I knew, deep within I knew that were I to defend him, her worries would only increase and she might go so far as to ban him from the house.

As his own family had done.

And it would be done for the *right reasons*, to her.

I had no need to be that kind of bastard, so I just sighed and said, "It's how all men are, Aunt Mari. And women. I learned that long ago."

"Bren, all I meant was—"

"I know what you meant." And my voice was more sharp than I intended. "Ma tells everyone I'm simple. Do you think that, as well?"

She said nothing. Of course. I'd bet all those months of my silence solidified the truth of it in her view.

I nodded, closed the door and led her back to the portrait. "This looks good here. Leave it, if you like."

Then I returned to the pool house, climbed onto the roof and stayed hidden in the shadows, smoking, letting myself accept the idea that my aunt also saw me as nothing but damaged goods in need of protection. Foolish. Incomplete. One to keep close because he could not be trusted to care for himself. In need of someone to watch over him.

And what's even worse? I could see no argument against it, for deep within I felt she was right.

Crash and Burn

Not two weeks later, I was in the kitchen, washing up, when loud voices burst from the bar. I paid little attention since Todd usually shut them down with a loud bark of, *Take it outside* or *Shut the hell up* or the like. But this time the only reply was a howl of, "Fuckin' cunt!" followed by smashing glass and a scream.

I bolted out to find Rocky backed into a corner, a hand to her face, near hysterics, as Todd fought to hold back a raving beast of a man. Shirt torn off one shoulder. Fists the size of fine hams swung through the air. Lorraine had also grabbed him as Bidwell danced around like a cheering section, giving off little yelps of fear.

Then the bastard hit Rocky and—

Da whipped his fist across Ma's face and her head snapped around and I saw blood and started yelling and—

I grabbed the baseball bat kept by the cash box as the bastard slung Todd aside and shrugged Lorraine off then lunged at Rocky. I bolted over and—

The bat smacked into the back of Pairdig's knee and—

The bastard buckled and wailed like a girl and half-dropped to the floor then—

Da turned on Eamonn, his eyes wild and filled with drink and punched him and—

The bastard's other knee cracked. I'd hit it from the side. The man howled and shifted away as—

Da turned his mad focus on me but he wasn't gonna get past me this time, no he wasn't and—

I was slammed against the wall. By Todd. Who yanked the bat from me and held me there, his eyes wide and angry.

"Get outta here!" he snarled.

I looked at him, stupid. Confused. One crack to his head and this was done. Why wasn't he letting me finish the bastard?

He pushed me, again. "Get out! I'll handle it."

I blinked and muttered, "Should-shouldn't you-you call the—?"

He spit and snapped, "Rocky, can you drive?" She nodded, quick and jerky. "Get him out of here. Both of you! GO!!"

She grabbed her purse from behind the bar, caught hold of my sleeve and pulled me from the place. It wasn't till we were in her Vega roaring down the street that I realized I'd actually been aiming to kill the bastard.

I was going to kill a man!

A man I didn't know!

All without a thought about the consequences!

Bloody hell!

He hadn't touched me. I'd stopped him with the first crack to his knee, but I was still after him like some wild animal and—

The para's eyes gleamed as he took aim and fired and another marcher fell and—

I chuckled. "I've mucked it up, haven't I?"

"What?" Rocky asked, her voice cracked.

"I should've stayed in back. Put a call to the police."

"Bren, that son-of-a-bitch *is* a cop."

I looked at her, startled.

"Ex-husband. Thinks he still owns me. I thought I lost him, but somehow—shit, somehow he always tracks me down and shows up and causes trouble and-and-and nothing ever gets done about it."

"Why not?"

"I told you! He's a cop! They-they-they always get away with it. With all kinds of shit, the bastards."

I finally noticed she was shaking with her voice verging on collapse, and she almost run up a curb. I put a hand to hers and said, "Rocky. Rocky. Pull over."

"No, I-I-I gotta—I gotta get us away—"

"Rocky." She seemed not to hear me, so I whispered, "Raquel, pull over. He's way behind us, now. Let's sit for a little. Catch up to ourselves."

She glanced at me, her breathing fast and uneven, then swung the Vega down a side road in a sharp little skid, just before Memorial, and shuddered to a halt at the intersection. And didn't move, for a full minute. Just sat there, like she was still driving, just staring ahead.

Until she began to sob.

I said nothing, just let her go till she was done. What could I say? That she was safe, now? I wasn't fool enough to think that. If he'd tracked her down more than once, he would, again. Best to say nothing than make some transparent lie.

Besides, I had the horror of knowing had Todd not stopped me, I'd be up for murder. Kills your image of yourself as someone who's in control. The one thing that kept me from careening into madness over it was that I'd been protecting someone, not out merely to hurt or destroy.

But still...

It took her just a few minutes to regain control. She pulled a packet of tissues from her purse and blew her nose then wiped her eyes.

"Sorry," she finally managed to grumble out. "But this means he-he-he probably knows where I live, too. I've had four jobs. Three homes. Last two years. *Colonel's* is the longest I been. At one place. Since I left that son-of-a-bitch."

"Can't you do something with a lawyer or a judge?"

"Like what? Last time he found me, I was in the hospital for a week. You think he got charged with assault? You think Internal Affairs gave a damn? One of his buddies even said it's my own damn fault for provoking him."

"Jesus, Rocky."

She nodded and leaned back, finally beginning to relax, a little. "Guess I'll have to move on, again."

"If I was you, I'd leave the state, complete."

"Can't. My momma's sick an' without me, she's got nobody, an' he knows that."

"She'll have nobody if you're killed. Have her move with you."

"She won't talk about it." She rubbed the back of her neck, still a bit shaky. "But Matty scared me, this time. The look in his eyes."

"Well, he won't be chasing you till he's healed," I said. "And may never walk the same, again, the way I clipped him."

She cast me a wary glance. "With the bat?"

I nodded. "I heard a crack."

Then her expression became incredulous. "You broke his knee?"

"Both, most likely."

"Good," and she almost laughed, then gasped. "Oh, no wonder Todd had me get you out of there. He don't want the cops to get a hold of you."

Oh, bugger me. Of course. Todd had seen it, straight off. Houston Police would have torn me apart, just as the RUC would with those who hurt or damaged their own, no matter how rightly deserved. I wondered what magic he might be working on little Matty to keep me out of it, because were I to be grabbed it would be bad for us all. My one trust was that Todd had no hesitation in doing what must be done to protect himself.

She looked me over, shaking her head. "And you seem so sweet and easy goin'. People really this hard-assed in Ireland?"

"In my part."

"You—you saved me. Thanks." She sat back, thinking. "I'm not givin' momma a choice. We're goin' someplace new. Like Colorado. I hear Aspen's real pretty."

"I'll help, if you like. And you can stay with me till you're set."

She looked at me and nodded. "Thanks."

She was good enough to drive, now, so first we went to her flat—*apartment* to get her clothes and such, then I directed her to my home.

It was a chill night so Angus was inside, but still he wound up at the back door, with a bark. Me just shooting back with, "Angus!" was enough to quiet him. Fortunately, Uncle Sean was at *Liam's Trough*, so no need for explanations, yet. She got the bed while I did the bean bags for myself.

And I have to say, it was a miracle Scott hadn't killed me for making him sleep on them, that night. I felt like I'd rolled down the side of a cliff.

I let Aunt Mari know what had happened and she took it in with her usual calmness. Then I went off to sell a couple of old lamps I'd rewired. When I came home, I found Rocky had bought an air mattress and quartered off some of the pool house for herself. And now she and Angus were best of friends.

"Just temporary," she said.

"I meant it, stay as long as you like."

"I don't think your aunt would approve, and I know your cousins won't. They came in while I was in the shower."

"Those little sneaks. They bloody well know they're not to come in when I'm not here. I'll talk to my aunt and uncle."

Which I did, the moment Uncle Sean was in the house.

He'd already been handling inquiries from the police about the *unknown boy* who'd *attacked a cop*. Todd had tried to take the blame, but Matty was being a bastard about it and told them what happened before going into surgery.

Leaving out how he was beating a woman, I'm sure.

It had been put forth that I was just a boy *who'd come in off the street for a beer and helped stop the bastard's assault.*

"The good thing is, that other guy in the bar backed Todd up."

"Bidwell," I said, nodding, figuring he'd use his lies to square himself an extra beer or two.

"And Todd's swearin' he had no idea the man was a cop. From what I hear, the DA's already damned perturbed 'bout the case. Officially. But the cops'll be watchin' us, now, and use any excuse to hurt us. Can't have you back there."

I nodded, saying, "I'm sorry."

"Don't be," Aunt Mari added. "I saw Raquel's face. She can stay here a day or two, till she gets her plans worked up, but no more."

"Yeah," Uncle Sean was nodding. "Brandi and Bernadette probably already told their friends."

"Is that a problem?" I asked.

"I just don't like the attention it's gonna bring. Too damn much goin' on here that ain't quite right an'...well..." His voice trailed off into a sort of discomfort and his eyes stayed off me. Deliberately.

That made me wonder, "Uncle Sean, am I not legal, here?"

They exchanged a look then Uncle Sean asked, "Why you askin' that?" And his attitude was all but screaming, *Do not expect an answer.*

I blinked.

Things began to fall together. Demands I stay in their home. Paid in cash. Mairead never writing me or referencing me in her letters. No form of identification on me, not even my passport. The only other people in Houston I'd been introduced to were the Landaus and some immediate neighbors, and it now seemed that was probably because Jeremy had met me when he should not have, and I'd been making repairs for their maids and gardeners. And even then, I was naught but *Cousin Bren, from Ireland.* As for my little sales, those were a near anonymous relationship with the dealers. I'd simply wandered along in my own way, hoping to maintain a quiet existence, and hadn't really considered the whole of it. To have it shown to me in full light—it was startling, to say the least. No need for more words.

My uncle's eyes stayed on me for a full minute more, and suddenly I couldn't see him as being helpful, but as a block of ice, and another to be wary of, like his son.

Finally, he continued, "Got any more questions?"

I just shook my head. Then we all got up and I went back to the pool house. Rocky had gone out seeking a new place or to talk with her mother or something, so I began work on a small radio I'd found.

And think.

Suddenly, I felt something like a prisoner. Didn't matter that I was eighteen and had ways of making a living, how could I make plans or go wherever I wanted with no identification? No legal standing? Invisible chains bound me to this area, and that simply would not do. I had to find a way to settle my existence and remove its limitations.

Scott came in that weekend, with bags of laundry. When he heard of what happened and that I was no longer allowed in any of Uncle Sean's bars, he took on his know-it-all voice and told me that it was because half the men working at his father's bars were paid *under the table*, as he called it.

"He keeps enough legal guys around to look good," he added.

"Is that normal practice here?" I asked, thinking if so then I could do the same thing elsewhere.

"Yeah, all over the border states," he laughed. "Lots of people yell about illegal immigration then hire 'em 'cause they're cheap. Farm workers. Housekeepers. Maids. Janitors. You name it. You're lucky you beat one of 'em out for that job. Too bad it wound up like that."

That's when Rocky came running in, saying, "I think I got myself a new place, down in Sugar—" Then she saw Scott and jolted to a stop. "Sorry, didn't know you were home."

"Just got in," Scott said, eyeing her. "Dad said you were stayin' here a few days."

Rocky got a cornered look in her eyes. "He told people where I am?"

"Just me, and I ain't tellin' nobody. Too many guys from my frat're from Houston. Already knew two of 'em when I pledged." He cast me a wicked glance as he headed for the door. "Almost time for dinner and then *Sanford and Son*. See you inside, Bren?"

I nodded and he left.

Rocky sank onto a beanbag, shaken. "I'm not safe anywhere."

"Scott won't reveal you."

"It'll get out, Bren. Word keeps getting back to Matty, no matter where I am. One day, he'll kill me. I know it. I'm gonna tell momma we're leavin', no matter what she says."

"Wait—you haven't told her, yet?"

"No. Dumb. Should've been workin' on her from the start."

"Does Matty know where your mother lives?"

She shook her head. "Maiden name's Martinez, and momma's in government housin'. There's a thousand with the same name."

"I'll help convince her, if you like."

She smiled. "Be hard to do. She don't speak English."

"Then stay on here till you've got her convinced."

"No. No, Matty'll work it out and make trouble."

That is when I had one of my more brilliant ideas. "What if I asked a friend if he's got a place for you? He's in Montrose and has a fine big home."

"A *friend*? In gay town?"

"Yes." Then I caught what she was thinking. "*Friend*, only."

She smiled and said, "I'd hate to impose."

"Let me call him and ask."

I used the phone in Uncle Sean's office rather than the kitchen, and Everett had no trouble with Rocky staying with him. We drove straight over, and he greeted her like she was the prodigal son. Offered a room far nicer than what I had.

"It's my throw-away room," he told us as we headed upstairs. He cast me an open look and said, "So if there's anything you want..."

"I'll see about it," I replied. I'd noticed that typewriter was on a sturdy table in the foyer, atop a nice linen cloth, and it looked well-dusted.

Rocky was beside herself at how nice the room was—and since it was to be for only a short time, no cost. In thanks, she made us a fine dinner of enchiladas, rice and beans...all from ingredients Everett had in his pantry.

"My grandmamma's recipe," she said.

Everett had her write it down, then he pulled out Coronas and I opened them with a bottle opener she had on her keyring. It was made of Lucite and had a scorpion encased in it. Seems Matty had given it to her and she kept it to remind herself of who he was.

"Honeymoon night, he hit me," she said. "He said he's sorry, but it was my fault. I thought it was."

"He was just lettin' you know what to expect," Everett said.

"I know. Just like that damn keyring."

"I think I lost the meaning, here," I said.

Everett took a sip of his beer and said, "You never heard that old story about the scorpion that asked a frog to carry it across a river? The frog didn't want to because he's afraid the scorpion'd sting him and kill him, halfway across. But the scorpion said he's bein' silly. *If I did that*, he said, *we'd both die.* Well, froggie saw the logic in that argument so agreed to carry the scorpion. It hopped on his back and off they went, and halfway across, the scorpion stung the frog. As he's dyin', the frog gasped, *Why'd you do that? Now you'll die too.* The scorpion responded, *It's my nature. You knew what I was when you agreed to carry me.*"

"That's me and Matty," said Rocky. "I got talked into returnin' to him so many times, now he don't believe me when I say no more."

"Well, I wouldn't worry about him, anymore," Everett said.

"Why?" Rocky had that edge to her voice, again.

"I know a couple of Houston's finest who are, shall we say, *deep undercover.* Told 'em I'd heard about what happened and knew the boy who'd hit your husband. Told 'em he was a Mexican kid. A friend of mine. And I'd given him money to return to Jalisco, *before I knew what had happened.* They huffed and puffed, like boys in blue do, but agreed Matty probably got off light. Said they'd pass the word along. They're really little teddy bears."

"But Matty's—"

"Oh, he's goin' on disability. Knee's wrecked. Won't be a cop, no more. 'Cept at a desk."

Rocky's face shifted from darkness to light in a flash. "Good. He loved bein' a bad-ass cop."

Everett turned to me and said, "You hit him just right, Pug."

I merely shrugged in answer.

He chuckled and wagged a finger at me, saying, "I don't ever want to get you mad at me."

"Not possible," I said, smiling.

She and I returned to the pool house to get her things—as if there was so much to get, just clothes, cosmetics and that air mattress. She'd had a couple friends empty her apartment and put her things into storage.

Once she was done packing, she collapsed on my bed and let out a slow sigh. "This can't be my life. It can't be. Runnin' from a man I hate."

"It's hard for him to chase you now, isn't it?" I tried to make it jokey but she wasn't in that sort of mood.

"He'll find me, again. I know he will. Even behind a desk, he can do it." She began to shake and weep. "How the hell did I wind up with a man like him?"

I lay beside her, my hands up under my head. Thought of how Da was with Ma, like a dog with a cat. But maybe it was more like two cats, because Ma was just as much back at him. Snarling and hissing and spitting and fighting, then suddenly loving and in need of each other.

Rocky was nothing like Ma. I couldn't see her using a skillet to inflict as much damage on Matty as he did on her. She'd curl up and hope it would stop. Until one day, it wouldn't. Da being killed was all that had stopped it with Ma.

I looked at her, whispering, "You'll find someone who loves you, without his fists. You're worthy of it."

She looked at me, tears streaking her face, and murmured, "I need to find somebody like you."

"Me? I'm not so good."

She shook her head. "You're kind. Gentle. Read books, like me."

She looked so lost. Hurt. Confused. Her fingers drifted close to my chin. Like she was begging for proof I meant what I said.

So I rolled over and kissed her.

I shouldn't have. I know that. It was meant only as a kindness, nothing more. But her fingers trailed around my neck and I felt something stir behind my heart and she kissed me back and her breath was like cinnamon and—

Joanna let me love her on the Ha'penny bridge and the world was scented with Spearmint and beauty and—

Her fingers traced up and down my back and sides in ways that made it hard to breathe, it felt so wonderful.

Now in my head I'm telling myself, *No, Brendan, not smart, not smart*. But when lightning dances in circles through your body, and your heart nearly stops from the beauty of it, all you care for is more of it. And so it came, from deep within me.

My left hand cupped her breast as her fingers gripped my belt to pull me atop her and her legs wrapped around my waist. She shoved my jeans down my hips to grope me arse. I pulled at her shorts, no longer capable of thought, just instinct. I don't know who was doing what-when-how-or-where, but I wound up released from my briefs and hard and ready and she guided me into her and the beauty of that entry overwhelmed me to the point I wanted to stay like that forever...but it felt so much better if I slipped in and back, like I'd seen—

Eamonn and Mrs. McKittrick as they fell back on her divan,

*grabbing at each other in ways lewd and vicious and not at all art
but—*

That's what she and I did. Steady. No hesitation. Over and over
and over and over. Her hands gripping me and kneading into my skin
and holding me tighter and tighter as I was trying to all but melt into
her while crouched atop her and her hands toyed down my back in
ways unbelievably tender and gentle as my lips crushed against hers
and she shoved against me and I pressed my face into the crook of her
neck and her nails dug into my scalp and I felt a shriek of exquisitely
wanton need—no, demand build within me so went faster and faster
and faster and faster until a rush from behind my balls raced through
every part of me and suddenly I was jolting and shaking and releasing
into her as she slammed herself against me, making it even better and
better and driving me near insane from the feeling of exquisite
tenderness dancing through every part of my body until she gasped
and slowed and drew me closer to her than anyone ever had.

And stopped moving.

As did I, for my heart was racing like mad and I was shivering
from the intensity of it all.

Breathless, we lay there. I could not think. I was frozen in time.
On the edge of madness. Barely remembered to breathe. Felt this
glorious sense of peace settle over me and did not so much as twitch
for fear it would all vanish and become nothing but a dream.

Finally, I was able to kiss her ear, quiet and tender. She let another
soft gasp whisper from her. Tears trailed from her eyes but she was
smiling, nearly laughing, so I figured they weren't from sadness. After
a moment, her hands drifted away from me and I rolled over to lie
beside her. I noticed her breasts were still caught in her bra and her
shorts and panties barely down her legs. My belt wasn't even undone,
so my jeans were tight below my hips and arse, and my shirt was
pulled up to barely expose my belly. How the devil we'd managed to
fit together still clothed like that was a minor miracle. It struck me as
so very wanton, I had to laugh. She joined me.

"Now that is what's known as a quickie," she said, the tips of her
fingers caressing my face. Then her eyes grew tender, with more than
a hint of wariness to them, and she whispered, "Did I take you away
from him, Pug?"

What? "From whom?"

"Everett."

I chuckled. "Since he's never had me, how could you?"

"Oh," sighed from her. "It's just...he loves you. I see it in how he looks at you."

I shrugged.

"But I'm your first woman. Right?"

"Was it that obvious?"

She giggled. Swatted me, then caressed my face. "No. It's just...you're a sweet boy."

I huffed. "I'm still a boy to you? After this?"

"C'mon...I'm near twice your age."

I had to shrug. "Sorry I didn't meet expectations."

"Don't be silly." She seemed caught between speaking and just looking at me, for a moment, then continued with, "This won't happen, again."

I drew back a little and she put a hand to my mouth before I could say anything. "No, really, you were fine. And I'm not sorry about it. But I'm gonna be leavin', and I don't want anything to hold me back."

"What if I join you?" Said without a thought.

She almost laughed and held my face in her hands. "You would, too, wouldn't you?" She kissed me. "Let's see how it goes."

Then she rose, fixed herself in the washroom as I cleaned up by the bar sink, and we took her things to Everett's. Where she made guacamole better than even Aunt Mari's and we spent the evening feasting on chips and beer and talking of nothing. Just nothing.

Everett drove me home, late, quiet the whole drive till we were parked in front. It's like he knew Rocky and I had joined together, I suppose, for all he did then was smile and say, "She'll be fine where she is, now," as I got out of the car.

I grinned and headed for the pool house.

Ten days later, Rocky was driving down Montrose when Matty roared up the other direction to ram her car, head-on. Then he pulled himself up on the driver's door and fired five bullets through the windshield into her before using his last bullet on himself. They said she died instantly.

For two days the news covered the story, both in print and on the telly. No one could understand why *a fine upstanding young copper who'd been given awards for heroism and community support suddenly went berserk*. There was discussion about him having to go on disability due to injuries that *happened outside of work*, but for which no details were forthcoming. It was also hinted by the police that Rocky was a controlling, manipulative little bitch who got what she deserved. Though they never actually *said* such a thing. Can't be held accountable for something not specifically mentioned. Matty was given a full honors funeral while Rocky was put into the ground with no fanfare and only through the help of an anonymous donor.

And what was worse? No one came to her defense.

Myself included.

To say I was torn to shreds by the whole story would be an understatement. In my heart and my head and my soul, all I could see was Matty firing into that little Vega, over and over and over until a brutal whiteness surrounded me and took me back to that bombing. Then every thought I'd had about my link to it...and reason for it...would dance over every breath I took. I could see nothing but my guilt. Nothing but my part in the catastrophe. For I was absolutely certain it was my crippling of him that pushed him to the point of death. That I should have known he would crash into the idea that since the life he'd wanted was over for him, so would burn Rocky's, as well.

No.

No, not *Rocky*. That's a child's name and she was nothing like that. Her full name was Raquel Anjelica Martinez. A woman who just wanted to live her life apart from a man who would not let her breathe without his authorization. A woman with simple dreams and hopes, unable to defend herself against a human beast.

A beast like my Da.

I locked myself in the pool house. Drifted in a cloud of apathy and self-loathing. Cowardly, it's true, but I could not face reality at that moment. It was as if I were a curse.

Could my parents have reached that stage, as well? Their fights could get violent, but in truth I never saw that depth of hate or self-destructiveness in Da. And Ma had not been so willing to just accept his brutality without some response.

But then, how could I really know? I'd been but ten years of age when Da was killed. And Ma had seemed truly bereft at losing him. I don't recall her ever even looking at another man, since, and certainly not in the way she had at Da, a few times. She had also defended his name against me far more times than I cared to remember, but had she actually missed him? I couldn't tell.

I felt truly rotten for bringing my parents' mess of a marriage into a comparison of the two, like there should be something in common between them when they were nothing alike. It was very confusing, and not having much in the way of pot, less and less beer, and fewer and fewer Marlboros left was not helping. But I dared not go out; the B-girls would be on the watch for me, and the anger inside was so tight I knew the moment they started their interrogations I would explode.

So the doors remained locked against them as well as Angus.

Oh, but did they try to get in to me. Knocking at the windows. Trying to see past the blinds. Calling my name like they were calling for a cat or dog gone astray. Scratching and whining at the door. I just sat and smoked and sulked myself into a mood of pure self-hate. Barely ate. Lost some of the weight I'd gained back. I cared about none of it. Everything seemed stupid and cruel and hopeless.

What hurt most was the thought that Rocky and I could have gone off and lived in Aspen and built a life for ourselves. It spun around in my head, over and over, mingling with my childish intention of moving off to live where Joanna went to university. And what did it keep coming back to?

That I'd been using them both to give myself an excuse to do what I was unwilling to do on my own. That each was a crutch, and I was too weak a man to stand on my own. My thoughts grew darker and worked their way deeper and deeper into my heart to tear it open even further. And my world grew black as coal.

Dear God, I hated so much in me.

Intervention

I'd like to claim my self-indulgence lasted months or years...but after little more than a week, Aunt Mari unlocked the French doors with her key—all without a by-your-leave, I might add—and calmly entered, with Everett. They found me sitting on the floor, deep into my second pack of the day. Beer and Marlboros, my steadiest diet. And it not even noon, yet.

She'd winced at how thick the smoke was then sighed, "Get off the floor, there, and have yourself a wash. Yer Uncle Sean wants to take ya for an interview, before he goes to *Liam's Trough*, and ya *will* go."

"Leave me alone." And yes, that really was my childish, pathetic response.

"No!" Aunt Mari said, now close to snarling. "Ya'll get up, 'cause yer goin' with—"

"Going where?" I tried to snarl it back, but all I could do is whimper. Jesus, was I worthless.

"I just told ya!" she snapped. "He's willin' to help ya find another position and—"

"I'm not after another position."

"C'mon, Pug," Everett sighed. "Don't do this."

All I could think to say was, "Go away."

Aunt Mari snarled, "No! Hidin' in here like a worm under a rock's doin' ya no good an'—"

"What do you care? You're not my mother, so—"

She slapped me.

Hard.

Well, not as hard as Ma could, and she had to bend over to do it, but it was hard enough to startle me.

"Yer in my home, young man, and my rules apply! I will not have ya wastin' away—"

I bolted to my feet, roaring, "I pay you for this room!"

"Not what it's worth, and not for much longer if ya don't have an income."

I was crouching into fight mode, so Everett got between us and pushed at me, "C'mon. Bathroom's over here."

But Aunt Mari was not done. "Make yerself human, again," she growled, "or I'll toss ya in the street, no matter what yer uncle wants. Then I'll have the place fumigated, from how it stinks of ya. DO IT!"

"You can try and—"

Everett shoved me into the bathroom, with a sharper push than I thought possible, from him. Straight into the shower. It was already going, and hot. When the hell had it been turned on? I was so shocked, I couldn't think of a response beyond a fine howl, as I was fully clothed.

"I'll be outside," he said, "Take your time."

"No," Aunt Mari called at me. "You're leavin' in ten minutes, either with yer uncle or all yer things. And I will not be careful when I heave them out, believe me. Nor will I pay further for yer medication, so ya can die in the street."

Then she stormed off. Leaving the door open. And of course the B-Girls were there, watching and listening with eyes as big as boiled eggs, Angus between them.

Everett closed the bathroom door, saying, "So, what are my little princesses up to, today?"

I muttered and grumbled and growled and whined, but having my clothes cling to me was uncomfortable, so I slowly peeled them off.

And I do mean peeled.

It finally hit me I'd not changed since Rocky's death. That they weren't already melded with my skin was more than amazing. Once I saw the filth on them, now I was undressed, I knew they would be for the trash, not the wash. Then I took the soap, lathered up—and lathered, again...and again, and shaved in the shower.

When I came out, still drying myself, Everett was behind the counter with a cup of what smelled like coffee. He nodded to another cup that had the tail of a tea bag in it, saying "Lipton's in your cup."

I tossed aside the towel and pulled on my briefs, followed by a pair of 501s. I actually heard him sigh but didn't care a whit.

"Why're you here?" I snarled. "My aunt call you?"

"No. I hadn't heard from you so came over to see if you were okay and—well, things progressed from there."

I got the cup of tea, tossed aside the bag, and noticed a pan of steaming water was on the hot plate. I poured more in as he offered up the container of milk I'd had in the fridge.

"You might want to smell it, first," he said.

I didn't. Just poured it in. Followed with sugar. And nearly wept at how lovely it was on my tongue and throat. I swallowed some down.

"Better now?" he asked.

I sighed and shrugged.

"Y'know, I knew Rocky, too—"

"Raquel," whispered from me.

He smiled. "Raquel. She and I talked a lot while she was with me. She let slip some things I don't think you know about. Like how at the last bar she worked, the same thing happened. Matty showed up. They got her away. She'd grown close to a bartender, there, and stayed with him a couple weeks before starting at *The Colonel's*. Got the name of the bar. Called the guy after...after everything. He didn't know where she'd gone and was shook up by the news." He gave me a pointed look. "I didn't ask, but my feelin' is...well...they grew very close, for a while."

I couldn't look at him as I murmured, "I got her killed. Tearing into Matty like I did, made him crazier."

"Don't, Pug. I'm willin' to bet he planned to kill her, that night. The way she described him. How she'd been away from him for nearly a year. That's what made him crazy. Stupid controllin' son-of-a-bitch couldn't stand thinkin' she might have got away. There's been so many times some asshole kills his wife and kids in the middle of a divorce, it's practically its own legal definition. All you did was postpone the inevitable."

"That's a harsh way to put it."

"But true. What's worse? I think it was one of *my friends* on the force who told that abusive fuck she might be in the Montrose area. So he got some of the patrol boys to keep an eye open and tracked her down. I should've known better than to trust a cop, even one I knew and had—well, had been with. That's what really hurts about this. Me askin' about Matty is probably what really set her up.

"The fuckin' uniform matters more than which way their dick points," he added, sipping more coffee. I could see his hand shaking from anger, even though his voice was even. "They don't really care about people, Bren. They don't really want to enforce the law unless they have to, or it lets them act like *Dirty Harry*."

"Who?"

"Clint Eastwood movie."

"Not seen it."

"Just reactionary right-wing crap full of stupid people. *Cops are right, everyone else is wrong* kind of thing."

"You've had run-ins with them."

He hesitated then sighed, long and slow. "Like I said, it's illegal to be queer in Texas."

"Do you know who it was?"

"I think so, from something he said. I'll get to the truth of it, next time I see him. So don't blame yourself."

I hesitated before asking, "Everett, did-did you pay to bury her?"

He took a long moment to answer. "Yes. She—uh, she took me to see her mother. We were close to gettin' her to leave."

"I told her I'd help with that."

"Might've worked better. Mama muttered *maricon* at me a couple times. Spanish for *queer*, basically. But Rocky feared you bein' seen with her'd get you in trouble, and nobody she knew had any idea who I was, so..."

"You know Spanish?"

"C'mon, Pug, I grew up in San Antonio. The city's more than half Chicano. You learn Tex-Mex by osmosis. She told Rocky— *Raquel* to go back to Matty. It was her duty as a wife. What bullshit. When it's your life on the line, you do what you must in order to live. That's the truth. If she'd really wanted to end it, she'd have left the state, with or without momma. Gone to Colorado, like she said she wanted. Instead, she'd get the same job in a dive bar, here in town, knowin' eventually he'd show up and she could scream about it. Get help. Protection. Sympathy."

"It's not right to say that!" I snapped. "She can't defend herself."

He glared at me, for a moment. "She said you were thinkin' of goin' with her. Were you?"

I said nothing, but that seemed answer enough, to him.

"Oh, Pug. Do you think she loved you? Or you loved her?"

That question jammed me in the heart. I hadn't really thought about it. Maybe, but...

But, no.

No. I liked her. I was comfortable with her. I'd have stayed with her. But loved her? Married her? No. That would have meant supplanting Joanna in my heart, and she wasn't—God forgive me, but Rocky wasn't enough to do that. Not to overcome Joanna's memory.

I guess he thought my silence meant *yes*, so he finally said. "Don't get lost thinkin' she was an angel followed by a devil, Bren. Those two had some sick game they were playin' at, an' it finally went south on 'em both. Now put on a shirt and your boots. I just saw your uncle look in the door. He's waitin' for you."

Then he headed out.

What he'd said, I could believe it. I just couldn't accept it. There was too much of it, and my part in this catastrophe was still too raw. Too real. I returned to telling myself I was only using Rocky as a means of escape. Joanna had asked me that, once. Or had she? Had somebody else? Christ, my head was too fuzzy to remember. And now I had to wonder—was I playing the same sort of controlling game she and Matty had?

If we'd been together long enough, would I have wound up hitting her? What little I got from Mrs. Haggerty about Ma and Da moving in on Nailors Row suggested they weren't yet physical in their anger. And I'd seen Ma drive my father to using his fists, sometimes. Couldn't blame it all on the drink, not if I was being honest.

Jesus, as if I wasn't already enough of a confused mess.

*****

I finally met Uncle Sean at the Gremlin, and we were off. I said not one fucking word the whole way. Nor did he. I got the impression this journey was not of his choosing, which almost brought a smile to me.

It was to Trujillo Motors and Auto Repair he took me, on Washington near the Katy Freeway, a fair-sized facility with five work bays, a line of used cars to the side and some junkers in the back. They dealt with European and UK makes, only. And did it confuse me to see Triumphs and Rovers and MGs with left drive instead of right.

It was owned and run by a round happy man named *Mr. Trujillo*, whom even Uncle Sean addressed as such. I was quiet, sullen and pissy. Not a great impression to make, but I cared not. However, I did keep to my manners.

Somewhat.

They needed a new mechanic, and Uncle Sean let him know I was the reason that Volvo hadn't been brought in, of late. A tall, dark, slim man named Rene Boudoin was in the office as they spoke. He was well into his fifties, with silver in his hair, but light on his feet and always smiling, to the point of irritation, and he spoke with an odd sort of accent that I later learned was Cajun. He gave me a look that showed he was hardly impressed, then led me to an old Sprite that kept dying.

"Can ya fix this 'un, cher?" he asked.

I grumbled but started the car up. It sputtered then died and I shook my head, saying, "This is just a vacuum leak."

"You think so, cher?"

I snorted. Took me all of ten minutes to figure out two hoses had been reversed and re-set them. Mr. Trujillo still wasn't completely sure but I heard him tell Uncle Sean he'd give me a try, *for old times' sake*, so I got the job. I was to be paid straight from the register, just like at *The Colonel's*.

I had nothing else to do with myself, right then, and the idea of working on cars, again, tugged at me for—

Joanna was at McClosky's, smiling as she said, "I knew I'd find you here. When you're troubled, you deal with it by working."

She convinced me to take the job.

And to be honest with myself, dealing with the poor way Americans treat cars like these, digging into a problem and finding the issue did a lot to take me out of my fucked-up attitude.

The one bad issue was I had to be at the shop by eight, Monday through Friday, then I'd leave at five, with an hour off for lunch. Which meant my late nights were no longer workable. I found that out when I'd start losing focus at about two in the afternoon after not having a good night's sleep. With it being a half-hour's journey by bus, with a change, I had to leave at just past seven to make it.

I finally saw that it was not so very far to walk, if I chose. Head up Shephard, since there was no short way across Buffalo Bayou, then left at Washington to follow the road. There were few trees for shade, so the main issue would be doing it under a steaming sun. But if I left at seven, I could make the walk while the sun was still somewhat low and hop the bus home.

What's funny is, I'd still get offered a ride, now and then, by an older man in a passing car.

That early in the morning? It was headshaking.

Another issue was not having easy access to the garbage people toss out, in the night. I finally figured I could still go wandering once a week, the night before a collection, and see what I could find. So that's what I did.

I drifted into a steady routine, eyeing the run-down homes and ratty businesses as yet unopen as a way to keep my mind silent during my morning walks. I soon figured it was best to wear my boots instead of sneakers. A city as rich as Houston and they don't even have sidewalks everywhere.

I got on well-enough with the other lads, though sometimes we had trouble understanding each other, thanks to our accents. I think they saw me as a mascot and not a worker, all paternal and a bit dismissive, like things had been with Diarmaid. And it affected me about as much as it had with him, which was little.

Rene was my supervisor, and working for him was not so bad as it could have been. In the beginning, I had the feeling he didn't truly believe me capable of repairing anything serious in those maddening British sports cars. Maddening, because they'd been designed so poorly.

Which I found funny.

I'd worked on Miss Cahan's Spitfire at McClosky's and knew how to make its ways assist me in working it well, so showed him a few pointers on how best to get to parts not easily gotten to. It wasn't till he saw me rebuild the fluid clutch assembly in a Volvo 122s and replace an MG carburetor in less than an hour, that he left me to myself, complete.

Hugo, the most aware mechanic, was from Guadalajara and close to my age. Lean and muscular with hair long, black and thick, he had a crooked arm. He'd broken it as a boy, and it was poorly set so the bone mended at a slight angle. It was no trouble to him, nor did it prevent him from working on an engine or transmission, but it looked odd. Except when he was riding his motorcycle; then he looked cool beyond measure. That and his easy grin got him notice from more than a few girls, of which he had quite the steady flow.

Then came Vinicius, who called himself Vinnie. Born in Houston by Brazilian parents. They owned a restaurant in the Sharpstown part of Houston, offering Brazilian fare, and he obviously enjoyed it. Past thirty, rounder than anything else, wary eyes under dark brows, he was too focused on his job to be much interested in anyone. Until his wife came by with his hot lunch. She was the evening chef at the restaurant and his perfect match in looks, while his opposite in manner. What was best? Sometimes she brought enough food for everyone. They had three boys and a girl and were happily working on a fifth child.

Tomas was smaller than me, in his thirties, and spoke very little— which was good, since his accent was the thickest of us all. He wore a wedding ring but said nothing about his wife or family. Hugo made sport of him, claiming they weren't real, but I came to realize he'd left them in a country called El Salvador and sent money home.

Like I'd planned to do and Aunt Mari had done.

Bernardo was the flash lad. Tall, lean, hair peeking from under his collar, strong profile, gray eyes and more than a little condescending. He'd been part of a wealthy family in Cuba till Castro came along. They'd lost everything and escaped to Miami, where his parents and sisters had settled in. But he hated that city.

"Too much like the poverty in Havana to be anything great," was how he put it.

He drove an old Mercedes he'd restored to near perfection, which I thought fit his attitude far too well. Till one day he informed me he'd only bought it because his wife worked for a family in River Oaks.

"I drop her off and pick her up," he said. "But I would keep getting stopped by police when I was in the area. Seems *something was always wrong* with this old Ford I had. I paid attention and never saw a fine car getting stopped, so bought this one. Repaired it and painted it, and I have not been stopped, since."

"Cops're idiots," Hugo'd said, smirking.

Bernardo smiled and replied, "No, superficial only."

I said nothing of my encounters with the RUC or what had happened with Raquel. I held no interest in explaining my life to anyone.

I got on best with Hugo. He lived off Alabama in a house made over into apartments, not far from a Mexican restaurant he loved. He took me there a few times, after work, riding on the back of his motorbike.

Oh, but did I love the freedom of it. Wind crashing around the whole of you. Moving in and around cars at speeds they couldn't approach in areas they couldn't fit. It was like a religious experience to me.

On top of it, girls flocked to Hugo and his bike, many of them joining him at his apartment. He had a bed on the floor and a couple of tables and a blacklight and posters and tapestry prints hanging from the walls and pot and wine and beer and everything was so cool and casual, it was like a never-ending party.

He even passed a few of his lasses over to me when he got focused on another, which felt a bit dismissive, but I wasn't going to turn them down. They were just holding and kissing and caressing in ways simple and kind and were as little interested in me and I was them. It was just nice to hold someone for a little, and half the time they spent our moments together talking about Hugo. How wonderful he was. Generous. All sorts of blather, like older versions of the B-girls. I'd just sit and smoke and listen, and more than once was referred to as like a little brother.

Now to be honest, on a few occasions it did go farther than chatting. I'm not going to say I pushed for it, nor was I upset at it happening, but never was it as fine as my one night with Raquel.

Or my dreams of Joanna.

Though I did quickly learn Paidrig's ideas about oral sex were ill-informed, at best.

A Saturday morning after a night with one such occasion, as Hugo and I were doing brunch at that cafe, he asked me, "You not all that into girls?"

I was eating some eggs ranchero and he had a terrifying burrito smothered in something that looked like tomato vomit. I shrugged, munched a bit on a slice of avocado, swallowed it down with a Tecate, and said, "I'm not sure what you mean."

"One you were with, last night—she snuck out early. Usual, they wanna lay in bed all night and cuddle and shit."

I just shrugged. Her parents didn't know she was out so wanted to be home before they rose, but no need to share that.

"The Irish got different views on makin' it?"

Again, I shrugged. "You never seem to need to—well, to go after a girl. They seem to come to you."

"I got good word of mouth. Took years to build that up. But you take care of a girl and she lets her friends know. And they come sniffin' 'round."

I smiled. "Well, I don't see that happening with me." Then I took another bite of my eggs.

"Naw, what I see happenin' with you is, you get to be their buddy. You don't want a girl as a buddy."

Which brought Joanna to my mind. Close. A friend. Or buddy, if you prefer. Our moments together had been perfect, even if I never did manage to do anything more than kiss her. None of Hugo's girls, each one sweet and lovely in her own right, had touched me in the same way. But what the hell—I was eighteen. I had time enough ahead of me to see if any other came close to Joanna's perfection.

Maybe.

"I have no problem with that," I said, then sipped more beer.

Hugo shook his head. "You're weird, Bren."

Which brought a chuckle to me.

Still, it was riding the back of Hugo's bike that I most enjoyed. When I said as much, he laughed and told me, "I'll teach ya to ride one, if ya want. But ya gotta be careful. Assholes in this town try to run us off the road all the time. Act like big-assed cars're the only vehicles allowed. Pickups with gun racks're the worst."

I shrugged and asked, "D'ya have to have a permit?"

He nodded.

"Well, that kills that, then."

"Why? Ain't you got a driver's license?"

I shook my head.

"Bren, I've seen you drive cars 'round the lot."

Again, I shrugged.

"Can ya get one?"

And once more, I shrugged. "What's needed?"

"Pass a test. Show you are who you are."

"Hard to do, that last bit, if you're from another country."

"Naw, we can get 'round that. Unless you *wanna* ride dirty."

I cast him a confused frown.

"Without a license."

I shook my head. "Too much could go wrong."

"Okay. Uh, you got a cousin you live with, right?"

I nodded.

"See if he'll lend you his. Make a copy. Got no picture on 'em."

"None?" It honestly surprised me.

Hugo shook his head. "They're talkin' 'bout addin' 'em, but till then—who's gonna know?"

I chuckled and asked Scott, the next time he was in from university. I had to tell him why, and he said fine. "So long as you let me ride it, some."

I agreed, and also said to myself, *No bloody way.*

So Hugo showed me all about traffic laws and moves and care against cars and trucks, and he was bloody right the way the traffic went in this town. On top of that, I had to focus to keep on the correct side of the road. But shifting and balancing and aiming his beast on two-wheels was not so hard. And the handbook for a driving license was an easy read.

All of which I kept quiet from my aunt and uncle. I wanted no chance of them refusing me the right to have my own mode of transportation.

I latched onto a 1966 Montesa Impala Sport for a hundred dollars. It was red and there was some corrosion, needed fresh struts, tires, spokes reset...but it was fun to fix and ran like mad. An airman had brought it back from Spain to drive but now had a wife, a baby and a car.

Rene let me use the shop's tools during my lunch break but would watch me. I thought at first it was because he feared I'd make off with something, but he finally squatted next to me as I cleaned the shifter on the bike and asked, "You work on these before, cher?"

I shook my head.

"But you doin' this with no instruction."

I shrugged. "Goes back together the same way it comes apart."

"How you gonna set the timin'? The brakes?"

"Got a book coming, for that. Detering's tracked down an old one, for me. Should be here soon. I'll work the engine and set it then."

He shook his head and wandered away. The other lads came around to watch, as well, but I just shifted into my focused phase and ignored them, and soon they'd stopped.

That little beast gave me my first true taste of freedom. Even more than skating on ice had. Sharp and fast, I could travel where I wanted throughout Houston. I felt the grand explorer, especially as I drove past cars lined up at gas stations, for I had no restrictions on which day I could refuel. It was glorious.

The response from Aunt Mari was wariness, but more from fear of my being hurt on it. She insisted I always wear a helmet, and to keep the peace, I did. Uncle Sean said nothing, just looked at the bike and me and frowned and went in to talk to his wife in a quiet voice. She may have responded just as quiet, but I saw them through the sliding door and while he was tight with anger—at me, I suppose— she was just as tight. I never asked what they spoke of because in truth, I did not care. And he never said a word to me about the motor.

Of course, I kept within the traffic laws, and would grow tense when passing a patrol car. Even after achieving my license, that continued.

However, the B-Girls definitely approved of my mode of transportation, though Angus hated it and would scurry away when I drove up. They saw to it I was outfitted with a thicker leather bomber jacket. Brand new, this one, and *no argument*.

"Our grandfather had one," said Brandi, completely ignoring the fact she'd said nothing about this when I'd bought that one from the second-hand shop.

"He was in World War Two," Bernadette continued, "in the Air Force. Bomber pilot."

I now half-agreed they made things up to support their points.

"That's why they call it a bomber jacket."

"He died a couple years ago."

"Heart attack."

"Your jacket's just like his."

"No, his had wool around the collar."

"He could take it off."

"No, he couldn't. It was sewn on."

"I saw him wear it without the wool."

"He just had the collar turned in, hiding it."

"No, that's not right..."

And off they went.

But now I was Mr. Cool, riding about town like I owned it—till an idiot in a Ford pickup decided to pull ahead of me, one morning, and turn into a driveway, forcing me into one of the five curbs in the whole of Houston. I tumbled, cracked my helmet and cut open my chin, and he got out screaming at me for daring to bump the piece of shit he drove.

To my horror, a cop was passing nearby and came over. I made like the cut on my chin kept me from speaking much, but still had to show him my copy of Scott's license. At least there was no trouble with it. In fact, he gave the bastard in the Ford a ticket and helped me stop the bleeding with a towel he had in his trunk. The bastard had no insurance, which I didn't mind since I'd not have filed a claim; no need to draw unwanted attention to myself. Instead, the cop made him give me two-hundred dollars.

Which I was more than fine with.

Except I had to walk the bike the rest of the way to work because the wheel was now out of round, and it wasn't easy. It also took days to find a replacement, which took most of the money given me. I got made sport of for some time, after that, except from Hugo; he took me to a shop to buy a real helmet.

"Not one of those stupid upside-down pan things," he snarled. "Might not be so lucky, next go around."

"You don't wear one, at all," I said, not liking the look of the gleaming golden thing he handed me.

"I been riding bikes since I was twelve. Got a sixth sense about cars and the assholes in 'em. You're just startin'. Play safe."

I eyed it, frowning. "It's bloody big."

"Naw, it's just like Peter Fonda's, in *Easy Rider*. Just no stars and stripes." Then off my confused glance, he added, "The movie, not the wrappers."

"Haven't seen it."

"Shit, Bren, don't they get movies in Ireland?"

"When was it showing?"

"Few years ago."

"That'd be in the middle of the Troubles."

"*Troubles*?"

"In Derry. Cinema cost money. Riots were more entertaining, and free."

"They got riots in Ireland?"

I looked at him, gobsmacked. "Yeah. There's six counties in the north, held apart from the rest of Ireland by the bloody English, and it's a big bloody mess."

"Shit, who knew?" Then he found a pair of thick gloves and handed those to me, as well. "Protect your hands."

I took them.

And paid for them, of course.

But his insistence—his concern, it cut through my reserve about my money, and his interest in helping me care for myself made me feel—I don't know how to put it except good. I knew he was right; I'd been lucky not to have been badly hurt to the extent I needed medical care. So he was like—well, almost like he was another brother helping me become part of this brave new world. Giving me another step to leave my old self behind. And in truth, I had no concern for its disposal.

None.

Because in truth, who I used to be, where I once came from, it struck me more as like a book I might have read long ago but had no interest in reading again. Put it aside in my memory and let it drift away.

And I wasn't sure how I felt about that.

Compatriot

Late in June, Jeremy returned to Houston from the kibbutz and his family held a Welcome Home party for him, inviting all of his friends and the whole of my Houston family. It was on a Sunday and I was supposed to go with them, but I'd zipped over to the shop to check a grinding noise I'd heard from the rear wheel of my Montesa; Rene gave me the okay to do it, now they trusted me. Turned out Hugo was there, as well, changing the oil on his latest girlfriend's car. So as we'd chatted, I'd called to tell Aunt Mari I'd meet them there.

Well, as I rode up, Jeremy burst from the house, howling, "You got a bike!" He all but danced around it, still chattering, "It's a Montesa! I never even heard of these till I got to Israel. Lots of guys have 'em—bikes like this. Rockin' all over Tel Aviv, Jerusalem, riding two or three on 'em. So cool! When'd you get it?! Can we go on a ride?"

He sat on it before I had the chance to respond. So I just slipped my helmet on him, hopped in front and took him for a spin down the block and around. To say I was on serious alert for anything that might cause an accident is to put it simply. I resolved to get a second helmet to have on hand.

Jeremy first wrapped his arms around my waist, then laughed and stretched them out as if he were flying.

"Lots of soldiers ride bikes like this," he called as we zipped along, his voice breathless. I didn't bother to mention he'd already said as much. "Two on each. Alive. Carefree."

"Am I not the first to carry you on one?" I called back.

"Naw. Not even the twenty-third or fourth. Yossi and I rode from Eliat to Jerusalem on his MotoTrans. This bike's a lot more comfy."

"I'm liking it."

"When'd you get it?"

"A few month back. Needed some tender care."

"She runs great."

"You want a turn at the handlebars?"

He hesitated then said, "No, no, I never drove one. Just rode..."

By this point, we were back at the house, so I stopped in the driveway. He hopped off and removed the helmet, and I saw a haunted, guarded look fill his eyes.

"Good idea to use a helmet," he said, his voice distant and—

Danny started away then turned to look at me and said, "Don't blame me, Bren." Then he vanished into the mist and—

Jeremy's voice was also soft and hollow as he continued, "Never know when you might take a-a-a spill. Or you-you never know what, and—"

Danny looked at me as he was getting in the car, his eyes wide with shock and anger and—

"Jeremy!"

We both jumped. It was his mother calling, from the door.

"Where've you been. Everybody's looking for you!"

"Yeah, mom," he called. "Right there." Then he cast me a sad smile and said, "Thanks," before he ran inside.

I hesitated then pulled a fresh pack of Marlboros from my saddlebags, as Hugo called them, and followed him in.

What a massive affair. There was barbecue in every form imaginable, both in the house and on the patio. Baked potatoes. Ears of corn. Steaming bowls of beans and borscht and salads and casseroles and desserts and breads and muffins, all well dug into. I was put in mind of Da's wake and wasn't so sure how to work my way around it.

Through the night I saw that no matter where Jeremy was, he was thronged by people. Talking. Laughing. His hand being shaked over and over and over. Now perhaps it was because I hadn't seen him since Christmas—or to be honest with myself, had ever really known him— but to me he seemed...I don't know how to put it, except...even though he was there in body, he wasn't. That he'd changed even more from Hanukkah. Quieter. Careful. And there was one moment when I caught him looking at me that I caught hints of horror in his eyes.

An expression I'd seen far too often, in Derry.

He'd come home without injury. To his body, at least. And his mother was beside herself with joy. No need for a strange Irish lad to say anything to make a wreck of that.

He was given pride of place throughout the night. His uncle, a charming man closely resembling him but near bald, drove in from

Austin with his family of three daughters. Jeremy was even shown deference by his father, his two brothers and his sister. But he never rose above this quiet, careful calm. As the night wore on, I found it more and more disturbing.

Like at Da's wake, everyone talked about his greatness and glory in ways so damned unreal. Refusing even a word that might be contrary to their praise. I started to feel angry and hurt and impatient with it all and finally had to get off to myself in a corner of the back yard. Get away from the ghosts surrounding me.

I knew that I'd been fortunate in that none of my close friends had been killed in the battles around Derry, but so many I'd known—well, was acquainted with—people who vanished from your thoughts the moment they no longer lived. Who counted only as memories. And my melancholy rose at knowing I was one of them. *That simple lad, Brendan, gone and forgotten.* Another ghost of the millions, in Ireland.

The area I chose for my solitude was near lost in shadows but had a patch of grass. I had just finished my third plate of this thing called fajitas—which Mrs. Landau had proudly said were prepared at some taco stand called Ninfa's—and I was downing my fourth or fifth cup of Shiner Bock. Fortunately, the mister had bought a few barrels during its last processing, for this party. I was close to asking him if he had one left at the end, would he sell it to me.

That or I was going to hit Todd up for a delivery of Valium.

God, what a beautiful night it was. Calm and clear with just a hint of the day's warmth. There were the mosquitos, of course, but I had a scented candle by me and had swiped on a fair bit of repellent. So I lay in the cool grass, my belt loose and a smoke in hand, staring straight up through tree branches spread far enough apart that you could see the stars. Well, the few Houston's lights would allow through their glare. But it was enough to calm me. Let me just be. Remind me of the truth of the world. Of existence. That nothing mattered but them.

I'd lit my second Marlboro when Jeremy slipped up to crouch beside me. His hands were shaking and his voice was cracked as he asked, "Can I—can I bum a—a smoke? Off you?"

His whole attitude told me he was not asking for a cigarette.

I slipped the box from my back pocket and offered it, saying, "Take one from the right."

He nodded and did and tore away the filter and lit it off the candle in moves so fast and desperate, it seemed he had inhaled half the damn thing before he sat back on the grass, beside me. He returned the box, saying nothing. I rose, found the filter, stuffed it in the box and put it back in my pocket. When he exhaled, I made sure to exhale smoke from my Marlboro.

"Thank you," he whispered. "Thank you, thank you, thank you."

I could see his hands were already steadier, and his voice calmer. "Yossi said—he said that, uh, that joint you gave us. Hannukah. Saved his life. So smooth. Gave me a chance to make my connection. Bring in more. Wasn't the same quality, but it worked okay."

He took another hit and leaned back against the fence. I noticed his father looking our way so made a show about smoking my cigarette.

"Your Da's watching," I murmured.

"He knows I smoke," Jeremy sighed. "Got the whole lecture on the legal shit. And what it does to your brain, lungs, heart, blood. He— uh, he knew the guy—my-my connection. He's doing eight to twelve at Huntsville, now."

"Over weed?"

He almost smiled. "This is Texas."

I lay back on the grass to look up at the stars, again. Whispery clouds were beginning to drift in.

He nudged me. "You want a hit?"

I shook my head. "I got a beer and my smoke; I'm fine."

"Then I'm gonna save the rest, if you don't mind."

I gave him a wave of my hand. "You want a real smoke, now? Cover it?" He nodded, so I gave him the pack. "Keep 'em. Just remember, there's two more on the right."

I finally saw a true smile on his face and joy in his eyes as he fired up a cigarette, patted my belly and rose.

"You're a lifesaver," he said.

I snorted at him. "Away on."

But I noticed through the rest of the party he was a great deal more easy-going.

Then July 4th he showed up at the pool house with a bottle of wine and a partial baggie and held both up.

"Celebrate? I owe you."

The family was gone to Hermann Park to watch the display, from which I'd begged off. I'd already begun to smoke and pace in response to the firecrackers and gunfire, but I wasn't as freaked out as I had been a year back. And Angus was there, barking and jumping at the explosions at the same time as me, so tending to him helped keep my focus off it. Plus, though it was a Thursday night, I'd arranged to have the next day off, giving me the weekend to recuperate, if I did go mad in any way. So of course, I motioned for him to enter. And Angus was happy to have two of us to protect him from the pops and cracks.

It helped that on the evening news there was a segment about a laughable attempt by the powers that be in Northern Ireland to come up with *a solution to the inequality in the area*, all without addressing how Paisley and his ilk would never go along with it.

The pot was good. Mellow. Would have been smoother through wine in a bong, which was Hugo's preference when *entertaining the ladies*, but it worked well enough. I sat on the floor, my back against a bean-chair, drifting. Finally at the point where I barely even noticed the explosions jumping in from around the city. Angus to my right. Jeremy to my left.

We talked about little or nothing. Him starting at University of Houston in August. Going in as a sophomore. Me, I was working on a troublesome Austin America and rebuilding the Montesa to where it was a tad more powerful, with Hugo's help. And complained that parts were hard to find for it. Him tending and expanding a grove of olive trees, not far from Haifa, and helping make oil from the fruit. Me running about with Hugo and his fanaticism about Tex-Mex food.

Which was becoming my fanaticism, as well.

By the time midnight was approaching and the gunfire and explosions were beginning to mellow down, Jeremy had settled next to me on the floor, both of us leaning against that totally useless bean bag chair. Angus was asleep. We were on what I thought was the last joint, so he took another toke and offered me the remainder. I brushed it away. I was now at the point where no sudden pops or snaps could attack me. He nodded and held it and a long sigh whispered from him.

"Thanks for lettin' me stay here. Be here. Through all the noise and crap. Forgot how loud it can get. How much it sounds like-like..." His voice trailed off.

I nudged him. Gave him a smile. He almost returned it.

Then he murmured, "My folks're havin' a barbecue. Again. That's all they ever have in this state. Set off fireworks and I-I-I just couldn't..."

"I know," was all I could think to say.

"It's all so different, here. Changed."

"I've not been here long enough to tell," I murmured.

"I was born here. So was my mom. Her folks came through Galveston back around 1910 or something. They were kids. Dad's from New York. They met when he did his residency. He decided to stay. And it was fine; nobody really seemed to care 'bout our religion. Now we get blamed for everything. Embargo. Hijackin's. Even Munich. Somethin' goes wrong, first blame the Jew."

"I can't see anyone doing that with you. You're too mellow a lad."

The smile finally forced itself to his face. "Never was."

I just nudged him in a friendly joshing manner.

He chuckled. "It's true. I was a terror, in school."

"You?"

"Yeah. Kids were kind of afraid of me."

"How so?"

"Long story."

"Got no place to be."

He chuckled and settled deeper into the bean bag chair and this long gaze came to his eyes.

Danny's gaze.

I looked away.

"When I was in sixth grade," he finally murmured, "this family moved in from Port Arthur and one of their kids was in my class. Kenneth Welchel. Found out I'm Jewish and started callin' me *Christ-killer*. Hell, I didn't even know what he was talkin' 'bout till I mentioned it to mom. Man, she tossed a fit. Went roarin' down to the school, but the principal told her it was nothin'. *Just kids being kids.* Then he said to me—I mean, my mother dragged me down with her to tell him what I'd been called, and I was embarrassed like you wouldn't believe."

I chuckled. "Parents love to cause their children hell."

"No shit. Anyway, mom had him explain what it means." He gave a nice long yawn. "Two-thousand years ago the Jews had a guy named Jesus executed by the Romans. That's why Christians call Jews Christ-killers.

"Now I knew a little bit about this Jesus guy. The way Christians see him. That he'd been hung on a cross till he was dead, and there's some weird crap about him not really dyin'." He nudged me to look at him. "We don't go along with that, but we're not as hard-assed as we used to be. Not at my temple." He shifted back to his thousand-mile gaze. "Anyhoooo, his explanation didn't make sense to me."

"Why not?" I asked, because truth be told, now that he mentioned it, I remembered the priests and nuns saying the same about the Jews.

"'Cause, I knew my history. Romans ran the world, back then. Jews couldn't do a damn thing without their okay. So I piped up like a little smart ass, *But the Jews didn't kill Jesus; the Romans did. You said so, yourself.*" He chuckled. "Maaaaannn, you'd have thought I spit in his face."

His chuckle became a laugh, and he took another drag of the joint's stub then sipped some wine before exhaling.

"Well, that principal bolted from his chair. Yelled at mom, *Get this little Jew bastard out of my office!* Said it so loud, half his staff looked around. That's when mom rose and said, very sweet and cold, *Unlike you, this little Jew is the product of a marriage.*"

That made me laugh along with him.

"Yeah. Then she took me straight to a karate class and enrolled me in it, and said, *Learn it; you'll need it.*"

"That happen with your brothers, too? And sister?"

"Nope. That's why it's such a shock. Nobody cared, not till that kid."

I just nodded.

"Karate got boring," he continued, "so I shifted to Aikido. Had lots of time to work on it. I got barred from the school. It took two weeks for Uncle David to make the district let me back in. Mom kept me current with my classes, so that was no problem." He was quiet, for a long moment. "Problem was with Kenneth—he'd gained converts. Lots of kids. Kids I thought were my friends started callin' me that. Whisperin' it. And the kids who didn't say it, who told me in private they thought it was awful what those brats were doin'? They let it happen." He gave a long deep yawn. "And the teachers did nothin' to stop it.

"Finally, ol' Kenneth and I got into it, after school. Right under the noses of three teachers. I think they thought it was time the little Jew boy got put in his place." Another long pause, then a smile. "I broke his arm. Compound fracture. That stopped the fight, all right. Blamed it *aaaaallll* on me. I was suspended for a month. Kenneth's dad threatened to file charges. My mother tossed another fit, but this time my father told her to shut up and see what happened. Then he took me to a shootin' range and showed me how to fire a pistol. We went once a day for a whole month. Thirty-eight revolver. Forty-five automatic, which hurt my hand with its kick. Shifted to a Ruger ten-twenty-two." He looked at me, pretty much stoned. I wasn't far behind him. "That's a rifle. Word got around. *Mess with the Jew, he'll mess with you.* You know what? When I went back to school, no one ever called me that name, again. Ever."

"Jesus, Jere..."

He sat forward, still cross-legged, still staring at nothing.

"Mom put down I'd won awards for my shootin' and had a black belt in Aikido. For the info. For the kibbutz. So when the Egyptian army started their build-up, IDF pulled me in and I was handed a GALIL and sent to Sinai. To stop any advance. I thought they were jokin'. Nobody thought the Egyptians were any good."

I watched him just sit there, unmoving. Barely breathing.

"They were wrong."

Then he looked at me, his gaze so intense I couldn't look away as he whispered, "You're not from Ireland." I frowned and almost spoke but he held up a hand and continued with, "You're from where all that trouble's happenin'."

I hesitated. "What makes you think so?"

"Your eyes. What's in 'em. It's the same like—like Yossi had after the war. He's back in Tel Aviv, workin' his parents' restaurant. Says he's gonna get too fat for the IDF to call him up, again." His voice went so soft I could barely hear it. "There's a difference, right? Ireland and the north?"

I just sighed, unable to think of what to say.

"But I'm right, ain't I? You *have* seen some things?"

He was almost desperate. I shrugged a *yes*.

"Then you understand."

That brought a smirk to my face. "Understand what?"

"What it means." He started breathing tight, almost shaking, again. "Bren—is that your real name? What's your real name?"

I had to shake my head. "I am who I say I am, I just don't know who I'm allowed to be," I murmured.

"Oh." He nodded. "Were you IRA?"

"Everyone's either IRA or UDA in that part of the world."

"You know what I mean."

I shook my head. "I wanted none of it. But it doesn't work like that. The choice is made for you; nothing you can do to change it. Or if you dare to try—"

Joanna kissed me, soft and easy, and Danny walked gently away into the mist—

I coughed.

Jeremy nodded then whispered, "You know what it means. You understand. I didn't wanna kill anybody. I didn't wanna hurt anybody. But I didn't get a choice and..." He sat still, his eyes boring into me. "Bren, I got nobody to talk to. Nobody who can understand." His eyes more and more like Danny's.

"I tried to talk with my dad, but he's busy and proud and mom's there but she's so nervous and-and she'd freak out if I told her anything, and my brothers and my sister, they're all fuckin' older than me and they-they-they got me on some kind of fuckin' pedestal. *One of Israel's heroes*." He all but growled that last out. "Pretty fuckin' hard to talk from top of one of them." It took him a moment to continue. "Can I talk to you?"

I gave a slight nod.

He still hesitated, then words drifted from him. "You know I fought on Yom Kippur. Rifle. Bombs all over. The whole nine yards."

He took another hit on the tiny bit left in the joint. He grew completely still, like in death.

"I killed on Yom Kippur," he finally murmured, his gaze no longer his own but one caught in battles from near a year past.

I figured as much.

"Scared shitless," he continued. "Caught on the side of a road. Saw this guy. Egyptian army. One of a dozen. Comin' fast. Howlin'. Got my rifle ready and aimed and boom. No more head. Shoulder hurt like shit. Who knew a GALIL could do that? Ofir said I wasn't holdin' it right. He-he-he was there with me and Yossi."

He shifted his gaze to me. "Why would I be thinkin' about that when I just killed a man?"

He was weaving under the pot's influence. He used the dregs in the baggie and remains of the other joints to roll another one. Fired it up. Drew it in, long and easy. Let the smoke whisper from his nose and past his lips.

"You've seen death...haven't you, Bren?"

My voice was soft as I said, "Brendan."

He looked at me, almost smiling.

"My full name is Brendan. Will be till I die." And I had to smirk at myself for saying it.

"Brendan?" He nodded. "Good. Don't like Bren. Don't suit you."

"Got a mate calls me Pug."

"Pug?" He snorted a near laugh. "That's even worse. I like

Brendan. It's right." He leaned closer. Offered me the joint as he whispered, "Have you watched someone die?"

I jammed my eyes closed and—

The PARA aimed and CRACK and blood splattered all over the ground before and Joanna struggled as flames danced-danced-danced closer and closer to her and—

I gasped and blinked and saw he was still holding the joint as an offering, so I took it and inhaled long and complete. Let it smother the rise of horror in my heart and mind.

My soul.

He looked at me. Needing no answer. "It changes you, don't it?"

I finally let the smoke out with a soft, "Forever."

He leaned back into the beanbag, resting his head against my shoulder. "Yeah. One second you're talkin' with your buddy; next second his brains're all over you. And it don't make sense. That was— that was Ofir. Sniper. Little flare-up. Almost got me. Almost."

"Yours was a war of defense," I muttered. "Mine's just stupid fuckin' hate. They can call it a war, if they want. The bombs. The killings, tit for tat. But it's just hate. Dogs fighting cats fighting rats fighting each other. Hate. And fear. And joyous cruelty."

Jeremy nodded and nestled closer to me. I lay my head atop his.

"I killed more people," he said. "Guys on the other side. Hundreds of yards away. My bullets. Their brains all over their buddies. Didn't know 'em. Probably had wives. Kids. Girlfriends. Even boyfriends. War brings out some funny shit in people." He gently shifted the sleeve of my under shirt up and caressed Joanna's name on my shoulder. "You love this girl?"

I just nodded.

"You miss her?"

I sighed and nodded. Leaned back more into the chair so my head was next to his.

"Why don't you go back to her?"

I didn't want to say it but the words drifted from me. "She isn't there, anymore. Never will be."

He rose to lean on one arm and look at me. "Is she one you saw...?"

Flames dancing—her fighting them—me being dragged away— someone screaming in my voice—

I jammed my eyes closed. Frowned hard. Coughed. Gulped in air. Swallowed and looked at the ceiling for comfort. Felt tears trail from my eyes.

Jeremy watched me for what seemed like minutes then took a last toke on the tiny joint. Leaned in. Put his lips to mine. Exhaled.

I breathed the smoke in. Not surprised. Not shocked. It felt natural and right. But I didn't look at him. I only let the air slowly seep from me.

"You know how I feel," he whispered, his fingers still caressing Joanna's name. "You understand."

I nodded.

He looked at me a moment longer then leaned in to kiss me. Soft. Gentle. Hesitant.

I let him.

His hand drifted over to touch my face then his fingers trailed down my neck and along my body. Caressed my nipples in a way that brought sensations to me I hadn't felt since Rocky.

I just sighed.

And let him.

He trailed down my belly to my jeans and undid each button in turn, slow and easy, still hesitant.

I did nothing to stop him. I was feeling a curious need building within me. Nothing desperate or vile. Just...there.

His fingers pulled my shirt up and up and up until he could kiss my nipples. Use his tongue on them.

That brought a sigh from deep within me.

He slipped a hand inside my jeans and felt me through my briefs.

All I did was breathe in deep. Begin to grow.

He slowly...slowly exposed me.

Stroked the length of me.

Kissed along my belly, sending shivers of joy through every part of my body.

Then he nuzzled my pubes and took me in his mouth, and it was almost like when I entered Rocky. But not quite. Nor was it like when one of Hugo's girls had done this with me. That had been nice and easy and fun. Something about his lips and tongue swirling around me as his fingers held and rolled my nuts in ways that were not only tender but invasive and brutally lovely in their sensations made me clench my arse and all but gasp from the pleasure of it. He kept at it and kept at it, working me into full and complete need.

Verging on wanton.

Whispering into a loss of control.

I didn't want him to stop.

I let his hands explore whatever part of me they wanted. My nipples. My arse. My thighs. No girl had done this in sync with polishing me. But Jeremy, his fingers never stopped roaming and caressing and touching and pinching and fondling as my own hands dug into my hair and gripped at it in near ecstasy. In my mind, I was all but screaming for him not to stop.

His lips and tongue worked more and more of their magic on me. Stronger. Faster. My breath grew shorter and harsher and deeper as sensations I'd felt since never engulfed me and dragged at my soul and tore at my heart exploded within like a monstrous wave of exhilaration building through me until I jolted and ejaculated with a near cry.

He kept working me, his lips not surrendering, making me squirm and whimper from the extreme tenderness of the lightning it sent careening throughout my body.

Then he rose up and pulled himself out, and within seconds he'd shot his own semen onto my belly. He spit mine out to mingle with it and mixed them together with his hands, smearing them over me. The expression on his face was soft and almost ethereal as he wavered there, then let himself wilt down to lie next to me.

And gaze at the fluids drying on my belly.

Trail his hands in it as he whispered, "This is life. Beginnin' of life. Beginnin'...we just ended."

Then he began to weep.

Cry.

Sob.

Bawl like Kieran when he was hungry or tired, and Ma would pick him up and hold him and let him cry until he was done.

Angus woke and whined but did not get up.

I held Jeremy, tender. He gripped me tight, desperate and lost. His sobbing almost silent. His tears nonstop. Soaking my undershirt.

And deep inside I wished I could join him in his grief.

I've no idea how long we were like that. Maybe an hour. Must have been, before he could even start to regain control.

Finally, he rose to sit. The weeping stopped. His breath was hard and he was hunched over, barely able to cast me so much as half a look, when he asked, "Have I just fucked things up between us?"

I frowned at him. "What was there between us?"

"Aw, fuck—I have..." He fought back more tears.

I had no words. Just kept looking at him.

What had finally caught up to me was how little I cared about what had just happened. Having sex with another lad and it seeming normal and natural. No confusion in me. The thought of being polished by a man had never once been entertained by me, even with Everett's gentle hints of what he'd like to do. The fact is, I'd always thought poorly of any man who would do it, because I figured that was what was done to Danny by Father Devil, or vise-versa, and it had crushed him. I think I may have been half afraid it would also crush me. Send me into the depths of sadness, like it had Danny.

But it hadn't.

It was nothing.

Just another form of release, and was with a lad who shared something deeper than mere understanding, with me. A connection far more important than love or friendship. Which certainly was something Danny had not shared with Father Devil. So it must have gone much farther than this and Danny not been a willing participant. His experience had hurt him. Scarred him. Confused him, even. I could see that now. That and the betrayals after were what filled him with such anger.

I halfway wondered if I might have felt the same way if I hadn't already been with Rocky and those other girls, whose names did not stay with me. If I hadn't enjoyed being with them. Could that be why I was feeling something like, *okay, it happened and so what?* It was just another experience, and not an unpleasant one.

Perhaps it was also because Jeremy and I now shared so much in our backgrounds. Had a deeper connection between us than with anyone else. He had revealed himself completely to me, and I to him more than anyone else I had, since Joanna, and I felt easy and calm and pleased that my first time with a man had been with him, a lad close my own age and in as much need of support as I was.

But now he was afraid we could not remain known to each other? No, that could not happen. It was silly to worry about anything so trivial as false morality when you could be gone in a flash.

So I yawned and whispered, "Well, have I gone running down the street, yet? Crying at your *abuse* of me?"

He eyed me, wary, and said, "...No..."

"Then don't be fearful. You're me China."

That brought a confused look to his eyes. "What?"

I rubbed the back of his neck, saying, "That's what me and me mates—me best mates in Derry called each other. They wouldn't let me get lost in my-in my thoughts or-or-or my projects but always made sure I was off with 'em to play footy or run about or just be lads together. They didn't see me as simple; just as Brendan."

"What d'you mean by that? Simple?"

"Stupid. Mental. Loop-de-loop."

"You? Why would anyone think that?"

I shrugged. "It was how I was called, and once a mind's made up, God help you trying to change it."

"So these guys, they were Chinese?"

"No. No, Jere, just something we read in a book, and we liked it and-and-and now you're me China."

He almost smiled. "Best mate?"

I nodded.

"You sure?"

I yawned, again, tucked myself away, re-buttoned my jeans and lay back into the bean chair to stretch as I said, "Well, we're not boyfriends, if that's what you're after."

He nearly chuckled and leaned into the chair, with me, one arm across my chest.

"Naw, not *boyfriends*. I like being just friends with you. Like knowin' someone who knows what I know. Knows what I feel. Like you got my back. What just happened was just a way of-of-of cementing that."

I snorted a laugh. "What a pile of shite. But tell you what, Jere— don't you think it better we cement our brotherhood over a pile of tacos?"

He sat up, grinning. "Poppo's?"

I grinned back. "I can do those. But are they Kosher?"

"Fuck that." He rose, pulling me up with him, then dragged me to the wet bar, soaked a cloth, raised my shirt and washed over my belly.

I started to pull away, saying, "What're yous doing?"

"No need to be sticky or uncomfortable," he said. "You might wanna change your shirt, though; that one's soaked." Then he added, "I thought Irish guys were uncut. You sure you ain't Jewish?"

I chuckled and shook my head as I said, "I'm special." Then I whipped my undershirt off and pulled on a button-down as he finished the last of his beer, which was probably warm, by now.

"No shit, Sherlock," he said, smiling in full, again. "And I promise I'll never pull this on you, again. Unless you want me to."

That last came with a wink.

I laughed and yanked him into an embrace. "I'll keep you to that."

Then I kissed him full on the mouth.

We led Angus from the pool house then rode off on my Montesa. Helmets on our heads, his arms around my waist, laughing. He had to direct me, and we ran more than a few red lights, but it was well-past midnight and the traffic was quiet. The darkness was comforting. The warm air soft against us. The neon lights flashing by, joyous. And the stars twinkling their approval.

And no one will ever be able to convince me what happened was wrong in any way, or that the taco feast that followed was not the best ever.

Life and Evangelyne

There wasn't a day, the rest of the year, without some atrocity tearing up the North, be it Derry, Belfast, any point in-between. The IRA, PIRA, INLA and RIRA had asserted themselves as being just as capable as the UVF, UDA, RUC and British Army in causing pain and suffering. Protestants shot Catholics and were shot, in return. Bombs went off at the hands of both sides, not only throughout the North but in Dublin, Monaghan and Birmingham. *Slaughter the innocent* was the mode of battle, if that's what you cared to call it.

Internment was now never-ending. Men and women snatched then tossed into prison without trial, which might get a tiny blurb in the papers, always with the British view claiming, *More terrorists caught in our push to make safe the place we'd made into the jaws of hell.* Of course, that last part was left off, as was any comment on it being Catholics who were treated as such and rarely Protestants. The attitude in the States seemed to be, *Just another day in the Mother country. Nothing to see. Drop a coin in the bucket and move yourself along.*

The more that happened, the more conflicted I was to be free from it all. It was difficult to know that at any moment my brothers or sister, there, could be maimed or killed for being in the wrong place at the wrong time. Or lifted by the Army for no more reason than their address or name. And there was naught I could do to alleviate the nagging worry.

What's odd is, not once was I concerned about Eamonn being in prison. Nor Colm or Danny, since with them I was still torn by that bomb. As for Ma—to be honest, she was impervious.

Mai's letters continued to be careful, with tidbits about Rhuari learning Gaelic off some subscription service, and Maeve caught in another scrap at school and being lectured by the nuns on behaving more like a lady.

According to her, Mai wrote, *she asked the nuns why she had to behave like a lady when Lonny Dillon could act the horse's arse. She was punished with a switch and Ma said it was right to do to her, but when they got home Maeve says Ma treated her like a queen. Brought in pastries from McDougal's and Chinese from the market shop! Seems she'd had her own run-ins with the nuns at her school so was proud Maeve had her spirit.*

Then there was Kieran, who was already causing trouble with the RUC thanks to cans of spray paint.

It seems PIRA likes him because he's small, steady with his hands, has a bit of talent in composition, and is willing to lay down a message anywhere they can get him to. Maeve says she's seen him balanced on two larger lads' upstretched arms adding a slogan to the highest point on a gable wall, neither of them actually holding him. Which made no sense to me so I asked her about it. She said he was just standing on their palms, as easy as could be. He may be eight years-old, only, but he's got no fear, that one.

Ma has a phone, now, and the number is at the end of the letter should you wish to ring her. It was Rhuari got her to agree, of all people. He told her it would give her more access to Eamonn. He's quite clever when he wants to be, our Rhuari.

Which I thought had already been decided...

Father Jack has said he would pay it on our behalf, so I will send him the money by cheque, each month. Maeve says Ma still fussed and fumed for days when it was announced but did not turn away the company man when he finally came to install it. Once it was done, I called and spoke with Maeve about Kieran. She just laughed about it and called him a feral dog, chased by the Army and the peelers, now and then, but they have yet to either catch him or, apparently, figure out who he is. To my fear, Ma encourages him. She says he's a true artist in his work, and when he's older they might let him design a mural. I never know when Ma's telling me straight or bragging for naught.

The rest of the time, Ma was referred to with a *She's doing well* sort of comment. And I never found mention of me, or what had supposedly happened with me. Which I suppose made sense, but wouldn't the powers that be wonder why no letters from me or money sent home or anything? Seemed to me that would be as suspicious as me writing home from Houston. Or were they never truly interested?

Then, as if in answer to my questions, came a letter where Mai mentioned there was a rumor going around that I'd been taken prisoner by the British over that bomb. The story went like, I'd been seriously injured in the arrest so had been held in a secret location, to heal, and now was undergoing interrogation in one of their well-known *unpublicized prisons*. Many were they who believed it and felt it wrong to do that to a *simple* lad.

For near two years? That made no sense. It would have made far better to have me buried in a secret grave by the IRA. But then Mai mentioned that a young Catholic soldier home on leave was executed by the bastards, and they got plenty of stick, over it. He hadn't been one of the squads or paratroopers; just home visiting his mother on her birthday. It was even in the local papers. So I suppose them spreading the rumor I was alive and under the thumb of the Army was to deflect some of the poor opinion against them, over that stupidity. Though how that might help made no sense to me. I said as much to Aunt Mari.

Her response? "I'd let that go, were I you. Let the Brits be on the defensive."

In the next letter, Mai mentioned more of the story, like how it had come out that *our Brendan* had only been planning to leave Derry and gone to a pastry shop to buy something for the train trip and accidentally been caught in the blast. But the British had somehow known I was Catholic so had slung me into a PIG and carried me off while the fires still burned, like I was a prize they'd caught. And now they refused to admit I'd been arrested but said only that, *We cannot offer information on detainees under the Special Powers Act.* To say that fed nicely into the suspicions and conspiracies all people in the Bogside held against the British would be an understatement, for I was not the only one thought to be held like that.

It put me in an odd state of emotion. I was actually hurt at how I'd been bundled into such a transparent lie. But I had little choice but to remain silent about it, so as to keep up the pretense. The only evidence I had to offer that the story was nonsense was myself, and I was caught halfway between heaven and hell, unable to determine for myself which would be my next destination. All I could do, right now, was wait and see and hope change would come.

Unless I could figure out a different path to take, which was also proving bloody well impossible.

Eamonn remained at Long Kesh, but hints were offered by Mai that the Provos wanted him in there. He was helping to organize the other lads, inside.

Our Eamonn?

Who couldn't hold a secret to save his life?

That seemed a great deal of responsibility he was being allowed. However, the British and fools running the prison being the usual horses' arses thought themselves intelligent and in full and complete control, so all Eamonn had to do was say something like, *Join with us and your lot will be better, for we protect our own.* Then if the Brits overheard him, more time was added to his so-called sentence. To everyone's pleasure.

My letters to him are returned, unopened, Mai wrote. *So I've begun sending them to an intermediary and he slips them in when he visits. Then Eamonn sends letters out with him. When I receive them, all are written between the lines on old letters I'd sent, but the ink is like a light red in place of my blue pen. Not easy to read but I've been able to work it out, with Tur's help.*

To my shock, he actually seems happy in there, our Eamonn. Before his arrest, he was aimless and unsure of anything, except that he was angry and it was enough to follow PIRA or OIRA or whatever it was. Leaving Queens was not his best choice, and skulking about or tossing stones and firebombs were hardly a good substitute. But inside he's found new meaning in helping the Provos. Of course, when the guards get wind of his actions, they shift him into solitary and dig at him for information on why he's recruiting. Seems it also adds to his stature that his "younger brother is being held by the British in some secret place." I hope that's not true. Now I take care to ask Eamonn for nothing but to know if he's doing well. And he says he is.

Christ, I wanted to find a way to speak with him. Some of the stories I'd been reading, per the Red Cross and rights organizations—when the papers bothered to ask them for a quote—hinted at true horrors in those cells. My little bit of time under arrest and knowing how Tur's longer period had damaged him—and now my brother caught in a place that was a hundred times worse? That could not be made better by Mai's assurances he was doing well.

Never was there word about Colm, Danny or Paidrig, or even wee Eammon. And I didn't ask Aunt Mari to raise question about them. A phone being set up for a known terrorist's mother had already put the spotlight on my family, I'm sure. So I kept on top of the news as best I could, which only rarely mentioned the names of those killed or arrested, and hoped for the best.

I found just one other person beyond Jeremy who was truly aware of the horrors happening in the North. Rene. That was only because he read both of Houston's newspapers. Uncle Sean had canceled *The Post* and now would allow only *The Chronicle* in the house.

"Too damn liberal," was his explanation.

So Rene got to where he'd bring in the previous day's copy and I'd read it during my tea—my *lunch break*. They also came in handy for mopping up oil.

Rene rarely spoke. With anyone. His sole concern was caring for his family and keeping them separate from the shop. I don't think he was ashamed of where he worked so much as he didn't want any co-mingling. And I'm sure his main worry was Hugo and his way not only with the birds—with *girls*—but also with shrugging everything off.

Hugo knew it and laughingly told me, once, "Responsibility. It's his middle name. It's real funny he's like that, 'cause he was born in the Big Easy."

"Where's that?" I'd asked.

He'd given me a horrified look. "New Orleans! That's what they call it, there. You didn't know that?"

I'd shrugged. "Maybe you're *too* easy for him."

Hugo'd laughed and said, "Ain't no such thing. He's just another white guy, at heart, but with a tan skin."

I had no response to that. To me, both of them were tan in place of my burn, for one of the lesser joys of being out and about in Houston was how red I could get, even with lots of Coppertone.

It wasn't till we were having a Christmas celebration at the shop and he'd had his second glass of this punch called Sangria that Rene even showed me a photo of his family. Him, his wife and their six children posed in front of their massive house in Pearland, south of the city. Two of the lads had wives and children also clustered about, and his own wife, Louise, was dead center of the group looking as proud as a mama cat with her litter. She was older than Ma but still lovely, with skin like light coffee and eyes dancing with laughter.

"That's Albert," he said, pointing to a man taller than him by a foot and well-fitted. "Oldest. Resident at MD Anderson."

"One of the hospitals, isn't it?" I asked.

He nodded. "Cancer. Gonna be an oncologist. That's his wife and those his two kids. She works a post office, near them."

He pointed to a woman who was darker, rounder and warier than Louise, continuing with, "They only got one car so he rides his bike to work. Keeps him tone. She oughta join him, but the kids and job keep her busy."

Next he pointed out Alonso, who was stockier and shorter than *Albie*, with a steadiness to him that was soothing. "He's a cop with HPD. Has been for six year. That's his wife and two more grandkids." He pointed to a small woman and twin girls who were identical.

I shook my head, thinking about the B-girls, and said, "I can't imagine dealing with real twins."

Rene chuckled and pointed to another lad, saying "Anatole's in the Marines. Okinawa." I had no doubt of that, because he was built so solid he didn't look real. Beside him was a tall young woman who looked elegant and confident in herself, with fine cheekbones and dark eyes that held a steady, amused gaze at the camera.

"That his wife?" I asked, pointing to her.

Rene laughed. "Evangelyne, my daughter. She's at UH. Favors her mama more than me. Not just in looks, but smarts. Got a head for Russian. Goddamn Russian! Whole new alphabet, even."

"Sounds like a mate of mine, learning Chinese. Not even an alphabet, he tells me, just symbols. It's mad."

Rene just nodded.

"He's at U of H," I added. "Ask her about Jeremy Landau, in the languages department. Maybe they know each other."

"I will," Rene said, thoughtful, "but it's a big campus. No, *Tole*'s got no wife, yet, but he's still young and frisky, enjoyin' himself."

He pointed to a trim young man with a bright smile and neat features. "Aristide's two year behind Vangie. Just joined the Air Force, so he's down San Antonio. Didn't make it to the academy, but he's thinking he'll serve a year then apply to the officer training school."

Seated on the ground, cross-legged and grinning at nothing was a chubby lad with semi-kinky hair done in a half-Afro. "That's Arnaud," said Rene, his voice growing soft and careful. "Still in high school."

"That's a big house for three people."

"Vangie's with us till she's done with college. Dunno what we'll do after that, cher. So what's your family like? Not your uncle's, but..."

I stretched and said, "Da's dead—" I caught myself about to say more and shrugged. "That's it."

"Damn, boy, you an orphan?"

I shrugged. "Free to make me own way."

What else could I say that wouldn't be both a lie and the truth?

"You born on Groundhog Day, ain't ya?"

I chuckled. "That's what Aunt Mari said. How'd you know?"

"Your application. How old you gonna be? Nineteen, wasn't it?"

I nodded and sipped more of the Sangria. It was sweet, like candy, but I liked it fine enough.

"Then I'm gonna throw you a real Cajun birthday, cher. My place." He whipped out a new pocket calendar and looked up the date. "Ooooh—on a Sunday. Bad day for it. Day before? Saturday? We'll do the whole three pots, an' I got some andouille sent me by my sister. Be a full feast. Bring your cousins, if they up for it."

"It's not so big a deal, Rene..."

"C'mon. Don't mind *you* meetin' my family." He leaned close to whisper, "You ain't like these other clowns. Bring some friends. I'll draw in Lon and Albie and their families. Make it a real go. Start to Mardi Gras."

"Mardi Gras?"

"Shit, Bren, ain't you heard of Mardi Gras?"

"Uh, yeah, I have. But it's in New Orleans, isn't it?"

"I'm from N'Awlin's, cher. It's happenin' wherever I am. 'Sides, the kids're goin' down, weekend 'fore Lent. Visit my sister. This'll prep 'em, right. Ain't been down, forever."

What could I do but agree? Because...well, why the hell not? I'd been in Houston over two years, bodily if not mentally. It was time I learned more of the world around it.

And of course I knew Joanna'd have gone, which put paid to it.

Aunt Mari and Uncle Sean begged off, and I was not about to inflict the B-Girls on Rene's family, not yet. But Scott was in for the weekend, so he, Jeremy and I headed down to Pearland. Scott had a Key Map in his GTO and *knew exactly how to get there*, so we let him drive. Down the 10 to the 45 past downtown to exit at Reveille Drive and aim south. And we drove.

Passing Hobby Airport.

And drove.

Passing long low houses and open fields and strip centers and non-stop flat land.

And drove.

By this point, I was sure we'd missed the turn, somehow. But Scott was in his *know-it-all* temper, and damned if it didn't turn out he was right. My guess is, we were halfway to Galveston by the time we turned left and left, again, and then right and then down a half-dark street until we pulled up to a postal box with the address's numbers on it. The thing was stuck in the middle of thick shrubbery and hovered over by massive oak trees. I'd never have found the place on my own. Nor would I be able to find my way back home, if need be. Christ. There were plenty of cars already parked along the road, so we found a spot around the next corner and bolted from the GTO to head back to the place.

The house looked small from the front. Single-story wood frame atop a short foundation to keep it off the ground. A solid wood deck painted in tan and brown. An area of gravel was in front of the deck, where Rene's Dodge pickup was parked. A brick-laid driveway to its left led to a separate garage. It gave off a sense of isolation, which was no surprise.

We were met at the front door by Louise, who was even taller than I thought and wore a flowery Mumu, as she called it. I could smell something like heaven wafting from the back yard and bouncy joyous music of a type I'd never hear before, with it. More voices were happy and loud.

"So you be Bren," Louise said as she grasped my hand.

I nodded in answer, saying, "Thanks for havin' me."

"Oh, I love your accent. Happy birthday."

"Cheers."

Then she looked at Scott and Jeremy so I introduced them. She focused on Jeremy and said, "Vangie told me 'bout you. And here seein' you, I almost thought you and Bren were brothers."

I cast Jeremy a glance. This was the first I'd heard he'd met the man's daughter. He just smiled and winked at me.

She led us in through colorful, comfortable rooms that rambled on and on and on to the back, with a different cat in every corner, none of them willing to do a thing more than watch us pass.

"There's a few more people than we expected," she said. "Mostly neighbors invited so they don't feel the need to call the police over the noise. Albie's on call so his wife and two're here, and Tole's come in from Okinawa. He just re-upped for another four years, so they give him some leave. Hope y'all like jambalaya."

"Oh, I love that shit," said Scott.

Louise cast him a look, so Jeremy jumped in with, "I've heard the best jambalaya's made at home, from scratch, with love from the cook."

She smiled at him and said, "Sounds like you got a future in politics."

Jeremy just chuckled.

Louise led us out, and now I got a serious idea of how long the house was. Its massive yard also encompassed the lot behind it. Open space framed by big, solid pecan trees and shrubs. Two barbecue pits going, one holding a pot of some heavenly nectar and Rene so happy and focused on it I barely got a nod of welcome from him.

Louise introduced us around to her family, and I could see the photos did none of them justice. All had smiles to put the angels to shame, but Evangelyne outshone them all. Dancing eyes, clear and dark. A form every woman should be envious of. And a manner so casual, free and easy, I almost felt as if I'd known her forever.

Jeremy did the formal introduction with a simple, "Vangie, this is Bren, the guy who brought us together."

She laughed and said, "Good to meet you. And thanks for connecting me with someone who's having as much trouble with that department as me."

"Half the professors think teachin' Mandarin with a twang is no big deal," Jeremy chuckled.

"Or that formal Russian, which would have been fine under the Tsar but has nothing to do with the Politburo, is the only way to go."

"We're called the Commie Pair, there."

I shrugged and said, "I got a—" about to mention Rhuari's Gaelic lessons then remembered I was supposed to be an only child so continued with, "I know a lad learning Gaelic, by subscription."

"You know any?" she asked.

"No, I've no head for languages." Then coughed. "I fix things."

"Bein' able to do that is more important than you'll ever know."

Then she led me to the food and filled my plate and a bowl with ham, étouffée, gumbo, shrimp and crawfish (which looked alike, to me), crab legs, seafood pot, pan-fried rice, chicken wings and breasts but no legs—*drumsticks*. Louisa also saw to it my bowl was never empty of red beans and rice and cornbread and Falstaff beer to go with it. Christ, with one helping I could feel how full I was in my cheeks, and I was sure if I looked in a mirror a basset hound would be looking back.

She positioned the three of us at a card table with Tole, who was even more built than in Rene's photo and had a face that was all angles. Jeremy spent most of the night talking with him about Hong Kong, since Tole had been there.

Scott just ate and drank.

There was a small band of three men—one with a squeezebox, one with a violin and one with a washer-board that he scraped up and down—and they played Creole and Zydeco music, which sounded the same to me, to be honest, but I was smart enough not to say so.

More than once, I flashed back to the Celebration Fleadh. Jesus, more than five years prior. The singing. The dancing. The joy felt by all. The fond memory of Joanna stealing my cap came up to caress me, this time, as did her laugher with her friends. Escorting her home. For once, I could put Charlie's chasing of me in a corner to be forgotten, and just let life be as it was.

The evening chill set in, but they kept the party going. Scott danced over and over with the twin girls, and Jeremy took Albie's wife (I think) for a spin, as well. When Rene and Louise finally joined in, Evangelyne asked me to join with her in a dance.

"It's not hard," she said, her voice gentle. "You just move."

I laughed. "I've never been one for dancing."

But she laughed and dragged me into a loose embrace. Showed me how to swing my hips and near-bounce on my feet as we traveled around an area of packed earth by the garage. I noticed one of her brothers—Alonso, was it? No, *Lon*—he gave me the wary eye as he swung around with his happy wife, but I cared not. And it seemed there were plenty of women and girls lined up to take over dancing with Scott and Jeremy—and Anatole. No, *Tole*. Him especially.

Through it all, Arnaud sat off to one side, smiling and watching and nibbling at a never empty plate of what they called *mudbugs*. His face was a mess from them, but he seemed not to care, and I thought him the luckiest lad in the world.

Closing in on midnight, Evangelyne—Vangie, as she liked to be called—and Lon and Tole began talking about Mardi Gras, coming up. Tuesday, week. They were heading to their aunt's house in Mid-City for a long weekend. It sounded wild and crazy and fun.

I was nibbling on a beignet, feeling mellow and safe, so actually asked, "So how far is it to New Orleans?"

Tole shrugged. "'Bout three-hundred and fifty mile."

Lon shook his head. "Aunt Catherine's ain't so far. More two-sixty."

Vangie laughed, her smile sparkling bright as the sun. "Lon, you never did have a sense of distance."

"I drove that road. Don't take five hours clear to her shack."

"That's before the double-nickel. Now it'll be seven."

She stretched like a cat waking from a long lazy nap. I could not help but watch.

Lon gave me a cool, cock-eyed glance. "You thinkin' of goin', Irish?"

I shrugged. "I'm just on me bike. Sounds a bit far to travel, for that. Is there a train or bus?"

"You could come with us," Vangie said.

"You crazy?" Lon huffed. "We'll be packed in my car, as it is."

"Plenty of room, Lon. Kids in the back, seat down."

"Six adults? For that far?"

"No, it's no worry," I said. "I'll not impose."

"C'mon, Bren," said Vangie, sitting up and almost excited. "It's a chance of a lifetime. See N'Awlins with a family that's both Creole and Cajun. We'll make it fun for you. Like a full birthday for our own little Groundhog."

"You better ask Aunt Catherine," said Lon, his voice taking on a warning. "Her shack ain' so big an' there's others comin'."

Jeremy came up, more beignets in hand, powdery sugar laced over his chin, and asked, "Where ya'll goin'?"

"Mardi Gras," said Vangie. "You comin'?"

"Middle of the semester?"

Vangie gave a gentle shrug. "I'll miss two labs and three classes, but I'm ahead in them all. Been plannin' this for months."

"Damn, Vangie," Lon snarled, "you gonna bring the whole city in my car? The way it gulps gas? Gonna cost a hunnerd dollars just to get there."

"We'll all chip in, Lon. And we'll make do on where to sleep." Then she cast me a wicked glance. "When we *do* sleep."

"I-I-I dunno," I said, feeling too much of the spotlight on me. "Maybe next year's a better idea."

Jeremy nudged me. "Oh, go on. Take some time off. Have a blast. You'll be glad for it."

"C'mon, Bren," Vangie said, getting excited about the idea, "you can be our mascot. Show us the Quarter through your Irish eyes. Daddy, talk Bren into comin' to N'Awlins with us."

Which he did.

Dammit.

Got me leave through Thursday, saying, "You'll need it." Since no one was listening to my protestations, I finally let the excitement take me over. I bought a rucksack, stuffed in some clothes and such, and set off to meet them at their home on a cold Saturday morning. The ride down on my Montesa left me bloody well frozen, but Vangie met me at the door and warmed me up with tea and muffins and jam and eggs.

It amazed me how she could feast as well as any and make it seem right and proper. She wasn't delicate, like Joanna. With some space from our time together, I could see I'd been putting her on this pedestal to worship her beauty and qualities I'd thought were ladylike. Suddenly, that seemed inappropriate. A bit dismissive of her humanity.

But Vangie? She was full-on human. She was real. She wore a simple peasant blouse and loose jeans, with light sandals on her feet, untouched by the cold. Her hair was pulled back in a tight bun, a bright scarf wrapped around it, giving her a look of exquisite sophistication. No makeup from what I could tell. And she buttered her muffins the same as I did, then bit into them in ways that were honest and uncaring as to what you thought of her.

And to my shock, I found I liked that.

Lon arrived with a wagon similar to Aunt Mari's, but an Oldsmobile. If it got the same mileage as hers, I feared the twenty I offered for gas would not take us far. But I'd brought just two hundred with me and had no idea how I'd get more if it was needed. Only he seemed happy with it, saying, "Thanks, Irish," and some of the wariness left his eyes.

Only some.

His wife and three kids piled its top with suitcases, not only theirs but Albert's—Albie, the doctor—and his wife's. And two more kids...and oh, Christ, and I couldn't remember their names. The wives' names. Lon's was a month. June? May? April! Lon's wife. Right. And Albie's? Oh, God...

Fortunately, Albie called, "Monica, grab the cord," and I was spared that embarrassment.

My rucksack joined the cases on top, and a tarp was tied over it all, good and tight. Apparently Lon and Albie, both, had been scouts. We *adults* sat in the front seats, three abreast; the kids piled into the back, and there was still space left for more. I marveled at it, for Mr. Devlin's estate car would have carried but half as much, and I'd thought that was large.

Then off we went, up to the 610 and then around to the 10.

And if I'd thought I had an idea of the spaciousness of America while in Houston, I quickly saw I'd been fooling myself. The long flat drive, for hours and hours. The endless fields and farms and trees punctuated only by the occasional truck stop or exit to cities like Beaumont and Lake Charles and Lafayette and Baton Rouge. There was one section miles and miles long that was just a bridge over marsh water, as far as you could see. That made me very nervous, and the longer it went the more certain I became that we'd never find land, again.

Lon had cruise control, so the car ran like it was on air and not pavement, and the seats were not uncomfortable. The heater was good enough to keep us all warm, and Albie and Lon took turns driving.

Vangie was in the rear passenger seat with me, so I nudged her. "Do you not drive?"

She chuckled then sweetly said, "My brothers're paternalistic, misogynistic twits who don't think a woman can handle a car like this."

"C'mon, Vangie," Lon snarled, "it's got a three-fifty, not a four-banger like that piss-ant thing you got."

Albie chuckled as he looked back at us from the seat he called shotgun to pat Monica's leg, saying to Vangie, "We seen how you drive."

"I'm not the one with a dozen tickets to his name," she shot back. Then she smiled at me, saying, "Helps to have a brother who's a cop, with things like that."

"Vangie..." Lon's voice carried a real warning, and I could see him glaring at me in the rearview mirror. "Maybe your buddy can drive, some. You ever handle a real car, Irish?"

It sounded like a challenge, so I just made myself chuckle. "Wrong side, mate. I'm sure we'd do a head-on, with me."

"Yeah, right, all you guys drive on the wrong side of the road."

I said nothing more, not even when we stopped for gas just past Lake Charles at a truck stop. I just went inside for the loo and had to pass through their shop, and dear God—the wealth of things available! Covers for steering wheels, gloves, rugs for your car, license plate holders, a dozen types of motor oil, antifreeze, tools, key chains, snacks, sodas, beer—Jesus, you could get lost in it all.

In a bloody shop in the middle of nowhere! Madness.

Once I'd done my business, I bought candy and sodas for all...to the tune of five dollars! Highway robbery—but maybe that's where the phrase came from. Then we headed on and I focused on the scenery and remained quiet the rest of the way.

Without question I was not welcome by Lon. It was obvious from the looks he kept casting me, in the mirror. Being between Vangie and Monica, my feet straddling the hump in the floor, I began to wonder if he knew I'd been the one to wreck Matty's knees. Everyone in the bar had known I was Irish, and how many lads the likes of me could there be, in a city like Houston?

Well, I was caught in a station wagon in the middle of nowhere with a pack of people I barely knew going to a city I'd only ever heard about, and I had joined in with it after next to no thought. It was a bit late for panic, now. So I scooched down in the seat to rest my head against its back and closed my eyes, amazed at having jumped feet first into such a situation.

Joanna would have been proud of me.

N'Awlins

Their Aunt Catherine owned what they called a coffin home in Mid-City. Long and narrow, it was. Two stories with a small porch in the front, painted a light blue with white trim and set well-up on blocks of concrete. A small white fence surrounded the tiny front garden, with steps leading straight up from the street to the front door. A driveway to the left already held two cars and a truck, and nearly a dozen people of various colors and sizes and ages roared from the house to greet us. I was introduced to so many in so full a rush, their names whisked right past.

I was finally led inside to meet the woman, herself—tall, strong, elegant, with cheekbones sharp enough to cut cheese and hands so finely drawn, they were mesmerizing. Her silver hair had strands of black mingled in, a little tabby cat was always curled over her shoulders, and she carried such a strong sense of serenity, just being next to her made me feel at ease with the world.

All the furniture had been shoved to the walls with more folding chairs brought in, and there were pots of jambalaya and gumbo always simmering on the stove. Chairs had even been set up in the narrow hallway, facing each other in pairs, and a room on the very back had a sign reading *private*.

"Aunt Catherine's room to herself," Vangie told me. "When she's had enough of us, she goes in there and you stay out, on pain of death."

"I'll keep it mind," I'd chuckled, fighting back the urge to ask if I could borrow it, for the moment.

We were arranged upstairs—boys in front, girls in the back, married couples in between. Our beds were mattresses covering the floors, with a sheet and a blanket, each.

The cars stayed where they were, for we were but a couple blocks from the streetcar on Canal Street and all insisted it was much easier to get hauled to the quarter than drive and spend an hour finding a place to park. So a good dozen of us went chattering along a street of houses similar to Aunt Catherine's, cars lining the sides so tight you'd think they were shoved in sideways. Then came a wide boulevard with the streetcar lane down the middle...and dozens of other groups waiting at the stop.

Meaning, it took three of the bloody things passing before we could all board, the first were so packed. We mixed with even more festivalgoers coming up, beers got passed around, and I wound up with beads draped over my neck, from whom I have no idea. Someone had a squeeze box and there was singing, not only till we boarded but down the whole trip.

Which turned out to be not far. We could have walked it faster.

It wasn't the nicest area of the center city where we jumped off, but down a block across the avenue and we were into The French Quarter, mostly low buildings of brick with fine terraces and balconies climbed over by ivy or hung with ferns and lights gleaming everywhere, even though it was day. Decorations of every bright color you could image hung from every space, and no matter where you turned there was some fine aroma demanding your interest, be it food, perfume, or something very illegal.

Oh, and if I'd thought the streetcar was packed, this was out of control. Men in nothing but a strap of cloth around their groins and high heels, with masks or makeup or both. Cops in short sleeve uniforms and hard hats, even in the chill, with batons out ready to be used...or fondled by the men in high heels. Women showed their breasts and men their dicks to people crowded on balconies, who would toss down what Vangie called Krewe doubloons and beads. I was groped and grabbed and hugged and kissed by both sexes, and I was handed a massive orange drink in a curved glass by a priest who turned out to be a woman with short hair and laughing eyes.

"You look like you need this," she said.

"Thanks," I managed to gasp.

"Oh, you're so adorable, if I ever did switch teams, it'd be for you." Then she kissed me, tongue and all, before gliding away to join with a group of other priests—well, more short-haired women dressed as priests and having amazing fun.

Vangie actually had to reach over and push at my chin, saying, "Take a sip, Bren."

I did. And it was nothing but juice. I finished it in seconds.

Vangie noticed and laughed. "Careful, those got a kick."

She took the empty glass and put it on a table where five men were seating, scream-chatting. One handed his nearly full one to her and she gave it to me, but by this point I was beginning to feel a buzz so knew I'd best take care.

Jesus, but our celebration Fleadh had been a quiet Sunday get-together, compared to this near riot. The thickness of the crowd ebbed and flowed, always on the edge of chaos but never quite there. Then as darkness filled the Quarter, the lights took over and a soft mist brought a layer of magic to it all.

Which was hard to savor with so many people jostling about. So many hands grabbing at me. So much noise and laughter and scream-chatting with bloody fucking joy like—

Heading down William, that Sunday, like a parade off to a party and—

Someone screamed, "I know you!" and—

"I know this hat!" and my NASA cap was grabbed off my head and I spun around, and it was Joanna, laughing and—

I jolted around to see nothing but people.

Except I'd heard *her* voice! Bright and sharp and real. For a moment I was thinking, *Where is she? Where did she go?* But how-how-how could she be here? This was all so different and-and-

And wrong!

The intensity washed over me and knocked me sideways and-and-and when I saw couples dancing to a street band it was—

Girls in costume dancing Irish jigs in perfect harmony as—

Music flowed down the street and from bars and restaurants, combining in a maddening cacophony of glorious insanity swirling around me to the point it was suffocating because—

Singing and songs floated from every corner and from within homes, and The Dubliners were there, and Tommy Makem sang "Four Green Fields" and—

I bounced against a brick wall and was jolted by some heavenly aroma and looked around to see sausages and onions offered by vendors off their carts, sizzling and rich as—

Kids grabbed toffee apples off Wellington Street and were made sick by their richness and—

A group of men passed wearing leather chaps and supporters and headdresses and—

I was in my finest trousers, jumper and tie topped by my NASA cap, wandering through it all and the noise of the people and the music and the laughter and stomping feet of dancers was too happy to be real because we were only walking down William with banners and joy and calling for the end to internment and—

Firecrackers exploded near me, followed by hysterical laughter, and my breath went fast and I let out whimpers because they were—

Real bullets tearing through men and boys and red blood flowing and people storming around me and Colm in panic as—

I slammed my head against the wall.

Twice.

I had to stop this collapse into the past. I desperately needed to breathe but couldn't from the noise and realized I hadn't brought my pills with me and I was drowning in the crush of people and the slashing memories and I slid down that wall, my back to it, until I almost fell into a side doorway and could crouch in a shadow and cover my ears to even begin to be able to think, again, as I quaked within and no longer tried to stop it.

Somehow—I don't know how—I managed for my mind to locate a stage of blankness by resting my head on my knees and covering my ears. Short, sharp breaths would burst from me and my heart pounded and every fiber in my being shook. It was too much. Cough.

There was too much. Cough.

So many people. Cough.

So much noise. Cough.

Too deep to swim through. Cough.

"I hear Paul McCartney's in town, recordin' with Linda." It was Vangie's voice drifting in past the chaos.

I said nothing. I think it was the second time she'd told me of this, but I'm not sure. Finally, she put a hand to the back of my neck, cold but gentle, saying, "You okay?"

I managed to shrug and make myself say, "Fine." But it was obvious I was lying.

She curled around to sit on the stoop. "I'm not so sure 'bout that..."

I finally managed to look at her. Shook my head. Said, "There's so bloody much of it. People. Noise."

Memories.

She nodded. "Sensory overload. Happens to the best of us."

I think I chuckled, then words spilled out. "I was-I-I was remembering a celebration. All over my neighborhood. People dancing. Singing. Music and drink and food for all. Wandering about. And it all felt right. It felt joyous and happy and even relieved. It had meaning and intent. But this? This-this-this is just sloppy and so fucking loud and indulgent and—"

Cough.

"Oh, Bren. You been thinkin'."

I'd hardly call it that, but still I shrugged a *yes*.

She laughed. "You don't come to Mardi Gras to think. You come to enjoy life. There's three-hundred and sixty days a year to contemplate the world's deeper meanin' and people's real intentions. Wednesday begins Lent. Self-denial till Easter. People are just partyin' so they can build up enough joy to take 'em through that."

"Sorry. I-I-I guess. I-I'm not used to so much of this...of this enjoyment."

She rose and guided me to my feet. "You need some quiet time. C'mon, I know a place we can go."

She took hold of my jacket and led me up a narrow street to what was barely a pathway lined with houses and cars badly parked. It was so much like the back alleys and side roads of Derry, it was disorienting. There were fewer people about but you could still hear the din from the Quarter, just in a softer mode. The buildings were run down badly, and the bars here were not as packed. Which confused me, for the music from them was just as pleasant and alive. But no one seemed demanding of joy or fun...they were just...just...just being.

Allowed to just be.

We stopped and listened at one small bar as four old black men played the loveliest of melodies in front of a gentle audience. It was bright and happy, and soothing. Just in words I didn't understand.

"This is Creole," Vangie whispered. "These men are masters of it. Song's called, *Je Suis Un Homme d'une Grande Familie*."

"What. What language is it?"

"Creole. There's some French in there."

Joanna knew French. She would have translated for me.

"It's nice," was all I could think to say.

Vangie let the song whisper past us for a while before continuing, "When I'd stay at my auntie's, I'd come down here on warm nights, when the air's so still it's like it doesn't exist. All you can feel is the heat and the tenderness, and between the songs, you can hear the night callers from as far away as Pontchartrain. I'd sip a coke on ice, with lemon, and let the melodies wander through me. This...this is New Orleans. True and alive. Mardi Gras is just one long party for a few days. This is forever."

I nodded and murmured, "It's more like Derry, now."

I walked through the night with "The Banks of Claudy" on my tongue and the murmur of cows irritated I'd awakened them with my pathetic voice.

I leaned against the door frame and rubbed my forehead into it, saying, "I don't want to think." Cough...dammit!

Vangie just cast me a sideways glance. "You said Derry. What part of Ireland is that?"

"North."

"Like Belfast?"

I nodded. "It's also Londonderry."

"Oh." She was quiet for a moment. "Isn't that where a bunch of people were killed? Protesters? Army went after 'em?"

The Para aimed and blood splayed.

I rubbed harder against the frame, nodding. I noticed the music had stopped.

She touched my arm, soft like Joanna once had, and said, "Bren, they're at break for this set. Let's go walkin'."

I nodded and realized I was still holding the orange drink. I hadn't touched it. Its sides were wet with moisture and the fog was settling in, thick and near boiling in the night air—

Like the thickest there could be in Derry and—

It was growing chill, and I was glad for my bomber jacket. I let her draw me down a street. Drifted into the mist.

Let peace grow within me.

Saw how the half-dead buildings began to look elegant and welcoming, as if they were only sleeping, before, as—

The homes were dark, made beautiful by the night's shadows as I wandered by. Homes once with families living there for generations and—

"*This* is like home," I murmured as we strolled through the mist. "Here. This."

"You homesick?"

I huffed a laugh...and fucking coughed. I wanted to say, *No, don't be ridiculous.* But, "Yeah. Never thought I'd be, I was so glad to get away. So glad to have it all behind me."

"I grew up in Houston. Know the city, all over, but I love comin' here. Feels right. Safe. Houston's got a small plantation town mentality in too damn many ways. Some of them hateful. But no matter what, I'd still long for home."

"But you can return. I can't."

"Why not?"

I told myself I shouldn't say anything, but my filters were bolloxed so I murmured, "I fell in love with the wrong girl, and now I'm banished."

"Girl?"

"Yeah."

"Hmph. I thought you and Jeremy..."

At that, I had to laugh. "Everybody keeps trying to put us together. Brothers. Lovers. He's just a good mate."

"Makes more sense."

"Yeah, him being Jewish and me Catholic..."

"That don't mean nothin'."

"It does to *his* mother."

She chuckled. "You sound like Bren, again. Ready to head back? Or if you want, I'll lead you to my auntie's."

"No, I-I-I'll be fine, now."

"You sure?"

I nodded. And coughed. But drew in a deep breath and held it. And kissed her.

Nothing major, just a peck on the cheek.

She laughed and pulled back and said, "Bren, you don't have to prove to me you're straight."

"It's nothing to do with that. Just—thanks. That's all. Talking me down from my madness. I can handle the crowds, now. Even handle being mauled like I was. Christ, I had hands go where no hands have gone, before."

She laughed. "It's 'cause you're cute, cher. *Adorable*."

"Why does that not sound like a compliment?"

She laughed, caressed the line of my chin and gave me a soft peck on the cheek.

I blushed and said, "Don't get close; I'm a hex on people."

She shook her head, sighing. "You're too sweet for that."

Then she took my hand and it was back into the breech.

We suffered through two more days of that madness, crawling into Aunt Catherine's minutes before dawn to collapse on the mattresses. Snoring and roughing it. Men draped over men so much like Eamonn and I had once slept, I welcomed it, while women chattered at all hours. I drank more Hurricanes and was so well polluted by Tuesday morning, I didn't even think to be bothered when one of Vangie's cousins joined me in the shower to share the hot water. A lad named Tavian who was lean and tough and hard, with the face of an angelic demon and skin tanned dark from the waist up.

"Construction," he told me as he soaped up then ran the bar over my chest. "Build ya up. You could so with some."

"I'm happy as I am," I said, taking the shower head to run water over me. The nozzle attached to a hose and hooked just above head level.

Tavian took it from me and rinsed himself off, saying, "You're Houston, right, cher?"

I shrugged a *yes*. He nodded, grinning.

"Been there. Never wanna go back."

"It's better than where I was."

He chuckled and turned the nozzle on me. "Everywhere's better'n where you was, till you're happy with yourself. Then everywhere's just right."

I got out and took my towel as I said, "It's nice to think that."

He followed me, shook the water off in the chilly bathroom, soft-punched my shoulder where Joanna's name was and left, water still trailing down his back. I wrapped the towel around me and came out to find a queue with both of Vangie's brothers and wives in it. They eyed me, wary, and cast a glance after Tavian then back at me.

I just shrugged and said, "The water's still warm, but I'd wait ten minutes for it to be hot."

Then I went to my corner and pulled on clean clothes.

That day was the big parade, with costumes even wilder than I'd already seen. It was a fight to get close enough for a view, but worth the push and tumble of it. Floats were decorated to garish perfection, and coins and beads and candies were tossed to the crowds. I wound up weighted down with near two-dozen strands around my neck and well over twenty doubloons.

And more bloody Hurricanes. By the fourth one, I was wishing for nothing but a Coke or even some piss-water beer.

Wednesday was early mass with ashes. Some did confession, though I did not, and then came the long drive home.

Lon set the cruise control and we glided along at what they called the Double-Nickel. This time I was lying in the back with the kids, half sleeping off all the alcohol in my system. We had pillows, though not enough for all, so parts of me were made use of, as well. I wouldn't have known we'd passed across the Texas state line had a highway patrol car not run up behind us, lights flashing.

We pulled over and I opened one eye to see a man in a tan uniform and what struck me as a cowboy hat pass by, glaring through the back window like he was searching for contraband. No one else in the car stirred, from what I could tell, so I did nothing, as well.

I heard the officer say, "License and registration."

Lon murmured, "What's the problem, sir?"

"Illegal lane change."

Which was bollocks. We'd stayed to the right the whole way since that never-ending bridge, the soft thump-thumping of the tires on the road's joints helping lull me into a near stupor. Cars whipped by us at much greater speeds, the whoosh of them only adding to the sleepiness of my mood.

"Where ya'll headed?" the officer asked.

"Houston."

"Where from?"

"New Orleans. These're my family, my brother and his family, my sister and a friend of hers, from college."

Then the officer gasped and said, "You a police officer?"

"Yes," was Lon's reply.

"In Houston?"

"Six years now."

"Just-just a minute."

He quickly returned to his car, where squawking voices were barely heard, then he returned, his manner much more pleasant.

"Here you go, Sergeant Boudoin. I'll send word down the line."

"Thank you."

Then our car started and we drove off. That's when Vangie's cool voice purred, "*Down the line*. Nice of him."

"You wanna get stopped every twenty miles, or so?" Lon snapped. "Or you wanna get home, tonight?"

She let out a deep sigh and said, "Fine, Lon, fine. Thank God for the Brotherhood."

Neither of them said another word the rest of the drive.

We reached their place just as dark was settling in and piled out of the car. I did a long stretch and quietly asked Vangie about what had happened.

"Cops look out for each other, Bren," she said. "They also look out for black people havin' too much fun or lookin' too prosperous."

"I thought black was African. Does it apply to Cajun?"

She smiled, nearly laughing. "You're such a sweet, innocent boy."

Well...there was the end of that conversation.

I joined them for a light dinner then headed back to the pool house on my Montesa. Got in about eleven, near frozen to death, again, and thought I'd have a nice long hot shower. But the moment I tossed my rucksack on the bed, Uncle Sean came slamming at the door.

"Where you been?" were the first words from his mouth.

"New Orleans," I said, put off by his demanding manner.

"All by yourself?"

"No, I went with friends, if it's any of your business."

"It's very much my business. Who're these friends?"

"Uncle Sean, I don't understand why you're asking—"

"You should've discussed this with me, first."

"Why?"

"We've been in a panic for days, tryin' to find you. Takin' time away from my business. Thought maybe you'd been grabbed and sent back to Ireland."

He was angry. Not as bad as Da would have been, but close to the same level as Ma after I'd gone off to Claudy—and it put my back up, to use a phrase I'd heard.

"Why would that happen? You said I was legal."

"I never said *legal*. I said don't ask about it. Just like I haven't asked how you got a license to drive that goddamn bike, though I got a pretty damn good idea. If you'd been grabbed, you'd have caused us all kinds of trouble."

And there it was. "So I'm *not* legal, in any way?"

He just got angrier. "What the hell do you think? I thought you were smart, Bren. Your visa expired over a year ago! David Landau said to leave it be. Do nothing. You're white so you won't be bothered so long as you keep your head down. But just runnin' off? Not a word to anybody? Us callin' all over town tryin' to find you? Callin' attention to you? If you'd been stopped, it wouldn't take some cop two seconds to figure out you ain't supposed to be here."

Now I was pissed. "So where am I supposed to be?!"

"You're supposed to be as invisible as possible. Runnin' around with a bunch of black people's contrary to that."

"Black people? What're you on about?!"

He hesitated then snapped, "Jeremy came by. Wanted to see if you were back from New Orleans, yet. He wouldn't say anything more, and I know Rene's from there, so I called the shop, yesterday mornin'. Should've called there, first thing, but my wife didn't want to get you in trouble. Instead, I find out you're gone to Mardi Gras with his kids and their families."

"Well, if you knew that, already, then why'd you ask where I was!? Who I was with?"

"You don't get it! A white boy with a bunch of black people—that screams for the cops to ask questions."

"They're Cajun."

"Don't matter! There's only two colors of people in this town, you little shit—white and the rest. You'd be smart to remember that." He turned to the door then stopped and snarled over his shoulder, "Don't ever do somethin' like this, again. If you do, I'll see to it you're sent back."

"Do it!" I snapped back.

That made him turn to me, frowning. "What?"

"Do it!" Now there was a snarl in my voice and not one thought in my head as I spoke. I was burning on some instinct and continued with, "Turn me in. Send me back. Explain to your officials how you had me living under your roof for well over two years and yet had no knowledge I'm *in the country illegally*. Call them now. I won't have this hanging over my head."

"Now you listen to me, you little shit—"

"I didn't ask to come here! I was brought, with no say in the matter, and you treat me like I'm a prisoner."

"We were helpin' you."

"You were helping the IRA keep me hidden, is all! It was that or a bullet to the brain, wasn't it? For botching their stupid bloody operation! Killing someone I loved! Don't threaten me with sending back, because you know bloody well it'd be to my death and that would prove YOU NEVER GAVE A TINKER'S DAMN ABOUT ME, YOU OR ANY OF—!"

He punched me. Sent me crashing to the floor. My ears rang something fierce. I could barely focus on the carpet. Not even Da's fists had brought that much pain to me.

I sort of made out that Aunt Mari had joined us and was saying, "What're you two on about? You can be heard through half the city."

"This selfish little shit doesn't give a damn about anybody but himself."

I forced myself to sit up, my breath short and harsh. There was blood in my mouth. I let it drip over my lips and down my chin as I glared at him and growled, "Make the call."

Both he and Aunt Mari looked at me, her confused, him not.

"You have a phone," I continued, my voice low and cruel. "Turn me in. Send me back to Derry. Do it, or bloody well shut up about it!"

Uncle Sean's fists bunched and he started at me, again, but Aunt Mari spun him around and ushered him out. She came back to me, wet a towel, and started to clean the blood from my face but I pushed away from her.

I felt betrayed. Brutalized. I'd begun to build up a new world, not understanding it was on sand. Just untold lies and half-truths and no real foundation to steady me. And now I was being treated like some fool worth nothing because I hadn't understood that. I could think of nothing pleasant to say to her.

Her voice was soft as she said, "Bren, he was worried for ya."

I wiped some blood from my lip. "I can tell."

Her Irish caught up and her voice grew sharp. "Ya could have left us a note to let us know where ya were. It wasn't right for ya to just disappear, like that."

Ma slapped me, over and over, screaming, "Where've you been?"

"So it's *my* fault."

"What did ya think? Yer mother told me ya could be like this, always off to yerself, doin' as ya wanted, but I never thought ya'd throw everything we've done to help ya aside without a thought. If ya'd—if ya'd just told us this is what ya were plannin', we could've told ya what problems it might cause."

"And you'd have told me I couldn't go, is that it?"

"It was a foolish thing to do. Yer here for yer own protection."

Still all my fault. Bloody fucking hell. "It may be best I leave."

"No." That had startled her. "No, here yer safe."

"So long as I remain a ghost? There but not really there? Here but not really here? *Don't you dare to live, Brendan, it might cause trouble.* What sort of life is that?"

"It won't always be like this."

"Never promise what you can't deliver, Aunt Mari."

"Why're ya bein' so contrary? All was goin' well, as it was." Her voice so filled with hurt, it cut through my anger.

I sat up, legs crossed, took the wet cloth from her and cleaned my face as I said, "Going well, so long as I kept to being your prisoner."

"Brendan!"

"What else would you call it? Keeping me here, locked away. A form of solitary that isn't but is. So long as I stay to myself, all is fine. But then I broached the rules. Unwritten rules. And now I see the four walls around me. I'm fine to work. Fine to fix things. Fine to have acquaintances. Or friends, so long as they're friends you *approve* of. No lovers. No life."

I looked at her in a way I know was cruel and hard; I saw the soft flinch in her jaw and eyes. It had no effect on me. I was like ice when I asked, "How long is my sentence?"

She shook her head, saying, "That-that's not what this is about."

"Isn't it? My brother's in Long Kesh, courtesy of Her Majesty's finest. But even his time has a limit. Does mine?"

"Yer not in a jail!"

"What else would you call it?! Are the bars any less solid and cold when put in place by family?"

"I told ya, it's not forever. But ya don't understand this town, Brendan. It's a different world to the one yer used to. It was years before I fully understood how the city works, and yer uncle—he just wants to protect ya."

Which was a lie as bold as I'd ever heard. And coming from my aunt, it cut even deeper. So deep, I dared not say a word in response. I just looked away. Felt the cut to my lip was growing sore but had clotted.

I rose to my feet and went to the sink to rinse out the cloth. Give me something to focus on. Something else to think about.

But all I could see was that I was a living ghost.

I had no idea what to think or say about it. My mind drifted into complete silence. I just knew that once again I was being told by others who I could and could not be around.

I actually chuckled then murmured, "I guess I should read *Jane Eyre* and learn more about my situation."

"Brendan."

"Who're you talking to, Aunt Mari? That's no more my name. You told me so, yourself."

"I thought ya understood."

"So did I. More the fool, me."

She could think of nothing more to say, so rose and left. I didn't look at her. Just heard the door close. As if nothing had happened. Just let things be. Let the boys calm down and maybe it will all work out.

And I knew that is how she wanted our lives to continue.
As if nothing had happened.
But for me, everything had changed.

Prisoner

Wariness slammed into my head. While I was fair certain Uncle Sean would not make the call to send me back, as the danger to himself and his expanding business would be far too great, no matter how knowledgeable or connected David Landau was...I needed some clarity before I made my next step. I grant you, I'd heard enough real threats in my life to know when one was hollow, but still I kept my movements careful.

A couple days later, one of Mairead's letters arrived, and for all my happiness at being away from God-forsaken Derry, I still loved to hear the updates on my family. Now more than ever, to remind me of where I'd come from. Give me at least something of an anchor to who I once was. I didn't want to lose that, yet.

Bits in the papers and on the nightly news continued to reference the violence all over the North, with bombings on a near daily basis. No one seemed to catch the lesson that such things only increased the anger and need for revenge, as Protestants were murdered by the IRA, PIRA and INLA while Catholics were murdered by the UUUC, UVF, UDR, Tara and SDA and every other variation on the alphabet. God, himself, couldn't have kept track of them all.

Direct rule became permanent, with London making decisions for a land hundreds of miles away that suffered from the idiotic decisions London had made fifty years earlier. Now there was no possibility of power sharing to be allowed by either side. No shock there. I think the only surprising aspect was the fight between PIRA and OIRA over who would best represent the Catholic population they both were bleeding dry. Wolves fighting over a flock of sheep.

Not that the Loyalists weren't like rabid dogs fighting each other, but they were well-protected by those using them to maintain their power.

Mairead wrote that Eamonn had finally been released from Long Kesh only to be immediately re-arrested under the Special Powers Act.

The new charge? Conspiracy to commit terrorist acts, putting him right back where he was. Apparently, they noticed he was not as low-level as they thought, and since the case against his weapons-running was falling apart on appeal, the Crown just started over. This time using what little they knew of his activities inside the prison to better hone their lies.

Rhuari was sinking deeper into his books, never mentioning how often he was rousted by the Army or RUC. Even when Mai called and it was him who answered, he'd allow as little information as possible, to her, and hand the phone straight over to Ma. It was Maeve who knew all and reported all in an anger that was founded not only in self-righteousness but cold control. Even at the age of fifteen, she had learned from Ma how to focus her words in ways that made even the RUC uncomfortable.

As follows, from Mai:

Maeve was off to a shop up the Strand Road when a fit young constable, who apparently fancied himself quite the lad, paced her with his jeep and became, as she says, too familiar with his words. Offered to take her to a nice private cell. Rather than curse him, she'd kept walking, saying, "Y'know, if I get put up the pole by you, I'll know how to prove it's your child and I'll have the courts force you to provide for me and the wain till she's of age. Wouldn't that be lovely?"

He shouted, "Stupid Taig cunt, dunno what you're talkin' about."

"Blood tests, ya dumb fuck," she'd said. "Read up on HLS testing and how they've begun restricting enzymes and can now identify the parents of any child. I wonder how many bastards you've spread about? Should be fun proving you're daddy to half of Catholic Derry."

"What bollocks!"

"No, it's science. Education. You can read about it in the library. You do know what one of those is? Or are you the type, you never opened a book through all your school days?"

"You need to shut the fuck up, you fuckin' slag."

"I'm aimed to be a Sister, and it may well be someday I'll be the one caring for you when you've been brought in with your tadger cut off from having raped one too many girls. Make you a lass instead of a lad."

He'd bolted from the jeep and slapped her. In front of not only a nearby army patrol, which wouldn't have been much of a deal, but a number of women, who began raising bloody hell. It looked to them as if he'd attacked her without cause, and something had to be done about it or there would be a female riot. It got so loud and angry, the patrol had to come over to quiet things down, and a supervisor got called in.

And our Maeve played it up, half-lying across the ground, blood streaming from her nose, a look of pain and disbelief on her face, all of it caught by a photographer for the Times! It was a nice mini-scandal. What's better? The craic is, that constable wound up transferred to Armagh, where no one would care what he did to whom. Or what was done to him if he dared do it.

I actually chuckled when I read it.

In the same letter:

Not to be outdone, Ma's been caught up in a couple of protests, and was interviewed for some BBC program during one. She touted it long and hard. Poor Ma. Her comments were short and meant nothing, and it was presented on a Sunday morning program, so was little viewed. But you'd think she was an international celebrity, the way she goes on about it. I've kept an eye out on the local news, but there's little dealing with The North available on Canadian television.

On a side note, Maeve revealed Rhuari's now speaking the Irish with a priest who comes twice a month from the Republic. There's talk of a school for the Irish in Derry, much like the one in Belfast, but no one seems to have direct knowledge of it. I think it would be too late for him; it's meant for primary and up. And if he's planning to teach it, he's years from being able to.

But knowing this helped me pull from Rhuari that he <u>has</u> applied to Queens to stand for a degree in teaching, so one never knows. As for Maeve, she is serious about the possibility of nursing school.

Kieran is quite out of control. Father Jack's been brought in to ferry him to school, as he won't attend, otherwise, and that seems to be making an improvement. I offered to have him come live with us and attend the local school with his cousins, but neither Ma nor he seem interested.

Now I have a bit of craic to pass along. I've heard that Father Demian—you remember him; he was the priest at Da's funeral—he was shot and badly wounded in Nottingham, a few months back. Some lad came up to the door, he opened it and the lad shot him in the gut. Or lower, if one story is correct. Maeve told me of this, and she's trying to find out more.

In another letter:

I got a post from Maeve that Rhuari is seeing a lass from Pennyburn, off Bruncrana. They met during orientation at Queens, or registration or something; she's not clear about that. But it does mean he's been accepted. By the saints, getting information from him is like finding a chicken feather in a goose down pillow. But if anyone can do it, our Maeve can. Ma doesn't even know about the lass, yet.

Now us. We're looking at a house in the Scarborough area, to purchase, with a good-size yard and room for us all. Better schools. Uncle Shamus has contacts with a couple realtors so we should find something soon. I hope so. Michael Paul starts his first year, in September, and Jordan Allwyn begins kindergarten. Toronto is exploding and they along with it. I can't believe they're growing up so fast.

She'd included photos of two healthy-looking lads with thick hair and more their father's looks than hers. With them were photos of little Aisling Marie and her latest, Stephen Gregory. All looking happy and more than well-cared for. Nothing hidden in their eyes, that I could see.

There was also a photo of Uncle Shamus and his wife and brood—five girls—all lovely in a simple way. He bore no resemblance to Ma but I could see aspects of Rhuari in him. The manner in which he stood, like he wanted no bother from anyone.

I compared it to another snap Aunt Mari had hanging on a wall, of Eamonn, Mairead, and myself standing before Ma and Da, with Rhuari as a baby in Ma's arms. Mai's eyes were bright and hopeful, as always, while mine were stark and cold, like I was looking for an escape route. Da's hands rested on Eamonn's shoulders, and I'd say my brother was trying to hide how afraid he was. It was not a happy photo, worse even than the one taken at Da's wake, and it haunted me.

Mai's letter continued:

Overall we're doing well, up here, though there are times I miss Derry something terrible. The neighbors and the craic and the corner bars and the like. But Tur and Gerald are discussing a second shop, already. And Uncle Shamus is in great demand, with his cabinets. Once that was raised as a possibility, I told him we were making a trip to visit all of you in Houston, his pick of June or July. We'll set the date, shortly, and my four will be with us.

If it's no bother for us to stay with you, Aunt Mari.

And the answer was to be *of course not*. So it was arranged for them to come in mid-July. I suggested she warn them of the brutal heat in Houston, but I don't think she mentioned it.

I wanted to write Mairead as Brennan, her cousin twice removed—or three, whatever. Fill her in on my new world instead of Aunt Mari doing it. If she did. See if I could find out more about the circumstances of me being shipped here. But she never would tell me the address. And the post came when I was off working. So I figured I'd have to wait till she came down to visit.

Fortunately, I still had some contact with patience.

I continued to work at Trujillo's, and Rene treated me almost as a son. Hugo and Tomas called me the shop favorite, as if it had nothing to do with my being better at the repairs than they. I laughed and shrugged it off. I'd been through worse with Diarmaid taking credit for my work.

What they didn't know was, I'd become friends with Vangie, and I think this was her father's way of keeping an eye on me. For when he sensed I was planning to meet up with her after work, I'd suddenly get the hardest and dirtiest cars assigned to me. Then I'd have to go home and get cleaned beforehand, so we'd have to meet later than I liked, and by ten I'd be knackered.

A couple times I even fell asleep in a film we were watching, half from being tired and half because she liked these foreign things with subtitles where next to nothing happens. Swedish and French and Italian and Japanese. Christ, there was one—wasn't even a new film— where this man and woman walked around talking and talking and talking, in French, about something that happened last year. Maybe. That one—I actually may have snored, she finally started going to those with Jeremy, only. Which Rene didn't mind because he'd figured out Jeremy was gay.

As for my aunt and uncle, I think they believed their threats had put me in my place, and I did nothing to change their assumption. I would always tell them when I was going out, so as to remind them that I was on their leash, like bloody Angus when out for a walk. And as Jeremy was also friends with Vangie, it was always him I was meeting.

I think it finally bothered them, for one Saturday Aunt Mari said to me, "You needn't tell us every time yer goin' somewhere, Bren."

"Don't want you to think I'm gonna vanish, again," I'd replied, and not in a kind way.

She had looked away, hurt. I almost apologized, but Uncle Sean was close by, glaring at me. He knew my information was for his benefit, so I shrugged and left.

As for the B-Girls, whether I liked it or not there was no way to shake those little terrors. At least I was able to keep them focused on ice skating and shopping for me some new clothes. It still seemed I was naught but a human doll to them, in many ways.

But then Brandi turned thirteen and I sensed more was happening. She would take my hand, at times. Then Berni would then take the other. Or if we hopped out for lunch at this cafe near the River Oaks Theater, they would order the same salad and each offer me a bite. At the same time. Almost as if daring me to say yes to one and not the other. I'd accept neither, to be safe.

Then came an occasion where Scott, in his wicked mode, suggested they ask one of their friends' older sisters to come by to *become acquainted*. Oh, they shot that down fast.

"We're not matchmakers," said Berni.

"And the only girls I know like that are too superficial," Brandi added. Apparently, she'd been reading the dictionary.

Berni nodded. "*So* much makeup. What're they trying to hide?"

"Exactly. And the old lady dresses?"

"Oh, they are, aren't they?"

"And I think they all do single blouses, no layering!"

"Pathetic. Don't they even try to keep up? I've never even seen one with a triangular scarf."

"They use square ones you have to fold, like their mothers do."

"Totally pathetic."

"And you want to hand Bren off to one of them?!"

"Honestly, Scott, I thought you liked him."

I just looked at him and shrugged, and he stayed quiet about it from then on. Smart of him.

I think he knew I was seeing Vangie, when he made the suggestion, and was just playing the maggot. After all, he and Jeremy were mates and never once did I ask Jere to keep silent about it. But I couldn't read his intentions so just ignored anything he said that might have seemed like he was trying to make trouble. Like a comment from him at dinner, once, about this new perfume he could smell on me. Which made Aunt Mari cast me a look and Uncle Sean tighten up.

But to my shock, Brandi shot him down with, "Honestly, Scott, we've been trying for months to get Bren to stop using Right Guard as his scent."

"And you want to make fun of our work?" Berni added.

He actually went into shock, I think.

I couldn't tell if those two knew I was dating and were supporting me or just being contrary with him.

Of course, I couldn't read Evangelyne, either. Couldn't tell if she knew I truly liked her. Not as I had Joanna, to be sure, but as a fellow traveler. First a friend and maybe more. I didn't know. I mostly enjoyed being near her. But whether she understood that or if she was merely being cool, I had no idea. For not once did she hint at anything more than friendship.

But dear God, the calmness and understanding in her. The lack of pretense. The good humor. Most of all, her acceptance of the world as it was. Some would call it sophistication; to me, it was a casual tolerance for the stupidity of others coupled without a willingness to let them have any form of control over her.

It was brought home to me when we were waiting for Jeremy at the Galleria before heading in to see *Funny Lady*. I got there early and Vangie showed, soon after, so we went into a shop to waste some time till he arrived. I was thinking of a new wallet but the prices in that place were horrifying, so I was just standing around frowning at some very expensive boots as she checked out some purses when I heard, "What d'you think you're doing?"

Actually pronounced *What yew thank yer doin'*.

I looked around and it was an older saleswoman with yellow hair puffed into the size of a bowling ball speaking. She'd grabbed hold of Vangie and her expression was not kind. Nor was her voice.

Vangie was calm and easy. "I'm checkin' to see how many pockets there are, inside. Not enough, but thank you."

"Yeah, well, I got my eye on you." Again, pronounced, *Way-ell, ah got mah ah on yew*. Christ the way some of these people said things.

I went over, confused. "Vangie, what's up?"

"It's nothin', Bren. Let's go."

The saleswoman eyed me with shock. "Yew with herrr?"

I frowned and nodded. "Aye, she's a friend."

"She-yit," the bitch spit, "a waht boa-eh an' his bla-yack hoore."

Now *that* told me exactly what was up. A switch flicked on the beast inside me and I growled, "What the fuck'd you just say?"

The woman jolted and backed away, because I'm sure the look on my face was not kindly. But Vangie grabbed my arm and pulled me to the entrance.

"Bren, let's go," she snapped. "Come on. We gotta meet Jeremy."

I glanced between her and the bitch and thought for a moment to still make an issue of it, but Vangie's look was not as forgiving as I'd have expected. So I huffed and we left.

We were rounding the corner to the theater when Vangie snapped, "What the hell were you doin' in there?"

"The things she said—" I started, but she cut me off.

"She's an ignorant fool from Katy, who's never gonna do better than minimum wage. I'm way better than her and she knows it. That's why people like her do stupid things like that. I refuse to let those fools get to me in any way, shape or form. They aren't worth it."

I had nothing to say, in response. If Vangie didn't care about that sort of nonsense, who was I to say otherwise? Only she wasn't done with me.

"Now, if there's anything I do NOT need," she snarled, "it's some silly little white boy thinkin' he's gonna protect me like some silly little girl. Knight in shinin' armor showin' off how *not racist* he is for all the world to see. That the kind of complex you got?"

All right, that was enough.

"You think I'm racist?" I snapped. "I was angry because I was part of her nastiness."

That did not help the situation. "And what exactly is that supposed to mean? You upset because she thought you were with a woman who's black?"

The question flummoxed me. "I-I-I don't see you as that and—"

And I coughed. Dammit.

"What *do* you see me as?" And it was not asked kindly.

My brain was bouncing everywhere by this point, and all I could think to say was, "You-you're Vangie. Evangelyne. Boudoin. A-a-a woman who's doing a far sight better with her life than I am, mine. I really don't understand what the problem is, here."

She blinked, and I think she was startled. "But I thought you were doin' exactly what you wanted."

"I am!" Then I shrugged, even more confused, and added, "Partly. I-I-I don't really feel like I'm me own man, sometimes, but I got no question about you. I've nothing but admiration for you, on that. I like being around you."

"Why?"

I just shook my head and whispered, "I don't know. I have no answer for you. You just—you seem in control of your life while mine is madness. Maybe I'm just trying to figure out how you do it."

Her calm, even smile returned and she almost chuckled. "Oh, Bren. Don't put that much on me."

"I-I-I'm sorry for what I did." I said that, not really knowing what it was I was apologizing for.

She seemed to understand, for she caressed my face and said, "It's okay. But the next time some fool pulls some crap with me, let me handle it my way. I've been livin' in this town my whole life. I know how things work here, and you raisin' hell over some racist bitch sayin' what half the city believes is only gonna make things a hell of a lot nastier for us all. Okay?"

I nodded, even though I still was not clear on what she meant. But then we saw Jeremy entering from the garage and went to join him.

Still, I could not put my confusion aside, for what I'd told her was the truth. She *was* doing much better with her life than I was, and I had finally caught an idea of what Father Jack was getting at with me. And what I'd almost begun to believe when I was around Joanna. That I'd put limits on myself with no concern for whether or not they were valid. Yes, I still wanted nothing more than a decent job and family, and no question I would always be good at fixing things. But why did those have to be my only goals? Why couldn't I learn how to design cars and go to work for British Leyland or Jaguar? The crap they put out could use some common sense in how they're put together. Who was stopping me, other than myself?

Vangie was learning the Russian. That meant a lot of study and patience, for it was a whole new alphabet and structure. Like Jeremy and his Chinese. Oh, the fun they would have over burgers at Poppo's, cursing each other in their respective languages while I sat like a fool, listening.

An ignorant fool.

Unworthy of either.

Why not go off and learn French or Spanish or even Swahili, just to say I have? Not everything had to be for a reason, even considering the constraints now put on me.

What brought it home clear to me was Everett, when he dropped by the house with the oil painting he did of the family. It was in rich shades of browns and gold, with Uncle Sean and Aunt Mari flanking the B-Girls and Scott beside them. A lovely work that wound up in pride of place over the mantlepiece, with the B-Girls making sure there were appropriate knick-knacks placed about it.

"You can't put that vase there! It's too tall!"

"Oh, those figurines take away from the painting."

"Flowers? Really? They die so quick and we don't want that."

"Oh, I saw the perfect carved crystal at Sakowitz."

"I remember that. It's Lalique, isn't it?"

"Yes, and clear so it won't distract."

"And it was only a hundred dollars!"

And in unison they cried, "Mom, can we go to Sakowitz?"

I stayed to one side, watching Everett enjoy the hell out of their little drama. Aunt Mari did, as well, and it went a great long way to making her even happier to have him around, though Uncle Sean remained stand-offish.

Rett still had a devil of a time accepting the kind words sent his way. As if he was embarrassed by anyone thinking him worthy of praise. I asked him about it as we headed out to his barge of a Chrysler, after dinner.

He'd shaken his head and sighed, "You need more of an ego than I got to be a real artist."

"Why is that?" I'd asked, and truly did not know what he meant.

"You gotta believe you got somethin' to say. Somethin' that's important to the world and has to be seen."

"Aren't you happy with how the portrait turned out?"

"You didn't see how many times I started over. All the mistakes I made and had to cover up. Compared to Sargent, I'm still working in crayons."

I had to shake my head at that. "Well, I just know that if there had been anything wrong with that work, those two little devils would have torn it to shreds with five words. Instead, they're arguing over nick-nacks."

He'd laughed and said, "Right about that. No, it's just been a rough week at work, that's all. Had two ad campaigns completely restructured at the last minute because *I didn't present a head of lettuce correctly*." He snorted. "Drove me nuts."

"Sounds like you're ready for another job?" And I deliberately put it as a question.

He'd sighed and said, "This is all I'm really good for."

"Rett, my cousins put the lie to that."

"You're sweet, and I understand it..." He unlocked his car and opened the door then just leaned against the roof. "It's hard to get worked up to do what you want to when you're trapped in a situation."

That hit me and I coughed. Then made myself say, "Drawing vegetables into advertisements?"

He chuckled. "I love the way you said that. *Ad-VER-tiss-ments.* Makes it sound like it means somethin'."

That's when Scott roared up with Jeremy; he'd come in, from Austin, that morning. They stopped in the drive and popped out of the car's windows.

"Hey, Bren," Scott yelled, though he didn't need to. "We're gonna grab a burger and go see *Great Waldo Pepper.* You up for it?"

"I just ate, but I'll have some ch—fries," I said. Then I had one of my more brilliant thoughts and jumped around to face Everett. "Rett, make a painting of Jeremy and his family! His father's a doctor. His mother's a CPA. His uncle's a lawyer in Austin and Washington. They could get word out about you." I dragged him over to the GTO, saying, "Oi, here's a true artist. He did that painting of me and just brought one over of your family, Scott."

"Cool!" Scott cried then he nudged Jeremy. "Let's take a look."

They rushed inside, and while I don't know much about gay men, I did notice Everett cast Scott only a polite smile, while it warmed greatly when he looked at Jeremy.

And was returned, in kind.

My China convinced his brothers and sister to pay Everett to do a portrait of their parents for their anniversary. As a thank you, he fixed dinner for Jeremy and me, when my China brought photos of the family for him to use. I brought Vangie—well, we both brought her, officially—and the two of them got along fine. She loved his home. *His condo,* as she put it.

He made a beef wellington with asparagus and creamed—no, *mashed* potatoes and a brown gravy. Paired with a good wine and what he called a sorbet for dessert—really just raspberry ice—but I did find it hard to keep from asking for brown sauce.

He then did sketches of all three of us, but Vangie was the only one allowed to take hers with her; mine and Jeremy's went in his book—his *portfolio.* A large valise filled with sketches of faces he'd done, all of them amazing in quality and depth.

From that day, Everett was part of our little group.

On the surface he seemed happy, but now I could see he was still living alone and working at a job he did not love. Ten years older than me—or eleven—and feeling limited.

"I don't really have what you'd call good friends," he told me, not long after. "A lot of people I know, but nobody real close."

I was at his condo waiting on Vangie and Jeremy. We were going to see *Day of the Locust* then have dinner at Bennigan's. He was on the couch, sipping some wine; I was stretched out on that easy chair, with a beer.

"All the years you've been here?" I asked.

He shrugged. "I'm not easy with people. You're the first person I've met that I want to know better." Then he quickly added, "Just *know*, not be with. Know, like Evangelyne. She's mellow."

I had to chuckle at that. "When she wants to be."

He only smiled. "And Jeremy's nice. Lovely boy. I've caught your expression in his eyes a couple times. I guess it's what happens to kids in war?"

I just drew in a deep breath and shrugged.

He nodded. "Still careful. Like me. Nobody my age. Nobody gay, like me. It's almost like I'm scared of 'em." He hesitated then added, "You had friends, I bet. Back home."

I shrugged. "I thought so. But people change and...and soon you don't know them, anymore."

"Have you?"

"Maybe." Then I huffed a laugh. "Probably."

"I haven't. I'm still that scared sixteen-year-old kid out on the street." He cast me a side eye. "You'd never do that to me, would you, Pug? Cast me out?"

I shook my head. "It'd be like kicking Angus, and I don't believe in abusing animals." Then I cast him a wink.

He chuckled. "Yeah, that's me. Shaggy ol' dog, beggin' for pets."

"Wasn't how I meant it."

"I know. I know. It's just me in a mood."

"You rather stay in? We can see the movie tomorrow or Sunday. I could pop to Kroger's and get some things..."

He shook his head. "I like the distraction. Like running out and around with the-the three of you."

Then we heard Vangie's Civic run up, outside and we both sighed and got ready for another evening of togetherness.

So Everett was feeling lonely. It made sense. I'd seen him just stand still and look at nothing, for a bit. More than once, lately. And he still had nothing good to say about his work. Well, that was not what I wanted for myself, not now or even when I reached his age. But I began to wonder if that had been what I was truly aiming for?

Nothing much; just an existence. That's all I'd been living the last few months, life on hold till I could talk to my sister, person to person.

Then that night, as we trouped back into his condo at one in the morning, all of us feeling groovy—and I care not what the B-girls say about that word—I saw him give Jeremy one of the same looks he'd given me.

As did Vangie.

"What was holdin' Everett back?" she'd asked shortly after, when we were headed to her car. "Jeremy likes him."

"Does he?" I'd asked.

"C'mon, Bren, you must've seen it."

"Well, I'm no matchmaker. When he's ready—or when Jere is— they'll connect."

"I bet they already have."

That stopped me. We were next to her little Civic, my Montesa behind it. "What makes you think that?"

She glanced back at Everett's place, smiling. "Wasn't Jere right behind us?"

I realized he hadn't followed us out. I had to chuckle. "You think?"

"I would not be surprised." Then she gave me a peck on the cheek, got in her Civic and left me to wonder. I stuck around for five minutes more, but no Jeremy, so I shrugged and went home.

I guess she was right.

Connection

I continued to see Vangie through February and March into April. *Just meeting as friends*. Going to discos, where she was the much better dancer. Films. Dinner. A few times, I'd join her family for an evening—but only at Rene's request. On those occasions, as the B-girls had once made a big deal about taking a gift when invited to someone's home, I usually carried down a bottle of rum. That went over *very* well, with Rene and Louisa, both.

I grew to know Arnie well enough for him to actually look at me with a near smile instead of a scowl. He even sat by me, once, and let me cut up his meat. Then he insisted I watch him eat it. Apparently, that was his seal of approval.

"He gets locked in his own little world, sometime," Rene told me.

All I did was shrug an okay.

One Saturday, Vangie drove the three of us down to Galveston and we walked around a town that was decaying, at best. Though it did have a nice enough beach and waterfront, Castlerock is far lovelier. The houses not as drab and gray. A feeling of joy about it instead of depression. And the water seemed bluer there than here. But it was a pleasant day, and Arnie tired himself out bounding around in the sand so slept in the back seat on the drive home. Which was good, because it took near two hours, the 45 was so backed up.

One night after a film, I took her by *The Colonel's*, and introduced her to Todd and Lorraine, who was now full-time. Rocky had not been replaced.

Todd was unchanged from the last time I'd seen him, except for his hair being longer and straighter, if that was possible. He shook Vangie's hand, then as she headed for a table held me back to ask, "Your uncle told you anything 'bout havin' the place redone? He had people in here measurin' things. Down the strip center."

I shook my head. "He doesn't share his plans with me. I don't think he even shares them with my aunt."

"Be nice to know if I gotta start lookin' for another job. Been a while since—I mean, I been here six years. Near seven. I got no idea what's goin' on, out there."

"Todd, this place wouldn't be *The Colonel's* without you."

"I don't think he wants it to be, no more."

Then he'd started prepping our order.

Lorraine brought Vangie's white wine and my Shiner Bock with a special flourish of her tray. Her bangles clicked softly along her arms as she laid down little napkins instead of cork coasters.

"Our new thing," she said. "Touch of class." Then her voice went conspiratorial as she leaned in close and muttered, "For this place?" She'd huffed a laugh.

"Miracles happen," I'd smiled.

She'd giggled and wandered away.

Vangie shook her head at me. "You worked here?"

"For a few month."

"Why'd you leave?"

I hesitated then grinned. "I went to work with your Da." Which was not a lie, really.

She'd chuckled and sipped her wine as I took a swallow of beer and we'd sat and talked about nothing.

It's funny, but no memories of Rocky or that night came at me. It was as if they'd never existed. I could still have the occasional flash back to a thought about Joanna, when sparked by something similar, but my connection with Rocky had been so fleeting, I don't think it had a chance to bury itself in my heart. I'd grieved for her; that was enough.

Through all this time, it was not until a cool Saturday night, early in May, that I had Vangie back to the pool house. Probably the last till November. You could smell the heat building in the city. Feel the thickness growing in the air. But there was breeze enough to minimize it, laced with none of the *glorious aromas* from Pasadena or Texas City, for a change.

While I was still set to talk with Mairead about my situation, I'd also asked Jeremy to let me know when his uncle was next in town. I wanted to speak with him about a *legal matter*. Confidentially, of course. Facts and information were never bad to have, and if my uncle wouldn't make me legal, perhaps an attorney could. I had money enough to pay for one, I thought. And it was time to settle who and what I was, here. If Uncle Sean wouldn't do it, I'd handle it myself.

Turned out, David Landau was bringing his family to visit on the July Fourth holiday, as well. And even better? He was open to speaking with me. Since he was Uncle Sean's attorney, I'm sure he had an idea of what I'd be asking. But I'd requested confidentiality, so I wasn't the least concerned that Uncle Sean would find out what I was up to. I was feeling more in control and starting to think of plans for my future.

Vangie and I had dinner at Vinicius' parents' restaurant, a plain open space with simple tables and food the like of which would feed you just off the aroma, along with a couple glasses of wine. So we both were in fine spirits as she drove me home, and made a bit of sport of me, on the way, saying, "You ever gonna get your own car?"

"I'm working on something," I'd replied, grinning.

"What kind you lookin' at?"

That struck me silent, for a second. "I don't know. I like Uncle Sean's Volvo, so maybe something like that. They're easy to repair. I'm not so impressed with the Gremlin, he's got. It's already giving him trouble, but he's not a light driver so it may not be the car's fault."

"What about a Civic?"

"Too new, for me. Couldn't afford one. I'm also thinking maybe of a Jeep. Mr. Trujillo just sold one that's six years-old for a decent price. They're basic, but reliable."

"Reliable in that you get a backache if you drive anywhere in one."

"But they're the car won World War Two, according to your father. So I might be able to get one from Army Surplus."

"That sounds pretty cheap-ass."

I laughed. "That's the point. I'd go for a Sprite, but they're the devil to work on. Same for MGs. And Beetles have no power. I rather like the Toyota Corona."

"Which one's that?"

"Sort of slopes forward in the front. Boxy-lookin'."

"Oh, yeah. Those're cute."

"And they're fair comfortable. One got brought to us for body work, and I drove it around the lot. Seems a good car."

By this point we were to the house, so I said to Vangie, "Come on in, I'll show you me digs. I got some wine, too."

She nodded and parked and followed me through the gate to the pool house. It was past eleven, so we kept our voices soft. Uncle Sean would be at *Liam's Trough*, right then. Or maybe the *Tricolor*, his first bar. Probably till after two; they'd been having problems with the till in one or the other and he was checking on it. What was best? Not even a huff from Angus.

"I thought boys all want sports cars," she whispered as we walked up the gravel drive. "Like Mustangs or Camaros."

"A Barracuda?" I murmured. "Nice, but they're with a three-speed gear box, aren't they?"

"No idea. I looked at one from Sixty-seven and it was automatic. Little V8. Almost bought it, but I was gonna do so much commutin', I went with the Civic. Great mileage, and so glad I got it, now."

I nodded in agreement, unlocked the door and led her into the pool house. The first words from her were, "Man, you were sure of yourself."

"What d'you mean?" I asked her.

"Look at this joint, so clean and cool. Like you're expectin' company."

I looked around and honestly had no idea what she meant. It was tidy, sure, but hardly what I'd call clean. All I said was, "Dunno why you said that. Tomorrow's my cleaning day."

"Your cleanin' day?"

"Yeah. Every Sunday." I stopped short of telling her I'd been raised this way and had become more-so since first seeing Joanna. Even kept my part of the boys' room as neat as I could, and it extended to here, without a thought. That Vangie should make such an issue of it surprised me. Maybe that was why boys back home had called me looner. Seems being so focused on clean wasn't what people normally are like. Like Scott bringing home months worth of laundry instead of a week's worth, now, and his room being in a state. Or Uncle Sean and that bloody Gremlin, and enough said about that.

But then Aunt Mari was neat about her home. And the girls were the same. And thinking of it, Mai had helped Ma keep the old hovel we'd lived in from being too far gone. Then with the new house, both had focused double hard. Her, even while working her job and pregnant, while Ma had fussed that she, herself, had been worked to the bone.

So I just added a shrug and said, "I can't live in filth."

She looked at my shelf of projects as she said, "So you're a Felix."

It took me a moment to understand she was referring to a character on a TV show. What was it called? *The Weird Couple*? I'd only seen an episode or two, but American humor really did nothing for me. Mainly because I didn't understand half the jokes.

"Is that a problem, then?" I asked as I motioned to the bean bags. I said it only for fun. Her dark eyes gave no hint of disparagement or distance, but instead were sharp on me in a way I found made my heart's rhythm increase.

She floated down to one then dropped her purse. Her skirt whispered around her legs, trying to find just the right position to make her look her best. As if she could ever look anything less. Nails as red as her lips. Her hair gliding about her face, framing it in ways that only added to her loveliness. I froze at the sight of her, lost in just appreciating the picture she made.

Until she leaned forward and asked, "Bren, you really gay, too?" Her voice was so sure the answer was, *Yes*, I actually wondered if I was.

I sat against a stool by the counter, almost laughing. "So being clean makes me a poofter, is that it?"

"*Poofter*?"

"Man who likes men."

She shrugged and continued with, "I don't care one way or the other, but if the only reason you're seein' me is to lay a fake trail..."

I laughed. "What the devil is it with you Americans? I'm neat, I don't run about cussing up women and yakking about your football, I got no problem with men like Jeremy or Everett likin' me, I enjoy bein' around a woman who isn't blonde, and that makes me queer?"

"I've never seen you with any other girls, and Everett's definitely interested in you."

I put up my hand to stop her. "As I said, he's a friend, and a good one. But he's nothing to me, that way. And now that he's with Jeremy..."

"Only because he looks like you."

Shite. I had to admit, I'd wondered about that. Apparently, it was obvious to her, as well. So I said, "I just don't see it. I'm Catholic, he's Jewish. I'm Irish; he's American."

"It's not religion or sociology, Bren; it's appearance."

"I still can't see it. As for girls, I've been here not even three years and you've known me for but a few month. Rest assured, I've been with others." I wondered if I should suggest she ask Hugo, but I decided it's best not to. Don't want to be seen as a chatty lad.

But she had to ask, "How many? Girls. How many?"

Nosy little thing, wasn't she? But in response I held up five fingers and whispered, "That's all you'll get from me."

"C'mon, Bren, you can trust me. Haven't you taken even one walk on the wild side?"

This was starting to get my back up, for there was no way I would reveal what happened with me and Jere. "Why do you keep asking me that?"

"The way you look at Jeremy, sometimes. Like he could be more than just a buddy."

I shot back with, "Have *you* taken that walk? Like with a girl?" Her response was to merely offer up that cryptic smile, which I took to mean, *Yes*. "Oh! Well. There's an image'll stay in my mind for a while." I turned away, mainly so I could get a moment's respite from her steady gaze. It was starting to make my heart race, and my cough was returning. "Now, I've got red and white. Would you care for one or the other?"

"Whichever."

I pointed to my stereo. "If you want to put on some music."

I heard her rise. "Nice set-up."

"My one extravagance." Which I'd found in a pile of trash behind a house and rewired, at a cost of maybe four dollars, total. But no need to sound too much the penny-pincher. Though my curiosity was growing. "Why the interest in me and Everett?"

"Just wondered."

Me arse. I half think she was testing me for some reason or other, and I'd no idea why. I dug into the fridge and pulled out a Chardonnay, a Rose and something I couldn't even spell let alone pronounce. I got two glasses out and turned to see she was looking through my LPs.

She noticed my large number of cassettes and reels of tape. "Not many eight-tracks."

"Reel-to-reel stuff has some I borrowed and transferred off a few." I opened the Chardonnay and poured her a glass. "There's a player under the table that I connect, once in a while, but for the most part, the cassettes are easier to deal with."

"You got some old stuff here. No ABBA. No disco."

"ABBA?" I asked as I poured myself the last of the Chardonnay.

"Swedish group. *Ring-Ring*. Just won Eurovision."

"Ireland won that, a couple years back."

Then she pulled out an LP, saying "I know," as she put a *Grateful Dead* LP on the turntable and set it to going.

I heard the first chords of *Box of Rain* as I brought her the wine. "You like them?"

"I like *Badfinger* more. Don't tell my momma." And she settled back on the bean bag, a leg tucked under her. "She thinks anything not Cajun or Creole is crap."

I sat on the floor, next to her, my legs crossed, saying, "I never spill secrets."

"I noticed." She sipped the wine, set it down, pulled her bag up and dug into it to bring out a little glass pipe with a tiny bowl. "I bet you got lots of them."

I gasped a laugh. "You're a bold one, carrying that around and this being Texas."

"And me not bein' white?" I shrugged, then nodded. She grinned. "Helps to have a brother who's a cop. Got more wine?"

I hopped up to bring her the bottle of chardonnay. She poured a bit into the pipe's bowl then packed its holder with some pot. I lit Marlboros for the both of us and set hers on an ashtray then handed her my lighter. She fired up the pot and inhaled it through the wine with a tiny gurgling sound.

"Vangie," I asked, "was it always harsh, being black in America?" Then I took a turn at the pipe.

"What a question," she murmured, smoke drifting from her in light wisps as she looked at me. "Don't you have black people in Ireland?"

I exhaled. "Not that I know of. Some of the British soldiers're black, but they're as big of arseholes as the white ones."

She gave me a curious look then leaned back, her dark curls shading down to her bare shoulders, her eyes caught in a blissful gaze. She finally exhaled and added a sigh to it. "Black people were slaves, here. Not human; just property. A lot of white folk can't get past that. Especially in states that fought to keep it goin'." She chuckled, soft and easy. "Y'know, in Louisiana, if you have even a drop of Negro blood in you, you're classified by the state as black. A man could be as white as you, wouldn't matter. You should hear what people say when they find out. Like they've been insulted."

I felt the pot beginning to wash over me, relax me, take me by the hand and lead me into peace. I leaned back against the other bag. Her eyes drifted with me.

"Your problems're religion, right?"

I had to chuckle. "And political. And historical. Can't separate one from the other.”

“Why is there so much hate there, Pug?”

“That’s what Rett calls me,” I said, feeling near joyous over it.

“I know. I heard.”

I looked back at her, tried to smile. “I had mates from school and not a complaint between us. Then all of a sudden we had no contact. We’re the same lads we always were. The only thing that changed was, we grew aware that our views of God were not the same. How we should treat each other was not the same. And we learned well how to fear each other for no more reason than that. One of me Chinas said...”

“Chinas?”

“Mates. He said the rich were using fear to keep us poor, and we were too bloody stupid to see it. I wonder if it’s that simple.”

“Is everyone there like that?”

I shook my head, and despite my usual reticence I found myself saying, “I’ve a younger sister engaged in the peace movement. It’s barely started but she says there’s been progress. I also have a brother keeping himself out of it, much as he can. About to go to Uni.”

“Doesn’t sound like any progress, from the news.”

I shrugged. “It’s the beasts howling at each other who set the tone, not those who want peace.”

She slipped down the bag to beside me and lay her head back atop it, her eyes drifting away, again. “I guess so. We still got the Klan and other rednecks fightin’ to put civil rights back fifty years. Did you know Deer Park has the biggest chapter of the KKK in the country? Tiny-ass town like that.”

“Those the fellas in the white sheets, right? Crazy flag and all?”

She smiled and nodded. “Stars and bars.”

“Oh? Todd has that in the back of his truck.”

“That bartender?”

“Yeah. Didn’t know it’s for them. Shite. Flags’re stupid things to worship. Tricolor. Union Jack. Brings about nothin’ but chaos, death and destruction.”

“Luchshiy sposob uderzhat’ zaklyuchennogo ot pobega,” she said, “ubedit’sya, chto on nikogda ne uznayet, chto nakhoditsya v tyur’me.”

I turned my head to look at her. “Y’know, try as I might, I can’t figure out what the fuck you just said.”

She giggled. Her face was dreamy and soft, like she was visiting a world as yet untouched by anything so human as hate. *"The best way to keep a prisoner from escaping is to not let him know he's in prison.* Dostoyevsky. All these people fightin' each other—they're like pawns on a chess board. Protectin' kings and queens and knights and bishops, and always the first to die. None of them realizin' it's all just a game. That none of it matters. Not really."

"That's a cheery thought."

She turned her head to me. "If it does matter, you get hurt. Crushed. Controlled. But if it doesn't, they can't touch you, and you control them."

Her hair cascaded down around her face. Her eyes were half closed. Her lips so inviting. I couldn't help but to reach over and touch her cheek. She smiled, shifted her face into my hand and gave my palm the slightest of kisses.

Fire shot from it through the whole of my being and I drew close to her and kissed her full—

And my history washed away from me.

I can't truly explain the depths of what I felt as my lips connected with hers. It's like I was reborn and now meant to be with this woman. Protect and worship her. Give her my love forever. She was the third person I'd met in all this city who truly understood my background. Not the Irish of it or the manner in which I grew up or even the religion behind it all. I just knew, like with Jeremy or Rett, if I told her of my feelings—of my concerns as I'd lived in Derry—she'd not need an explanation of them. Just as I finally saw I needed none in regards to her encounters with the idiots of America. We were two who could easily become one and be each other's support through a hideous world.

Dear God, the warmth of her. The smell of her. Like grass fresh mown on a summer's day, touched with the lingering scent of honeysuckle still on the vine. I'd felt not even the hint of this with Rocky, as lovely as she had been.

I shifted to nuzzle her neck, my hands slipping into her hair, and I whispered, "I would destroy any man who hated you."

She pulled back, her eyes now wary. "I don't think you know what you're gettin' into, here."

I leaned into her, touching my forehead to hers. "I don't care. You are the first woman I feel complete with since I've been here. I can't explain why. It's just—that's how it is. But the choice is yours to make, and I'll honor it, no matter which way you decide. Just don't make your choice from a wish to keep some form of control. I've already seen more than once how close we are to death. Never let fools make you wary of loving or being loved."

Now, she eyed me with amusement. "Love? A few dates and you're talkin' love?"

Shite. Overstepped it there, I did. "In a symbolic sense," I shot at her, trying to seem more dignified than I felt. I grabbed my wine to sip from it...and give me a diversion.

She laughed, reached over to turn off the lamp and grabbed me by the ears and lay back, pulling me atop her. "You're an idiot." Which I near proved by almost spilling my wine on her. I set it on the floor then molded my body to hers.

"I do me best," I said, smiling. And lying there, with her hands still gripping my ears, I felt both like a king and proper fool.

She must have sensed it, because her face grew tender and open. And her fingers caressed around to my hair and ran through it and down to my neck to clasp fingers behind it, and even in the shadows I could see her looking deep into me. "This is probably a mistake."

I brushed her lips with mine. Tasted the hint of white wine still on them. Smelled the mixture of Spring and Mary-Jane with a dash of sweat. Felt the smoothness of her skin as I held her face in my hands. And I whispered, "There's little in life that's not, but still it seems to work out."

We kissed, then she whispered in my ear, "Don't ever say you love me, again."

"I won't—I can't promise such a thing."

"Most guys would rejoice at being told that."

"You haven't noticed I'm not like most?"

She trailed her fingers down my spine to the small of my back, making me as hard as any rock or stone in Ireland. I crushed against her. Nuzzled her breasts.

"Then make me one promise," she sighed.

"Anything."

"Let Everett join us, sometime."

I jolted back to look at her. "What the devil? Are you his pimp?"

"I just want to see what happens."

"And if I say, *No?*"

"I'll know you're just as uptight as any other boy I've dated, and all I am is some brown sugar, to you."

Now I huffed, irritated. "I don't even like *The Stones*. Notice, I don't have one of their albums."

"Brendan." Oh, shite, she's using my full name. "I just want to know if it'll be okay with you."

I looked long and hard at her—then shrugged. "I don't know what he'd want to do with the both of us, but..."

Her dark eyes focused hard on me. "You mean it?"

I grabbed her glass of wine, sipped from it, and continued, softly, "I'll invite him over now, if you like. I'm sure he's waiting by the phone."

She rose up to lick my lips, sending screaming lightning straight into my heart. "Not just yet," she whispered.

I held her tighter and whispered back, "This is no mistake, Vangie. Something this real could never be."

She laughed, pulled me down to her, wrapped her legs around me and grabbed me arse. I gasped and nuzzled her breasts and slipped my hands to her hips, and we kissed and caressed for only a minute or five-hundred, inching farther and farther away from the point of turning back.

Oh dear God, the fire in my heart as finally I slipped up her dress and she pulled back my shirt and I undid my trousers and she removed her bra to reveal the loveliest pair of breasts ever I had seen. Perky and with nipples in a perfect "o" that pointed at me as if to emphasize how far behind I was in the undressing. Off went my shoes, and a moment later all I had left on me was my briefs, which barely held me in check; and all she had left on her was her panties, which actually looked so lovely on her, I hesitated at removing them.

She lay back as if to say, *It's up to you.* So I drew my fingers up her legs to entwine them in the panties as she did the same for me, and we revealed each other in unison and the simple, beguiling, quiet beauty of the moment stung me, deep.

Then she curled her hands around my hips and whispered her fingers up the length of me, and it was all I could do to keep from exploding, right there. I lay atop her, crushed myself against her, kissed her lips and eyes and neck and breasts as she ran her fingers up and down my spine, her nails digging deeper and deeper even as she gripped me arse and drove me mad.

We kept that up for I don't know how long before I entered her. This time there were no questions in my mind. This time, with her wrapped around me, it was too right. Too correct. And slipping in and out and in and out as we both grew closer and closer to the moment of

madness, I knew nothing could ever come between us.
Nothing.
Nothing.

Blunt Reality

It was the end of a brutally hot Friday when Rene came up to me, his face all seriousness and intention. I'd just finished repairing the clutch on an Austin America and was washing the fluids off me, as well as some of the sweat. I was hoping for a shower before my date with Vangie; she'd already queued up at a theater to buy tickets for *Jaws*, with Jeremy and Everett. Apparently, this was *a big deal*, as they put it, and they wanted decent seats, so I was to bring pizza and sodas, since the film wasn't till after seven. I thought it silly, but she was my girl and them my best mates, so you do what you must.

Rene caught me just as I was drying off. I'd already worked it out where I could call in the pizza, jump in the pool, dress and collect it by six. Carrying it on my Montesa meant it wouldn't be as hot as I liked by the time I arrived, but I could park near them and we could feast before the crowd began ushering in. His face told me I wouldn't make my schedule.

"Cher, can we talk?" whispered out of him, as if he were embarrassed.

I only nodded a *yes*, casting a glance at my bike.

He led me to a corner. Propped himself against a wall, on his left arm.

"You been seein' lots of Vangie, last couple month," he said.

I nodded, now wary.

"You two gettin' close?"

Well, this moment was due to come, so I said, "I like her. A lot."

"How you mean?"

I know she told me never to say it but, "I think I love her."

Rene sighed, his eyes locked on me. "She told you her plans?"

I nodded. "She's strong in the Russian. Wants to join the State Department. Maybe go to Moscow."

"That ain't gonna happen if she's got a husband and kids."

I blinked, and the world all but vanished.

I hadn't really considered the reality of me marrying her. I'm not legal, and I seriously doubted the Soviets would let me in, given my past.

Rene seemed to know what I was thinking, so he continued with, "She been to your place. More'n once."

Oh, shite. "I'm surprised she told you." And I coughed.

"*She* didn't." His voice now had an angry, cutting edge to it.

I looked hard at him. Gossip strikes, again. None of the lads in the shop knew I was seeing Vangie, and I knew Aunt Mari would never have talked about me, which left my uncle. He must have seen us or heard us, even though I was always careful to bring her over when he'd be out at one of his bars. Was he spying on me? That added a layer of distrust I wasn't ready for.

"Evangelyne's of age," Rene continued, "so I can't tell her what to do with her life. But you know what I'm gettin' at, cher. Question is, you so selfish you'd make her give up her dreams for you? You oughta be clear, up front. Right?"

He walked away.

It took a moment for my brain to wake up to what had just happened. My heart was well aware and was keeping silent almost to the point of not being there. I felt a soft tingle up one side and tremors down the other. Because the one comment that stuck with me was, *Would I make her give up her dreams for me?*

Christ, what a bloody idiot I was. I *had* been thinking of asking her to marry me. But I hadn't thought beyond that. What it meant. Even if Jeremy's uncle could get it straightened out, she'd never gain employment with her Foreign Office. My stain would mark her. And Rene had pointed it out so simply and quietly, I kicked myself for not seeing how obvious it was.

I managed to pull my thoughts together enough to drive to the pizza shop, order the pizza and sodas and have them delivered to Vangie, Jeremy and Everett with a note saying, *Sorry, can't make it.* Then I rode home, stripped down to my Y-fronts and let myself fall into the pool. I had to think, and this heat was keeping me from being able to focus on anything but my misery.

I stayed in water up to my chin, eyes closed. I thought of lying on a floatation pad but didn't want to bother with lotion to keep from burning. None of which was a conscious thought; it was all just, *This'll be fine.*

The thing was, I did love Vangie. Not just her eyes or smile or breasts or anything physical about her. I loved how steady she was. How she knew what her life was going to be. How kind she had been to a lad she barely knew.

And maybe the fact she told me not to love her brought the reverse effect. I'm not smart enough in that to know for sure. And...to be honest with myself...I'd received no indication she felt the same back to me. So Rene's concerns might have been for nothing. Except it felt as if he believed she did.

And he wanted me to be the one to shut it down.

But how could I?

Which was answered with, *Why shouldn't you? You're the one driving the situation.*

Of course.

The smart side of my brain just had to kick in with something so simple. *How crazy are you, Brendan? How needy? You're together what? Six weeks? Yet here you are wanting her to become your family and Trujillo's your job, without even thinking about what she'd planned for herself. Rather arrogant of you, wasn't it?*

It was.

So why was I so upset and—

"Bren, are you gonna stay in the pool all night?"

I opened my eyes to see Brandi standing by the diving board. She'd walked all the way around to it, without me knowing. I looked around to see Bernadette at the other end, also watching me.

"It's been a long day," was my answer.

"I thought you were gonna see *Jaws*, tonight," Bernadette said, her voice wary. And how the devil did she know that? I hadn't shared my plans with them. Scott wasn't here and I knew Jeremy hadn't said a word to them.

I shook my head. "I'm not fit to enjoy it. Another time."

"Is that girl coming by?"

"Bernie!" Brandi hissed. "We agreed not to ask him."

"Just wondering. She's so pretty. We saw her, one night, when you walked her out to her car. And asked Scott if he knew who she was. 'Cause we couldn't ask you. You wouldn't have told us."

And here I was, thinking I'd been so bloody careful. Now it seemed the whole fucking family knew about Vangie.

Fucking hell! "You two've been spying on me!?"

I started for the side ladder. I needed some kind of movement to break the growing chain of fury in my chest.

That made Brandi hurry around to her sister, whining, "Oh, Bernie, you tattle-tale."

"But I just wanted to know," Bernadette shot back at her.

Brandi yanked her towards the house. "I don't care. We agreed not to mention her." She knew they'd set me off.

"No, *you* agreed. I just said *Okay*."

"That's an agreement."

"No, it means you do what you want and I'll do what I want."

"Oh, you're impossible."

Then they closed the door to the kitchen, behind them.

I sloshed from the pool, angry. I half-noticed they were peeking out the kitchen door's window at me as I stormed back to the pool house in my soaked briefs. I didn't care, the little devils. I slammed the door closed, locked it, drew the blinds, and stood in the middle of the room, dripping wet, chilled, fighting to calm down.

Why was I surprised? Why was I angered? Those two had always butted their noses into my life. Never left me to myself. Always chattering about it and casting judgement my way every chance they got. Why was my existence of such importance to them? Why was it *anyone's* business who I loved when it had nothing to do with them? It's criminal that anyone thinks they need to know all of your secrets and control your world when their own is in chaos, and life could end at any second.

I don't know how long I stood there before I decided I needed to get away from there. My skin was dry, briefs only damp, and I felt clammy. And cold. Cold in a space behind my heart, where something had been torn out and shredded into nothingness, and my world had shifted.

Again. And again, without my agreement.

Finally, I dressed myself in jeans and an undershirt, pulled on my boots and stormed into the house.

Aunt Mari was finishing the dishes from dinner and looked at me, saying, "Thought yer out with yer friends, tonight."

I all but growled, "Plans changed."

"Ya hungry, then?"

I shook my head. "Where's Uncle Sean?"

She huffed. "More nonsense with that Gremlin. Had to take it in the shop. We should've bought new instead of used."

"Rene said nothing to me about it."

"It was a late call, and nothin's being done about it till Monday, anyway, so I'm sure ya'll wind up handlin' it."

I coughed then took in a deep breath to regain some sense of control. It was Uncle Sean who'd told Rene. Bastard. Finally I was able to ask, "Any-any news from Mai as to when she's bringing the family down?"

"Oh, she rang me. It's been put off. They found a house so are focused on that. And she's soon to have another child, so I think they'll come down for the Centennial."

"What? She-she's not to come, at all?"

"She'll be down next Fourth of July. It'll be two-hundred years since the foundin' of the country. That'll be a celebration."

Christ, everything I'd planned was collapsing around me. I had to get out. "I-I-I'm goin' for a walk. Maybe up *The Colonel's*."

She looked at me, frowning. "Ya all right?"

"Why shouldn't I be?" Stupid response, Brendan. Stupid.

"I don't know. Ya just seem...upset."

"It-it-it's been a long week, and hot."

Her voice was concerned as she said, "Ya were in the pool for some time. Till the girls bothered ya. What did they say?"

I just waved my hands in the air and headed for the door but she stopped me, saying, "Bren, I know it's been hard for ya, these past few months, but it will get better. Nothin's permanent."

I could not hold back a sneer as I replied, "I learned that long ago."

I stormed out, but rather than walk I mounted my bike. My intent was just to ride around, maybe have a burger at *Prince's*, but still I wound up at *The Colonel's*.

Todd was tending bar and Lorraine was serving. They greeted me and I nodded back. A young black lad had my usual seat at the end of the bar, so I sat midway down, my mood darker, and it was all I could do to keep up any pretense in good manners.

It was slow, that night, and Todd was on edge. He made a call, took a call, then started chatting with me about nothing. My job at Trujillo's. My plans for the evening. I let him know I'd be interested in some pot and Valium, maybe some blow. Something to help hide the growing hollow behind my heart. He only nodded, in answer.

He said he was still seeing that girl in Jersey Village, and it was sounding serious. He was even stockpiling cash to put as down payment on a house. Planning to marry her, sounded like. Just what I needed to hear, others working up a future together as mine threatened to collapse around me.

No, it *had* collapsed. I didn't want to put Vangie in the position of choosing between me and her life. But that's what it would be. Better to back away, before we became too serious.

As if having sex wasn't.

I wanted to vanish from here. Not wait for Jeremy's uncle to come but get rid of my projects, pack my clothes, hop my Montesa and ride to the west. I'd heard you can disappear well in California, and I'd like to see the Pacific—as if it's different from the Atlantic or North Sea. Anywhere but bloody Texas.

It's the middle of 1975 and it's still ugly to be a white man with a black woman. A city the size of bloody Houston, skyscrapers aiming for the sky, big plans for the whole east side of downtown and freeways and expansions of the port and money flowing like water, and they're still a gossipy, snarling hamlet of ten-thousand, out to make sure I was never to be a lad unto himself. Left alone to live his life. Too damned many others felt it their duty to instruct me on what I may think, say, believe or do. Or whom I may love. As with Joanna, it was the world against us.

That sounds childish and tragically romantic, our own new edition of *Romeo and Juliette*, but that story—what, four hundred years old now?—that story was a harsher truth than anything written before or since, and I include the Bible in all of this. Love means nothing to those who choose to hate. It matters not which part of the world you're in—London, Houston, Tokyo, Sydney, Rio, Nairobi, Jerusalem, New Delhi, Belfast or bloody Derry—people were the same in all of them. Demanding conformity to the exclusion of divergent personality. All wrapped in an existence that didn't dive a damn about such childish things as your own wants and needs.

Rhuari was playing the game right, seeing a nice Catholic girl who lived to Derry's north, away from the worst of *The Troubles*...and Christ, what a stupid, silly name for atrocities committed by animals of the worst sort. But there it was and unchangeable, so live with it or howl at the wind, as it were. But I could see Rhuari achieving what I'd only dreamed of—a life where you and yours are left alone to just live. Same for Mai and Tur, now well-established in Toronto, and Maeve planning for nursing school, even while living with Ma at her worst.

Eamonn was stuck in neutral at Long Kesh; no telling for how long. Or was he? From the sound of Mai's letters, he seemed to have adapted. Built himself into a leader of sorts for—oh, Christ, was it

PIRA? OIRA? INLA? I couldn't keep any of it straight in my head. But he was somebody to others, and even to himself.

But me? All I'd achieved in my nineteen years was to become a pariah. A ghost belonging nowhere. Stateless with no possibility of change coming, thanks to my own foolish choices. A man made invisible because he could not see the reality of the world around him. Touting his desire to be left alone, even as he thumbed his nose at convention and dared the world to do anything about it.

And wasn't that what I always really did? Ignore the demands of the church, the politics, the IRA, the UDA, the fucking Brits? *I'll do me unto myself, thank you very much, and you leave me be.*

Except they fucking hadn't.

But then I wondered—could it be that what I thought I wanted, I didn't want? That I hadn't brains enough or awareness enough to see that fool part of me? That contradiction? Jeremy made a quote about that—what was it? A poet saying something like, *So what if I contradict myself? I'm large enough to contain multiples.* Something like that; I'd have to ask him, for I sure as hell contradicted myself.

I had to fuckin' laugh. Jeremy was making his own life with Everett, even as gay men were derided and attacked and lied about. I don't think his parents knew, yet, and I did not want to be around when that came to light. Or maybe I should be, to give him support in case they reacted like Everett's parents had. But he'd survived a war; I doubted their displeasure, if there was any, would keep him from doing as he wished.

I noticed Todd gazing at me with his wariest of expressions and realized I'd probably been sitting for half an hour staring at my bottle of beer. I had to break this or become a true loony remembering amazingly stupid things and howling at the moon over imagined injustices. So I asked, "Does Bidwell still come by?"

Todd shook his head. "Got fired, so no money."

Like me Da. "That never stopped anyone from drinking."

"Depends on what else you got goin' on," Todd muttered, like he's deep in thought.

Okay, time to shift away from that subject. "You-you think my uncle really will redo this place?"

That broke his gaze and he let out a long sigh. He shook his head and turned back to polishing a glass. After a moment he edged over, still cleaning the same glass, not looking at me.

"You are a fuckin' idiot," he snarled, soft and hurt. "A goddamn fuckin' idiot, fallin' for a fuckin' black girl in fuckin' Texas."

"Careful, there," I said. "You can't help who you love."

He leaned against the bar, his arms stretched straight. "Bullshit. You can't help thinkin' somebody's hot an' you wanna fuck 'em. Love's a choice. It's always a fuckin' choice."

"I wanted her to marry me," I said, a hint of warning in my voice.

"Goddamn fuckin' idiot. Makin' a marriage stick is hard enough an' you wanna make it harder? Fuckin' stupid. All the shit goin' on in the world to make things hard enough for you an' you gotta make it harder?"

A snarl billowed up from behind my heart and before I could stop myself, I said, "What the fuck would a junkie dealer know about it?"

He tensed then shrank a little.

"I got busted," he said. "Dealin'."

That killed my anger. "Bloody hell, Todd..."

"I'm out on bail. DA's offered a deal, and I...fuck me, but I'm gonna take it. Lets me keep my job. My life. No jail."

"Um...good?"

"No. That girl in Jersey Village. All I said tonight? That was bullshit. She don't want nothin' more to do with me."

Now I felt the proper bastard. He'd said everything was fine with her, but his answers to my questions had been vague themselves.

"Todd, I was wrong to say what I did. I'm sorry."

It took him a moment, but he finally looked at me and shook his head. "I can't figure you out. I known you, what? Two years an' still can't figure you out."

I huffed at that. "Nor can I."

He looked around. "I thought I'd like stayin' here. Thought it'd be my own little hideaway. But it's not. Your uncle's a weak man."

I chuckled in near derision.

He continued with, "He's weak 'cause all he thinks about is makin' money. Anything that might hurt that, he won't go up against it. He's gonna stand aside and let it be. I can't stay here. Soon as I can set it up, I'm movin' back to Albuquerque. Maybe Santa Fe. Start over where nobody's seen me for years. Homcomin' sort of thing."

So he could move on while I couldn't. I felt something almost like envy...or anger. Not sure. "I'll be sorry to see you go."

He looked at me, his eyes full haunted. "You walkin' home?"

I shook my head. "Got me motor."

"You don't get hassled on the way?"

"Just by assholes who think I've no right to the road."

"Be careful." He poured a shot for himself and one for me, saying, "You don't belong in this country, Bren. 'Least, not this part. You ain't asshole enough."

We raised our shots in a toast and downed them.

"Alba-qwirky, eh?" I asked.

"Albuquerque," he said, not smiling.

I nodded. "I'm thinking I might off to California."

His eyes grew almost tender. "You'd like it there. I know you would." His gaze held on me, for a moment, then he added, "Sorry it turned out like this."

I smiled at him, paid for my beers and headed out into a still warm night. At least I was in a slightly better mood as I gazed down Shephard. I'd enjoyed my walks along that road.

Like the walk I'd taken when I only dreamed of Joanna beside me. And the one we took up to the circle fort. Walking along the back streets of New Orleans with Vangie only reminded me of my wandering through Derry at night, alone, enjoying the darkness and solitude. All gentle times. Times when there was no one around to trouble me or those I was with. We were just unto ourselves. As life should be. I could see me setting out to walk for the rest of my life. Even thought of leaving my Montesa at the bar and making for home—shanks-mare, as Todd put it—but didn't want it to be out for someone to mess with and—

Footsteps raced up behind me and a blanket was slung over my head. Before I could do more than cry out, a fist punched into my gut three times, doubling me over, and rope was wrapped around me, securing my arms to my sides and my legs at my knees. I heard a car roar up, then I was thrown into its trunk to land face down. As I gasped to find words to say, the lid closed and off we drove.

Seems chaos had decided to reassert its control.

Schooled

We turned right then left and another left before driving straight, to head south. The sound was muffled but I could tell when we passed over the bridge at White Oak and then could make out the sounds of highway traffic. That was the 10. After another sharp turn to the left, the car thrumped over bumps in the road, again and again, before shifting to the left and speeding up to start cruising down a highway, going east.

It was midnight-dark and the blanket was some rough wool. I tried to pull it off by rubbing my head over the floor, but no good. The way they'd bound me, they must have known I'd do them a damage once the boot—the TRUNK, dammit—was opened if I had half the chance.

I managed to find a sharp metal edge in a fender so caught the blanket in it, at eye level, and used it to tear open a bit of a hole. It cut me, above my right cheek, and I felt blood trail from it, but I finally was able to see a bit of the trunk. Filthy and rank from sour oil and fumes.

The obnoxious whine of a country-western song assaulted my ears as I peeked around. The edge I'd used had been the inside of the left fender that had been crumpled in, and there was hole in it. I maneuvered about to look out it but could see little more than the tops of black trees passing beyond it, obscuring whatever it was behind them. Bright signs screaming to *buy this Chevy* or *that detergent* or *our home* or *your next best life insurance policy* were brightly lit. Freeway lamps were near non-existent. Highway signs too high up to read. In fact, I saw nothing to let me know how far we'd gone for what seemed like hours till I caught a bit of an exit sign for the 10 West to downtown whip away.

Before I could even think of what that might mean, we whooshed under an interchange, exited the freeway and curved around then drove down an impossibly straight road that desperately needed to be redone. On and on the car rattled, tires squeaking and flumping. The stinking refineries now overpowered the fumes of the car's exhaust, stark and harsh in their odors. Church steeples covered with floodlights whipped by as well as power and phone lines, barely visible against the midnight sky. The occasional big truck roared up and past, loud and obnoxious.

What's odd was, throughout this I wasn't so much scared as confused over what the bloody hell they thought they were doing, and who was it doing this to me. I knew I wasn't being robbed; I had little cash on me and nothing like a watch or other jewelry. Nor did I think I was going to be killed; they could easily have done that in the parking lot. This seemed closest to the stories drifting around Derry about lads carted off in a similar way to be interrogated and punished for some slight or other by either one of the Republican or Protestant groups, some of whom *did* wind up dead on the side of a country road.

Like me Da.

Was this how he might have been taken? No, he was too powerful for such a ridiculous kidnapping. He'd have been promised a drink, and all they'd need is a bit of something in the whiskey to calm him till he was secured. Then they'd have their fun. Was that what would happen with me? No, no, this wasn't Derry. So what the fuck was going on?

Dear God, we drove forever and ever, and the stink of the refineries and the exhaust threatened to make me heave. I coughed and fought to keep my breath steady. I was starting to go mad as we turned to the left and, after a short drive, turned to the right and went into a tunnel. The echo of it actually scared me, for it seemed tight and permanent till we came out the other end. Still on we drove, barely turning once then finally again and again, both to the right, and I saw a sign pass that said *Jesus Saves*.

Arseholes and idiots? I wondered. *I guess we'll see.*

Then we pulled off to something rough and noisy. A gravel drive. Did they make entire roads of gravel in Texas? It sounded and felt so much like the one leading up to Evangelyne's home but I knew we hadn't gone that way and—

The car skidded to a halt in the gravel and the lads in front piled out. The back popped open and I was dragged out to flop face down on the grit before I could look about. I kicked and pulled away and one of them cried, "There's a hole in the blanket!"

Someone shined a torch—*flashlight* in my face, blinding me, and snarled, "You son-of-a-bitch!" And he kicked me in the side.

I was dragged in front of two other cars' headlights, blinding me further, so could never make out better than the silhouettes of several men of all shapes and sizes. Beyond them were some odd-shaped bars, hanging with chains. Thick black oak trees hovered above us, their gnarled limbs seeming to mock me.

Throughout, I twisted and yelled and used every variation there was on the word *motherfucker,* demanding they let me alone and go have sex with themselves, but to no avail. I was slammed against the side of a newer car, and three of them held me there as they undid my bindings. The blanket was yanked away and a cloth wrapped around my eyes, then my boots were yanked off and my jeans were torn away, literally ripped. Bloody hell! What the fuck was this? Was I about to get buggered and killed, like those lads from the Heights had been?

That's when I let loose with, "Fucking queers! Cocksuckers! Think you'll get your jollies off me, you fuckin' wankers!?"

Their only answer, besides laughter, was more punches and kicks to my sides. If I'd tried to say a word after the fourth or fifth boot to my kidneys, I'd have hurled, I'm sure, and I'd sooner die than give them the satisfaction.

I was dragged from the gravel then over a rough patch of grass and dirt to be slapped face-up against a large tree. And bound to it with rope wrapped 'round both the trunk and myself. My arms were yanked to hug the tree and tied in place, as well, after which a rope was wrapped around my neck to immobilize my head. Then they tore my shirt in half, down my back. My legs were still free to kick and my feet could paw at the dirt, but otherwise, I was caught, completely. The bark dug into my skin. I felt ants beginning to crawl on me. My throat was raw and drier than dry. And the warm breeze already had mosquitoes whispering up to feast on this newest offering.

Then one of the men slapped my head against the tree, the bark scraping my face. It hurt but more in a surprising way than a painful one, and I felt blood trail down my forehead and cheek to soak into the pillowcase.

"We ain't gonna fuck you, boy," he snarled, his breath reeking of cheap beer. "Much as you might like it." Then he slapped me arse, hard.

"No, we just don't like white boy nigger-fuckers," said another man, to my other side.

Another chimed in with, "You like fuckin' cunts with black skin?

We gonna show you what happens to white nigger-fuckers in this town, boy. We gonna fix it so's you never go near anything as black as that cunt, again." His breath was harsh from whiskey and chewing tobacco.

I heard another car drive up and doors open and close. More men crossed the gravel, almost casual, and there was murmuring for a few moments, then silence.

Fucking silence.

Until something *whished* and there was a sharp sting my back.

"What the fuck yous doin'?" burst from me.

They laughed as more of the vicious sharpness licked my legs and arse and back, like a razor slicing into me, again and again.

They were fucking whipping me!

I howled, "Are yous outta yer fuckin' minds?! What the fuck're yous doin'?"

A quiet voice added, "Can't take a hint, Irish, you gotta take the punishment."

Irish, he called me? No one I knew addressed me as that.

Except...

Oh, Christ, except Lon.

Vangie's brother.

But that wasn't his voice. Was it? I-I-I couldn't remember. It'd been months since Mardi Gras and he'd barely spoke to me, even then and—

More of the stinging cuts sliced into my back.

"Cut it out! Get off me!" I screamed. "I'll fuckin' kill yous!"

"You an' what army, asshole?" sniped another man as more of the bloody razors cut me. My back. My arse. My legs. My heart began to scream. Not pound—shriek in opposition to the pain. I could barely keep my breath. Coughed, over and over. Could no longer choke out curses and demands. My stomach heaved and I cried out in pain...until absolute fury kicked in and I snarled, "How many of yous. Got your tadgers out. Pullin' on 'em? How many? Got your cocks. In hand. Hard as stone?"

More cuts against my arse. More against my legs. I jolted but continued with, "Bet yer dicks. Yer dicks're. Like wood. They are. You'll go home. Pull on 'em. Long an' easy. Thinkin' of me. Me arse. Gettin' beat."

But my heart was pounding mad. I was dizzy and my words grew soft.

So damn soft.

Could barely breathe. Or swallow. Or even cough.

My head exploding until...

Until...

The world drifted...drifted...to a point where I felt the pain but didn't feel it. Knew it was there. In my head I knew. But I didn't know—not really. Like it's...it's...

It's—

Charlie drove up and nearly hit me with his car and he and his mates piled out and that fucking Para groped me arse and balls then went for Danny's and he was tearing at us till Father Demian slapped at me with a rosary, over and over, face-back-body-legs, howling, "Why didn't you come to me? You knew. Down deep you knew so why didn't you protect him? I'd have been happy with you instead of that weak child of a boy, but you always knew better than anyone, didn't you, and don't blame me, Bren, don't blame me, don't blame me as white enveloped me and I was slung back and—

I was on the ground. Face up. I think. The blindfold still covered my eyes. I was so bloody cold. My chest was shredding me to bits. My arms were lifeless. Tingling. I could barely breathe. Words sliced at me—

Goddammit, I told you!

He's bullshittin'.

Heart trouble.

I goddamn warned you!

Not that bad.

Can't find a pulse!

Shit!

You're not doing it right!

Pressing against my chest.

Breathe in.

Breathe out.

Get off me as the para shoved his hand up me arse and—

Breathe in.

Breathe out.

Fuckin' shite yer breakin' me bones and—

Soft groans whispered from deep inside me.

Despite the blindfold, hideous white light fired into my eyes. I had to close them. Then hands forced open my mouth and shoved something under my tongue. Felt like a tiny pebble. A pearl? Like an oyster does? Make something lovely out of hardened snot? My mouth was closed and words kept coming—

Didn't do that much.

C'mon, he's fakin'.

Look-it his fuckin' lips!

Clean him off!

Shit!

On my belly. Dirt in my face. Searing pain as water sloshed over my back. More water. Rubbing the skin. Fuckin' peeling it off, they were. Whimpered from the pain.

In the car.

I rose. Levitated. Light as air. Drifted along. The blindfold loose. My eyes half-open. Dirt and grass and gravel whispered past below me till I'm suddenly facing the midnight sky cut through with crooked branches and beyond them a blanket of stars casting their gentle light down on me.

The stars—

As I walked to Claudy. My companions, they were. Bright and happy, even if they were on the other side of the clouds, for I knew they understood me and took joy in me and my sad little attempts at life and would always be there for me as they were at the Circle Fort and on the walk home. No judgement. No gossip or hate. Just happy to be there. Maybe I could join them—

The blindfold was pulled back over my eyes and something wrapped around me. A solid, crackling sheet of something. I was pulled into the back of a station wagon, the blindfold shifting, again. Could see windows curl up to the roof, in the corners. Had I seen this before? Seemed familiar. A blanket was laid over me and I kept hearing—

I warned you, I goddamn warned you.

Takin' him to a hospital?

Like this? You loco?

Hope he pulls through.

It's bullshit.

Don't want no murder charge.

One less nigger-lover's a good thing.

Hey!

Did somebody punch somebody? Was that what I heard?

Get his clothes.

Fuck!

Burn 'em.

Sound of someone big running across the gravel as the car door whispered closed, at my feet. Naked feet. And legs. And all of me. And the engine started and the AC came on and I grew cold again.

I think I heard myself ask, "Where am. Am I to be. Buried?"

That last one invited a punch to my head, followed by a snarl of, "Shut the fuck up."

A voice sounding so familiar.

Too goddamned familiar.

But my head was shattered. I couldn't think. Couldn't focus. There was a buzzing fog. Not one coherent thought. So I just let the floor embrace me. The crackling sheet hold me. As I heard the doors to three more vehicles slam close as they started up.

I finally realized my arms were free. My back pounded with pain. I somehow managed to think of removing the blindfold, but when I began to push it up my head a hand swung around and smacked me, and that voice growled, "Leave it on."

I started to roll over and he shoved back, spitting, "Stay down."

I couldn't think to fight him. My heart and head were too lost to me, pounding and aching and kicking at my soul. So I stayed. But every foul word I could think of rang in my head for what seemed like hours. I cannot say for certain whether I spoke them or not. I'd like to think I did.

Now pain shot through every part of my body. Tears fell from my eyes. I think they were tears. Might have been blood. I finally realized I still had the sleeves of my shirt on. I pressed one against the cloth over my face and wiped at them, as best I could. There was nothing to say, so I said nothing. Just let myself drift along in the back of that car and—and—

A peck on the nose, and Joanna said, "Meet me at Marianne's."

Why didn't I say, *No, come with me now*? So many times I'd thought of how I could have saved her, but truth was making itself known. I couldn't even save myself, so I'd have wound up as dead as she now was. Maybe that would have been a blessing on all concerned. One more martyr to the cause and—

We were backing up? Already? Slowly. Then I heard the creaking of the gate and understood we were at the house.

I heard the rear of the car slide down and I was dragged to the back of it. The blindfold almost came off but was yanked back over my head, complete, then I was lifted up and carried into the pool house...without the crackling sheet.

I was settled carefully onto the bed. Face down. Lights left off.

"Satisfied?" It was Uncle Sean's voice.

"It'll have to do." In that voice.

"If he don't pull through, we're all fucked. I told you—"

"Yeah. Right. Makes all the difference." Then a hiss near my ear of, "That was for Matty, Irish. Hope we meet, again."

"Get the fuck out! I don't want to see your ass, again. Ever."

"You won't," was the soft, vicious answer.

Then I heard the car door slam, and it start and drive away, and the gate creak closed. That is when the blindfold came off my head and the lights were turned on. And I managed to look around to see—

Aunt Mari coming up behind Uncle Sean, asking. "What happened? What's going on?"

"In the house," Uncle Sean snapped.

She saw me on the bed and jolted. "Brendan? Oh dear God, what happened?"

"In. The. House!" Then he took her by the arm and dragged her out.

So I lay there, shuddering, cold despite the warm air. He had set the AC to going. I'd have told him not to bother but I knew soon it would be blazing unless he'd done it, so there it was. My back was blazing with pain, which became twice as bad if I even tried to move, so I just lay there. My heart and lungs were too unwilling to let me even think of what next to do.

None of this had meaning. My thoughts were scattered and sharp and fast and confusing. I honestly thought that they would never regroup. That I'd lost my mind, complete. I had no concept of time. No idea when I'd arrived or sometimes even why I was on the bed, face down. I sleep on my side, not my belly. Why was I like this? It wasn't comfortable. But I could not move.

Could not move.

It was still dark when Aunt Mari came in with rags and soapy water, Uncle Sean behind her. She could finally see how completely I had been sliced and diced. Her gasp made me smile, and I caught a glimpse of her giving him a glare so cold and hard, I thought he'd die from it.

He should have.

Then she started tending my wounds.

Dear God, did it hurt. But also felt good. The water, warm.

Helping calm the screaming pain to where it merely throbbed.

I dared not speak. I was sure I'd make no sense. Or worse, use my harshest words. I did not wish to be held accountable for them. Not yet. Not now. My mind was still too separate from my body and I wanted to know more of what all this meant.

And wanted to know why *they* were saying nothing. Not to me. Not to each other.

Nothing.

They worked in tandem, and their silence grew terrifying. I remembered Todd's words. *He'd stand by and let it happen.* Then Uncle Sean's reaction over New Orleans. And his threat. His fist on me for not doing as he said.

As Da had done.

And from it grew the cold certainty he had known what was going to happen. Might even have been there. And the thought was so matter-of-fact, it brought no additional pain or confusion.

I finally thought to look at the clock radio by my bed. 5:22. When did I leave *The Colonel's*? Eleven? Eleven-thirty? I don't think I really noticed, but even if they had driven around some time before meeting up, I couldn't see me being bound to that tree later than twelve-thirty. Had they been whipping me that long? I had no idea. But surely no more than half an hour. More than that and I'd be dead.

Or *had* I died? Was that why they stopped? Was that why they were suddenly afraid. It's one thing to beat up a simple Irish lad, but to kill him? That might be a bit much.

Clarity drifted closer. Something had happened with my heart. Had it stopped in response to the pain of the whips? Had I suffered an attack? Had I been unconscious for hours?

I told you. I warned you.

And a pebble in my mouth. Under my tongue. Make a pearl.

A pill?

I noticed the small container that held my nitroglycerin tablets was on the table next to the bed. I kept it in the medicine cabinet. Hadn't needed to even think about it, in months.

And the top was only partly on.

No.

No, no, I knew my uncle was angry with me, but for him to help in something like this? To let them nearly kill me?

Your uncle's a weak man.

The belief burrowed deep into my soul. They had stopped

whipping me the moment I had a problem. How could they have known that merely from being told I had heart issues?

I warned you. I told you.

They wouldn't have known when to stop. They were drunk fools having fun with a Taig. Who'd have kept on and on till he was dead. Why would they think all I'd need was a pill to be made better and not a trip to hospital?

I warned you. I told you.

In a whisper that could have been his voice. Could have been.

Oh, God...oh, God...oh...

I drifted into white nothingness. Cold and alone, my thoughts just out of reach, with Dr. Gilbert seated by me, his face cool and simple but his eyes angry and—

Did he give me a shot? My arm stung, but every part of my body roared with anger at the world and pain and confusion and—

And—

Daylight peeked around the blinds on the French doors. I was on my belly, and Aunt Mari was carefully washing my back. I felt warm soapy water whisper over my skin and then me arse and then thighs. It smelled of medicine. Stung like medicine. I groaned.

She shifted on the bed and I tried to rise up but she kept me down. "Stay still."

I let myself lie on my belly, my face half in the pillow. The memories rushed into my mind. Cold and silent.

"How ya feelin'?"

All I did was grunt and give a slight shrug of my shoulders and grimaced from the pain of even that little bit. I was hungry, but not so much that I wanted to move to get any food. And thirsty, but with the same thought.

More warm water was smoothed over me as I fought to bring my mind back to the moment. Then a soft patting dry, and after— the spraying some cold ointment on my cuts.

That stung.

I tensed and rose to lean on my elbows and stayed like that for I don't know how long before the first words whispered from me.

"He knew."

"What?" It was obvious she hadn't been listening for me to say something, not that she was avoiding the question.

"What they did to me," drifted from deep within my heart. "He knew. They were going to."

She hesitated, then her voice was softly innocent. "Who knew?"

She hesitated!?

No.

No.

I should have said nothing more. That was answer enough. But still, "He was there," whispered from me.

"What're ya sayin'? Why're ya sayin' that?"

I could not look at her. Her voice grew lost and afraid.

Why am I saying that?

She knew who I meant, and she wouldn't give me an answer. Just an evasion. So, it's true.

Fuckin' true!

Fuck!

I pulled my pillow close under my chest and sank onto it. "He-he-he wasn't at *Liam's Trough*. Last night. This morning."

"Yer uncle? Yes, he was. But he doesn't go in on Sundays."

Sundays? Then I heard church bells in the distance.

"What day is it?" I asked.

"Sunday morning. We're off to mass, shortly. I just came in to clean yer—yer injuries. They're doin' well."

So I'd lost a day. Of course. My bet was, I'd been given something to relax me. Settle my heart. Or something. I didn't know for sure. Didn't want to know.

"Friday night. Was Uncle Sean. At *Liam's Trough*?"

More dithering, from Aunt Mari. More hesitation until, "No, he has-he has a man doin' the close, now. Good man. He did drop by *The Colonel's* to see how Todd was doin' and—and—"

To make sure they got me. She'd forgotten she'd told me he was going to see Rene about the Gremlin. I almost chuckled. I guess he saw me as a gremlin, as well.

"They took me. Took me to the east. I could smell the refineries. Strong. For hours. Miles away. Then straight here."

"Brendan..." Her voice trailed off at saying my true name. Speaking as my aunt and not some distant relation. As someone who'd been kind and decent to me...and that made the horror of this even worse.

She sighed and ran a hand into my hair. And stopped. And pulled her hand away. "Oh, Holy Mary, there's damage to yer head. I never saw it, in the curls."

I near laughed. "Nothing to worry about there. That's the last place I can be hurt. Stupid, stubborn Irishman. Too bloody thick. No, *simple*."

"I-I-I'll get fresh water and—"

"Don't!" shot out of me, followed by a gentler, "Don't. Please. You've done enough." Then I added, with a snarl, "So has your husband."

I didn't hear her move, for a moment, then finally she said, "Bren, after ya started seein' that girl, Sean began hearin' things. Comments made by regular patrons. Another bar he's plannin' to invest in—they-they-they wondered if he was plannin' to shift it into a bar for blacks and-and were pullin' back. It made him worry, but he didn't say anything to ya. Didn't warn ya. And now he feels responsible for this happenin' to ya."

Aunt Mari was lying to me. I could hear it in her voice. So careful. Unsure. Repeating what she was told. What the two of them had decided. That or she still thought her husband was a man who'd do what was right. It didn't matter.

He knew what was planned for me. Warned them about my heart. Was probably there, to take care of it should something happen. Make sure they didn't do me too much damage. Just enough for everyone to feel vindicated and back in control. Just enough to leave him and his alone.

But my heart *had* kicked off and scared them. Assault is one thing; murder, another. I could not merely disappear, could I? Too many people knew of my existence. Questions would be raised. The situation too odd. And unlike the IRA, there was no cohesion in the ranks by all concerned to keep it silent.

I had nothing more to say to her, and I could tell from her uncertain actions she had no idea what more to say to me. The silence grew, held in place, threatened to engulf us within it, permanently, until finally she rose and left.

I heard the door close. And a wave of hideous sadness swirled up from deep within. Exploded to engulf me and...and...

I began to sob.

I used my pillow to keep it silent, but shuddering gasps of sorrow took hold of every part of me, even as my heart whimpered and my body moaned. I could not stop them.

I was alone.

Joanna was gone from me.

Evangelyne gone from me.

My family gone from me.

My friends gone from me, and my world shattered, again.

I was surrounded by darkness. Blinding, brilliant darkness. I could see nothing. Touch nothing. There was only abandonment. And all I could do was weep like a child.

I don't know how long I lay there before the need to pee became too overwhelming to set aside. *Get to the toilet or it's in the bed, and you don't want that.*

I rose slowly, ignoring the stinging pain in my back and the objections from my chest, and forced myself up to my feet then went to the toilet. Leaned over the basin against the wall and let it continue until I was done. I almost felt light-headed.

At least I saw no blood in the piss.

I leaned in the doorway. Noticed the AC was running as best it could and my circulating fan was also on. The air promised another day of heat and humidity. I pulled the top sheet from the bed. It was now crusty with dried blood but still I wrapped myself in it, managed to slowly...slowly climb out the hatch onto the pool house's rooftop.

I crawled to an area hidden under the thick tree. The tin was cool to my feet so I lay back on it. Oh, dear God, how glorious it felt. How it soothed the throbbing pain.

Through the crooked, grasping oak trees, I watched light clouds cross the sky. Felt the morning breezes stir and caress me. Birds flew about, calling. Squirrels danced above me. My heart slowly grew less unhappy. Less demanding. Almost to where it did not even hurt.

Then I turned onto my belly to watch the cranes dotting the skyline, with buildings leaping up and up as Houston reinvented herself. And redevelopment wasn't just downtown but also to the west, around the Galleria, and to the south, down by the medical center. Business was good thanks to the recent oil crisis and Houston was the wave of the future; just ask anyone, they'd tell you of the glorious plans being formulated, even for the east areas of the center city. And talk of approaching financial difficulty was derided with the purest of arrogance.

As Vangie had said, this was a town caught in the past, where white and black mingled no more than necessary and the law was on the side of those who broke it. If you didn't follow the rules, you'd wind up strapped to a tree and punished by those too easily offended by anything they disliked.

Men and women may walk the world's halls of commerce

wrapped in the modern armor of business suits and briefcases, but at heart too many were still trapped in the feral hate and fear of their fathers and grandfathers. I kicked myself for ever thinking this country would be any better than the rest.

By this point, the blood on my back had issued a call to every damned mosquito and fly across the city, so I slipped back inside and stood before my fan, to help against the growing warmth. It felt good whispering over the stinging cuts, and I luxuriated in it. Thinking maybe, maybe, maybe if I didn't move it would all vanish into nothingness.

Church bells rang, calling liars to worship. Dogs laughed in with mocking tones, knowing full well the truth behind the hymns that would be sung. Word was surely passing from church to gathering to community of how yet another fool had been shown his true place in God's universe. Something they just knew even Jesus would say was right and good.

I noticed a little cassette player on my work counter and touched it. A tape had become tangled within and shredded, so it had been tossed in the trash. One mistake-one problem and it became worthless. Like so much in life.

Still half-wrapped in that sheet, I stood before it—I didn't dare sit on a stool, yet—took a small screwdriver and worked off the cover to look at the inner workings. Pieces of tape were caught everywhere. Using tweezers, I picked each one out, some so tiny they were near invisible in the mechanisms. Some had even been caught in the gears, tight and immovable. I had to work them free. Once I had everything out that I could get to, I used a can of air and a soft brush to clean out the dust and residue, then I reset the pulley and gears. By the time I reattached the cover, it looked all but new.

I found an old cassette cleaner tape and ran that through it, and it seemed to work fine. So I tried my *Iron Butterfly* cassette, a copy I'd made from the album—

And the damn thing chewed it up. Shredded it and mangled it in complete destruction. Furious, I slung it across the room. Shattered it. Put a hole in the wall, as well. It had let the cleaning tape through, like it was playing with me before destroying another tape that held more meaning for me. Well, now it truly was garbage.

It's funny, but that bastard cassette player had helped me finally allow the reality of Vangie's loss to sink in. She and I were beyond repair, no matter what I wanted. But wasn't that the truth of all life?

Things, people, relationships, none were easy to fix. That realization forced out everything I'd ever wished or dreamed or prayed for, with Vangie.

Now I understood why it was impossible, between us. Any plan I might make for us to get away from this madness would have meant not only that she make a sacrifice for me. Give up her future for me, a lad hardly worthy of it. We would be flipping the bird against everything the society of this country preferred. We'd be fighting forever with those who hated those who did not conform to their narrow world. I wasn't being heroic or strong in going against the demands; I was merely a fool for not really seeing it, before.

Like I hadn't with Joanna.

Sometimes, no matter how much you want to fix something, you simply can't. You have to admit it's beyond your ability to even think of how it could be handled, and all you can do is let it go. Toss it in the bin. Find something else to work on.

And that fucking infuriated me.

Exposure

I finally realized the sun was well up in the sky and my room was warm. What little work I'd done on the air conditioner had helped it put out cooler air, but more was needed. At least my heart seemed back to normal. No palpitations or anger at any movement I made. I felt sweat trail from my face and body. Touched it and found that it was slightly pink. The raw marks around my wrists from the rope still held their imprint and the raw spots seeped blood onto the countertop. There'll be stains there, now.

That would not do. I'd have to scrub them away.

Finally, I decided the best way to rejoin humanity was with a long, cool shower to wash the blood away. So I dropped the sheet and set only the cold-water tap going, and God, did it feel good to stand under. I also washed my hair. Which set a cut near my temple to bleeding, but not so very bad. The chill water did so much to soothe my injuries, I wanted to keep standing there. Let it pound on me. Refocus my mind on the here and now and put aside the confusion haunting me.

I thought for a moment I might pull on some shorts and soak in the pool, but the B-Girls would soon be back from mass and I did not have the stamina to handle their questions over my injuries, or their advice or their snarling little arguments. My blinds were closed, but was my door locked? I couldn't remember. I'd feel so much better if I knew for sure, so I turned off the shower and walked into the main room, wet, completely naked, and—

Everett was standing there!

I near went through the roof.

"Sorry, Pug," he said, "didn't mean to scare you. I knocked..."

I wrapped a towel around me, snarling, "How'd you get in here!?"

"The door wasn't locked and you didn't answer..."

His voice trailed off when he finally noticed the scrapes on my face and chest. I would have sworn Aunt Mari *had* locked the door when she left.

He kept on with, "I-I-I-we came over, yesterday, but your aunt said you'd been sick so I thought we'd just-we'd..."

I slammed the door shut and rammed both latches into the frame. Which gave him a good look at the marks on my back. He actually gasped.

I spun on him, my voice a low growl as I said, "You're not to say one fuckin' word about what you've seen here, do you understand?" He was about to argue so I cut him off, my voice shaking from the anger in it. "You tell anyone, I'll swear before God it was you did this to me!"

He went flush. "That's a fucked-up thing to say!"

"I mean it, Rett. You understand me?"

"Then you better get dressed, 'cause Vangie's down at Jeremy's, an' they're gonna bring over a nice hot chicken soup made special for the flu."

I howled, "Aw, Christ, she can't come in! I can't let her see—"

He nodded and pulled me away from the door. "I'll tell them to wait. Maybe meet me at the *House of Pies*."

"I'm not going out!"

"Of course you're not. Right back."

He left.

I leaned against the counter and, despite me trying to keep every bit of control I had, I began to throw anything I could put my hands on. Tools. Items to repair. Cans of WD40 and oil. Money. Wallet. A dirty plate and glass I hadn't washed. More holes in the paneling. All like a child, but I could not even think of stopping until I was exhausted and sitting in a heap on the floor, shaking like a terrified dog.

I didn't notice Everett return, not till he sat beside me on it, tender and easy, and handed me a washcloth to wipe my face. I was pouring sweat, again, stained with blood. May as well dye all my things red, now.

After God knows how long, I was able to look at him. I'm sure he saw someone close to madness.

"Am I allowed to ask you what happened?" he asked, his voice gentle but his eyes holding almost as much anger as mine, and I felt the bastard for having snapped at him.

"Some men. Grabbed me. Tied me to a tree and..." I made the

motion of flicking a whip to finish. No need to mention the heart failure or whatever it was.

"Jesus fuckin' Christ." Even though he was whispering, you could hear the anger boiling in him. "Fuckin' Texas." He took in a deep breath before asking, "Over Vangie?"

I shrugged and muttered, "Not just her."

"Matty?" Again, I shrugged. He crouched beside the bed. "You didn't call the police..."

I shook my head. "If I file a report with anyone, they'll find I've overstayed my visa. And I will not be deported with these injuries on me."

"You-you-you're not legal?"

I shook my head.

"And you were sneakin' into gay bars?"

"Just the once."

"Son-of-a—" he sighed and ran his hand through what hair he had left. "Okay. Who dressed your wounds?"

"Why?"

"Couple're bleedin'. Look deep. You might need stitches. You got any ointment? Bandaids?"

I motioned to the toilet—*bathroom*. He went in and dug through the medicine cabinet to find a box of bandages...and more Bactine.

"Oh, for God's sake," he moaned, glaring at it, but he brought it with him. "Lie on the bed. Face down."

"Everett..."

"I know my name! You may not trust me to keep a secret but—"

I stood up. "I'm sorry for that. I should never have threatened you. It was wrong of me." I was drifting close to tears.

"Shut up!" He finally added, "I can't say I'd have done different." He froze, for a second, and all but choked out, "There's lashes down to your calves?"

I nodded. He let out a deep breath.

"Lie-lie face down. I'll remove the towel. Spray some of this on."

I did and he lifted it away, and I heard a near hiss being drawn into him. It took him a moment, but then he did nothing more than gently spritz that stuff over my wounds, stinging the fucking hell out of me. Then he bandaged the worst of them.

I told him all that happened, as he worked, but made it sound as if I passed out from the panic and pain, and that Saturday I'd been near delirious. The bottle was empty by the time he and I were done.

"Now pull something on. Nice an' loose. 'Fore I forget I'm your nurse."

I stood up, feeling a hundred times better, and slipped into my pajama bottoms, keeping them light around my middle. "Thanks. Rett, I-I-I know it's cowardly not to make a report, but—"

"But nothing." His voice had an edge as he snarled, "You're smart not to. I know how cops work. I fuckin' know."

I huffed a near laugh. "Do you, now?"

He sat on the edge of my bed, his eyes locked on me, then asked, "Did I ever tell you about bein' gay in Texas?"

"Some. Your family locked you out."

"Yes, but that's everywhere. Families doin' that."

I shrugged, went to the bar and found an unopened bottle of wine in a corner. Apparently, I'd thrown it but it hadn't broken. A white. Chardonnay. Vangie's favorite. Perfect.

I didn't care it was not yet noon; life was too upside down for tea and biscuits. Hell, even a fry-up. I pulled some cheese from the fridge. Then I dug up a box of crackers and a knife. I set them on a plate, carefully sat next to him on the bed and cut slices to go with an apple I had as—

Eamonn cut slices from the apple and popped them in my mouth and they were juicy and sweet and—and—

I froze. Dunno how long. I do know his eyes were locked on my face as he quietly said, "Y'know, I was also sneakin' into gay bars when I was seventeen."

I managed to focus enough to say, "Hardly the same."

"True. What's more, I looked like I was fifteen, just like you, and back then drinkin' age was twenty-one. 'Course, that never kept me out. 'Specially when I started runnin' around with a dyke named Jimmie. She was of age and had a car and, as you know, I was sleepin' on couches. We'd go huntin' together. Her for a woman she was crushin' on who might be at this bar or that; me for a man who would take me home. Put me in a real bed, for the night. Let me...let me think I was loveable." He hesitated then grinned and added, "Preferably one who looked like Robert Conrad."

I managed to say, "Dunno the name."

"*Hawaiian Eye? 77 Sunset Strip?*" He sang the tune to it. I shrugged. He shook his head. "Really came into his own in *The Wild, Wild West*. Got me to love bondage, baby."

"I-I-I'll remember that." I tried to make it a joke, but I don't think

I succeeded.

"Don't worry; it's all fantasy. Anyway, by the time I was nineteen, I had my life somewhat under control. Goin' to art school at night. Job at Frost Brothers, in their shippin' department. Room just north of San Antonio College. Even a little money, for a change."

"A room?"

"Yeah, in a house. Upstairs. Shared the bathroom and kitchen."

"Like a bedsit."

"Is that what you call 'em?"

I shrugged a *yes*. "Didn't know you had those here."

"Anyway, one night, Jimmie and I went out and hit a bar on the north side, off Broadway. She'd heard her girl liked to go there, and I hadn't been to that one, yet.

"I shouldn't have gone; I wasn't in a good mood. A couple guys at work had found out I was gay and...well, they weren't bein' nice about it. Neither was she, once we got there and she found out her girl had gone and got married. We argued over somethin' and I stormed out. Planned to take the bus home.

"Only a guy I sort of knew was in the parkin' lot, smokin' a joint. We chatted. I took a few puffs. All very dangerous and decadent for the mid-Sixties. Years in prison, if you're caught. He said he had some more smoke in his car, so I went with him. He wasn't bad-looking and seemed cool, and I didn't want to come across as a dope who wasn't okay with the latest dope.

"Two of his friends were there. Also smokin'. Newports. Minty. Disgustin'. Just like the both of them. But it covered the smell of the pot. Passed another joint around. They said they'd give me a ride home, so I got in. Brand new '65 Impala, 4-door. Lots of room."

He paused for a long moment, his eyes locked on something far away. I did not move.

Finally, he continued with, "They took me to a dark, quiet area of Breckenridge Park. Grabbed me in places I didn't want. Yanked my jeans down. Tore my undies off. And...and...and they used me. Mouth. Ass. Everything. Even though I told them I didn't want to."

"Christ, Rett."

"Yeah." A smirk crossed his lips. "On a side note, they're the reason I prefer men who are circumcised. One of them had never heard of soap and water, and there is nothing dirtier than a filthy uncut dick."

"Okay, that was ugly."

"You have no idea," he whispered. Again, he was silent for a long

271

time. "They dumped me back at the bar when they were done. It was closed and everybody was gone. Busses weren't runnin'. Didn't have money for a cab. I hurt all over and felt filthy and-and-and I flagged down a cop and told him what happened." Another long silence before he said, "He talked me out of makin' a report."

"Talked you out of it?"

Everett nodded. "*Men can't be raped in Texas*, he said, *only assaulted. And since you're queer, you could go to jail instead of them. It's illegal to be a homo-sexual, here.* Then he made it even worse by askin' me, *But c'mon, isn't that what you queers like? Makin' your guy be with you? Isn't that how you screw?*

"I had no fuckin' idea. This was before I really understood what bondage was, and I wasn't all that experienced in anything else, and I—and I'd cum when they were fuckin' me. I couldn't believe it, but it happened. So I stupidly listened to him. I still hear him sayin' it, every now and then. Remember thinkin', *Yeah, I guess so.*"

He refilled his glass with wine and topped off my own, saying, "I've been fucked up ever since."

I had no idea what to say, so just watched him.

You could almost see a casual attitude fill his face as he continued with, "I went a little crazy. Drank a lot. Wound up gettin' fired from Frost's. Lost a couple other jobs because they figured out I was gay. What made it worse was, I saw the fuckers who raped me. Around at clubs. They even tried to get me alone, again, once. And I said nothin'. Even though I knew they were doin' this to other guys, like me. Guys dumbass enough to trust 'em.

"I stopped goin' to bars. Sometimes, I'd connect with gay men from work or someone in art school, though once I did pick up this gorgeous black salesman when I bought some shoes at Penney's. Sloe eyes and a dick to die for. Another time, when I was workin' at a newsstand, I got this amazingly beautiful Persian student pilot to stick around, after closin', and let me suck him off."

"Persian?"

"Iran sends their pilots to San Antonio to get trainin' in fighter jets and stuff. At Randolph, I think. He came back for repeats. Till I was let go. But I kept away from the bar scene till I graduated art school. By that point, I couldn't handle San Antonio, no more, so I moved to Houston. Start fresh. Whole new life. All that bullshit.

"Problem is, you carry your baggage with you, no matter where you go. And I did. Still do. With some of the guys I pick up—

sometimes I get—I get angry and pretend I'm hurting them. Doing to them what was done to me. It's a good thing Jeremy don't live with me. I've managed to keep that side of my personality away from him."

All I could do was shake my head and murmur, "I never saw any of it in you."

"I'm calmer now. Comes with age. Next birthday, I'll be thirty. You're invited to the funeral."

"All this—is that why you helped me and Scott that night?"

He didn't look at me as he said, "I suppose. I could see what was happenin'. I'd seen *Lunatic* get other guys, that way, and done nothin'. Guess I'd just had enough and wanted to stop it. At least once."

His eyes shifted to catch mine. "I also wanted to see what you'd say, and I could tell right then and there, you keep secrets. That's why I like you, Pug. I know I can trust you. I don't have many people like that in my life."

I just smiled my thanks.

"I told you all this shit because—well, the God-awful truth is, cops don't like to be bothered by people unless they can be brutal or heroic. What's more, one of them probably was a cop. There to let his fellow officers know Matty got his due. Because God knows they'd never be able to prove you did it, not in a court of law. And if you do report this, they'll come after you instead of him. May even get you deported. They protect their own, those bastards, no matter what."

"What do I do, then?"

"Do you know who they were?"

I hesitated before saying, "I-I-I never got a good look at them."

Rett noticed the hesitation and nodded. "Well, the legal system's out, and revenge don't work unless it's against the right people and you know they can't escalate things, on their side. And cops always escalate things. Third choice is, accept it and move on."

"To another town, like you?"

He shook his head. "Houston's big enough to get lost in."

I nodded.

He finished his wine and said, "It's up to you whether you say anything to Jeremy, but you will need to talk to Vangie."

"She's angry with me."

"Of course she is. But I think she'll understand."

"Will she understand I was thinking of quitting her?"

He gave me a long look before asking, "They threaten her, too?"

I just shrugged.

He nodded, long and slow. "Talk to her, Pug. You and she have a lot to discuss, and be honest with her. She's worthy."

"She can come over, if she wants. The gate code's 3-9-7."

"I know. Part of the family, remember?" I half-smiled at him. "Don't you wanna come with me? Treat you to some pie."

I shook my head. "Hurts too much to sit much. Besides, my bike's still up at *The Colonel's* and—"

"That—is that where they grabbed you?"

I nodded, and I could see the question slam into his face. *How did they know you were there?* He looked at the house, by reflex. I shifted my focus from him, because I didn't want him to know I was sure of what he wondered.

"When you're ready to get it," he said, his voice absent, "I-I'll give you a ride."

"Thanks," I said, and saw him scowling as he left.

I pulled a pair of gym shorts over the pajama bottoms. My clock said it was 12:25, and the family usually returned from mass about one or just after. Time enough to be a bastard.

I managed to pull on an undershirt then cranked the AC to max, but I was still trailing sweat when she finally came to the door and God, the image she made when I let her in. Hair pulled back and tied with a bright scarf, peasant blouse off her lovely shoulders, long strap to her purse hanging down, plain tan slacks, golden hoops dancing from her ears, her lips painted red. Her expression was harsh...until she registered the damage to my face. Then she shrank, a little.

"Rett told me, but..." Her voice went too quiet to hear.

"I wish I could say you should see the other guy," I said.

"Did you see who did it?" she asked, her voice wavering.

I shook my head. "Blindfolded. When it did come off, lights were shining in me eyes."

"What about voices?"

Can't take a hint, Irish, you gotta take the punishment.

I tried to answer but couldn't think of the words.

She didn't seem to notice. "Are you all right, now?"

What could I do but shrug?

"And this was Friday night?"

I nodded.

She moved around me and touched the shirt, saying, "May I?"

I took in a deep breath and nodded. She lifted up the back, only a little, but it was enough. I could hear the sharp breath. She dropped the shirt's tail, tears in her voice.

"I can't believe it. I heard of things like this and-and learned about them. Usually done to black men before a lynchin'. But today? These days? Here? Still?"

"Just a scratch or two, right?" Tried to make it a joke. Again, don't think it worked.

She sat on the edge of the bed. I offered her wine but she brushed it away, so I plugged in the cork—then unplugged it and poured myself some more. I stood at the counter, waiting.

It seemed like hours before she said, "We wanted to see you, yesterday, but your aunt didn't think we should."

Of course. Can't let word get out too soon.

"I talked to my father," she continued.

Well...here it comes.

"He says he spoke to you, Friday. Bren, do you—do you think he-he-he set this up?"

I was shocked. "No. Why would you even ask that?"

"The timin'."

"He wasn't the only one unhappy with me."

"But he's the reason you broke our date, right?"

I just sighed, but that was answer enough for her.

She nodded. "You shouldn't've cut out on me, Bren."

"I-I-I had to sort things out."

"About what?"

"You and-and me and-and—"

"You couldn't talk to me about it?"

"I-I-I didn't—couldn't figure what I needed to decide and—"

"If you'd joined us, we could've discussed everything after the movie and this wouldn't've happened."

Wouldn't have—what!? What the bloody hell?

"Not that night, anyway," I snapped.

"Ever. Instead, you wussed out. I really thought better of you."

Oh, that cut deep. I shot a glare at her. Why was she going on at me, like this? "Any decision I made would have been to your face."

"Any decision *you* made? All on your own?"

"It was up to me."

"Was it? Daddy said you were thinkin' of marryin' me. If we'd talked, that would've come up, wouldn't it?"

"...Maybe..."

"Are you still?"

"Still what?"

"Thinkin' of marryin' me?"

Somehow I knew this was not being considered as a proposal.

"Vangie, I-I-I've lived near three years as nobody. How could you marry someone who's naught but a ghost? I thought of making myself legal, but for all I know I'll still be carted back to the North."

"Legal? You're an illegal immigrant?"

"I overstayed my visa. Can't go home, and now..."

"What did you do that's so bad?"

"Nothing, but sometimes even that's too much. Either way, it would not have worked out. And then there's-there's-there's what you plan for your life. I'd be wrong to take you away from that and—"

"Did those animals beat these thoughts into you?"

I shook my head. "I've been beaten before."

"Like this?"

"When you're nine years-old, it's always like this."

She rose and came up to me. Her eyes were tender, a bit of sorrow behind them. "So, it *was* my daddy who got to you."

"He—Rene—he just helped me see the-the reality of it all."

"Reality? He had no idea what the reality was, and neither do you. Thinkin' I was yours, to begin with. I thought you knew better. That we were just havin' fun."

Just having fun. I was never hers, nor she mine. We were...we were just having fun.

"But your Da...even he thought..."

"Daddy? Well, he'll never do that, again. He needs to learn to trust me. I was fool enough to think he already did."

I murmured, my mind not really with me, "Fathers are mad creatures about daughters. Before mine died, my brother and I were on the wrong side of his anger more times than I can count. But I don't recall him ever laying a finger on my older sister, even when she got between him and Ma and us boys."

"This the family back in Ireland?"

"Northern Ireland."

"So what happened to you, last night—"

"As I said, I've been beaten before."

She sighed. "Those stupid, stupid men who did this to you. They're just some wild dogs who think they're provin' something by attackin' a puppy."

The pack of dogs snapped and barked at the tom as it hissed and spat and howled then spun into a raving thing of claws and teeth, startling the beasts, for moment, and tearing into them with mad fury before they swirled around to destroy it only to find it had used the moment of indecision to escape.

I gave myself a smirk. I'd had no such chance, and her comment had brought a frown to my face and I near growled, "You see me as a baby dog?"

She shook her head and sighed. "Bren, I see you as tender and sweet, and a little damaged. A bit needy. I enjoyed bein' with you. We had fun, together. But I never should have let it go as far as it did, because never once did I think of you as a partner for life. I even told you not to love me."

No. "No, you said not to *say* I loved you." Christ, Brendan, that was a desperate response.

"Which is the same thing," she snapped. "If we'd talked, I'd have reminded you of it. I honestly thought you understood. But like any man, the second we get together, you think I'm yours and everything that's gonna happen is up to you. And I hate that attitude in men. I'm never gonna let a man own me, like that."

I could think of nothing to say, in response. Just looked at her.

She sighed and shook her head. "Sorry, that was uncalled for. It's just, when daddy told me what you said, I'd have told him the same thing. And really think he'd have let the word out and they'd have had no excuse to go after you."

I felt a bit dizzy so leaned my elbows against the counter and held my head in my hands...and fucking coughed. Her comments struck me so wrong, I could barely breathe. I was beginning to shake. I couldn't believe it. Anger started to boil inside me.

"You think you're the only reason they did this to me?" whispered from me, without a thought.

"What else could you have you done to deserve it?"

That was for Matty, Irish.

"Crippled a cop." I should not have said it. Should never have said a word. But control over my voice was not an option, at that moment.

That made her hesitate. "What do you mean?"

I looked at her and my heart screamed *Shut up, Brendan, shut up, shut up,* as my voice went low and cruel. "Ask Lon."

I knew he'd lie, but Vangie was friends with his wife and would find out the truth. If she wanted to. That was the question.

She grew tight. "I don't understand."

I was crashing into a sorrow deeper than I'd felt since learning Joanna was gone, and I could not allow that. Could not bring that to Vangie. But there was a creature inside me that had control of my voice and said, "His station wagon is so big and quiet." Where they lay me on a sheet that crinkled and...of course. "And I'm sure his tarp keep my blood off the floor."

She caught my meaning, then. "You...you're sayin'..."

I smiled, cold and cruel, reveling in the knowledge I was giving her, and sneered, "My aunt and uncle will be home, soon. May be best you leave. Don't want the gossips to claim I'm still having my *sugar brown*."

She slapped me.

And backhanded me.

Then stormed out.

Set two of my head injuries bleeding, again. I could feel the blood course down my face and over my jaw and around my neck to stain the undershirt.

I know I should have felt the utter bastard, for what I'd just done. At least bleak and sad and worthless. It wasn't her fault I'd gone running wild in our...our what? Friendship? Acquaintance? Whatever. Instead, here I was joyful at having snapped back at her casual dismissal.

And yet...halfway wanted to die.

Self-care

Monday morning, I found a pay phone on West Gray and called Trujillo's. No way in hell did I want anyone in the house to know what I was doing, anymore. The receptionist answered and my message was simple.

"It's Bren. I quit. Goodbye."

Then I hung up and walked from there to *The Colonel's*. I wanted to get my bike before the sun was too high in the sky, sure, but I was also fair well convinced Todd had turned me over as part of his deal and I wanted to be nowhere near him. That's what he'd been hinting at. His phone calls. Felt regret, just not enough to give me warning.

I wore a dark shirt and loose gym pants, in case I began bleeding, again, and pull-on tennis shoes because the bastards threw out my boots as well as my torn jeans and shirt. It was not an easy journey. My back, legs and arse ached and stung, especially when I began to sweat, but I forced myself through the discomfort by letting it take twice the time it normally would have.

It wasn't till I got there that I realized I didn't have my key. It had been in my front jeans pocket and I hadn't even thought about it. Shite, Brendan, kick your brain into gear. At least they'd brought my wallet back with me. I was able to force-start the bike, and I had another key at the pool house.

I kept to myself, the following week. Finished work on the few projects I had left and sold them. I felt no regret over the smashed cassette player. Now that Vangie'd put me in my place, it was too bloody appropriate, so into the trash with it.

The B-Girls weren't around. In my confused state, I'd forgotten they were off to some camp up in Conroe. Scott was interning at a bank in Dallas, for the summer, so I was troubled by no one but Angus, at that moment. I made myself help Aunt Mari on whatever she needed, but silently. She noticed yet said nothing; just cast caring, worried looks my way.

That hurt me more than Uncle Sean's part in this. She was my mother's sister. The caring one, like Mairead. Yet not one more word from her about what had happened. It took all I had to be anywhere near her. No lunches or dinners in the house. No soaking in the pool. Just sitting on the roof and smoking pack after pack of Marlboros. I'd had foresight enough to buy a carton of them enroute home from *The Colonel's,* and they kept me from crashing into an impossible depression.

I looked in the paper under *rooms to rent, unfurnished and furnished.* Found one of the latter down below Alabama, past a massive highway interchange. I popped over, on a Thursday, played up the Irish to the landlady. Not that I needed to. She looked in my eyes, said, "You're a sweet boy," and took my first and last month's rent.

I moved there in the dead of night, on Saturday, after I'd cleaned the pool house of every trace of me. Told no one I was doing it. Angus sensed I was up to something and kept trying to get me lost in petting him. Didn't work. I wanted to be gone before the B-Girls returned. If they had found out my plans, they'd have trumpeted it in both the local papers.

It's not like I had so much to ferry. All my clothes fit into a duffel bag, and my tools were in a handyman's satchel. By this point, my injuries were healed enough to sling the larger one over my back without extreme discomfort and strap the other to the rear of my seat. Angus followed me to the gate, whining. I gave him a final pat then rolled my bike a block away before starting it up and leaving.

I felt as if I were escaping.

My new room was in what had once been a fine old house. Two stories with great pecan trees around it, not twisted branches like those bloody oaks. An open porch in front on both levels had round, sturdy columns, with a porch in back that was also both levels and enclosed by screens. The exterior was painted a soft pink with tall, black-trimmed windows that had screens on them. No air conditioning, but with them open enough breeze entered to where it mattered little, thanks to the shade.

So long as a fan was going.

A plain fence of wrought iron encompassed the yard, with a creaking gate at the head of the broken sidewalk. There were patches of grass all over, strewn with pecans. I saw a couple of other tenants gather them and eat them straight from the shell. I'd never been a person for nuts, but I tried it and the taste was nearly heaven. A ragged gravel driveway led up to a shabby garage filled with garbage and junk, above which was a two room flat accessed by a rickety staircase.

My room was in the back downstairs quarter, and half the size of the pool house, but I had a large bed, dresser, two chairs and a table. I shared a bath with a lad in the front room on my side of the house, and the entrance I used was through the kitchen. A foyer with a grand staircase separated me from the other side, and there were four more apartment rooms on the second level, all geared to house single men or women. A closed-in area of the back porch had a six-person dining table, and everyone shared the kitchen. It cost but fifty-five dollars a month, bills paid, so I had nothing to complain about.

Mrs. Glendon was the owner. She was near seventy and no taller than my chin—and as noted, I'm not the tallest lad ever. She wore caftans made of the lightest silks and cottons, always in soft pastels that complimented near translucent skin. Thin gold and silver bracelets clicked by the dozen up and down her arms, her fingers were never still, and she carried the scent of lavender in her nearly white hair.

The house had been her family home, but fortune brought about having to subdivide it to make an income she could live on. She kept the rooms to the other side of the stairs from mine, and it was rare to see her in the kitchen. But she was always smiling, always chatty in a non-invasive way, and always a bit distant, even when collecting the rent.

The lad in front of me was named Eldon, and I could get nothing more of a name from him. He was very tall, very thin, skin tanned dark, and poorly dressed. And also very still and quiet to the point it could be spooky. But his large black eyes missed nothing, and the one time I caught a glance into his room I saw stacks of books everywhere. He lived off disability and was barely making a go of it; I got the feeling Mrs. Glendon let him slide on his rent more than once.

Above him was Myron Phelan, a thin lad with cerebral palsy who had, apparently, insisted on that particular room even though climbing the stairs was difficult for him. I don't think he was more than my age, with a body half-twisted from his condition. Still, his eyes were sharp as a hawk's, as was his profile, and he took care of himself in every way needed. Mrs. Glendon referred to him as, *Independent to a fault*.

Since Uncle Sean had used the same phrase on me, I asked her what it meant and she responded, "Won't take help, even when it's needed."

"What if they try to force it on you?" I'd asked.

She'd merely shrugged and wandered back to her room.

Above me was a bright focused lad named Richard Markowitz, who worked in food service, liked to be called Rick and *was only staying until he knew whether or not his new job running TSU's cafeteria would be made permanent.* He was stocky, red-haired, wore glasses over a nose Mrs. Glendon referred to as Romanesque, and sported nice suits that barely covered the hair on his arms and neck. I noticed in him a tendency to become so focused he would pay no attention to anything else around him. Rather like me when I was fixing something. He was also Jewish and had solid plans for his life, and kept Kosher so never made use of the kitchen.

"No offense," he'd said when I'd offered to make him a burger as I made one of my own, "but this kitchen has seen too much that's not right for me. There's a deli down Richmond I go to for dinner. Recommended by my rabbi as the closest to Kosher place in Houston."

I didn't make the offer, again, though I did join him at the deli a few times and found I truly loved their chicken soup with matzo balls, though it drove him near mad the first time I asked for a slice of lemon to put with it. I'd learned to prefer that from the many cans of Chicken Noodle soup I'd prepared for myself.

Above Mrs. Glendon's quarters were two women, one of them named Mrs. Kendall, older, black, large in many ways and on Social Security. She was once a cook in a diner and knew how to whip up meals fit for the Gods. On Tuesdays and Fridays, she would gather us together and make a feast from whatever we brought to her. Meatloaf smothered in tomato soup, with potatoes and carrots and peppers and onions. Tuna casseroles with macaroni and cheese or rice, mushroom soup, more onions and baked to a crispy covering. Spaghetti with meat sauce that had carrots in it! I'd never have thought to do that, but it gave the canned sauce a whole other taste and made the meal better than good. And while she partook of the meals, not once did she bring her own ingredients for it, and she kept the leftovers. When I quietly mentioned it to Mrs. Glendon, she took me aside and said, "She's preparing it, so that's her contribution."

I felt the fool for not having realized that was how she helped make her miserly check extend for the month.

Behind her was Miss Sauvage, a thin maiden-lady who always dressed well before leaving her room, even if it was merely to see what post had come. Her hair was in what she called a French Twist, and she wore little jewelry. Oh, and she insisted her name was pronounced *Soh-VAHGE*. We all humored her.

She worked at a nearby fabric store, to and from which she took a cab, and knew how to make clothes from whole cloth. I figured her to be of Ma's age, but her haunted eyes made me wonder if I might be underestimating. And while her skin was not so wrinkled as Ma's, the lines flanking her mouth were deeper and the crinkles around her eyes were not from laughter. She made me feel sad every time I saw her.

Mrs. Glendon had a granddaughter named Sonja, who lived in the garage apartment, was very tanned, very bulky, and surly at the best of times, but who would come to help her, on occasion. She was well-past forty, making me wonder if I'd underestimated my landlord's age. But while I was peeling cucumbers to help Mrs. Kendall prepare a salad of sliced luncheon meats, cheddar cheese, lettuce, tomatoes, carrots and onions (she did love those last two in everything), and diced olives, no less, she happened to mention Mrs. Glendon had her daughter *at a very early age*, and then she'd been made a grandmother not twenty years later.

"Such a scandal for the family, back then," she said. "She's lucky she inherited this house. She should've give the girl up for adoption. That was the best thing done, back then."

I said nothing, just cut cucumbers as she made a dressing from herbs, olive oil and lemon juice. But I decided right then there was no chance of me sharing any part of my life with Mrs. Kendall and her loose lips.

I found somewhat steady work with a second-hand shop up Fannin, near downtown, repairing TVs and radios and appliances and the like. *As needed.* Again, I had to do a free repair for them to prove myself, but this time I played up the Irish and said, "Lookin' for meself a place to make a bit o' money 'fore I decide to settle here." Completely up front, so they couldn't say they didn't know what they were getting, with me.

My hours were noon to five, normally, and they would also buy some of the things I'd found and fixed. Mrs. Glendon even let me dig through the garbage in her garage for whatever looked promising, and I'd give her half. Sonja was grumpy over me being in the place but said nothing.

I kept to myself the first few months, and I'm happy to say I was allowed to be. I focused on my work, read the full central library, and watched a small black and white telly I'd found that needed but a bit of tinkering in order to turn on. My reading focused on mysteries and crime, science fiction and fantasy, horror and adventure, even classics by Dickens and Twain and Stevenson. I got to know some of the librarians by name, and they would make suggestions. I'd say nine times out of ten, they were good. As for the telly, I stuck with the news and police detective programs.

My mood at the time? My emotions? All I can say is, on the surface they were steady, quiet, like the Foyle whispering past on a cool spring morning. To be honest, that is all I wanted right then. Nothing in the way of coherent thought or emotion. My fellow tenants, whether by intent or not, indulged me.

Except for Rick, who loved to pontificate on everything, once he was done with his day's work. He was the most in control person I'd ever met and seemed to like having followers, of a sort. Many a time when he set out to do something, he'd insist Myron and myself come along, as if to bear witness...and I mean insist to the point of near tossing a fit.

On one occasion, he dragged us to a strip club on Loop 610, somewhere. An ugly low-slung block of a place, darker inside than the night sky, with girls gyrating in high heels and little more. All he did was sit there with a single beer, watching. They'd come up to him and to me, trying to get us to buy more of their shite beer or watered whiskey, and begging tips be stuck in their G-strings. Not one of them even began to interest me, and after but half an hour, he said he was ready to go. Since we were in his car, we went. Myron grew quite agitated on the trip home, and I hold no blame to him; not one of the girls had come close to him. I think Rick caught on, for he never insisted we go there, again.

Eldon would join the table during dinner, but never did he say a word. The closest I ever got to having a conversation with him was once, when we were both in the kitchen—him to get a drink of ice water from a milk jug he kept in the fridge, and me to grab a can of Dr Pepper. He'd looked at me, smiling, and said, "I bet you've never had a lonely day in your life."

I was so taken aback by even hearing the sound of his voice, all I could think to say was, "Only my share."

He just shook his head and returned to his room.

Sonja just stayed snarly.

That's not to say I isolated myself. Those Tuesday-Friday meals could easily draw me into hours of fake-chatting with them all. Which

I actually enjoyed, especially since a Friday dinner helped me make it through the maddening fireworks of Fourth of July. Billie Jean King had won at Wimbledon in a massive blow-out against a man, and that was far more important to all.

We'd also chat about NASA's Mars adventure, and how more Apollo flights were planned, including docking with Russia's Soyuz craft. Then there was this new dance called *The Hustle*, that Myron insisted was being sung by football players or something. Miss Sauvage went on a bit about a new polyester fabric called Trevira, that was fire-retardant and easy to care for. In short, nothing too deep or meaningful. The exact sort of discussions I needed.

As for Northern Ireland, the IRA had a truce that wasn't one. The Protestant UVF and UDA had a family fight the same as PIRA and OIRA'd had, with more dead thanks to it. The usual tit-for-tat shootings and stabbings, with the Army still killing Catholics at will. Some new Protestant Action Force was enjoying its slaughters as the IRA had run-ins with the British and more Protestant sub-groups popped up. But it was not quite as vicious as 1972 had been, and it was of minimal interest to the others, so I left all thought of it in my room. It's not as if there was anything I could do.

That may seem cold, since most of my family was still caught in that hell, and I give no excuse for it. I was still too caught in my aunt and uncle's betrayal. I kept track as best I could on the bombings and deaths, to check on family and friends. And saw how casual the news was about the slaughter of the Miami Show Band members by Protestants, as well as other civilians caught in the crossfire. I also found that the central library received copies of The Washington Post and New York Times, which carried stories in more detail, so I kept track as best I could.

I told myself that had I seen any story even hinting at Rhuari or Maeve being hurt, I'd have contacted Aunt Mari. But I never had to test my claim.

I suppose I could have maintained contact with Jeremy and Everett, but I didn't want to put them in a position where they might have to lie about me. And Everett's connection with the family was too tenuous to test like that. So I stuck to my little area, the Kroger that was closest, and kept my head down when on my Montesa. Seems being on the other side of the 59 was like a wall keeping those in River Oaks and even Montrose away.

Work I did for that shop was more by rote than anything, it was so easy. Rewire a lamp. Solder a broken connector. The usual nonsense. But they were happy with me, and altogether I made enough to get by. I also fixed a few things for Mrs. Glendon in her apartment, gratis. She was always very appreciative, and having her smile at seeing one of her truly ancient lamps come to life without blinking or her aged console TV work without flickering pleased me to no end. She also had an ancient crystal radio that stopped working and took a lot of focus on my part to bring back to life. I wasn't fond of the sound coming from it, but she was overjoyed. I think she'd had the damn thing since she was a girl.

I also discovered the joy of wanking. Masturbating, if you will. Not that I hadn't before, but now it was near every night. Dreaming of a fine woman I might have seen on the street coming to me and making use of me. I was more aware of the varieties of sexual positions with female bodies, now, and proudly pretended to use every damn one of them. What was best was, this way—using fantasy to fulfill my needs instead of a live woman—I need never worry about hurting someone, or them getting hurt on my behalf. And while I sometimes missed having the actual touch of one, it proved to be satisfying enough.

By Thanksgiving, my sadness was dissipating and my comfort with the others in the house was close to warmth. It was my suggestion we each pitch in a bit of cash for Mrs. Kendall to buy a fine turkey to go with the potatoes, carrots, green beans, mushroom soup, yams, butter, stuffing, onions (of course) and cranberry sauce from a can. Miss Sauvage used her usual cabbie to take her to and from Kroger's, to fill the list, then Mrs. Kendall pulled together a feast.

Mrs. Glendon showed me a Norman Rockwell's painting, saying, "This is what she's aiming for, so we need to set the table just like this."

Well, while it wasn't exact, Mrs. Kendall was pleased, and we all enjoyed every bite. Including pecan pie. I'd never had it; Aunt Mari had always made pumpkin to end her meals.

What I found interesting was, the only person to have family come visit him at this time was Rick. He had a sister, her husband and their five children stop by when driving home to Los Angeles. From Disney World in Orlando. In a Winnebago.

"So stupid," Rick said after they had left. "Disneyland is just down the 5, but they just had to go to one that's at the other end of the country. I'm the only one with sense, in my family."

I merely nodded and smiled. Like I was simple.

No one ever appeared for Myron or Eldon, but I got the feeling neither expected any. Same for Mrs. Kendall and Miss Sauvage. Even at Christmas.

Mrs. Glendon had a small tree delivered to sit at the base of the stairs, and everyone put ornaments on it. I bought some from a gift shop on Westheimer. The tree never wound up being as rich-looking as Aunt Mari's, nor was anything more than a row of lights put up, outside, to celebrate, but I enjoyed it fully. We picked names from a hat for gifting. I drew Miss Sauvage and found her a nice spring-like scarf at Woolies, which she seemed to like. I got a copy of *The Dubliners* from Eldon; I think it was one of the books on the floor in his room and he'd just wrapped it. Didn't matter; I'd read nothing by James Joyce but heard he was good.

New Year's was gentle. Only Rick, Myron and myself made it to midnight to share a glass of Manischewitz grape wine. Which I was not fond of so only sipped, but it pleased Rick.

They knew nothing of my birth date, so I passed into twenty with no fanfare. It being a Monday, all I did was read and have a shot of vodka. I thought of a joint but didn't think that would go over well, and I had no pills or blow—though to be honest, I'd felt no need for them in months. Nor had I needed one of my heart tablets. The solitude had become my drug of choice. Associations, not friendships, my preference. So a quiet night to myself made it one of my better birthdays.

I know I was off licking my wounds like that injured tom probably had after his encounter with that pack of dogs. I wanted— no, I *needed* the peace to regroup my thoughts and try to understand my place in this world, though to be honest with myself, I wasn't consciously trying. It was more like I was drifting, with no urgency to do a thing more than let the world pass me by. I'd seen what happens when you try to make plans.

It all went well until one day, after I'd been there a full year, I arrived home from work to find Everett sitting on the porch steps, looking the same as ever, but with a near scowl on his face. I stopped in the driveway and hopped off the bike.

"Hello, Pug," was all he said, quiet and easy before he rose to usher himself over to me.

"How'd you find me?" I asked.

"I found you six months, ago. Saw you on your scooter and—"

"It's a motorcycle."

"And followed you. I'd have said somethin', then, but I knew how you were feelin' and I didn't want to fuck things up. Of course, I didn't expect you to take my comment so literally."

I frowned. "What comment?"

"Houston bein' big enough to disappear in. Y'know, your aunt and uncle are worried sick."

"Are they?"

"Cut it out, Pug; you're not that callous."

"Then you don't know me so well."

"For God's sake," he snapped. "We havin' this conversation here?"

I huffed and headed to the back door, pushing my bike. "Come on in."

He followed.

I led him into my room and he glanced around, not impressed in the slightest. "Have you been *here* all this time?" I frowned. He raised his hands, in surrender. "Sorry. Seems...comfortable."

"It's been all right."

"New friends?"

I shrugged a *yes*, still not happy. He could tell.

"Home from work, already?"

"I keep me own hours."

"That must be nice. But not very lucrative."

"I'm doing well-enough."

He nodded, not believing me. "Okay, fine, we'll do it this way. Your sister's in town."

That kicked my mood out of me. "Mai? You've met her?"

He nodded. "Her, her kids, her hubby, who's a real cuddle-bear, by the way."

"They told you who I am?"

"No! But I'm not stupid. Hell, I'm practically one of the family, thanks to you, and they let their guards down just enough for me to figure it out. I think they think I helped you disappear. Your aunt keeps askin' me subtle little questions that I'm not supposed to know are meant to pry information past my supposedly impenetrable wall of silence. Even Jeremy's given me a nudge or two while tryin' to find out. It's almost cute."

"Why didn't you tell 'em where I was?"

He huffed. "Since you don't tell tales on me, neither do I, you. I honestly thought you'd have said somethin' yourself, by now. But then, I also know how complicated family life can be, so—so—well, shit, why haven't you?"

I shrugged.

"Quiet as the grave. Normally, that's what I like about you, Pug. No bullshit out of your mouth, so none out of mine."

"So you—how much d'you know?"

"Aside from what happened to you? And who was probably behind it? And talkin' to Vangie? And hearin' what you said to her? You proud of that?"

No, but I could find no way to admit it.

He took in a deep breath. "Okay...well, let's just say I know enough to know I don't want to know any more. I just...I thought you outta know your sister's here. Okay?"

My head spun as I murmured, "Okay. Uh, thanks."

"Jesus, Pug, don't you even want to see her?"

I went weak and dropped into a chair. My voice barely registered as I said, "How?"

Everett squatted before me, his hands on my knees.

"Easy. You get on your bike and ride over to your Aunt's house and knock on the door and when she opens it say, *Hi, how you doin'; what's for dinner?*"

"I can't."

He sighed as he said, "Your uncle, right?"

The glance I gave him was sharp enough to let him know he'd made the correct assumption.

"You'd let *him* put a wall between you and your family?"

I rolled my eyes. If only it were that simple.

"You don't really know them," I murmured. "Know what—" I cut my voice off and lay my head in my hands.

Everett's voice grew calmer as he said, "*Them?*"

I pressed to my forehead with my thumbs. "I-I-I just—" I was beginning to shake. And cough, dammit. Every fucking wound from a year back had been ripped open, again.

"I know, Pug. I mean, I don't *know* know, but I have my suspicions. This time, at least, I was smart enough not to nose around. It's just—you wouldn't be doin' this for your uncle. Or your Aunt. You'd be doin' it for your sister and nephews and nieces and brother-in-law and cousins and friends, and don't be a pussy, Pug. Don't make me think less of you. Please."

"And if I don't go, you plan to tell 'em where I am?"

"No," he snapped. "But I would stop admirin' you. I would stop bein' proud of knowin' you. I would stop—I think I'd stop lovin' you."

That jolted me. I looked at him. "Loving me?"

He gave me a sheepish shrug. Then he added, with a wink, "Don't tell Jeremy—as if I need to say that to you."

"Don't you love him?"

"Of course I do, but it...it's different. With him, it's a partnership. With you, it-it's so much mixed together. Admirin' you, wantin' to protect you, care for you, afraid for you, hurtin' for you. Afraid *of* you. Almost like you're my own child, but mixed in is-is me wantin' you. Wantin' so much for you. With Jeremy, I'm comfortable. I never could be, with you. If that makes any sense."

None in the least. But still, I took in a deep breath and rose. And nodded, saying, "I'll go, soon as I clean up."

"You'll be glad."

"Will I?"

The look he cast me was haunted but tender. "If you want backup, Jeremy and I can be there."

I shook my head. "I'm not that poorly."

"I know," he sighed. "I knew that the night I met you."

Then he hugged me and left.

I showered and shaved, except for my mustache, then dressed up nice and rode over—and spent half an hour down the block trying to convince myself I should go that last fifty feet.

Because I was terrified.

How would I be greeted? Would Uncle Sean send another fist into my face? I wasn't fool enough to think I could stop him or avoid it. Nor would I let it pass without violence, in return. Would Aunt Mari layer me with guilt and pain? And the B-girls, dear God, they'd probably tear me apart for leaving them. I wasn't even so certain Angus would be happy to see me. And I had no excuse to give them for vanishing except I needed to be alone. Which is fair pathetic. So what do I do?

What do I do?

Then Mai sat in the front bay window...and she looked so little-changed my heart tore into me in ways I'd never felt possible.

The B-Girls joined her, chatting in their argumentative way, and she was so calm and easy, with them, and kind...and instinct took over and I started up my bike and rode up to the door and rang the bell.

Angus barked and Bernadette opened it and I said, "Howya. I hear you got company."

And she screamed, "MOM!"

Understandings Made

To my surprise, Bernadette and Brandi bounced around happy to see me. Of course, they were also *just furious*, which they let me know, over and over in the same breath. Aunt Mari rushed up with a hug and *was glad to have me home*. Scott was in his usual *were you gone?* manner, and Angus was beside himself with joy and insisted on many a petting and lots of kisses.

All wanted to know where I'd been, which was no surprise, but my only response was, "Here and there." After the fourth or fifth time of hearing it, they got the hint and moved on. Uncle Sean? He said not a word. Nor did I want his attention in any way. But Mai was—she was my Mairead.

"By the Saints, Bren, you look so well," was her immediate comment. Letting me know the pretense was to be kept. "Much better than when you were brought over." Then she hugged me and continued with, "I was so worried when they said you'd vanished, and not a word from you."

"I just needed to be with myself, for a while," I muttered, so happy to be caught in her hugs, again.

"*A while* is how you put it? A year?" Her eyes were dancing with so much joy, I couldn't help but respond with smiles of my own. That's when I noticed she was well along with another child.

"How many is this, now, Mai? Ten?"

"It's numbers six and seven. Twins." She pulled me into another hug to whisper, "And Tur's aware these are the last."

My voice was just as soft when I asked, "The church allows contraception?"

Her hands were so tender on my face as she laughed, "Oh, Bren, don't be silly. We live in Canada, and there are so many ways to bend ancient rules and regulations that won't actually break any of them."

"I take it you like it there."

"Love it, except for everyone driving on the wrong side of the bloody road. Just can't get used to that nonsense."

I was then slung into the bay window. Angus lay across my lap, demanding scratches to his belly, and I was peppered with questions by her as to what I'd been doing. I told her everything I could without spilling secrets.

Or my address.

I learned Rhuari had married his lass up in Pennyburn and felt a twinge of envy at him doing what I'd wanted to do with Joanna so growled, "I guess he had to be married so young, eh?"

"No, it was only from love," Mai told me, a bit of chiding in her voice. "Her name's Bridie, formerly a Harkin. Her Da's a teacher at Magee and her mother does photography—news and portraits and such. Even *my mother* thinks she's a lovely girl. Just two months younger than him. She's sendin' me photos of the wedding and maybe, maybe a copy of a film her mother took. Eight-millimeter, but Shamus has a projector so it'll be fine.

"Maeve says it was small but sweet. He'd been seein' her since he sat for his A-Levels, the little sneak. Both are bound for Queens, in the Fall, and will stay with a maiden aunt of hers, in Belfast. He's already found himself a post at an off-license, in the evenings."

That sent a chill through me. "An off-license, Mai? In Belfast, in the middle of The Troubles?"

She grabbed her glass of iced tea as she said, "He'll be fine." Then she sipped some in far too controlled a way. I was about to argue but she cut me off with, "Maeve says so." Then she cast me a look that near made my heart flip-flop.

"She's not women's auxiliary?" I asked, refusing to believe for a second she could ever fit in with that crowd.

"Don't be daft. She—um, she knows a good friend of *our Brendan's*." Said with another careful look.

I went along with her. "Good friend of his, is it?"

She nodded. "Colm O'Faelan."

"Colm?" Christ, suddenly I realized I'd not thought about him in months. Close to a year. Then I remembered I'm not meant to have known him.

She nodded. "He's a bright lad. Moved up in PIRA, since I left Derry. Has more than enough connections. Can make promises, even."

I didn't mean to say it, but I was still taken aback so whispered, "I'm shocked he's willing, after what happened."

"Why would he not be?" she asked, her expression even more

careful. "That bomb goin' wrong was not my *brother*, Brendan's, doin'. And it's fully understood, now that everyone's calmed down. Well, understood by those who want to."

She took another deliberate sip of iced tea, which Aunt Mari had always made too sweet and strong for me, and turned to face me, eye to eye. "She was also close to Danny Gallagher, another friend of our Brendan's." Then she took a deep breath and put a gentle hand on mine and said, "Unfortunately, he was caught in an own-goal, six month back."

That was a punch in the gut. I whispered, "Danny?"

Mai nodded, her eyes hurting for me. "He-he was helpin' set another bomb—well, both he and the lad who built it."

No. No, it would have been Danny who did the building. He'd been good with electrical work and his apprenticeship. So if he'd been making up bombs for the IRA, I could see him becoming his moody self then losing concentration and—

The child bounced against the car and white filled the world and silence descended and—

And all I could do was let out a long, slow sigh and murmur, "I missed that in the news."

"It wasn't much mentioned. It happened not long after Danny was accused of shootin' Father Demian."

At that, I almost laughed. So he had tracked the bastard down and fixed him. But why had he waited so long? Had he debated doing it, for all that time? Or had he finally just reached the point where he had to take some action for his own well-being? An attitude I could easily understand. Still I leaned back, more sad than I'd been in months.

Mai carefully kept on with, "Rumor is, the lad Danny was with had gone off the rails. He'd deliberately given out the wrong warning for bombs they'd planted. Several innocent people, both Protestant and Catholic, died. So the Brits were chasing after him, and then Danny for Father Demian."

"The old bastard lived? Grassed on him?"

She nodded. "It's thought by many the IRA took care of the problem. Two birds with one stone. Others think Danny was out to top himself, and the other lad was caught in it. I can't believe that, though. He was always such a nice lad. Well-behaved."

Before I could stop myself, I snarled, "And that bloody priest is still walking around."

"Bren! It's a wonder the man wasn't killed. Took him months of rehabilitation to be able to walk, again. He's now retired to a flat in the Vatican. Handles paperwork of some kind."

"Good."

"What're you on about?"

My brain caught up with my heart and said, "Nothing. I just never liked him."

"*You* knew him?" And her voice was sharp.

I was barely able to keep myself from saying, *Aye, and he was a devil*. But only barely. "I-I-I knew of him. God, poor Dan—um, poor lad."

"He did have his moods," Mai said, carefully.

I nodded. The one positive was that Father Devil had no more access to boys to molest; just other priests. I wondered how well *that* would go over. Perhaps I could ask Everett to dig into the bloody man's continued existence.

Then Tur came waltzing in, looking half-again his size when last I saw him, but strong with it. And his face was as bright as Mai's; no more of that haunted look I'd seen on him. He'd been napping in the pool house, along with his five. Ranging from ten months to seven years, all were more the image of him than my sister, and none of them took me as *their cousin twice removed*, at first.

You can't fool a wain about people, not really.

We had a great meal of pot roast, potatoes, carrots (can't get away from the damn things) and salad, with an almost-decent beer flowing like water and conversation a-plenty. The twins flanked me and continued to pester me with as many questions as you might expect from an agent for MI-5. They also made sure I understood that each had a boyfriend who wasn't worthy of them. And they had been taking dancing classes where the boys were just impossible. And both insisted I go ice skating with them, again, so they could show off their moves. Along with more than a thousand other details that flew right past me. For once, they did not begin their usual back and forth, nor could I get them going. It was head-spinning.

But it did keep me from drifting into too deep of sadness over the understanding that Father Devil had finally killed me China. Not with a bullet or a knife or garotte, but with words and actions of years ago. And the only one being held to account was the true victim.

All of my anger against Danny, over Joanna, vanished. For what good does it do to keep angry at a ghost?

And there was Colm, enveloped onto another probable path to

death. I'd read where it looked as if the British were now shooting to kill those they knew—or even suspected—were part of the alphabet crew, albeit on the Catholic side, *not* the Protestant. That put him in deeper danger, but enough said about that.

At the same time, Scott was also chattering about adding some weight, and that he was to graduate in the coming year. And how his pledge to a fraternity helped him with contacts, so that he'd already fielded job offers from three banks in Dallas.

"Just home for a few days to see my cousins, spend Fourth of July, then it's back to the Metroplex. Intern at Republic." Spoken as if I should know what it meant and must be impressed.

"You like it up there?" I asked, during a break in the B-girls' interrogation.

"I prefer Austin," he said, "All the Landaus are there, right now. Gonna watch fireworks over Town Lake, or somethin'. But reality is, there's not much goin' on there besides UT and the State Government. Maybe in a few years. I want to be in the center of the action. DFW's goin' strong and my girlfriend's from there. Turtle Creek." Again, spoken as if I should know it. "The Metroplex is the place to be. I'll bet it's the biggest city in the country in twenty years. You should hop up for a visit."

"How far is it?" I asked.

"Oh, don't drive. Catch Southwest; they're real cheap."

But Brandi chimed in with, "Oh, no, no, no, they're tacky."

"The stewardesses wear hot pants!" Bernadette added.

"Not many girls look good in those."

"But they still wear 'em."

"Yeah, like Janelle Farmer."

"Oh, the perfect illustration."

And praise the saints, they were off, with Scott given no chance for rebuttal.

Angus sat with his head in my lap the whole time, accepting bites of the roast but seeming more afraid that I might sneak off, again. I kept his ear tickled as much as I could.

I'd arrived just after they'd returned from a trip to NASA, and now they were excited for the fireworks over Hermann Park, day after next. Sunday was America's Bi-Centennial and it was going to be massive, this year, so Mai talked me into staying the weekend. I'd have to sleep on the couch since they'd taken up every available bed. I'd rather be home, popping valium to sleep through the holiday, but I hadn't brought any with me. Not even a joint, and oh, did I feel the need for one. Especially now I knew about Danny, Colm, Maeve and Rhuari and how I was, even to Mai, officially no more.

But at the same time, it was so good just to be near her and Tur. Connect with my family, again. Who I was—used to be. No, still was, but playing at a part. I'd be Brendan Kinsella till I died, and that was that. So I gave in.

We sat around to quietly talk the evening through. Tur told me how they'd only needed a driving license to cross the border into America. And how they'd passed through Niagara Falls and spent two days in New York City and another day in Washington, then Nashville, New Orleans, and finally here.

"Ten days, it took," he said. "Two-thousand miles. Tiring, since my wife refuses to get a license to drive."

"I don't need to," Mai smiled back. "Our new house is close to a grocers and the bus is good enough for me. But you have a motorbike, Bren. How did ya manage that?"

"He's had it for years," said Brandi.

"He goes all over the place, on it," Bernadette added.

"But he needs a new helmet."

"The one he's got is so old."

"And ugly."

"We saw a really cool one that had wings on the sides."

"And the face of an eagle, on the front."

And the next half-hour was made up on the need for me to replace my perfectly fine helmet with one they thought to be acceptable, which we would buy tomorrow, no matter what.

Finally, one by one people wandered off to their rooms, and soon the house was quiet. Dark. Easy. The B-girls had dug some of Scott's old clothes out of a box in the attic for me to change into, and they were being washed. It would be interesting to see how they fit, now I was more filled in. Sheets and a blanket had been draped over the couch, for me, with a cushion for a pillow. All so very nice and casual and happy, I should have slept like a baby.

But my head was chaos within so I sat in the bay window, to think.

Do too goddamn much thinking.

Its shades were up and the moon was out, and in that alcove I felt quiet. Still of heart. There was light enough to just make out my portrait was no longer on the wall by the fireplace; the painting of flowers was back. The family's portrait was still above the mantlepiece, and everything else was exactly where it had been before I left, except Angus' bed was gone. I vaguely wondered where he now slept. No matter; this would always be the comfortable home for people and family to visit and sit and enjoy themselves. Like you'd find in a manor house.

Like Joanna's had struck me.

A funny thought hit me. People say, over and over, money can't buy happiness. But never acknowledge that it can buy comfort and that can be a path to happiness.

Sometimes.

Not always.

Not when others have chosen to force themselves into your life. Like the British had done, in the North. Even well-off Catholic families had learned that harsh lesson.

Poor Danny.

I felt there should still be some anger behind my heart over what he'd done, but the sadness was too strong. He'd been me China. One of me best mates. Damaged by a bastard meant to protect him. To guide him. And he was no more. I wondered how his Da had taken the news. His Ma. His sister—her being the only one I honestly thought might have wept for him.

And then there was Colm. Now thinking himself important but only another pawn in a war over nothing, with a target on his back.

And dear God—Rhuari, somehow calmly going about his life as if the Troubles meant nothing to him. And Maeve plowing ahead without distraction. And Kieran going wild.

I thought to say a few words to the Virgin for them...but I'd stopped praying. Couldn't remember the last time, outside of mass, where I'd whispered my wishes up to God. Was it at my first dinner with the family? With Aunt Mari and hers? For Joanna? What words did I use? I couldn't remember. I wanted to say something for my Chinas, my brothers, my sister, but couldn't think even of how to begin.

Except to cough. Again. Dammit. But I'd had sense enough to bring some pills in my wallet, wrapped in a tissue, so I was safe, there.

I looked around the room. It was neither proper nor honest, anymore. All was alien to me. I hadn't been gone all that long, yet I couldn't believe I'd lived here. And that it was so bloody chilly.

I reached across and drew the blanket around me, hoping to ward off my shaking. I leaned back, thinking of that day. The day I'd learned what Father Devil was. The day I'd stood aside and let Danny wander off by himself and—

He looked around as he disappeared into the mist and saw me before he got in the car and glanced behind me and I turned and white surrounded me as I was screaming and he held me as Colm punched me and he pulled Ma back from me and—

The stairs creaked, jolting me. I wasn't asleep, only in that near state close to it. I looked at the stairs to see—

Uncle Sean coming down.

I bolted to my feet to face him. There was a soft lamp in the kitchen to keep the darkness from taking over, but it was behind him. So while he could see me, well enough, thanks to the window's light, I could make out little more than the shape of him in the shadows about us.

"You ain't told us where you been," he growled.

I shrugged.

"Stayin' with that queer friend of yours?"

"I'll thank you to keep a civil tongue about Rett. He's been more decent to me than you could even think of being."

"After all I done for you?"

"What you did for me still shows on my back! Care for a look?"

"Keep your voice down!" He then gave a long sigh. "You really think I had somethin' to do with it?"

"I think you were there," I said, "and stopped it when I collapsed. Do you want special thanks for saving my life, after putting it in jeopardy?"

He sat on the arm of the couch. A bit more of the kitchen light shone past while still sheltering him from my view.

"When you left, I was glad," he finally said, his voice cool and matter-of-fact. "My wife wasn't, but ain't much to be done about it. Police report? Missin' persons?" He snorted a laugh. "She just had to let it go. And I was relieved.

"Till I got a call from the local FBI office. Lookin' for a kid named *Brendan Kinsella.* Knew he was related to my wife. Knew I had an Irish boy stayin' with me. Had me come in. *To talk.* Wanted me to bring that Irish boy along.

"I told 'em I didn't know where that *Brendan* was, an' that Brennan had returned to Ireland. They didn't believe me. Showed up at the house a couple weeks later, wantin' to talk with him. Said

Dublin had no record of him enterin' the country. A British spook was with 'em."

It seemed he wanted me to say something more, but I only glared at him. I felt no need for this conversation.

He finally nodded. "I showed 'em the room upstairs. They asked about the pool house, so I showed 'em that. All clean. All neat. Too clean an' neat. They started askin' if I'd let that Irish boy work at *The Colonel's*. I told 'em it was part of his therapy; get him used to dealin' with people, again."

That actually made me laugh.

He nodded. "Again, they didn't believe me. They think I helped you get away with assaultin' a police officer. That's when I brought David Landau in and they backed down. A little. It's lucky I was the only one here. Your aunt don't know 'bout it."

"You don't give her much credit, do you?"

He stiffened with self-righteousness, obvious even in the dimness of the room, and his voice grew cold and hard. "Y'know, Trujillo's got raided by immigration. Two of the guys deported."

That jolted me. "Which two?"

"You really care?" I said nothing. He finally continued with, "Hugo and Tomas. Rene thinks you turned them in."

"He's a fucking idiot. Anyone who knows me knows I would never do that."

"Yeah, I know. Border cops was really lookin' for you. Those two were just luck o' the draw. Good thing is, that helped verify who was behind all that shit, so I could get it shut down."

"Are you going to say it was a cop causing you pain?" I asked, oh, so sweetly. "Perhaps the one who brought me here in his station wagon?"

He almost smiled as he nodded. "I kind of figured you knew who it was. Stupid bastard shot himself in the foot, with that stunt. Hurt the whole goddamn department. I used to give nice donations to 'em. Pension fund. Help out wounded officers. Orphans and widows. All that shit. Thought it could protect me. But he set the ABC breathin' down my neck. I now gotta make sure everything in my bars is a hundred percent perfect. Cost me shitloads of money. So...the last time they come lookin' for a donation, I told 'em why they ain't gettin' another. He got himself transferred to a desk as they investigate him."

Again, it's like he wanted me to speak and was irritated by my silence.

"Told Rene, too. Dunno what all happened, but he quit and moved back to N'Orleans, soon after. An' that daughter of his—"

"Evangelyne."

He eyed me. "She's off to Washington. State Department, Jeremy told us, real happy for her. He thought we were hidin' you, 'cause of the feds; thought I'd pass it onto you. I didn't know she knew him, too."

"Would it have mattered? You achieved your goal."

"I didn't want nobody hurt."

I had to fight a laugh.

He noticed and took in a deep breath, saying, "All right, all right. You, a little. Put you in your place. Just didn't expect as much as they did."

I could barely keep my voice level when I spit, "What'd you do, barter with them? Pay them? Lay down guidelines? *No more than five lashes per inch of skin?* You ask for some of your money back after seeing the damage they did me?"

He rose and growled, "Keep your voice down!"

"I didn't ask you to come talk to me."

"Goddammit, Bren, I gotta live and work in this town. It took a lot to let you come here 'cause it broke all kind of laws, but—"

"Did *I* ask you to?"

"Your mother did, you ungrateful little shit. She got hold of my wife and we agreed to get you out of the country; to hide you."

"Why?!"

"There was people on our own side pissed as hell. Believe you me, if we had left you with them, you'd be six feet under, right now. We kept you alive and cared for you, and then to have you trash everything and endanger us? Threaten my family's livelihood? It was worse than ungrateful. It was destructive."

"You told me none of this," I growled. "How was I supposed to know—?"

"You got told more'n you should've. Thanks to my wife. You had more'n enough information to understand how important it was to keep a low profile!"

"No, no, no, no, no, you don't put this back on me. Giving me half-truths and semi-lies. Telling me nothing I could hold onto in order to make plans or—"

"What plans did you need to make? You weren't supposed to be here; you weren't even well. Still aren't."

"As your friends proved." And I fucking coughed.

"They weren't my friends!" He took a deep breath and let it out before continuing. "Just a couple guys at the bar. Saw you with that girl."

"Evangelyne!"

"Keep your goddamn voice down! They told me what was bein' planned."

I advanced on him. "Who? Who was it? Bidwell one?"

No, he wasn't there, that night. Or was he? I couldn't recall.

Uncle Sean didn't budge, except to bunch his right hand into a fist. "You ain't gettin' names, boy. All you're gettin' is what I'm tellin' you. They wanted me to understand it was nothin' personal against me or my family."

Ain't gonna hurt you much.

Just put you in your place.

Bidwell. That *was* his voice. Fucking Bidwell. Who saw me cripple Matty and did his gossipy bit to help himself out of a small trouble. *Just let me be part of it.* The son-of-a-bitch would love that.

"So I made a deal with 'em," Uncle Sean snarled. "Warned 'em 'bout your heart. Didn't want you left there to get found in the mornin'. Get it in all the goddamn papers."

"You give them some of my pills?"

"To be safe."

"I still near died." Another fucking cough.

"I know. They *did* go too far with their end of it, but there's nothin' I can do about that, now." He rose. "Sometimes you gotta make hard choices and hurt people in order to protect those you care for. Now, I'm not sorry 'bout any of this. It's half your own damn fault."

I couldn't keep the sneer from my voice as I said, "Isn't that always how it is, with a coward?"

He stood there, for a moment, tensed enough to hit me, again, and I made myself ready for it. Instead, he sighed and said, "You're movin' back here."

"Are you bloody mad? Why should I?"

"We'll put you in the room upstairs. I want you here the next time those Fed bastards come snoopin' 'round. An' you'll tell 'em who you are. *Brennan*. McGabbhinn. I'll give you a bio to repeat."

At that I snarled, yanked off my shirt and turned to show him the marks on my back. Even in the soft light you could see the scars. The words hissed from me. "And how about I show them this?"

"You won't."

I turned back to him. "You so sure?"

He nodded. "'Cause you know as well as me, they won't care. It's somethin' for the local cops to handle."

He remained a block of nothing in the kitchen light. I felt like I was floating.

"I don't understand," I said, soft and breathless. "What good does me staying here do?"

"Told you. I want this shit over *Brendan* or *Brennan* settled. I want my business back to where it was 'fore you came. With the ABC off my neck and no more shit from Washington. I'm gonna have David Landau make you fully legal. Get you a green card and social security number. Helps to have a Jew lawyer who knows people who know people. But till it's all done, you'll work at *The Colonel's*. Paid normal, with taxes out. Path to citizenship. Whatever. Everything legal. And it'll all get done under your new name."

I snarled, "My name is Brendan Kinsella."

He shook his head. "So far as I'm concerned, he died in that explosion, was carted off an' buried, nice an' quiet. Couldn't have a Catholic body show up in a bombin' aimed at a Protestant group. Especially one with connections to the IRA. Brits'd have a field day, in the papers. Great propaganda tool.

"So you are Brennan McGabbhinn, now. Born in Letterkenny. Relatives in Dublin took you in after an accident that killed your father. Decapitated him. Seein' it sent you off your head and exacerbated a heart condition. 'Cause of my *charity work* for Ireland, an' how you're a third or fourth or somethin' cousin, by marriage, the Church asked if I'd sponsor you here. Get some specialized treatment for *an injured boy who went a little off his head.*

"It's thanks to complications in your illness that you wound up over-stayin' your visa, but it was a medical visa, so that's easier to get corrected. It'll mean some fines an' court costs, but it's doable."

My brain went automatic. "Then you got a passport for me—"

"Expired. Gonna have to work you up a new one. That'll take a while. An' we'll have to explain we thought you'd gone home but instead had another psychotic break and just vanished. Till today. May mean goin' before a judge an' makin' nice with the State Department. A few political donations. But I can get it settled. If you're here. Available for them to talk to whenever they want, and back up everything I said."

"You want too much. I-I-I won't do it. I'll leave this fucking city."

His voice grew soft and like ice. "I seem to recall *Brendan* had a younger brother. Nice kid, I hear. Smart. Goin' to college in Belfast. Got married to a sweet girl. Mai loved tellin' us all about it. But a Catholic boy in a Protestant town? Name linked to an IRA offshoot? These days?"

I actually felt ice spread throughout me and had to fight to keep my voice level. "You do anything to hurt my brother, I'll see to it the whole world learns what you've done and how you got a good lad killed and—"

"The IRA is all who matters in that, an' who they gonna believe? Me? A man who's given them money an' helped in ways you don't even know about? Or you? A disturbed young man who can't even prove who he is?"

"But—but it—it's Rhuari. He's done nothing to you."

Now he advanced on me, both fists ready and reminding me so much of Da I actually expected him to punch me—and I just knew if he did I'd lose any sense of control and tear into him and wind up dead, or worse.

"Listen up, you little shit," he growled, his voice barely audible. "You been nothin' but a disruption since you came here. Bringin' that fag into my house. Attackin' a cop at my bar, over his slut of a wife. Chasin' 'round with a black girl for all my neighbors to see. I got the IRS auditin' me over donations to NORAID. I spent more in lawyers in the last four years than my whole fuckin' life. I want it stopped. Now. An' if that means me bein' a motherfuckin' asshole to do it, then I will be a motherfuckin' asshole. Family or no family.

"But once I know for sure that it's all done, that I'm free an' clear, you can do whatever the hell you want, go where you want, even move to fuckin' Canada. I know your sister'd like that. Fact is, so would I. So think about it. *Brennan*. Choice is yours. Make the right one."

Then he stepped back, gave himself a shake, and went upstairs.

I sank back into the window, barely able to breathe. Coughing. My brain blank. I couldn't make sense of any part of it. All that ran through my head, over and over, is that I had been officially removed from the family. *Dead and buried*. Something I thought I'd already accepted and wanted, but now was torn apart by and wanted to fight.

And if I did, Rhuari would pay the price.

Rhuari.

My brother.

Oh, God, Oh, God, Oh, God, what was I to do?

He was already in danger enough. Kinsella is not a common name, and both Eamonn and myself could be connected to that bombing, with little trouble. I'd long had the impression the IRA and UDA had worked out a deal—*You leave these alone, we'll leave those alone,* kind of thing. Help each other's protection rackets. *See? We protect people. Pay us or things might get nasty from the other side.* All it would take is one well-placed message letting it be known a certain little off-license clerk's brother had surely been part of the murder of a Protestant leader, and not one of those sons-of-bitches in the bloody alphabet could prevent it.

Sweet, quiet little Rhuari.

And my fucking uncle would be the one to aim the gun if I didn't agree to kill who I was.

Oh, Jesus God, that bastard.

That bloody goddamned motherfucking bastard!

Captured

I didn't sleep, that night. Just sat in the window and let the horror of what my uncle had revealed settle into me. Not one coherent thought to remember. No angry declarations in my mind. Nothing. It was like I was a cyborg shut down to regenerate.

When Aunt Mari came down to begin breakfast, I forced myself to rise and help her, still silent. On auto-pilot, as it were. We did a full fry-up for the lot of them, and I think five words passed between us in the doing of it. A couple of looks she cast my way solidified the impression that she knew everything Uncle Sean had said to me.

And was willing to let it happen.

What can be said in answer to that?

I remained there the weekend, still blank of mind. Isn't this how computers work? You input the information, set it going and it quietly works out your answer, in the background? I honestly have no idea. I just know my movements and words were more reactive than from real thought, and there was nothing contrary from me.

Throughout, there was food like I'd never seen before. Scott's old clothes were a bit tight, but that was acceptable, according to the B-girls.

"They look good on you," said Bernadette.

"Better than on Scott," Brandi added, nodding.

"His leg's are too skinny."

"But you could lose a little on your tummy."

"Now don't be silly. His belly's just right."

"No, he needs to control his weight now, or he'll look like daddy."

"Oh, you're putting down daddy's looks?"

And off they went.

And I felt nothing about it.

I did get to know my nephews and niece, not to mention Tur and Mai, again. Michael and Jordan were the hardest on me, one being seven and the other six. Michael was built like his Da, stocky and unmovable, with russet hair and energy to last a lifetime; Jordan was slimmer and also russet-haired, but smarter in how he refused to play his brother's older-boy games. No brogue to either of them, though when Michael was flustered or angry, a hint of it would peek through.

They liked to play baseball. In the morning. Before the heat rose. We used the front yard, since the pool owned the one in back. I knew a little about it from having seen it on the telly, but they still had to fill me in on the finer details. Both boys were mightily excited about a new team coming to Toronto and already had plans to eventually become players for them. For some reason, I had no doubt they would. They were in a better world.

Michael's preferred position was catcher, and Jordan's pitcher. Scott was assigned short stop, Bernadette as first base, Brandi as cheerleader, and nothing more, thank you. Which left me as outfield and first to swing the little bat they had, trying not to make a fool of myself.

Many's the time they rolled about in laughter at my lack of prowess or, dare we say, coordination.

Tur and Mai watched from folding chairs on the driveway under a massive oak tree, sipping beers or tea and calling support for us all, as Aunt Mari sat on a blanket, close by, tending to Aisling, the charming brat. Stephen was caught in the Terrible Twos, and no one was pleasing to him except his great aunt. Fortunately, Anthony was only beginning to crawl.

It was hard to believe Mai was not yet four years older than myself, for she seemed to have fitted easily into that of matron. Especially considering her growing girth. But the looks she cast Tur, and he her, promised they would be happy together for the rest of their lives. Nothing of Ma or Da about them. I think it helped, them being in a city that had a future instead of naught but a past.

And I felt all the more hollow for it.

When eleven came, there was a mass exodus into the house to make use of the air-conditioning and drink gallons of Aunt Mari's overly-sweetened iced tea or lemonade (which none seemed to have any issue with but me) and beer for the adults who wanted it, whilst making sandwiches from meats laid out across the kitchen counter, with potato chips and olives and pickles. I long learned to do half-tea-half-water over a glass of ice, so I could enjoy it well-enough and face no questions from the B-girls over why I wasn't having any.

After this was a nap then came time in the pool, in which I was much more popular since I'd stay in the shallow end, wearing one of Scott's dark undershirts and a pair of what he called board-shorts—which the B-girls thought were just the coolest thing—and play with the little ones as the rest frolicked in the deep end.

Then Uncle Sean broke out the barbecue and cooked burgers and hot dogs and steaks, with toasted buns, to refill everyone. It was all so normal and natural, at times I wondered if any of the horrors of my past had really happened, and if maybe I'd only dreamed the argument between me and himself.

Still, I avoided him, through this, and as we ate allowed the B-Girls to continue peppering me with questions about what I'd been doing the last year, for they sensed my answers were too deliberately vague. I would smile and quickly work out a way to get them to disagree about something or other and off they'd go, distracted. It was almost a fun little game.

Sunday was Mass, to which I was all but dragged. Then more of the pool, more of the same food until late in the afternoon, when we all piled into Tur's green, five-year-old Travelall to make the trek to Hermann Park.

Along with what seemed like the whole of Houston.

We found a spot to picnic on in the midst of the crowd, and Aunt Mari broke out sandwiches and her salads made from potatoes and from macaroni, and we watched a fireworks show that was massive and wild. I caught no effect from the explosions and the noises on Tur and Mai, but they still rattled me. I found having a beer in one hand and a ciggie in the other helped to stop any spin into madness. By midnight, Sunday, I was ready for a month's sleep.

I called into the shop on Monday to say I'd not be in till tomorrow, but it turned out they'd closed for the day. They just hadn't thought to tell me. So I remained at Aunt Mari's to see Tur, Mai and their brood off home in that bloody Travelall.

We never had another moment to ourselves to talk, try as I might. So I was left to myself to decide what to do.

When Scott was dropped to Hobby Airport for his return to Dallas, it was near twilight, and dark by the time we returned to the house. As Aunt Mari and the B-girls wandered inside, I kept Uncle Sean next to the station wagon.

What I said was, "All right, I'll be your ghost. But working at *The Colonel's* is no part of it. I won't deal with Todd and—"

"He ain't there, no more," said Uncle Sean. "Got sent to Huntsville. Six-to-eight years. Stupid shit sold an undercover cop a joint in the goddamn parkin' lot."

The news made me both sorry and glad—and angry, on top of it. So much for the deal he'd brokered.

He continued with, "You'll be backin' up the new guy four nights a week, Monday through Thursday. Name's Winston. I got someone else to handle the weekend. He's bigger'n you, better able to handle the rowdies without a weapon."

"All right, then. How am I to be paid?"

"Check every Monday. Thirty bucks a night, room and board."

"But how do I cash a check? I've no bank account."

"Do it in the register, end of the night."

I shrugged an okay. "I'll be back by the end of the week. Just need to let my friends know where I'll be."

"They won't be showin' up here, will they?"

That got me raring up. "Why shouldn't they?"

"For one thing, the pool house needs to be available, so you'll be in your old room. I don't want 'em traipsin' through the house."

"They're decent people, all of them."

"That's part of the deal."

"Then it's off."

"Don't be an idiot, *Brennan*. One phone call, you get sent back to Dublin, and your momma loses two sons, one of 'em twice."

"I'm from Derry," I growled.

"Not. Any. More." Then he patted me on the shoulder and said in a voice calm and kind and loud enough for Aunt Mari to hear, "We'll expect you for dinner, tomorrow. I know the girls'll love to see you back here, again. I bet they'll even want to clean your room."

Then he headed inside, leaving me to seethe unto myself.

My instinct was to vanish, again. Go to another town or state. Dare them to find me. Only it wasn't just me under this threat, now, and that my uncle would not make that call to target Rhuari was a risk I did not want to take. I hadn't seen eyes as hard and cold as his since Da's, though at least my father's had been from the excuse of being filled with drink.

I don't remember riding back to my place. My brain was back to thinking, trying to figure a way out of this that wouldn't rain catastrophe down on one and all. Turning myself in would raise noise in the press as the Brits trumpeted having caught another terrorist.

Good PR for their cause and the devil with reality. So Rhuari'd soon be found out and gone after by some idiot on the Proddie side. I knew full well not even the IRA at her strongest could protect him. Of course, that might happen, anyway. But something told me Rhuari was smart enough to keep as quiet as possible.

As he always did.

Dear God, I wanted to talk to him. Needed to. Christ, I had to hear him say he was that smart. But I didn't know Ma's phone, and the only number I could think of was Mrs. Haggerty's up on Nailors Row, which was no more. I could have found Father Jack at the church office, but then I'd have to let him know why I was calling, and then he'd know that I was *not* dead, if he did not know already—and I did not trust him a whit.

It was near four in the morning before I accepted I was trapped and drifted to sleep.

I told the shop I'd been called home. They were sorry to see me go. They said. I doubt they meant it. They never had been comfortable with me; it was my abilities that had kept them from backing away.

I let Mrs. Glendon know I had to leave and her distraction almost vanished.

She lay her fingers light against the base of my neck and murmured, "You're a very sweet boy. I'm sorry to see you go. But no refund on the rent you've paid, or deposit."

I grinned. "I expected none."

I bought sacks of onions and carrots from the Kroger and gave them to Mrs. Kendall, saying, "These are tonight's contribution, and Friday's. I'm off."

"How sad," she said. "We missed you, Friday."

I shrugged. "I'll join you, Friday week, if that's all right."

"Just let us know. I'll make an Irish stew. And Colcannon."

"Sounds perfect." And I had to fight from tearing up.

Since when had I become so emotional?

Miss Sauvage, Rick and Myron were not home by the time I was set to leave, and Eldon only watched through a window as I hopped on my bike, my duffel bag over my back and the tool holder lashed to the back of my seat. I waved to him; he did not wave back. I smiled and left.

And felt like I was going to my grave.

Uncle Sean was right; the B-Girls had cleaned the room at the top and made the bed, and a tiny fridge had been added, with snacks and

Dr Pepper. An air conditioner had also been set in a window. This space being so much smaller, it actually did well.

As I still had my key, I walked straight up and inside to unpack. Before I was half done, they were at the door.

"Are you really back, Brennan?" asked Brandi.

"*Brennan*?" I joked. "Why so formal? It's just Bren, right?"

"We've missed you," said Bernadette.

"You just missed having me to boss around," I said, with a wink.

"Are you staying?"

"Daddy says you'll be here for a while."

"You're not gonna go running off again, are you?"

"Not even saying good-bye."

"That was really rude."

I shrugged. "You're right; I was. It won't happen, again. And how long I stay depends on your Da."

"What's he got to do with it?"

"It's his house. I'm just inhabiting it."

"So are we."

"But you're family."

"So are you."

"Not by much. Didn't he mention that part?"

Brandi gave me the hard-eye before saying, "Did you and daddy have an argument?"

"Is that why you left?" Bernadette added.

I barely hid a smile as I turned to them and said, "Now, now, little ladies, some things should be kept private."

They drew closer to each other and Bernadette said, "What'd you argue about?"

"Did you not hear what I just said?"

"But you made up, right?" asked Brandi. "You and Daddy?"

"I'm here, aren't I?"

Bernadette glared at me. "You're not answering our questions."

I smiled wide and said in a tender voice, "Because you're asking things that are none of your business."

"If Daddy hurt you in some way..."

"What's between your father and me is between your father and me."

"You did have a fight, didn't you?"

Brandi slipped up behind her, saying, "We heard Mommy and Daddy arguing about it."

"After you left."

"They were being real quiet."

"But it's over Daddy hitting you."

"That's not what she said," Brandi hissed. "It's something else."

Bernadette snapped back, "It was something that hurt him."

Brandi turned to me. "It's those scars on your back."

That jolted me. "What d'you mean?" And my voice was sharp.

"You were dipping Aisling in the pool and I was sneaking up on you, underwater, and your shirt rode up a little and I could see lines across your back."

Bernadette nodded. "She told me and I looked, too. They're healed but they're there, and there's even a couple on your legs."

"Did Daddy do that to you?"

"Is that why you left?"

I dropped onto the bed, feeling as if I were floating. I had to draw in a deep breath before I said, "There's nothing you need worry about. What matters is, I'm here. And I'm fine. And I'll be staying."

"You're still not answering our questions."

"I've given you the answers I will give." And I turned as close to stone as I could.

They looked at me for what seemed like forever, then Brandi said, "Mommy asked us to tell you dinner'll be ready at five."

"Leftovers."

"We'll be having them all week."

I nodded and they left without another word, not even between themselves.

I let myself smile over this. Uncle Sean wanted me here? I'd be here. And at some point I'd make certain the girls saw my shirtless back, in full, *by accident*, driving home what they pretty much knew their father had done.

I deliberately made dinner as light and carefree as I could, telling the B-Girls more about my former housemates. Joyous little anecdotes to build up each one's peculiarities.

How if ever I had a question about something I'd ask Eldon and he would have an answer. "He's an encyclopedia, that lad."

And how Rick had fought for months to make his position at TSU permanent and now was fighting to be freed from his contract so he could take a position at Baylor.

"Oh, that's in Waco," Bernadette said.

"Very, very Baptist," said Brandi.

"Jeremy was thinking of going there but didn't like it."

"Said he'd have to go to Austin for church."

"It wasn't church." Said with a massive sigh. "He called it services."

"No, that's not right. It was something else."

I had to say, "Synagogue?"

"No, that's not right," said Brandi.

Bernadette jumped in her chair and said, "Temple!"

"Yes, that's it! Temple! He found three of them in San Antonio, when he was considering Trinity."

"I'm glad he chose Houston."

"Me, too."

"Aren't you, Bren?"

Both cast me a look that demanded an answer. I smiled and nodded.

I still ate my chicken with a knife and fork, sending them into eyerolling heaven, and praised Aunt Mari's macaroni salad as if I hadn't had it but the day before. Uncle Sean said little, and I caught the B-Girls cast the occasional wary glance between him and myself, as if to wonder why.

So... their distrust of him was being manifested beyond repair.

After dinner, I met Uncle Sean at *The Colonel's*. The floors had been stripped, repaired and stained dark; gleaming new tables filled the space; the bar had been polished, the walls painted black, and the ceiling was white. Ferns were hung about to give the place a bit of humanity, and the front windows were clean of all covering, so any and all could see in.

And no more pool tables.

Winston looked so much like he was a college prep lad, I was surprised to find he was thirty, had a wife and two children, was a Methodist Layman, and loved motor sports. His blond hair was cut short, he wore white button-down shirts and black slacks, and he had the straightest teeth I'd ever seen on a man. He fit in perfectly with the new look of the bar.

Lorraine had been replaced by two lovely slim girls of indeterminate age, origin, or interest in anything but their own conversation, and the regulars had become *clientele*. A selection of foreign beers and fine alcohol was behind the bar as was an even greater selection of wines. A cook and two helpers made rather costly burgers with tiny fries in a redone kitchen. Even the parking lot was repaved, and the line of shops adjoining the place were in the process of being built up to be leased. It was a bit of a shock.

I thought for a fleeting moment about talking with Uncle Sean about letting the—*renting* the last space of the shops, as I'd once considered, but my memories of the area were still too raw, and I honestly wanted little to do with him. It was enough for me to arrive, lock up my bike and enter the place to work my seven hours, as they now closed at one.

It could get busy but could also be close to tedious. I kept Winston stocked in the various forms of alcohol as well as fresh glasses and plates and kept the tables clean, like a glorified busboy. At least they had a steady dishwasher.

Winston was not the chatty sort, which I preferred. I took up Rocky's habit of bringing a book to read when things were slow. I got a few odd looks from them, but since they never had cause to complain about needing the tables done or more beer chilled or the garbage emptied, they left me to myself.

I kept going to Friday dinners at Mrs. Glendon's, and even brought Everett and Jeremy along with me, to introduce them. I found Everett had kept my location secret, and Jeremy was aware enough to not ask questions of me. He just went with the flow.

Rick had been hired to a NASA facility in Huntsville, Alabama, so two college students had taken over his room and mine...and never wanted to join in.

"Meal card," I heard one of them say to Mrs. Kendall, when she asked, and nothing more.

Not that I cared; in fact, that was the only one I ever saw, and was only the once, so can't say for certain the other existed. Except they must have; Mrs. Glendon would have insisted on having the income, so the dinners were a bit more sparse. That is, until Jeremy and Everett began bringing things to cook, as well.

Jeremy convinced me to join him in Aikido, Saturday mornings. Learning to drop and roll and twist and throw people. I never got much good at it, but it was fun and he was a joy to work out with. It helped me trim down a bit, for as Brandi had pointed out, I was starting to grow something of a paunch.

I returned to making my rounds of the trash cans on the nights before collection, but on my Montessa. I bought a set of saddle bags to sling over the seat and fit what I could in there. Then I waited till morning to bring them up to my room. I also put bolts on both my doors, to keep out any late-night *visitors*, especially once I learned the room on the other side of the toilet had been made into yet another living space.

I let the next year pass by quick, with Christmas and New Year's subdued affairs. I turned twenty-one with little fanfare but a new nephew and niece. Mai's twins had decided to be born on my day. I was happy for the distraction of it.

Maeve had begun to write Aunt Mari, herself, to keep us abreast of the goings-on in the North. It was more of the usual bombings and chaos, with Eamonn going on the blanket in protest of prison actions. He'd become quite radicalized. Negotiations meant to change everything went nowhere, and finally Maeve's own peace group joined with the group who'd won the Peace Prize.

That bit, I was able to follow in the news. It seemed everyone had been hoping they'd succeed until everyone decided they hoped they wouldn't because of childish actions and attitudes fostered, in part, by the press. I was beginning to believe both sides were too vested in the struggle to seek an end, as both the IRA and UDA had grown to love the profits in their protection rackets. Without saying so, Maeve let us know the off-license Rhuari worked at was paying a nice penny and, as I suspected, both sides had worked out which shops could be destroyed and which left alone.

My one happiness was how Rhuari's was one of the latter.

Because of word about the space shuttle being tested, Everett organized an excursion to NASA for me and the crew at Mrs. Glendon's. Rick heard about it, roared into town and bought tickets for the tour, *at a discounted rate*. Everett rented a massive passenger van and I paid the gas. Then on a fine Saturday late in April we headed over.

When Aunt Mari had said it was 25 miles away, it hadn't seemed like so far, but getting there took near an hour, thanks to traffic on the 45. Then down the long, long road leading to the Center and seeking a place to park, as there were tourists and buses all over the place. And getting to the line for entry. Apparently, we were not the only ones excited about the grand new space program. But since we had a package tour set up, we were shown in detail one of the few places in the world that looked to the future and not the past.

Of course, Rick acted as if the whole experience had been his doing. As if all of NASA was his. It was quite humorous. But it was worth every penny.

Of course, the tour ended in the gift shop, and I purchased another cap for myself, this one of the Space Shuttle.

Then came Scott's graduation at UT. I got an even truer sense of the size of Texas as we drove to Austin, with never-ending rolling hills of a hundred shades of green and brown and non-stop sky in the distance. The B-Girls told me all sorts of tales along the way—like when we passed through a town called La Grange.

"It had a whorehouse," said Bernadette.

"Marvin Zindler raided it, last year," said Brandi.

"It was a big scandal."

"All these Aggies got caught with their pants down."

"On camera."

"As Marvin Zindler ran around saying *MAR-vin ZIN-dler*!"

"*EYE-witness News!*"

And they giggled.

I half-thought they were making sport of me, but Aunt Mari chimed in with, "Just some adult boys doin' what adult boys do, as other adults decided they shouldn't do it."

"You think prostitution's all right?" Uncle Sean asked.

"I think it's the world's oldest profession and won't be goin' away, so best to work with it than against it. None of the boys was underage or married, so it should have been of no one's business but their own."

"Father Tony would disagree." Which brought a startled look from me. Since when had he been dealing with a priest? He didn't even go to mass, anymore.

"Father Tony knows nothin' of real life," Aunt Mari had snapped, in answer, "an' would do well to remember that."

Which ended the conversation and made the B-Girls' eyes as big as saucers. Not another word was said the rest of the drive.

Of course, the ceremony was big and lavish and went on forever as the heat of the day made more than a few of us melt. There was speaker after speaker I'd never heard of and never wanted to hear from, again, then came the long, long procession of graduates gaining their diplomas as their names were called. Christ, made me glad I'd left school early.

Finally, it was over and we found Scott in the crowd with his girlfriend, Trisha, who was blond of hair, tan of skin and very chirpy, and who was actually his fiancée. Which pleased my aunt and uncle, no end. The B-Girls were a bit huffy but polite and peppered her with a thousand questions in their best interrogative manner. Poor Trisha had no idea what she was getting into. Scott was set to begin work at a Dallas bank in two weeks, so he and she planned to *jaunt off to Cabo for a few days*. I think it's in Mexico, but I never asked for fear of looking the fool.

The drive home was long and quiet, but I dozed during much of it, with the B-girls flanking me and each using a shoulder as a pillow. Aunt Mari kept staring straight ahead, saying nothing.

My one thought was, *Good*.

Jeremy's graduation was the following weekend, and that came close to being a true joy. First of all, it was indoors and they had the air conditioning running at full blast. Everett and the crew appeared, saw me and made themselves known to us all, much to my delight and Uncle Sean's discomfort. But Aunt Mari was gracious and the B-girls were ecstatic to actually meet the people I'd told them about. New victims to interrogate.

Myron loved the attention and made up a number of ridiculous answers to their queries. Mrs. Glendon, Mrs. Kendall and Miss Sauvage cast me more than one dubious look, each, but soon mellowed into chattery gossip with the two. Everett and I became Eldon's wall against the girls.

They joined with us in the *friends of the graduate* seating, off to one side, and we had a joyous time. Howled *Jer-e-my, Jer-e-my* in our loudest voices when he walked the stage, so much so he was able to locate us in the crowd and wave.

Through it all, Uncle Sean was seething.

Once it was done and the auditorium was emptying, he dragged me off to one side and growled, "I told you I didn't want those people around—"

"This is not your home. And they are friends of both me and Jeremy, so I've kept to my end of the bargain. When will I see proof of you keeping yours?"

That slowed down his spin into anger. There had been no hint of anyone coming asking after Brennan. Not even a whisper. I'd begun to think Uncle Sean had been lying to me.

"It's takin' time. We have to—we have to get your birth certificate from Dublin, and they're not respondin' to our requests."

"What d'you need that for...?" Then I remembered. "Of course. You can't send my old passport in. They'd realize it's faked, and might send the bad lads back your pads. You're starting from the beginning."

He just glared at me.

I shrugged. "Ask the church; they have sway with the Taoiseach."

"I-I'd like to keep them out of it."

"Why? They helped get me here, didn't they?"

He jolted. "What makes you think that?"

"The church has its fingers in everything, in Ireland, so you'd think they'd have an interest in making sure that—oh, that everything's well and good. Unsullied hands, for them."

He eyed me. "I'll suggest it to my lawyer."

"Do it now. I think I saw Mr. Landau down with Jeremy's family."

"What makes you think he's workin' on this?"

"You said he was, remember?" Said with a smile, then I returned to my friends.

Jeremy could only swing by to say, *Hi*; his family was having dinner at a steak house with him as guest of honor, of course. It turned out he had already been hired by Champion Oil because he was somewhat fluent in Mandarin. They wanted to send him straight to Hong Kong, along with a delegation to discuss business opportunities.

"It's as crazy as hell," Jeremy laughed. "They speak Cantonese, there."

"But they speak English, too, don't they?" I asked.

"Yeah, but it'd make more sense to meet in Shanghai or Peking. I think I'm goin' along just to make sure their negotiators aren't pullin' shit behind their backs."

"Can you do that?"

"We'll see. But it's like tryin' to get somebody in South Texas to understand a cop in South Boston. Dad went there for a medical conference, once, and got lost so stopped a cop. He had to get him to write the directions out because he couldn't understand what the guy was sayin'."

I chuckled. "A mate and I had a run-in with a Para from Liverpool, ordering us about, and it's like he was gargling his words. He was about to shoot us before Colm realized he wanted a light for his fag."

Everett glared at me, cockeyed. "Fag?"

"Cigarette. That's what they're called, over there."

He nodded but still gave me a side-eye.

Jeremy was set to leave the following week, so we gave him a full going-away party at Mrs. Glendon's, the Friday before. Mrs.

Kendall worked up a feast of what she called Chinese food—chop suey and crispy noodles (all of which I knew was from a can but tasted...interesting), hot and sour soup (which I think was also from a can), stir-fried rice with shrimp and peas, and the ever-present carrots and onion, steamed rice, dim sum, egg rolls, and fortune cookies bought from a Chinese shop in the Sharpstown area, and even chop sticks. Turned out Everett had driven her there, the night before, and was paying for the party, in whole.

"Can't exactly say goodbye to him at the airport with mom and dad around, can I?" Everett said as we set up a line of card tables in the foyer. We then put folding chairs around them. The dining nook was too tight for our full group.

"His parents don't know of you, then?" I asked.

"I don't think so, but I've never met them. What's your impression? They more like your aunt or your uncle?"

I shrugged. "Probably Aunt Mari."

"Well. Then they might tolerate me."

"Oh, come off it, Rett. You're part of the family and—"

He shook his head. "Your uncle won't even speak to me. Just casts me angry looks when I'm there. And your aunt is always watchin' me, especially when you or Scott're around."

"But, hey, the girls love you."

"Only because I indulge their princess fantasies. Spoiled rotten, those two. Won't be long before they're holy terrors." He unfurled tablecloths over each table. "No, this is my family. In this house. I'm just Everett, to them. Not gay Everett. Not some *other* being you need to be wary of. I'm so glad you brought me here." He hesitated then smoothed out the tablecloth. "You're not wary of me, are you, Pug? I'm just Everett to you, aren't I?" And he cast me a sideways glance touched with hurt.

I huffed. "No, you're Rett."

He smiled. "I wish."

Soon everyone was set and helping themselves to the feast, and I was amazed to see Miss Sauvage and Eldon were masters with chopsticks, even more-so than Jeremy. They helped everyone else learn, except for Myron; his palsy seemed to be advancing so he required use of a spoon.

On top of this, Eldon actually spoke to Jeremy, telling him, "They also teach Mandarin in schools, over here."

Jeremy merely grinned and nodded, his mouth full of noodles.

"The symbols are the same as Cantonese," he continued. "Just different styles." He used a paper napkin and his sticks dipped in the soup to work one up. "These are the same symbol, but Cantonese is delicate and precise. The Mandarin is simple. More graphic-style. And Mandarin has but five levels of tone while Cantonese has eight or nine, and the tone is important to the meaning. Do you understand what I have written, here?"

Jeremy looked at the napkin and slowly said, "Nǐ xǐhuān nǐ de shíwù ma? Do you like your food?"

"And what does this say?" He pointed to the other section.

Jeremy frowned and looked harder at it, then said. "It's more complex. Not sure how to pronounce it. *Is my meal pleasant to me?*"

"Close. It is the Cantonese way to say, *Do you like your food?*"

"Did you teach Chinese?"

"No. No. I read a few books. Listened to some tapes. Cassettes. You may have them. Listen to them on your journey."

"Yeah, please! That'd be great."

Eldon all but bolted into his room, then a moment later set a couple of bags holding books and cassettes next to Jeremy, then said, "Happy Birthday," and sat back down.

Jeremy almost told him it was not his birthday, but Everett put a hand on his and said, "Eldon that's real thoughtful of you. How long you been studyin' Chinese?"

Eldon focused on his bowl of soup and managed to mutter, "Since I learned Jeremy learned it."

"You learned a language like that in just the last few months?"

Eldon shrugged and sipped some soup.

"That is amazing."

Eldon blushed and sipped more soup.

Jeremy dug through the books as Everett asked, "Eldon, do you know any other languages?"

He shrugged.

"French? German? Spanish?"

He shrugged a sort of *yes*.

Everett turned to me. "Bren, why didn't you ever tell us?"

"Didn't know," I said. "I only spoke to him in English."

Eldon looked at me and asked, " An labhraíonn tú Gaeilge?"

I squinted and smiled. "Is that the Irish?"

He almost smiled.

"No," I said, "I never learned—but I've a brother studying it.

Would you—would you write to him? In the Irish? He's in Belfast."

I got the barest of nods from him, and knew Rhuari would have to write to him, first. So I wrote a letter to Maeve, as Cousin Bren, and let her know about Eldon, including the address. Said he's looking for a pen-pal, in Gaelic. To my joy, not three months later, during our Friday night feast, Eldon showed me a letter from Rhuari, all in the Irish.

"He does good," he said. "Punctuation is off, but good."

"What's he saying?" I asked.

"He likes his school. Loves his wife. They have a white kitten so he put in this poem, *Pangur Bán*."

"Messe ocus Pangur Bán,
cechtar nathar fria saindán;
bíth a menma-sam fri seilgg,
mu menma céin im saincheirdd

"Caraim-se fos, ferr cach clú,
oc mu lebrán léir ingnu;
ní foirmtech frimm Pangur bán,
caraid cesin a maccdán."

"There's more to it, but that's the important part."

"What's it mean?" I asked, looking at the letter over Eldon's shoulder. And wasn't Rhuari's handwriting precise?

"Oh, it's about a monk and his white cat," Eldon murmured. "Each taking joy in their profession. The monk writing; the cat hunting mice. It's Ninth Century. Not Irish Celtic, more Gaelic. General Gaelic. And he shared it with me."

He was so pleased, for the first time in my life I knew I'd done something completely right.

But back to that last evening with Jeremy.

Jesus, how pleasant it all was. Chatting about nothing. Laughing at nothing. Myron loosening up enough to scoop refried rice into his mouth and chuckle when some stuck to his chin. Mrs. Glendon sweetly cleaning his face like she would a toddler. Mrs. Kendall ladling out the soup then meat and rice with the flourish of a master chef. Miss Sauvage getting tipsy off half a bottle of *Tsingtao*. Jeremy and Everett nudging each other with near kisses and feeding each other. The various aromas from the food enveloping us in comfort and hominess. I felt more at peace than I had since—well, since that breakfast just after the battle for Bogside, with Eamonn and Tur and Jackie and Aidan as Mai cooked, when it looked like we might just be all right and there was talk of a fleadh. The army was protecting us, then, and we'd become masters of our fate.

If only we had known, then, the opposite was true.

I finally understood how right Everett was. This was what a family should be. Warm. Comforting. Accepting. Supporting. No demands you lie to yourself to be what they want. No threats to make you conform to the future they've plotted out for you. None spoke ill of the other. None refused to accept the peculiarities in us all. I can't say it was love I was feeling, just then, only safety. For I knew these people would hope as well for my wishes and dreams as I would theirs.

It only underscored how much of a prisoner I was, in that attic room. How trapped by fear and loyalty and worry. My one prayer was that it would not be for very long.

We sat around that line of tables for hours, even after every bite had been finished, drinking beers and wine and talking and talking and talking about the world and ourselves, unwilling to break the lovely spell of contentment that had surrounded us. Even Sonja was a pleasure to be around, and got on so well with Everett, it was like she was a different person, all-together.

Finally, Mrs. Glendon grew weary and wandered off to her room. Mrs. Kendall did the same; I was surprised she stayed as long as she did after working over a hot stove all afternoon. Myron offered to help clear up, but Eldon and I insisted we'd do it, so he laboriously climbed the stairs, casting looks back at us laced with a smile.

Once we had all the dishes back into the kitchen, Eldon folded up the tablecloths and collapsed the chairs as I broke down the tables. Then he and I were about to take them out to the garage when we saw Everett and Jeremy in the kitchen, holding each other, forehead to forehead. Eldon stopped, set his chairs down, crossed to them and embraced them both. I could just barely hear him say, "I'm so happy for both of you." Then he came back, picked up his chairs and continued outside. I winked at Everett and Jeremy and followed him out with both tables.

I was fair certain Jeremy did not go home, that night.

His parents had their own going-away party for him, to which I was invited, as were Scott, who was fresh back from Cabo and as golden as a lab can be, and Trish, who was just as shiny. That affair was nice and everyone was pleasant, but it struck me a group of people gathered together, all with the same thought and contemplation, nothing unexpected or untoward. Just in perfect order.

Soon after, Jeremy was en-route to Hong Kong.

And I had one less visitor to my prison.

Stasis-not

One thing that drove me near mad was not having a workspace for my repairs. The main attic had poor lighting and was too hot, even with me keeping the door open, a fan running cool air from my room, and a couple of lamps on extension cords. Aunt Mari said I could use the kitchen, and I considered it, but my inner neat-freak (a moniker bestowed upon me by the B-girls) pointed out that cleanup would be difficult, at best. The pool house was for visitors only, now, of which there were a few; none of whom were introduced to me. The garage was for the cars.

I complained about it to Everett and he set up a space for me to work. It was a room upstairs but had a big, lovely window untouched by shade, and his air conditioning was centralized. His only request was that he be allowed to do sketches of me.

"I love how you get so focused," he said. "Like that day you were working on my typewriter. The world just vanishes around you. No wariness. No pain. No anger. Just this Zen kind of peace. I wasn't even there, so far as you were concerned."

"And that makes me the psycho," I said, smiling.

"No," he said with a sigh. "Just someone who knows the best way to handle the world is to ignore it."

He would also feed me. Pastries and tea. Cottage pies. Fish and chips from the frozen foods section of Weingarten's. Almost like he was trying to fatten me up to use in some barbecue. The only thing was, when I work I forget to eat, so I actually lost weight, once he let me begin.

There were also short letters and cards every week, from Jeremy, which he would read to me. Like Ma had read the letters from Aunt Mari. It was like a little holiday, each time.

Each one of our group got those, myself included. Seems he had little else to do between business meetings. Friday nights, we'd share them. Somehow, he made certain different information was in each one. Like hopping the bus to Stanley, a British-y beach area on the other side of the island. Or Kowloon's Jade Market and nearly being harassed to death by people demanding he buy this bracelet or that ring or a special statue to bring him luck.

"They're always startled that I speak Chinese," he wrote. "Then they begin talking so fast, I can't keep up. It's close to insane."

Another time, he told us, "Found out I was born in the year of the horse, according to the Chinese horoscope. It's supposed to be good. I now have a banner outlining it. In English on one side and Cantonese on the other."

He also included little cards with his letters, outlining the Chinese horoscope by years. Everett was horrified to learn he was born in the year of the rat.

"What's he tryin' to tell me?" he'd cried upon reading it.

I'd laughed. "Look at mine. I'm the goat!"

Miss Sauvage put a gentle hand on my arm and said, "But it means something different to them. Goats are peace-loving, kind, popular..."

I'd chuckled as I said, "Not so sure about the popular."

"Don't be. Silly." Myron said it as he tried to give me a light punch on the shoulder.

"They're also helpful and trusting," Miss Sauvage added, with one of her rare smiles. I thanked her with a nod.

Eldon mentioned to me, only, when he'd get letters from Rhuari, as well. He'd write of how he was doing with his studies and married life and his job and Bridie's aunt being a bit too nosy about when they planned for children, and how Bridie was also taking courses in computers. Learning how to make what he called punch cards for them.

That word was in English, not the Irish.

"He could not work out how best to translate it," Eldon told me. "It may be something that cannot be well-represented in Gaelic."

"Does he tell you what they're for?" I asked.

"They're used to input data to produce reports, process invoices and checks to be printed, monitor budgets and manage class registration. I don't think they'll be used much longer. His wife mentioned magnetic tape is being developed to store data, now, and other programs are coming so data can be input directly into the system."

Amazing. Rhuari handling the past of Ireland and Bridie, the future. I actually felt a bit of pride over my brother and sister-in-law being so well-grounded in the world. And found it interesting he was more open with a pen-pal than he was with his own family.

It kept on like that when Jeremy's trip was extended a week. Then several weeks. And then went to four months. Then six, and it began to look like they'd keep him there forever.

At the beginning of the fifth month, I was at Everett's, having brunch, as he called it—poached eggs, toasted muffins, bacon, sausage, beans, slices of cheese and fruit and glasses of champagne, as if it were a party. First time we'd done that but it felt fun, especially with it being cold and wet, outside.

I'd finished my plate and planned to work the afternoon on a hi-fi setup I'd found next to a trash can. I could already tell it would need a lot of work but was not beyond repair.

Everett had seemed odd throughout the morning so I wondered if he'd got a tough letter from Jeremy. The ones we'd shared at dinner, the night before had been rather unhappy with how long he was stuck in Hong Kong.

I'd put my plate in the sink and was about to head upstairs when Everett pulled me into the living room.

"I want to—want to ask you something," he said. "But first I want you to see these."

He opened a portfolio to show me sketches of Jeremy. Portraits and profiles of his face that were truly elegant. Lovely watercolors on thick paper, in gentle pastels. Pen and ink. Graphite. I already knew he was excellent in his talent. What I did not expect was how a great many were completely naked.

"I-I-I want to do some of these of you," he finally said.

I was seated on the couch, the pieces spread across the coffee table and floor, and felt as if I were invading Jeremy's privacy merely by looking at them. "Rett, I'm not so sure."

"Please." He grabbed another album from a unit of shelves and opened it to reveal actual photos of Jeremy in various stages of undress, again including full frontal naked. Lovely artistic black and white images of him standing in various poses or seated on a stool.

"I've been livin' off these since he left," he said, his breath quick and sharp, "and-and-and you and he look so much alike, it'd be like he's here."

"Hardly. He's in far better shape than me." And that was to put it mildly. While I'd toughened up a bit, there was neither softness nor fat on him, and I'd not realized the amount of hair he had from his navel to his groin and around his legs.

"C'mon, Pug, he ain't that much better. By the time I get done..."

"Rett, is-is-is he all right with you showing me these?"

"What he don't know won't hurt me, and-and I don't want you to tell him, so I know you never will."

"So what is this? You want to snap photos of me without clothes?"

"No, just sketches. I want to do sketches. Paintings. Acrylics. Maybe oils. No photos. A friend of mine in a poster shop has a client who likes my work. He's in Atlanta. He wants to start a collection and-and I promised Jeremy I'd never sell anything I did of him, but you-you and he are like brothers, and I can do more if you'll pose for me."

"But you could still use these photos."

"No, Bren, they're black and white and I paint in color. Please. Just a few? Poses different from these."

"Different, how?"

"Notice, he barely pays attention to the camera, mostly looks away. I'd want you looking straight out at me, at the person viewing the work. There's a secrecy to you. A wariness. The only time it goes away is when you lose yourself in some repair you're doing. I tried to catch it when I took all those shots, a couple years back, but that was all wrong."

"You did a fair job of it in my portrait."

"But not as good as I wanted and I'm still trying, but I don't quite have it. I want that in these."

"And for that I have to be naked?"

"It's what the client wants."

"Wait—is this an order he's made?"

He nodded. "A commission. A triptych. Nude, only.

"Fine, then go to one of your gay bars; you could pick from a hundred guys willing to do that."

"I don't want them. I want you. I want that look in your eyes. I love Jeremy, but he's not you. He'll never be you."

"Rett, I'm not..."

He put a hand up, for silence,

"You're right," he said. "I could find a hundred guys who'd drop their pants for a few bucks, but their eyes would not inspire me. Yours do. Jeremy's close, but if you look at what I've done you'll see, it's from love, not inspiration. And it shows. He's sweet, and what I've done of him is sweet. But his scars, they're different from yours. Painful. Knowing. But not wary. He's got no reason to be wary.

"I'd want to do you standing. Three directions. Facing me. Sideways, looking at me. And turned away, watching me over your shoulder."

"Oh. You want *those* scars."

"Oh, much more than that. Let me show you something else."

He grabbed a sketchbook. Offered it to me. I took it, more wary.

"Open it. Please."

I took in a deep breath and did.

They were sketches of Myron. Head and shoulders, he looked as if he was just another guy. But in the full-figure ones you could not mistake his legs were twisted by his infliction. Body crooked. Yet lovely. Naked. Showing not only the horror of what he was living through, but the cruel beauty of it. I could even tell he was circumcised.

"I-I-I didn't know he was Jewish."

"Oh, circumcision's fairly common, over here. For newborns. He has a spastic version that didn't start developin' till he was a few months old. His twin's doin' fine."

"Twin?"

He nodded, a bit on the sad side. "His parents pay his rent. Living expenses. To keep him out of their house."

"Bloody fucking hell. Why would they do that to him?"

It took him a moment to say, "He's an embarrassment."

"They banish their child for not being perfect?"

"It's not that uncommon, Pug."

I sat on an arm of the sofa. "When did you do all these?"

"I started way before Jeremy left. He was in the middle of exams and I got lonely. Went over and Myron was home. We got to talkin' and I started sketchin'. He loved being my model. Even naked." Then with a chuckle he added, "Especially naked."

"Christ, Rett, and here I thought I knew you."

"Don't ever think that of anyone." He hesitated then asked, "So— can I use you? Will you let me? Just some studies, to start. Then sittings."

"Sittings?"

"In the general sense. You'd actually be standing."

I took in a deep breath, still unsure of all this. On the one hand, it made me nervous to undress before him. Not because he was gay; I trusted him enough to not take advantage of the situation. It was more that he'd be making a record of it to put in someone's collection of naked men.

"And that's all it would be," I finally asked. "Sketches."

He nodded. "Graphite. Charcoal. Pen and ink. And then the real thing. In acrylics on board. I might take some pictures for skin tone, but that's it."

So I shrugged and said, "Have you any beer?"

He bolted into the kitchen and brought back a six-pack of Heineken. He set it on the coffee table.

"It's from Germany," he said. "Really hard to get."

I closed the sketchbook and unbuttoned my shirt. "Where do you want me to stand?"

"Your workroom has the best light."

I cast him a bit of the side-eye and smirked, "Have you been planning this for some time?"

"I-I'd been thinkin' of it."

"Let's get on with it, then."

I grabbed the six-pack as he pulled out a large sketch pad and I led him upstairs. He positioned me by the window, with it to my left, and set a stool across from me. Then I doffed my shirt, jeans and briefs, and he began to sketch away. And the hi-fi set got ignored.

What's truly funny is, I felt stronger for letting him do it.

It was mid-March when Jeremy finally returned, certain he'd helped his company score a major deal with some unnamed Chinese bureaucrats, thanks to him not only knowing Mandarin, which they spoke, but also picking up enough Cantonese to realize the local representatives were trying to double-deal them. He'd never let on he could understand what they were up to, but his boss was kept up in a fairly basic way on their machinations, so consistently came across as more knowing and savvy than they expected.

"It's not a perfect deal," he'd told me and Everett, "and we'll have to keep watch to make sure they keep their end of the contract, but it's a good start."

He was given two weeks before he was required to be at a desk so used it to find an apartment off Memorial Drive, not so very far from my prison. He bought furniture to compliment that his parents gave him, from storage, and we used his father's old Ford F150 to move things about. During those drives, he would chatter like a madman.

"Hong Kong's wild, man," he said. "Buildin's going up everywhere. People stacked on top each other, forty stories up. Streets so narrow you can jump across 'em in one leap. It's crazy. But they have a great transportation system. I never needed a car to get around. It was amazin'."

And on and on, half the time repeating what he'd put in his letters.

Now this being Houston, a car *was* necessary, but he wanted something special. He found himself a bronze Mercedes 450 SL. The owner claimed it was as good as new, but I checked it out and found it'd been in at least two smash-ups, neither serious enough to make it worthless but not for the price he wanted.

However, Jere fell in love with the bloody thing. Pictured himself driving about with the top off and his best sunglasses on. So I pointed out the damage and the man finally dropped the price enough to make me happy enough to let Jeremy be happy.

Especially since I knew I'd be doing the work on it.

Of course, the deal almost fell apart after the papers had been signed and a bank draft handed over because Jeremy overheard the man whisper to his wife, "Who'd of thought them two queers'd figure out how damn bad a driver you are?" as they entered the house.

He was about to go after him, but I grabbed his jacket and pulled him back to the car, saying, "Don't be an idiot. It's *us* fucked *him* over."

"But he said—"

"The damage isn't so bad, Jere. A bit of finesse at my hands, and this car'll be worth twice what you paid for it."

He looked at me, almost smiling. "I thought you were Mr. Honesty."

"When did I lie to him? Not once." And I batted my eyes.

He laughed and decided to have the car appraised and the bastard sent a note in the near future, letting him know how the *two queers* had scored off him.

Everett finished his triptych of me a week before Jeremy returned, actually done in oils and exactly as he'd promised. I did let him take close color photos of my arms and legs and face, but that's all he wanted.

"To get the skin tones," he said, again.

It was always interesting to see how far he'd gotten during the week. I think he made me look far better than I really was and kept in check the mass of curls my hair had become. He hinted he'd like me to shave my mustache, but then he relented once he started work on my face.

"It keeps you from being angelic."

I couldn't help but snort when he said that.

After that, he made time to help fix up the apartment in the evenings. I used Jeremy's father's tools and garage to put new shocks in the front of the 450, reset the timing, and smooth out an additional dent on the inside of the front fender that rubbed against the tire in sharp turns, making it shudder. I also noticed one of the rims had been damaged and replaced it with one from a junkyard. By Friday, Jeremy's apartment looked like something out of *Architectural Digest* and his Mercedes ran like it was fresh off the boat from Stuttgart. We decided to arrive at Mrs. Glendon's in it, to announce the return of the prodigal.

During this week, I'd caught the idea that Jeremy was hurt that he wasn't moving in with Everett. Nothing specific was said, that I heard, anyway, but some looks were cast from him to Rett. It was like the time apart had set each on his own path.

Then that Friday afternoon, Rett and I were having a beer in the kitchen as Jeremy did laundry in his own little machines, seeming as joyful as a new wife who'd just discovered the pure pleasure of clean clothes. An icy beer against my forehead, I was letting the cold of it seep into my soul as I calculated how much time I needed so I could stop by the pool house, shower and change and still be on time when Everett removed his shirt to reveal what he called a wife-beater. It was tight and I'd not seen him in one, before, and I noticed his slight tummy was trimmer.

"You been exercising?" I asked.

"What?" He cast me an odd look then chuckled. "Just workin' my ass off. No time to eat, much. And puttin' frames on those paintin's so they can travel."

"They turned out well."

He smiled his thanks and drank down half his beer. "He paid me. Money came through today. Got more in the bank than I ever had in my life." Then he cast me his usual sideways glance and asked, "Aren't you hot, too?" as he mopped more sweat off himself. "You'd think a place like this'd have a better AC."

"He's afraid to turn it on," I chuckled. "Cost of utilities. That'll change." I took a sip, glanced around to make sure Jeremy wasn't in hearing range, and leaned close to murmur, "He hasn't seen my back."

"I thought you and he were doin' Aikido."

I huffed. "More like him throwing me across the floor. But that's what sweatshirts and gym pants are for, isn't it? Little extra padding?"

"But he knows what happened, right?"

"I think so. Maybe Vangie told him some of it, but I-I-I haven't discussed it with him. Don't want to, yet. But if he sees the scars, I can't avoid it."

He chuckled. "Damn, Pug, nobody knows anything about you till you want 'em to, do they?"

I shrugged. "Not so much to know."

"Cut it out." Then he jolted. "Oh, Pug, we missed your birthday."

"It's no great shakes." I took another sip of my beer.

"But it is," he almost whined, as if it were his we'd forgot. "How old are you now, twenty-one?"

"That was last year, Rett."

"Right. Right. Okay, we'll make next year's a big one. It's important."

"How so?"

"You'll be past the age when you can say you're a boy, anymore. You'll be a young man." Then he shook his head. "Yeah, but you never were a boy, were you? Not even when I first met you."

"You put too much onto me, sometimes."

His eyes drifted to some unknown point and his voice grew absent. "Jeremy's twenty-three. He's not a boy, either. Not since I've known him. I get the feelin' Yom Kippur did that to him."

All I did was take another sip of my beer.

"I should've asked him to move in with me."

"Why didn't you?"

"I don't know," Everett said. He cast Jeremy a sorrowful look. And saw I'd noticed. And sighed. "I—my situation—I'm in a place where I don't know what that situation truly is."

"What're you on about?"

"You know, I've worked for that fuckin' grocery chain for eight, shit, *nine* years. Bustin' my ass. Last minute changes in the specials. Complaints from idiots about my layouts. Doin' more than needed to be done because I thought that'd protect me when they found out I'm gay. Like that'd be my insurance. But the last couple of days I finally realized they don't give a shit about anything I've done. And now? Now they're tryin' to force me out. So they don't have to pay unemployment." He cast me a smirk. "I'm lookin' back and can see just how miserable that fuckin' job made me. I whined, yeah, but I couldn't really see it, not while I was in the middle of it. Why the hell would I want to make myself indispensable to that?

"I'm good at what I do, Pug. Damn good. But because of this-this-this one aspect of my life, I feel like I have to take shit from assholes because I couldn't possibly have it as good anywhere else. And now I'm gonna turn thirty-two, and I've got nothin' to be proud of."

"That's a harsh assessment. Your artwork..."

He almost smiled. "I mean, career-wise. Havin' a guy like you as a friend, that does make me proud. Knowin' Jeremy loves me, that makes me proud. Havin' Jeremy to love. And my art. But I can't think of anything else that does. I can't think of anything from that job I'd put in a portfolio to show off my abilities, if I did ask for work at a graphics house. I don't think they'd go for my pieces of you, Jeremy, and Myron. It's silly; when I started, I was helpin' sell cabbage. I'm still helpin' sell cabbage. Not much to brag on."

"So what you gonna do?" I asked.

He was silent for a long moment, then said, "I'm givin' notice on Monday. They'll think they've won, but I don't care. I'm not gonna let people who don't count run my life, anymore. I'm not lettin' anyone." He finally looked at me with a sideways glance, his expression filled with hurt, and I could still see him wondering if there was some way to get me completely over to his side of the fence. But then he smiled and the expression softened as he asked, "Is that what happened with you in Northern Ireland? You finally saw what a fucked-up place it was and got the hell out?"

His question gave me a lot to ponder, because in truth it wasn't until I was here, with Aunt Mari, and had put a year's distance between me and the place that I had even begun to see how insane it had become. It's a horrible thing to consider, but deep within I knew that bomb had been my saving grace.

I told myself I'd been in the process of leaving, at the time, but it was really escaping. And Joanna was my reason—

Am I just a crutch to help you?

No.

And yes.

I honestly can't say I'd have left solely on my own. I could see where I was always too accepting on whatever new limitations had been put on my existence. Always with an excuse not to take a radical path to get away. Even after I was old enough to do so. Not until Bloody Sunday.

Had I stayed in Derry, I'd probably have wound up in the IRA or PIRA, or an H block or dead at the hands of God knows which side, since both were as apt to kill their own for not being in perfect accord as kill those they considered enemies. I'd gotten hints from Mai of Colm now being deep enough in PIRA to be specifically wanted by the RUC and the Brits, with a reward posted. And Eamonn had grown harder and more radical in his hatred for the Proddies while in Long Kesh; now he was in the H Blocks, and he was seen and treated as a hero by those who'd only recently arrived. That would suit him.

But what had caught me most was Ma's shift into warrior mother. Mai said little about her newfound religion, but it came across in her letters when she'd sometimes give a careful sigh at how Ma disparaged Maeve's peace group and its attempts to bridge the ever-growing divide between Catholic and Protestant in that snippet of land. And how she whined that Rhuari deserted her to live a life of leisure in Belfast, though I knew better from his letters to Eldon.

Translating from the Irish, of course, so there were few details.

She'd mention how Ma would make her weekly travel to visit Eamonn and Maeve would say she'd come home glowing about how well he looked and how strong he'd become in *The Cause*. Or how Maeve had been in a cutting argument with Kieran over him chucking stones at an army PIG, trying to get him to understand he could be hurt or killed if the soldiers inside felt too threatened, and Kieran's response had been that he only listened to Ma, not his *traitor of a sister*. So being away from that had saved me from being gently worn down from the unceasing nature of it.

Just before he'd left for Hong Kong, Jeremy told me a tale about frogs. If you put them in hot water, they instantly jump out. But if you put them in cold water and heat it, slowly, so very slowly, the frog adjusts to the growing temperature and doesn't move, not before it kills him. Suddenly I could see its relevance to Everett's situation.

And my own.

"You're smart to leave, Rett," I finally said. "And I've got some scratch put aside, if you need."

He smiled and shook his head. "There's somethin' wrong with this picture," he said. "Jeremy's the Jew but spends like a blond trophy wife; you're Irish and I've never seen anyone so tight with a buck. No, I've got the money from my art sale, and I'm gonna sell the condo."

"Is that why you haven't asked him to live with you?"

"Partly. Keep my options open. I've got some equity in it. Live off that. Take my time findin' another job. One I like. And if it don't work out—well, we'll see."

We'd left it at that.

I'd headed home, understanding he and Jeremy would collect me in an hour. In that Mercedes. Which would make for an unpleasant ride, because the folding seats didn't have room for a mouse, let alone me. But it wasn't to be so far a journey, and Jeremy wanted to show it off. So instead of the pool I had a nice long shower.

I thought back on Rett's comments, and now could see how blind I'd been during my time with Vangie. I'd ignored the looks sent our way. Paid little attention to the slow service and bad tables we'd gotten in restaurants. Not really understood the danger behind a cop stopping us enroute back from New Orleans. Hell, when you live in an area where five cops can handcuff, beat up, and toss a bound man in the Bayou to drown and have nothing done to them, you know the very idea of equality and justice is only a foolish notion.

But I'd been so lost in my focus on Vangie, the growing danger was kept in the background of my mind. Now that near three years had passed, I knew that if we hadn't left to live in a place more accepting, the strain would have ended us, sooner or later. No matter how much we loved each other. One can only go so far in their battle against the world before it crashes down on them.

That brought me back to Joanna. We'd both been aware of the conflict and people's attitudes, but we'd felt safe against it because we loved each other. Could the same have happened with us? Possibly.

I let the water pour over my back, growing more and more depressed at the train of thought racing through my head, because I was back to thinking of the arbitrariness of the world and existence. And saw heaviness and inertia and people fighting to keep things as they were as the main way people fought that reality, epitomized by the tit for tat killing and bombings in Derry and Belfast. Both sides saying, *You hurt me, I'll hurt you worse, then if you hurt me worse than that, I'll hurt you even more.* With neither side accepting that neither side would give in. It was a blind, depraved sickness in us all.

And nothing was going to change because men honestly do not want to. That entails contemplation and struggle in the midst of uncertainty, and they will push against it with a viciousness like you could never believe. I'd seen it at its worst in Derry. I'd received it at its worst here. Even Uncle Sean had shown himself vulnerable to it. And the justifications for it were ludicrous. If we give Catholics the same rights as us, we'll lose ours. If we blow up enough people, the bloody Protestants will back down. If we hurt you enough, you will agree with us. If we're angry enough, you will understand us. If we give you money enough, you'll leave us alone. In all of it, we are the righteous and you are not, and plenty are they who know nothing of the battles but will take sides and point out what's right and wrong for all to see.

It all made me so bloody tired.

And sad.

Unbound

We arrived to Mrs. Glendon's in high fashion, though me arse did not appreciate the ride. All were pleased to see the return of the prodigal...all but Myron. He wasn't displeased, but I had the feeling he now knew his time with Everett was done, which made me wonder if there had been more to it than just sketching and painting.

Mrs. Kendall worked up a feast, in celebration. No meat, it being very expensive, but rice and stir-fried vegetables galore, and soy sauce as the main condiment. We were well-fed. Miss Sauvage and Mrs. Glendon listened in rapt attention as Jeremy told his tales. Even Sonja seemed fascinated.

He'd been ensconced in an apartment overlooking Kowloon, with a maid who had tried to catch his sexual attention more than once until he convinced her he was not seeking a bride. So she'd brought her brother in, one Saturday, *to scrub the floors*.

In a very tight shirt, very cut-off jeans and lots of looks.

"I grabbed the bus to Stanley to get away from it," he said. "Stayed there, bored out of my mind, till I hooked up with some American Marines over from Okinawa."

"That sounds so exciting," said Mrs. Glendon.

"And a bit dangerous," Miss Sauvage added.

Jeremy's grin was wicked. "Not so much. I actually knew one of 'em, from here. It was crazy."

I noticed Everett grow still at hearing that.

"I'd just found out we weren't headed home, yet," he continued. "And I was pretty lonely. So we hit every pub along the boardwalk. We were pretty drunk when they invited me back to their hotel. In Repulse Bay. Grabbed a cab and jammed the five of us into it, and I stayed the night."

Then Jeremy cast Everett a glance.

"One room. One bed. All five of us. By the time I got back to my place, I was wiped out. So crashed. I think the maid got the hint. Her brother never showed, again, and she was actually nice to be around. Cooked a Wind Sand Chicken to die for."

Everett's demeanor did not change. If anything had happened between Jeremy and those Marines, he knew of it, already, so his new plans made even more sense to me.

Eldon sat to one side, throughout, half watching, fully listening. He even smiled when Jeremy mentioned how his books and tapes had added to his knowledge of Chinese and helped them. He'd already told me of another letter from Rhuari, but we waited till the evening was done before he read it to me, in his room...which was stacked with even more books, if possible.

Thank you for the detailed analysis of my report. You noticing I had missed a couple of accents and misused two words helped me greatly impress the people teaching me the Irish. One even suggested that when I matriculate, I might join them at a school in Derry to educate young children in the language, to which I readily agreed. Everything up till now has been very piecemeal and inconsistent. A physical school would help combine all roads into a single path. We will be discussing this for the next year or two, at least.

Bridie has just informed me I am about to become a father. This is frightening and yet I am intoxicated with joy. The thought of raising a child without the disparagement and rancor so rampant in my area is overwhelming and yet inspiring. I almost cannot wait.

I stopped Eldon at that and asked, "He really said that?"

Eldon nodded. "He had to join a couple of words to get the true meaning, but that is correct."

"Bloody hell, me little brother inherited me Da's gift of gab."

"He is very good at this." Then he continued on.

We expect the birth to be in September or October. Bridie's parents are very happy, as is her Aunt Roisin. I have not yet told my mother. She's been having difficulties with her health, lately, and I want to wait till we make a trip home, for a few days, in mid-May. I will have leave coming then, from the off-licence, and it will be out of term.

I have let my younger sister, Maeve, know and she is very pleased. She has begun Nursing School, so insists she will know everything she needs to know to help with the birth by the time Bridie is ready. We both chuckled over that.

"There is an addendum at the end with more information," Eldon said, his voice very careful. "About your mother."

"Okay," I said, growing wary.

"Have they told you anything about this?"

Which made me even warier. "About what?"

I could see him shifting back into full-Eldon mode. "Should I be the one to tell you?"

"That bad, is it?" He just looked at me, which obviously meant, *yes*. "Let's have it."

He hesitated, nodded and translated—

Maeve just rang me. My mother has been diagnosed with cancer. My sister was very upset so I was unable to find out what sort. I am going home for a couple of days to be with them both, and when we speak to the doctors about treatment. I was uncertain about leaving work so suddenly, but Bridie understands better than do I, and she insists Maeve and I must be with my mother when this is decided. It is difficult to know what to think or do in a situation such as this. I am sorry to burden you with my troubles, but it helps me see that my wife is correct. Until next time.

I think I stopped breathing.

Ma had cancer.

Bloody hell.

I hadn't heard word one from Mai or Aunt Mari, but surely they knew by now. For Rhuari's letter was from at least a week past. I felt as if I had been cut away from the family, yet again.

My mind went blank. I honestly could not formulate a thought about it, except to whisper, "Rhuari's a cool one."

"Very much." The sound of Eldon's voice startled me back to the moment.

I nodded. "Thanks for telling me."

Eldon nodded. I patted him on the back, from which he flinched. I held my hands up in a *Sorry* motion and he grimaced a smile then nodded, and I headed out to Jeremy's car—

To find him and Everett in a deep, quiet conversation by it. I made a show of lighting a cigarette and walking into the back yard to smoke. See if my brain could catch up with me. Or at least explain my serious lack of feeling about my mother's illness, and why I was still supposed to be ignorant of it. But the distraction of what was becoming a sharp yet quiet argument between them kept me from focusing my mind.

I knew one of 'em, from here.

Tole.

Anatole Boudoin. Marine in Okinawa. Jeremy knew I'd work out who he was referring to. But was he actually saying he'd been with the man, sexually? Was that some gay code between him and Rett? Rett had known Vangie, and she'd mentioned her brothers. So had it been a subtle signal to him that he and Jeremy were done and he had moved on? Careless about what any mention of her or her family might mean to me?

Jesus, Brendan, why're you caught in thoughts about that? Now? Your mother has bloody cancer and you're worried over whether or not two queers are breaking up? When you wanted nothing to do with that part of their lives and—

"Pug!" Everett called, casting a *Let's get going* wave to me, so I wandered back, finished my ciggie, hopped in the tiny seat and let them drive me home. It was the worst silence I'd ever heard, with Jeremy leaning on his door, Everett on his, and the space between them insurmountable.

And my head still blank the whole way.

I didn't go upstairs. I knew I wouldn't sleep. And it wasn't from my mind being trapped in thoughts or worries or fears or anything along those lines; I just could not physically settle enough to even think of lying in bed. All I could do was pace around the pool. It was still empty, not yet cleaned in preparation for summer, and it seemed to taunt me with its stillness. No water to slap into little waves. Nothing to distract me. So my mind was taken up by one word.

Cancer.

My mother.

Who was so harsh about any form of illness, I'd have sworn neither flu nor cold would even consider the possibility of trying to approach her, for her attitude would scare any health issue away. Yet here was the worst of them.

Some clock somewhere was chiming midnight. Time for sleep. Time for rest. Time to settle in and reset yourself for the next day.

I had to move.

Go.

Somewhere. Somehow. Not just be here. Not in jail. Not now.

Go!

So I hopped on my Montesa and rode away. Not with any direction in mind, but just to do something. It was madness to go riding about so late on a Friday night, with all the drunks driving about. But it would have been more insane to sit in my room and sulk.

I found myself at *The Colonel's*, but I had no interest in dealing with Winston's self-aggrandizement. Or the big, beefy jock who held my position over the weekend. Instead, I turned around in the parking lot and thought about heading to Poppo's for some tacos or maybe a Jack-in-the-Box two-for-a-dollar and—

I was grabbed from behind and a blanket slung over my head as a car drove up and—

I jolted.

It was well over a year since I'd remembered that and—

Then I was bound and tossed into the trunk and—

I grew breathless and looked around. Saw the lot full of cars and how much finer they were. Heard the music coming from the bar; not Todd's country rock but some weird melody mixed with a low-key synthesizer of some kind.

It was disorienting because it wasn't right and—and—

They grabbed me from behind.

I'd been facing south. Car'd come from behind me. Against traffic?

No.

Someone ran up.

I looked to my right. There was an abandoned store and empty parking lot before it. Had they been waiting there? I couldn't remember whether I'd noticed cars in the area, or not. I was too lost in my turmoil over Vangie and—

Someone ran up behind me and—

I'd been grabbed and carried to the right and bound and tossed into the car's trunk and the memories were like a flood crashing through a dam...memories I'd shunted aside and—

They turned right...then left...then left...and—

South. I remembered. They headed south.

South.

What am I doing?

They headed south.

What am I doing?

Headed south.

What am I doing?

Starting up my Montesa, crossing to the southbound side, turning and speeding down it at twice the posted limit. After a few minutes—

We crossed a bridge, hollow and far—

I was on the overpass at White Oak and ahead was the I-10 Freeway. I crossed it and turned left, onto the service road.

There was no traffic to deal with. The barest lighting. I passed a couple of streets and almost missed the freeway access, it was so crowded by shrubs and trees.

I merged onto it behind a huge oil semi. The slight hop of my tires whipping over the pavement dug into me as—

The tires thump-thumped over the pavement. I tore a hole in the blanket and peered out a tear in the left rear fender.

I adjusted my left mirror so I could catch the same view and saw glimpses of signs whipping away. Newer signs, not the same ones. But the freeway still curled around to pass downtown, cranes as plentiful as the skyscrapers already built, leaping to the sky, their lights softly pulsing.

I passed the 59 and stayed on the 10, still heading east. For miles I rode as the smell from the refineries increased and reached the 610 and—

We passed under the interchange and—

I took the first exit. Onto Mercury, it was. Not thinking, just following instinct.

A turn to the right onto a crap road barely wide enough for two cars, made worse by the shadows of night and—

The car's tires hit potholes and bounced over railway tracks at a fine speed. Jostling everything. Heavy trucks headed the other direction, making the car shiver as they sped past.

Why was I doing this? What was I hoping to gain from it? I had no idea. I was controlled by instinct. By subconscious demand. Mentally, I told myself not to continue, but I could not stop. Could not turn around. Just kept going and going.

The occasional semi approached me from ahead, headlights glaring into my eyes. But I kept on. I rolled over more railway tracks. And more. Passed bleak, black houses pumped up next to the road, bordering on derelict even in the midnight shadows. Dark shops. Closed gas stations. Empty strip centers behind wide parking lots. I came up on an open area and the road slowly curved to the left as—

Silence surrounded me, except for the car's tires and growl of its engine. Seeming to go on forever till we thumped over more railroad tracks—

And I passed more old houses. My breath grew short. Sharp. As if I'd run a hundred yards. The memory was growling at me. I could smell the car's exhaust. Feel it shimmer under me as my Montesa rumbled on and on until...

I came up on what looked like the end of the road and—

The car slowed and turned left.

I turned left. Still no thought in my head. Then—

The car turned right—

As did I and the road dipped into a tunnel.

I couldn't believe I was remembering this so precisely. So completely. To the point I felt as if it were happening, again, as they—

Drove on and on in silence, the stink of the refineries back to overwhelming and then—

I came out the other side, drove down and turned left onto a marginally better road.

My heart was now pounding, remembering the fear I'd felt. Not a visceral fear but more an intellectual question of—

Was I going to be killed?

The thought in the back of my head, again, as if it had never left. I hadn't admitted it to myself, at the time; I'd hidden it with anger and irritation. But I didn't have that, now. All I had was a drive…a need…a demand to see where I'd been taken. To know where it had been. So I let the fear spread through me, openly, honestly. Kept wondering if this was an intelligent thing to do. Might I be heading straight to the men who'd done that to me? Straight to still being killed?

It's easy to get away with murder in the city like this. All the years Dean Corll and Wayne Henley and David Brooks had disappeared boys, and no one gave a bloody damn except their families. Who were shunted aside. It would have taken nothing for me to vanish into a grave, like in Derry, and the reasoning I'd used to shrug that fear off seemed childish and pathetic.

Now—during this ride—even though I was on my own and deliberately heading down roads I'd never seen, my head and my soul were feeling every moment of the fear I'd shunted aside back then, and my heart was racing fast.

None of this was smart, as I had no pills with me.

So turn around!

No!

No.

Let my heart do its worst.

I passed the 8. Wondered if I'd missed my next turn, to the right. A sign passed me and in the mirror I saw it said *Jesus Saves*—

Saves what, I wondered, seeing the sign through the tear in the bumper. Arseholes and idiots?

To the next street—

We turned onto a gravel road—

And there one was. So I turned. My little Montesa did not like it; I had to drive a bit more carefully. I still managed to ride fast enough so the dust didn't have a chance to settle on me.

On and on, I continued...and then from behind some sad trees I saw a pole holding one street sign appear in the darkness. I stopped. There was nothing beyond this point. No lights. Even the gravel faded into black. I looked up.

There were the stars, glistening above me. Just beginning to guide the fullest moon there ever was up into the sky. Already hints of its light touched the tops of trees. Silent houses slowly grew visible, adding a bit more length to the road before me.

So I turned left and rode along, then swung around to the right as the moon grew brighter and the stars beamed down. I passed more bleak dark houses and began to think I'd gone too far and it was time to retreat when I came to an open space.

I slowed the bike. Carefully rode into a gravel parking area. Black, hulking oak trees lined it. Big. Uncaring. Like protective demons, their twisted branches casting a vaguely threatening sort of shade from the soft moonlight across—

Across a playground?

I could make out monkey bars. A slide. A merry-go-round. All positioned in a large rectangle of near-white sand bound by square logs of some kind. And at the far end of the open space, a white wooden building with arched windows in black trim beneath a simple tile roof. And with it a strong wooden steeple.

A church?

A fucking church!

I was there.

Could feel it.

They had taken me to a fucking church yard!

I looked around to see a line of houses across the street, all dark within. Dogs barked to warn me I better not mess with them, even though I had shown no sign of wanting to. I'd heard no dogs, that night, nor crickets or frogs. Perhaps this was the wrong site. There were churches like this all over Houston.

But then came a soft breeze, and the moon's light danced between the leaves of the center oak tree onto a cord of some kind hanging from a branch.

I rode over. Set my bike on its stand and got off to look closer. It was a length of rope hanging from a thick branch and tied to a massive truck tire. Two fat strands, and very much weather-worn. Dirt and dust had made it filthy, and the ends were frayed and—

My hands were bound around the tree and—

The marks on my wrists had long since faded, and I got the feeling this rope was much thicker. So it had nothing to do with me.

Did it? I was back to doubting my instinct. I circled the tree. None of it seemed familiar but—

They bound my arms around it and—

It had been wide, like this one. I embraced it with my arms but they only fit halfway around it—

But as I did, it grew dark and I began to shake. I bolted back, shivering, and looked up. The moon had slipped behind a cloud. But it already was returning to be with me.

And illuminate a hole in the tree, level with my knees. Knothole? Is that what these things were called? And there was something inside it, almost gleaming. I picked at it and pulled out a couple of tiny mold-plastic cars, two marbles of different sizes—

Never played marlies, so silly--

With wavy strips of color inside them and...and...

There was a key in that hole.

My breath went quick and shallow.

My heart pounded.

My hands shook as I dug it out.

No, it was two keys. One to the pool house. Christ, I hadn't even thought about that one being in my jeans or missed it and...and...

The other...

Jesus God, the other was to my Montesa.

Some child had found them and kept them and...and the stars and the moon had led me back to them. Led me back to where my world was shattered. And I all but stopped breathing.

Every fiber in my body tingled. Another soft breeze shifted the leaves and whispered around me and I felt as if I were breaking apart.

I looked at the houses across the road. None of them were new. Nor was that church.

So it really was here!

Here?!

This area of gentleness and ease? Where children played? So peaceful and calm and welcoming, even in the middle of the night?

The air was warm but I felt like ice. My breath grew calm. My heart slowed its beating. All of the tingling stopped. I realized I still had my helmet on.

I calmly returned to my bike, mounted it, cleaned off the key and used it to rev its engine to life. My final bit of proof.

Suddenly, I was drowning in anger.

No, fury.

Insane fucking fury.

I revved the engine and roared onto the open space to dig through the grass and sand, spitting it everywhere. Around and around. Across and back, again. Tore up as much as I could. The dogs went mad. Lights came on. People burst from the houses to see me and yell at me in words I didn't give a damn to hear. I said nothing, just tore up more of the grass and gravel before I sped off at top speed.

Let them call the fucking cops. Let them try to so much as find me.

Forty-five minutes later I was back to the house. I stormed up to my room, not caring about being quiet. Tore off my jacket. Tore my shirt at the pocket while doing so. I didn't care. It was too much a part of this world and I wanted it gone, so I tore more away. Each *shrick* of the material brought me a hint more peace.

My trousers were JC Penney specials, and so fucking middle-class. All those fucking houses around that playground had been fucking middle-class. So these, too, were torn. In moments, I was wearing nothing, not even my briefs. They were in heaps of rags on the floor, and I was weary beyond measure. I heard movement in the house so slammed the latch closed, then stood still in the middle of the room.

No one came up the stairs to me. Nor did I hear a voice. Let them settle back. I had much to think about and wanted nothing to disturb me.

That the people who had probably attended that fucking church would stand by and let someone be tortured without even a call to stop it, that screamed too completely of the actions and attitudes in Derry. A lad being kneecapped by the IRA? Keep walking. Sunday services with the devil Paisley? This proves we are Christians as we slaughter Catholics. Let some bastards erase a young man from the world for daring to date out of his religion or race? Well, it's just not allowed. Anywhere. So it had to be done. Nor would that attitude change.

It made me cold. So fucking cold. I was like ice. Quaking from the shivers. And that's without the air conditioner going.

I started the shower up, more by habit than anything, and looked at myself in the mirror. I was healthy. Physically. Clear skin. Some freckles had come along. Body more fit. My chin seemed stronger and the mustache—suddenly, it looked pathetic. Was this my one real act of rebellion? Fucking facial hair?

I found my scissors and ran water in the sink, ignoring the shower, then cut most of the mustache away. Ran a lather and shaved the rest. I looked so fucking weird once it was done. Had my upper lip always been so far from my nose?

Then I looked at my hair. Curls and—and more curls—and I cut at it. Along the sides, mainly. And over the top, but not as much. I began thinking of a *MyDolls* concert I'd been to at a club, with Everett, and some of the lads had what they called mohawks. So I cut my hair down to the point I could shave on both sides of a thick strip of it.

Which made me look comical.

But wasn't everything about me ridiculous? I very nearly shaved off the rest of my hair to make it official, but no.

No, that could be acceptable.

This was the look I wanted. A stripe of curls down the middle of my skull. I saw little scars in my scalp. Some from the bombing, I suppose; some from my lashing. Well-healed but visible. They looked right. It all felt right and made me joyous.

I showered and scrubbed my face and scalp and stepped into the room, stark naked and dripping water. Then I started up some Ramones followed by Patti Smith, flopped on the bed with my headphones, and let the music dance through me.

I thought of the Provos in the Maze, still on their blanket protest, demanding Special Category Status. Eamonn was amongst them. Might even be leading them, for all I knew. They wanted to wear their own clothes as political prisoners, not the bloody uniforms of the state. They'd been allowed that privilege until recently, then told they were now common criminals, not men fighting for their country's rights and freedom. And once again, as if to prove how stupid everyone was, it was escalating, tit-for-tat.

Beat us and we'll destroy everything we can in our cells.
Take away what we haven't destroyed? We'll sit on the floor.
Take our clothes? We'll wear nothing.

I'd now heard that they weren't even cleaning the fucking cells, anymore. Just letting everything rot with shite and piss. And the response was, *fine, we'll make art on the walls with our feces*. God only knew what the next level would be, but it was sure to be met with just as much stupidity from the opposing side. Keep it up until both sides are too weary to continue. That's the only way compromise ever comes about, really; both sides grow equally tired. And finally understand that the world really does not fucking care about anything.

So now here I was, approaching the same fucking habit. Should I do the same? Not bathe? Not clean my room? That would be silly. I was hardly a political prisoner; just a familial one. Like a king locked in his chambers by his royal Uncle. Better that than execute him, I suppose. So who should I imagine myself to be? *Prisoner of Zenda? The Count of Monte Cristo? The Man in the Iron Mask?* Considering my actions with Jeremy, once, maybe I was just Oscar Wilde in *The Ballad of Reading Gaol*. Ha! The Oscar Wilde of the mechanic's set. He never met a phrase he couldn't turn, nor I a screw.

Christ, I was pathetic.

But to be honest with myself, understanding that made me happier than I'd been in years.

The Devil's Haze

I honestly do not remember much about the next year. One day bled into the next with such ease and simplicity, it was impossible to tell them apart. I expanded my collection of records and tapes. Lived in the music at all times, even while working, riding my Montesa or living in my prison; all it took was a small cassette player in my pocket and an earphone. I continued to fix my items at Everett's, though none with the intensity I needed to help me think. I drank too much beer but didn't eat enough to add a gut. Smoked too much pot, but never fell into that haze of *it's all fine*. Got over having a snort of coke because I hated the aftermath.

Oh, and I was maniacal about keeping up with the Friday night dinners; they were my one true respite and all that kept me from careening into full riot. I could just let myself relax, around them. Just be. Know that they held no judgement over me. Unlike the glares I'd get from Uncle Sean and sighs from Aunt Mari over the Mohawk. As it should be.

Of course, my dinner companions also commented on my Mohawk, but the only response they got is a shrug and a smile...and that was fine, with them. Jeremy actually said he wished he had the nerve to do it, but he knew it would be very much frowned upon.

"Corporate Houston," was his excuse.

Instead, we'd go to discos and bars, gay and straight, and dance with girls and boys and each other. Never a thing more. And I got back to sparring with him and actually managed to throw him once or twice.

Then one day he took me to his shooting range, out near Katy. An area so flat and wide, it's like the world was really a smooth ball, all around.

"Officially, I'm still IDF reserves," he told me. "That's why I keep it up. In case the Arabs try anything, again."

"I've never fired a gun," I'd said, which is what led to the invitation.

The range was an open area with bullseyes on bales of hay, in the distance, and marked off spaces where you needed to stand. I was in a t-shirt and ragged cut-offs, while Jeremy wore boardies and what he called a wife-beater.

He had a sleek rifle and automatic pistol with an extra clip and—

The pistol sprang apart on the bed as Eamonn handled it and he said, "Forgot about the spring."

I eyed Jeremy's pistol, cold and tight, as he said, "I've cleaned it and the safety's on."

I'd already noticed...and was relieved.

We stood in our section and he fired off the pistol and managed to hit the bullseye every time. Then he'd offered it to me, asking, "You want a go?"

I shrugged, took it and held it like I'd seen him do.

"Line up the sight at the end of the barrel with the target," he said. "Hold your hand steady, like this." I cupped my right hand with my left, as I'd seen him do. "Take aim, hold as tight as you can, and pull the trigger. Just keep in mind, pistols ain't very accurate."

"The movies get it wrong?" I chuckled.

"Totally."

So I fired. Emptied the clip. I hit the target twice.

"Not bad, for your first time," he said. Then out of nowhere he added, "Y'know, Everett's not mine, now. Never was, really."

That gave me a start. All I thought to say was, "I'm sorry to hear that."

He nodded, replaced the clip in the pistol and took aim, again, saying, "He showed me the sketches and stuff he did of you. And Myron."

I shrugged. "I didn't expect it to be a secret."

"He's done stuff like that of me, you know."

Then he emptied the clip into the target, missing none.

The safest answer in the world is to say nothing when you don't want to lie about something, so that's what I did. I was also not happy about the smell of the bullets being fired. Too much like Bloody Sunday...too much...

Jeremy noticed my tension. Nodded. "You know anything about art?"

WTF?

I snorted. "You see any hanging in my room? I'm of the mind, if I like it, it's art. If I don't, it's not."

He chuckled. "I remember that portrait of you, by the fireplace. Why's it in the attic?"

"I'm not their favorite person, right now. And that thing's years old."

"But it's classic. Same for the one of your family."

"And the one of yours."

"Yeah. My folks really like it. I got your aunt to show me yours. Couple nights ago. You were at work."

"Why?"

"I wanted to-to see somethin'. And I was right. That's what convinced me. Everett never was mine."

He took up the rifle and fired off a number of shots, still straight into the bullseye.

"I don't get you," I said, growing wary.

"The work he did of me? Those sketches and paintings? They're excellent. Nicely detailed. Good use of color and brush strokes. Impressive. Same for the ones of Myron, and for the portraits of your family and mine. Lovely work made by a craftsman. But your portrait? Everything he did of you? There's layers to them. Tenderness. An ache. A beauty. A longing. Levels of meaning."

I felt the need to say, "Jere, there's nothing between me and Everett but friendship."

"Really? You share secrets with him."

"The hell I do."

"He's seen your back. I know what happened, but he's seen it."

"Not because I wanted him to. With him—fuck, it was only by accident."

"I know. And Vangie saw it."

"Because he told her of it."

"She told me. She also told me how you broke up with her."

I snorted. "Can ya break up with someone who was never yours?"

"Like me and Everett, huh?"

"I don't think it's the same."

"Don't you?"

I shrugged. "I dunno...you tell me." That's when I pulled my shirt off and gave him a good look, saying, "Anything like this between you and Everett? Or you and Vangie?"

He let out a long sigh and said, "You sayin' that's why you and she aren't together?"

I shrugged him a *yes*.

"Why didn't *you* tell me about it?"

I took the rifle from him and hefted it to my shoulder, as I'd seen him do. It felt wrong. Unwieldy. I gave it back and picked up the pistol. A Walther PPK, like James Bond. That seemed to all but fit in my hand.

"You should take this completely apart, next time you clean it," I said, my voice soft.

"Bren, I thought you could talk to me and me you and—"

"I didn't tell you, Jere, because I don't tell anybody anything. Not if I don't have to. I learned long ago that what people know can get around, and I wanted none of that about me."

"You don't think I can keep a secret?"

I just rolled my eyes, aimed at the target single-handed and fired off more shots. One actually hit the center.

"Jere, you know more about me than anybody else in this town," I said. "If I didn't think I could trust you, you'd know nothing. Besides, it's not about keeping secrets so much as not giving others ways to hurt you."

"Like you hurt Vangie?"

"You see. I knew things she didn't know...and should not have known. And I was a fucking bastard about it. For no good reason. And you now know that about me."

I handed the pistol back to him.

He nodded, sighing. "Got ya. Y'know, I'm still in contact with her. Even now she's in-in Moscow. And I'm pretty sure you caught what I was sayin', about the marine I hooked up with in Hong Kong and...well...is that bad, between us?"

I'd had to roll my eyes as I pulled my shirt back on. "C'mon, Jere, you're me China. The world is too fucked up to be worried over something so trivial. You could be here, today, and gone tomorrow, as you bloody well know, so what would it matter to any but those who don't matter?"

"You matter," had popped out of him so very fast. "I-I'd like to think I matter."

"You do! I'm telling you, whatever you do is fine with me. So long as you understand, I'm not gonna spill my guts every time I turn around."

He huffed. Then chuckled. Looked amazingly relieved and fired off more rounds with the rifle. Every one a bullseye. Then he stood next to me, not looking at me.

"So you and Rett never...?"

"No! Jesus..."

"I-I wouldn't blame him or you," he said with surprising tenderness.

"You don't believe me?"

"Well...I-I would have, except that stupid mohawk just kills my trust."

I chuckled. "You're the only man who's had me, Jere."

He smirked. "Yeah, well, you know the old sayin'—*incest is best when it's kept in the family*."

"Incest?" I'd snorted and sneered, "Arsehole."

He'd laughed and hugged me, and we'd stayed friends. Kept our family going strong.

It took a bit of work, but I finally managed to talk both him and Everett into a road trip to Austin, one Saturday, to see a punk band mentioned in a zine, *The Next*. Hoping it might reconcile them. As a buffer, I invited Myron, who said no because he wasn't feeling well, and Eldon, who had just smiled and gone off to write another letter to Rhuari. Which was all well and good, because it was a bloody long drive to Austin, made longer by it being night.

The band was at Raul's, by the university. We went in Everett's Chrysler. It drank the fuel, but as he put it, "This bitch is paid for, so it equals out." And it still ran as smooth as the first time I'd been in it.

He'd quit his job, our Everett, and begun free-lancing. More commissions had come in from that collector and word seemed to get around, so I'd posed for him, again. As had Myron. And, I'd learned, so had a few lads from the Montrose area.

Raul's was near the corner of the university's campus and reminded me of all the little corner bars in Derry, where Da had gone to get his fill...a single story of nothing. On the outside. Inside, was bare and open, but it was a great venue.

There were but three lads in *The Next*, Ty, Skip and Wil, and were all around my size, give or take a few inches, but they filled the room with their sound. Ty snarled. Wil pounded. Skip kept the rhythm. They yelled. They kicked around. The crowd moshed, even though there wasn't an official pit for them to do it in. But what a joy it was.

The song that made the evening for me was *Monotony*. Christ, did it speak to me in ways nothing else had. I bought a cassette they'd run and transferred it to my reel to reel to protect it.

Turned out they were from San Antonio and Raul's was the

closest gig they could get. Everett bonded with them, even more, flirting heavily with Skip while commiserating about how backwards that town was. Didn't look like there was a bit of reciprocation, though.

However, San Antonio did sound interesting—the Riverwalk, the Alamo—so I actually asked Rett on the way back, "Why don't we make a trip there? I've never been."

His simple response was, "Then catch a bus. No fuckin' way am I ever goin' near that town, again."

And that was that.

The next Friday we told the family of our trip and everyone was fascinated. When I mentioned San Antonio, seems I was not the only one who's not been there.

"I hear the Alamo is quite small," Eldon said, and unprompted! I was so shocked.

"It's about a city block," Rett told him. "And it's got a mural of John Wayne in that movie, *The Alamo*. Really cheesy. But the tourists love it, and the Riverwalk's close by. I liked going to *Casa Rio* more than *Mi Tiera's*. It's like *El Patio Tex-Mex*—little grease and easy to eat. What was better is *Schilo's*, up on Commerce. They even make their own sauerkraut and root beer."

"I never. Had sauerkraut," said Myron, finally rousing to attention.

"I'll bring you a Reuben, next Friday," said Jere, excited. "You like corned beef?"

"I don't know."

"Well, I love it, so I'll bring a turkey Reuben, too, and whichever one you don't like, I'll eat."

Myron just nodded. He seemed extremely tired. He even had to rest on the first landing before he could continue upstairs.

"That guy in my old room," I asked Mrs. Glendon. "His name, again?"

"Mr. Salinas," she said. "And he's hardly ever here. Does a lot of traveling in Mexico, I believe."

"Maybe you should swap 'em out."

"I've offered, but Myron is being Myron. Independent to a fault."

Can't argue with that.

Then a couple of days later, he didn't come out of his room, so after much knocking Mrs. Glendon went in to find him lying half on his bed, cold to the touch. She called me and I went straight over. She wept as I called the police.

Fortunately, the officer may not have liked my look, but he was fine with just my name and contact information, since I still didn't have the documents Uncle Sean had promised me. I said I was a friend who lived close by. The coroner came and Myron was taken away, wrapped in a sheet. While I felt sorry at his going I also felt relief. He must have been suffering.

I never met his family or his supposed twin, but Mrs. Kendall was beside herself with anger at them as she cooked that Friday's meal.

"Threw everything in trash bags," she hissed. "Dumped his books in a box and put 'em out on the street. Took a few things to Goodwill. Left his clock and radio and TV in the room. It was more like they were getting rid of a dead animal than a son and a brother." She was fighting tears. Letting them fall into the soup she'd worked up. "He was a good boy. He didn't deserve a family like that."

"They *weren't* his family," popped out of me. "*We* were. They were just relatives."

She looked at me, a bit taken aback. "What a thing to say." But she hesitated then added, "You-you really think so?"

"No question. He was happy here."

She almost smiled. "We should do something special for him. To remember him by. Will-will-will Everett and Jeremy be here, tonight?"

"Jeremy will. Everett—he's upset so..."

"Of course. He's such a sensitive soul. Myron so loved my cherry pie. But I won't have time to work it up, tonight."

I gave her a nudge. "If you baked one store-bought, I'd never tell."

She looked at me, thinking. "I could add more cherries and braise it with sugar-butter, the way he liked. Makes the crust such a golden brown."

I grinned at her. "Back in a jiff."

I picked up some sparkling wine, as well, and it worked out to the good. Everett forced himself to come, in memory of Myron, and Jeremy tended to him. Once the pie was doled out, with one slice left for Myron, we all raised a glass.

Rett wept. As did we all, to one extent or another.

We only learned about his funeral through the newspaper notice, and I'd bet ten-two-and-even it was a photo of his twin they used with it.

Dear God, as if I needed more excuse to hate people.

It wasn't long after that Ma finished her cancer treatments at Altnagelvin. Mai filled us in, telling Aunt Mari Maeve had to all but drag Ma there every time and deal with her constant complaining. She'd even suspended her nursing studies to care for Ma. Between what little was in Rhuari's letters to Eldon and Mai's to Aunt Mari, along with a few calls between the two of them, I got the sense things weren't going so well.

To my dishonor, I didn't care.

What mattered more was by the middle of my second year of punk, safety pinned t-shirts and rolled up jeans, I was bored with having to shave my head. Which wasn't easy. So I let it grow out and got back to growing a mustache.

My Montesa was also more and more in need of work, and the tools I had available in the garage were insufficient. As for getting parts, those were damn near impossible. After months of scrounging junk yards around the city, I'd located one up the 45 that had a couple of bikes similar to mine that I could cull parts from. But they weren't always the best fit and took a lot to make work. I needed better tools for that. That the grouchy old bastard who owned the place was dear with his pricing didn't help.

Randy-Ray was his name, and he had a ratty beard, silver-streaked hair and looked like someone had stepped on him. When I'd first come in, he'd yelled at me, "Get out. We don't want your kind."

"What kind's that?" I'd shot back without a thought.

He'd caught my brogue and said, "Wait, you Irish."

"And?"

He'd snorted. "C'mon in. What you want?"

He never did explain why he'd wanted me to leave. I saw him do that twice more to lads with long hair and tie-dyed shirts, but never to bikers in leather and black, no matter how long their hair was. Made no sense to me. Still, he had a rusted Montesa that had been cannibalized, already, but contained the part for the motor I needed. So from then on, his was the first place I checked.

I also noticed an old Peugeot 404 convertible sitting next to his mobile home/trailer office/whatever. Rusting. Tires flat. Windshield intact but filthy, and the interior gone to ruin. But it had a nice line to it and the body was not the least bit dented. It seemed to just be wasting away.

I asked him about it, one day, as I was paying for a muffler from a SEAT that I figured could be made to fit my bike.

"Wife's piece of shit," he'd snarled. "She's gone. So left it there."

"Gone? Left?" I asked.

"Passed. Been five years. Six."

I had noticed a trail bike in fair condition behind the office that was dirty from never being used, so got a bright idea and asked, "Would you like it fixed up?"

"Ain't worth workin' on," he'd snarled. "Piece of French shit. Just ain't got 'round to runnin' it in with the rest of the junk."

"I'd do an exchange."

He wasn't paying attention to me when he said, "Like what?"

"The trail bike in back. If you're not doing anything with that—I'd trade my labor for it. You provide the parts."

He snarled a sigh. "Why th' hell I wanna do that? She's a bitch."

"Sell it?"

"Who's gonna buy that piece of shit?"

"I might know someone, but it's got to be in good shape."

Of course, I was lying. But it seemed to catch his semi-interest. So we went out back and looked at the Trail Bike, only on closer inspection it was well beyond repair and I had to back away.

But now he had the idea, he said, "I can get parts on that thing, an' for your bike. Same place, usual."

"New parts?" I asked.

"Nope, but good. You get that thing to runnin' and lookin' even half decent, I know a guy. San Bernadino. But it's gotta be runnin', an' runnin' good."

I smiled. "Can I use your tools?"

"Ain't got much."

"Better'n what I have, now. Work on the car and my bike?"

He shrugged a *yes*, so I agreed.

I went two days a week, at first, cleaning the filth from it and testing the mechanical bits. Just a couple hours at a time since I'd have to work in the evening. Weekends were prohibited.

"Busy time," he said. "Don't need no confusion."

I was pleased to find the engine wasn't as bad off as it looked, though a den of opossums were not thrilled with me.

"I'll get 'em out, said Randy Ray. "Don't want 'em run off too much. They eat ticks and shit. No rabies."

The next time I came out, they'd moved to a shed near the trailer and the car smelled of some kind of camphor.

"Mothballs," Randy-Ray told me. "They hate 'em."

So I worked with the smell of that around me, then scurried home to shower it off, as best I could.

The 404 was a 1963 model with a four-cylinder inline motor, overhead valves, and side-mounted camshaft. Deterings Bookstore scrounged up a *Chilton's Auto Repair Manual* for the 404, fairly well-used but readable. It had a single carburetor and fuel injection, none of which looked like they were in so very bad of shape. Its paint was a ruin, of course, and all the hoses had to be replaced, but some WD40 handled making the doors, hood and trunk open and close without too much argument.

Of course, the engine block was thick with the oil in it, but by breaking it down complete, soaking in old oil—which he had plenty of sitting about—and rubbing the pistons and cylinders steady with a rag soaked in fresh oil, it slowly shifted back into decent shape. Did the same to the four-speed transmission. Then I set the car up with seats from a wrecked Mercedes.

It was a slow process, and soon I was at it three days a week, then four. I managed to force myself to work only 10 to 3, so I'd have time to clean up for *The Colonel's*. And I made sure I did as good a job as always, there, while keeping my distance from Winston and the steady flow of new waitresses.

But coming back to the house filthy and in need of clean up turned out to be a saving grace. For one hideous-hot August day, I rode up to the house to find a Ford sedan in front and three men in suits seated at the kitchen table having coffee with Aunt Mari.

I strolled in, covered in muck, and she motioned me over, saying, "Bren, come here please. These gentlemen would have a word with ya."

"For what?" I asked, wiping black sweat off my face. "I'm hardly presentable, and I've work, tonight."

One of the men, who looked like a salesman in the Macy's suit department, rose and offered me the least genuine smile ever.

"We need to clear up a few things about you being here," he said.

"What's wrong with me bein' here?" I played up the Irish. Uncle Sean had at least made good about getting me a green card and social security number, and I'd even filed taxes and gotten a nice return, so I thought I'd have fun. "I'm full legal."

"Gentlemen, this is Bren—" Aunt Mari started to say.

But the Macy's man raised his hand to stop her. "Please don't. I want him to tell us his name."

Oh, this was going to be fun.

"Who's askin'?" I shot back.

His fake smile widened, he pulled out his identification, and his bloody name was Charles. Brantley, but that part didn't matter; him being FBI, did. "Now, your name? And your ID?"

"Brennan McGabbhinn," I huffed and pulled the green card from my wallet. Same for my driving license. Everett had used his art skills to replace Scott's name with my new one. It looked ragged and was close to expiring but did well enough to surprise them.

"You got a passport?" snarled a burly man in a poor-fitted suit.

"What's this about?" I snapped.

The third man in a very well-tailored suit said, in pure Toffee British, "It's about you answering questions being put to you."

"I'm Irish," I growled, "so if it's you askin' 'em, ye can fook off."

Aunt Mari gasped, but he didn't even flinch. Just eyed me like a cat eyes a mouse it's about to feast upon.

"This is the United States, not Ireland," he all but purred.

"Nor England, so yer nothin' here."

"We want to see your passport," said the suit.

"Her husband has it," I said, playing up how weary I was. "Said somethin' about gettin' it renewed? Was that it?"

Aunt Mari nodded. "It lapsed before we sent it in. We're workin' with Dublin to get it handled."

"You oughta have it with you," snarled chunky.

"I got a green card. What more ya want?"

"Where have you been?" asked the Brit.

"None o' yer fookin' business," I snapped.

"It is our business," said the suit. "So where have you been?"

I glared between them then shrugged. "At a junkyard gettin' parts fer me motor."

"You got a car?" chunky asked.

"No. Bike."

Suit handed him my license. "It's for a motorcycle."

"Where's your helmet?"

"It's right there," I snarled, motioning out the back door. "Look for yerself."

"You vanished for a year," asked the Brit. "Where did you go?"

This time, I ignored him.

The suit said, "We'd like to know."

"Why?"

"Just tell us, Mr. MacLoughlin."

"McGabbhinn."

He gave me his fake smile, again. "McGabbhinn."

I sighed and said, "Nowhere. Just another house."

"Where?"

I knew he'd check it, and I didn't want to dance around the whole issue, so gave him Mrs. Glendon's name and address. I also noticed Aunt Mari trying so very hard not to look like she was writing it down. "Things was too crazy, for me. I was just...I dunno. I just needed t' be off t' meself. Still go there, Friday nights. Dinner. Keeps me steady."

"You didn't go back to Ireland?"

"And how could I afford a ticket?"

"But why not tell anyone where you were?"

I huffed. "Have you met her daughters? They could teach the likes of you a few things about interrogations."

That almost made suit chuckle. Apparently, he had.

"Where were you born?" asked the Brit.

I cast him a glare, but suit said, "Please."

"Letterkenny," I said.

"What brought you here?"

"Me heart. An' I-I went off me head."

"Why?"

"Me Da..." And suddenly I was thinking my own father—

Found off the Limavady Road, hands bound, tortured and frozen as the whip tore across my back and white enveloped me and I slammed against the wall as flames danced...danced...danced closer and closer and...and—

I was half-seated on a chair, and Aunt Mari was slipping a pill under my tongue. Christ, I hadn't had those memories in years. Now I was breathing hard. My heart going like mad. Confused as to what was happening.

Aunt Mari was in her scolding tone, saying, "Now see what ya done! Brought it all up, again, for the poor lad, an' him doin' so well. Ya can all leave. Talk to me husband an' his lawyer, from now on. Shameful, this. Shameful!"

"We can settle this," said suit, "if we may take his fingerprints."

She bolted upright and snarled, "I told ya! Talk to me husband and his attorney!"

They huffed and puffed, but they left.

And I was left with wondering why they wanted my fingerprints, now. After so many years. Like they were refocusing on tracking down Brendan Kinsella and wanted to prove I was him. Did they even have my prints? And why the fresh interest?

But then I wondered why I should fucking care. It wasn't as if I were going anyplace soon. So deal with it when it happened.

If.

I learned from Mrs. Glendon they actually had dropped by to talk with her about me, and she spoke only of how lovely and gentle I'd been while there. And quiet. Mrs. Kendall backed her up, as did Miss Sauvage. Eldon refused to even speak with them, to no surprise.

Uncle Sean never said word one about talking with them, or not. He seemed completely unperturbed by their latest visit. I don't know if that meant he'd shut them down or delayed them or what. I just didn't see them, again..

Then a couple weeks later, I got a passport. An Irish passport, not UK. Uncle Sean brought it to me just as I was about to head out to *The Colonel's*.

"You can leave, now," he said. "Everything's legal."

"Took you long enough."

His voice snarled, "You don't know what I had to do to get it."

"And not leave a trail?" I sneered.

He grew tight and glared at me.

I looked in it at the photo and grimaced. It showed a full head of curls and mustache. "How'd you get this photo?"

"When Mairead was here. We all took lots of pictures, and I found one that could be fixed enough. Now look at the date of issue."

September 1977. And an entry stamp for six weeks ago, to the US.

"Did Aunt Mari not tell you of the visit we had? This doesn't align with what I told them."

"I already worked 'round that. Said you were lyin'. They'll wanna talk to you, again."

"Have they already made an appointment?"

He growled, "Nope. Sooner you're gone, the better."

"Don't push all this on me, Uncle Sean," I snapped back. "You made your own choices, and forced many for me, as well. I feel no reason to thank you for them." I looked at the passport. Flipped through the pages. "I'll be off in mid-January, then."

"Here for Christmas?"

I nodded. "To be my last, and I've a car to finish working on, so..."

"I've already hired someone else for *The Colonel's*."

"Someone legal?" And I smiled at him.

"Don't push me, boy." Then he turned and left.

We spoke not another word.

Recall

It took me another two months to get the Peugeot to where, when I started it up...well, while it wasn't showroom perfect, it ran. With a set of old tires off a couple other wrecks, it drove itself onto a car transport. He'd sold it to the man in San Bernadino along with some other junkers, and he was happy.

My Montesa also was, I'd say. For she was almost like new.

It was just after our second Friday dinner of 1981 that I got home past eleven and saw a note taped to the back door. *Call Mai-Urgent.* With a phone number. I recalled her once saying Toronto was an hour ahead, but if it was that important, I'd give a try. So I popped another beer, leaned against the wall, and dialed the number on the kitchen phone.

It rang three times till she picked up, and before she could say a thing I popped off with, "It's a Friday night and I'm a bit drunk, Mai, so I make no claims to manners. What's it that's so urgent?"

I could picture her taking a deep breath to hold her tongue, as I'd seen her do so many times with Da and Ma and Eamonn and even me, on occasion. Then I heard her exhale and knew she was about to speak. I smiled at the picture it made in the back of my mind.

"Ma's cancer's back, and it's spread." And I just *hummed* and nodded. I suppose she'd dispensed with worries of the Mounties listening in, which made sense; I'd been *dead* for eight years. Why would the Canadians still be checking her phone?

She waited a moment then said, "You hear me, Bren?"

"I did."

"She—she wants you home."

I didn't believe a word of it, but still I asked, "Is she that bad?"

"If she continues treatment, she might last nine month, a year."

"And without?"

"We're not considerin'—"

"Not considering, me arse. I'm not that far removed from Ma's attitudes and angers. Has she agreed to do any further treatment?"

Another long breath and exhale. "She will."

"The fuck she will, and you know it."

"Brendan!"

My true name in a voice as sharp as Ma's at her worst, just then, but it did nothing to me. In fact, the news Ma was soon to be gone from this world infected no part of my core. My mother was dying, and the most I could manage was a shrug. And I knew it told in my voice.

"Without treatment, Mai, how long?"

She was silent for a long, long moment before the words sighed out of her. "Three month. Maybe four."

"I'll be home in a month or two, once I've arranged things here."

"That long?"

"Well, I can't drop everything and run to her, straight off, can I?"

"Why not?"

"Considering how I was got out of the country? You want me arrested the moment I land? No visits from me, then."

"Is that really still a worry?"

"If you want me to take the chance, fine. But I also have friends here to say farewell to..."

"Friends?" Her voice took on the pain of the world as she asked, "Do you truly hate her so much?"

I wish I did, because that would be an honest emotion, but I still felt nothing. However, I did think it only right to give Mai some comfort. She'd done so fine a job handling Ma and Da and the thousand other putrid hates in that corner of the world; for me to seem cold and uncaring felt a dishonor against her. And there was still the fact that my mother had forced through the saving of my life, for what reason I could not think except I knew it was not from love. I'd like to know why, and it was best to talk with her before she was too far gone.

So I made myself sigh and say, "I'm drunk, Mai. I can hear your words, but I can't feel them, yet. In the morning, I'll wake to the horror of it, but right now, I can't even feel me nose."

"I never thought you to be so cold."

I near snapped at her about the hypocrisy of caring for a woman who hated me, even if she was blood. And I do believe Ma hated me. Especially when she'd seen me smile.

You see, I'd come to believe that since she was so unhappy in her life, she despised the possibility of anyone else being happy in theirs.

I half believed that's why she'd pushed Eamonn to be part and parcel of a cause destined to destroy any and all around it, himself included. That his blanket protest had only almost worked I'm sure pleased her no end, but his misery during it was the greater pleasure. She'd fought against Mai marrying Tur, despite her being up the pole, I think because she could sense they would have the kind of marriage refused her. True, she'd hated them living in the hutch for so long, despite there being no place else for them to go. But Mai's spirit had never broke, nor had Tur's—not till internment.

What a poke in the eye that must have been. God only knows what she'd have done to Rhuari, had he not been lost in his books and then moved to another town, one that might have been more dangerous, physically, but was safer emotionally. And that he'd found support in a girl who loved him as much as he did her. Then there was still Maeve, who was the dutiful daughter and strong enough to remain to herself, and finally Kieran, who was the wild child she'd always wanted and nurtured and accepted in whole.

As for me? Sure, I'd taken her slaps and snarling words and given no reaction in answer. For all I honestly knew, despite the horrific manner in which it happened and the fact that she brought it about, she especially hated me for escaping that god-forsaken bit of the world. Plus, it was colored with the fact that I'd seen Danny kill Joanna and others, and it was Colm high up in the chain of command in PIRA while her first born, who was now a martyr to the glorious cause, was still an afterthought. Should he still crash into the ruin she'd envisioned for him, it would serve no purpose, anymore.

That Houston had proven to be no better a choice to live in was no fault of hers. America still traded on her image as the land of the free and open opportunities. And truth is, had I not still had some of Ma's destructiveness scarred into my soul, I'd have had no trouble here. This country loves white men, be they Celtic or Anglo or Germanic or Nordic, so long as they keep themselves to the norms she's laid down. To fall for a black woman was treason of the worst sort, save falling for another man; that is an offense punishable ten times over.

Of course, Mother Ireland was hardly perfect, being controlled with lies told by priests and anger frothed by nuns. Where history was more important than a decent job. With those who'd hate you for going to St. Agnes and not Christ Episcopal or Presbyterian Church of the Good Shepherd. Fear and hate care not whom they're used by, even if by both sides of a conflict, and many are they whose sole purpose in life is to make certain they are constantly involved in attacking everything they do not believe in. It's the devil's work, but aren't most men truly in line with the devil? Aren't we the ones who love to help the world prove life and love are as fleeting as a raindrop in a thunderstorm?

So in answer to Mai's snide little comment I only said, "Not tonight. No guarantee about tomorrow."

"Brendan, what's wrong with you?"

I almost yelled, "Not tonight, Mai!"

"All right, then! Will you try to get there sooner than you said? You don't know how important it is."

"Wait—will you not be there?"

"I just come back but I'm with twins, again, so can't fly."

"I thought the last twins were the last."

"They would have been had Tur and I not got tipsy, one night, and neglected taking care."

"Oh, Mai..."

"Let me tell you this—I will not have another, or Tur will find himself without something he very much prizes."

I had to laugh.

"It's not funny."

"I know," I said, still laughing. "So Maeve's on her own with Kieran and Ma? Christ."

"Rhuari's back, livin' in Pennyburn with his in-laws till they can find their own place. His post came through at the new school."

Which I already knew, thanks to a letter Eldon read me, that evening. Still, I said, "Oh, that's good."

"But it means he's tied to it, for now. Proving himself. Still, he has a car so can help some. Maeve says Kieran's barely around, so all she can do about him is worry. But her training's come in handy."

"Mai—is Ma really so bad?"

"You'll not recognize her, Bren."

Damn me, now I felt something of the bastard. "I'll do what I can to get home sooner."

And we left it at that.

So after I hung up, I took the pool house key, went outside, let myself in and climbed up to the roof to stand there and look out over a city so lost in rebuilding itself from nothing to something, it had forgotten what a city is supposed to be. A place for human beings to live and love and grow their families in safety and peace. A community meant not only to protect but nurture and aid in that growth. Instead, this was just a place to make money. Lots and lots of money, if you were the right sort of person. And assign you to nothing if you weren't.

The night air was sharp and alive. It stung my cheeks and fingers. The sky was clear, but the lights of Houston minimized the chance at seeing much in the way of stars. As it always would. And I'd learned the hard way that you had to drive dozens of miles to the west or north to dim them enough to view the sky as she should be seen.

I thought about what Ma's dying and Mai's begging me to go home meant. Could it be a new direction in my life? That was quickly shot down. It hadn't been all that long since the visit from the FBI and that Brit, so I'd be a fool to return as Brendan Kinsella. Now it was obvious I was still wanted for questioning in the bombing. The Brits had memories as long as the Irish, and the Irish have memories tracing back a thousand years. We know not only our neighbors but every slight that's ever been made against us and where our families come from, back ten generations.

Besides, if Colm was a part of PIRA I'd never be able to fool him into thinking I was Brennan McGabbhinn, and they might even want to speak with me about why I'd revealed Danny, despite it being by error. No, I couldn't pass as anyone but myself, while there. At least, not for very long. So my stay would have to be quick and careful. Best if I waited a while longer, until it was sure Ma was going to be gone, soon. I'd want to be around for her wake and funeral.

And answers to my questions might have to remain unknown.

It's about here I began to wonder if this was what my destiny proscribed. If I could be given a short time away from the hell of Derry to appreciate that same hell permeated every spot of the world, even the grandest, so that when I was forced to return I'd do so without hopes or dreams or prayers to cling to, just a brute version of existence meant only to prove how much like animals we truly are and—

"Bren."

I heard the voice but wasn't surprised at it. I turned to find the girls, each at their own window, watching me. They had taken over the two back rooms, now Scott was settled into Dallas or Grand Prairie or Plano, somewhere up there.

"Can't afford Turtle Creek, yet," he'd told me at his wedding to Trish. "But we will."

I smiled at the girls, knowing it was Brandi who'd spoken.

"Mom told us," said Bernadette.

I nodded.

"Are you going to visit?"

I nodded.

"Mom's going, Saturday," Brandi added. "You going with her?"

I knew she'd go. I also knew it would be best if I went alone. If I was found out at any stage of the journey, it would be as bad for her as me. And besides, she wasn't my mother but a cousin two or three times removed. Right?

So I responded to her with, "No. Soon after."

"Will you be coming back?" That was Bernadette. Perceptive little beasts, the two of them. After all, wasn't I an orphan, already?

"And how could I desert the loveliest girls in all the world?"

"You did before."

"And returned, didn't I?"

"Would you even be going if Evangelyne was still here?"

That caught me off-guard. "How come you to know her name?"

"Dad, when he was talking to mom."

"Back before you were hurt."

That made me hesitate. So they had known all these years and said nothing. Just tried to get me to tell them what they already knew. I was glad that I hadn't.

"She's the reason you got hurt, isn't she?" It was Brandi talking.

And now they were letting me know the poison I'd set between them and their father had taken hold. I could not think of what to say.

"It's a pretty name, Evangelyne."

"She was pretty."

"We saw her when she was leaving, one night."

"You walked her to her car."

"Real gentleman."

As if repeating that would loosen my lips.

"Where's your Da?" I asked.

"Still at the new bar, setting it up," said Bernadette.

"Supposed to open, tomorrow," Brandi said.

"It was supposed to open, last week."

"Well, when you hire cheap labor that's just standing around a hardware store—"

"Don't," shot out of me. "Please, don't do that."

"Do what?"

"Just-just-just don't say anything negative about anyone, not right now. I don't want to hear anything negative."

"You haven't answered our question."

"What question?"

"Would you still be leaving if Evangelyne was still here?"

Suddenly, her using Vangie's name bothered me, but I held my tongue back from spitting out *Mind your own fucking business, for once,* and said, instead, "We'll never know, will we?"

"What about Everett?"

I rolled my eyes. "What about Everett?"

"You're *really good friends* with him."

"He'll learn there are better friends for him than me."

"Can I ask you something?" It was Brandi, looking very intense.

Bernadette hung out the window to glare around at her, horrified. "You said you wouldn't—"

"It doesn't matter—"

"It's a violation of privacy!"

They kept at it till I had to snarl, "No, I haven't slept with Everett."

"Happy now?" snapped Bernadette.

"I hope so." It was Aunt Mari said it. Up in my room. Smoking a Kool and having a midnight beer. Waiting to talk to me. She'd been doing that more and more, of late, as if to paste over things she'd let happen and the secrets she kept. "And that now you'll say good night."

The girls grimaced, cast me a wave and vanished into the darkness of their rooms. I just shook my head, crawled back into the pool house and came out...and stood by the empty pool. I did not want to move. Did not want to face anything in the world, again. In the back of my head, a thought grew. An idea that I could become a statue and stand here the rest of my life and not be sorry for it.

Oh, if only it could be so.

Continued in

A Place of Safety
Home Not Home

About this Author

Kyle Michel Sullivan used to write screenplays, but shifted to writing books that range from sunshine and light (*David Martin*) to cold and dark (*How To Rape A Straight Guy*, which has been banned more than once) to farcical and insane (*The Lyons' Den*) to mainstream romance (*The Alice '65*) to a tale of tragedy and redemption (*Bobby Carapisi*). He has ventured into SF-Horror-Suspense with *The Beast in the Nothing Room*, done gay revenge in *Porno Manifesto* and worked up a vicious female revenge thriller in *Carli's Kills,* then taken Capitalism to its logical extreme in *Hunter*. He has also written murder mysteries (*Rape in Holding Cell 6, The Vanishing of Owen Taylor*, and *Underground Guy*).

Most of his novels are gay-oriented but not all. Many contain intense sexual content that fits the erotica category, but not all. Some are even romantic and tender. He's written what he's written, and each one of those books got him one step closer to this point.

He tries to build characters as vivid and real as possible and has a lot of fun doing it mixed with angst, anger, and amazement ... but that's the lot of a writer.

Other Books by This Author

General fiction
A Place of Safety-Derry
A Place of Safety-Home Not Home
The Alice '65
The Vanishing of Owen Taylor
Bobby Carapisi
The Lyons' Den
David Martin

Adult Erotica
Blood Angel series - Léonidès (ebook only)
                     - The Prussian (ebook only)
Carli's Kills
Hunter
The Beast in the Nothing Room
Underground Guy
Rape in Holding Cell 6
Porno Manifesto
Curt (AKA: How to Rape a Straight Guy)